Desert Dwellers Earth and Water

The second book in the Paintbrush Saga

Desert Dwellers
Earth and Water

The second book in the Paintbrush Saga

Sarah Bergstrom

LODESTONE
BOOKS

Winchester, UK
Washington, USA

JOHN HUNT PUBLISHING

First published by Lodestone Books, 2020
Lodestone Books is an imprint of John Hunt Publishing Ltd., No. 3 East Street,
Alresford, Hampshire SO24 9EE, UK
office@jhpbooks.com
www.johnhuntpublishing.com

For distributor details and how to order please visit the 'Ordering' section on our website.

ISBN: 0978 1 78535 745 9
978 1 78535 746 6 (ebook)
Library of Congress Control Number: 2017957124

A CIP catalogue record for this book is available from the British Library.

Design: Stuart Davies

UK: Printed and bound by CPI Group (UK) Ltd, Croydon, CR0 4YY
US: Printed and bound by Thomson-Shore, 7300 West Joy Road, Dexter, MI 48130

Contents

Prologue

FIFTY YEARS AGO

Lourdes grabbed her cousin's arm and turned her around, singeing Kari's skin with her glowing fingers, which resembled long flames.

"Ouch! Watch it, Lourdes!" Kari exclaimed, yanking her arm away. She grasped her injury tight as if to smother the pain and soon relaxed. Burns from fire reaume always hurt more than average, like a bolt of lightning that surged through one's whole body, but left a wound only at the point of contact.

"Oh, sorry," Lourdes mumbled, her dark eyes blinking rapidly, but she appeared too excited to be truly apologetic. "I've been getting the bonfire going and just forgot to switch gears ... It's just, well ... that's him! See? He's making the water boil! He's raising the water temperature on his own! Isn't he amazing?"

Kari's straight hair swung right and left like a blonde broom sweeping her shoulders as she stifled her irritation and scoured the gathering to find the mystery man. Storm clouds were fast rolling in overhead creating an early dusk. All of the woodland reaume were starting to prepare dinner before a bonfire that Lourdes had just produced in the middle of the village. Though she obediently searched, all Kari could think about was her stomach. "I thought you weren't looking for anyone, that you'd always stay single?"

Lourdes sighed. "That's before I got to know him."

Kari lifted a heavy bag off the ground and carried it to an empty wooden bowl, set away from the fire on a carved wood table. She untied a rabbit carcass from a hide belt around her waist and laid the body on the flat wooden surface beside the bowl, then dug in her backpack to find a knife with a stag-bone handle.

"So?" Lourdes asked, curling her hands under her chin as if she were shivering despite the intense heat. "What do you think?" She extracted her harvest vegetables from a woven birch basket and began preparing them.

Kari paused and traced Lourdes's line of vision to where her new love interest stood at another table further around the fire, also prepping his dinner.

"All right, he's pretty amazing. I'll give you that," Kari answered. No one had ever seen anyone from the air or ocean reaume before, and now here was a man who was both. His skin and hair were dark, like the black wolf that lived among their sister clan. His frame was thick with muscle and of medium height, very different from the tall, slender bodies of the earth reaume.

"Is he not the best looking man you've ever seen? You can say yes and I won't get mad. After all, you know I claimed him first."

"Claimed him? What is he, a piece of furniture? Anyhow, it doesn't matter what I think," Kari answered.

"Of course it matters! You're my cousin and best friend!"

"If you insist, then, I guess he's ... all right," Kari answered and began skinning her kill.

"Just all right?"

Kari shrugged. "Yes, all right He's too stocky for my taste."

"You mean muscular, exotic. He's eye candy after living with people so skinny they look as if they're about to pass out."

"You asked me what I thought! I'm just being honest. He's fine for you. Look at it this way, at least I won't be competition, because you know who'd win." Kari smiled, and Lourdes threw an acorn at her stomach.

"Well," Lourdes said, "it doesn't matter what you think anyway. Why should I care?" She dumped a load of vegetables into the bowl with some force. Carrot chunks flew everywhere.

"That's right, it doesn't matter," Kari said. Her cousin was such a hot head sometimes. She didn't seem to have inherited any of her dad's earth reaume traits. And how strange that no one had ever heard of the different types of reaume having children together until Lourdes was born, and now here were the products of two mixed marriages. Who could have guessed that could happen? And they were falling in love, or her cousin was anyway.

"So, why did this guy come here anyway?" she asked.

"That's the strange thing," Lourdes told her. "He's been here for months and as you know, last night was the first time we really talked. We walked up to Hot Springs and watched the sun set. He told me he actually flew here to meet me! We're the only two on this earth who share more than one reaume heritage.

"A match made in heaven," muttered Kari as she rolled her eyes."

Lourdes bumped Kari with her ample hip, but she recovered and tipped a carved wood pitcher of water over the food. Ringing the outer edge of the fire lay masses of large stones. Kari sifted through them with wool-lined tongs, plucking one after another, hoisting them over to the bowl and dropping them in. As she did so, the water began to steam.

"Do you know what he said?" Lourdes asked, eyes shining. "He said when he first came here to meet me, he didn't expect me to be so beautiful! He's perfect, I tell you, perfect!" She collapsed dreamily into a maple recliner, lashed together with sinew, standing near the cooking pot, and turned her attention to the fire.

"You can't end up with him. You'd leave me all alone here," Kari said, collapsing onto the chair beside her cousin's and wiping sweat from her rosy face.

"It's not like we're getting married already. We just met."

"So, if you didn't know about him, then how come he knew about you?" Kari asked.

"Do you remember that man who visited us from the palace last year? He was some sort of scientist. He came to ask about anomalies."

"Oh, you mean the ambassador, Einar."

"Yes, well, Einar told him about me. That's how he knew to come here. He also said to send any who had anomalies to the palace for an experimental treatment," Lourdes said and hesitated. "But then, no one who went with him ever returned."

"Oh, yes, I remember," Kari said slowly. Her expression shadowed with the darkening sky. A storm was brewing.

THE PRESENT

Part 1

Forest

Chapter 1

Earth Reaume

"How long until we get there?" Lahcen called to his brother and sister from behind, his black, wooly hair beaded with drops of water. He surfed an accumulating stream, drawn from the breadth of surrounding plant life.

"I suppose it depends on how many sirens we meet along the way to put you guys under a spell. It was Khalid's turn last time. Now it's you!" Qeriya teased, her mahogany eyes flaming with mischief as her slight frame wended around a tree to surprise him.

He skidded to a stop and sent a wave rolling towards Qeriya, but she back-peddled in time to avoid getting wet. It seemed Lahcen's ability to produce surf had waned from their time in the rainforest. What he managed here, in the old forest, was certainly larger than anything he could muster back home in the desert, but looked like a puddle compared to the wave he'd ridden during their stay with the fire reaume.

Her throat constricted as she thought of her newfound fire manipulating cousins and friends in the rainforest. They'd been through so much together. And it was hard to leave, but they had to help their parents before it was too late. The king could decide to terminate his 'guests' at any moment.

"Ha-ha, very funny, Qeriya," Khalid called, swinging from tree to tree like an orangutan, flaxen hair bouncing with each swing. His broad shoulders and slim frame curved effortlessly around branches, propelling him with super strength. "How was I supposed to know Anna put me under a spell?"

"Perhaps you're still under it. It sure took you long enough to tell her goodbye," Qeriya teased again. She navigated bundles of deciduous leaves, occasionally getting close enough to feel their feathery texture on her cheeks and hands; carefully avoiding getting tangled in the branches or losing her hold on Doctor Michael, who reclined in a floating bubble of air behind her.

Khalid didn't laugh. His prominent brow converged to make him look downright scary in the fluorescent light of a clouded sky.

"Hey, I was only kidding!"

"That may be, but, perhaps you have a point. I can't seem to shake her."

"You're going to have to, at least enough so that we don't end up turning back," Lahcen chimed in from behind, his surf spraying them. Qeriya moved a little faster to get ahead of him.

"Don't worry. I do miss Anna, but I've got it under control. So, our plan is to meet up with the earth reaume?"

"No!" Doctor Michael's voice came from atop his floating bed. Going through the human village will be much safer. The king will expect you to join the earth reaume. I'll rest easier when we're at the village."

"You're awake? I thought you were resting easy?" Qeriya asked, disillusioned.

"I've been awake. Who can sleep knowing a pack of soldiers could find us at any minute? Now that we're away from the fire reaume, we don't have the manpower we once did."

"Don't you mean fire power? Try not to worry, Uncle. We can deal with a skirmish if it comes our way." Qeriya tried to sound light, but felt a tremor of anxiety in her gut for the old family friend they'd only recently discovered to be their uncle. He wasn't completely recovered from the scourge of time spent as a prisoner of the king at the volcano. Ever since they had found her parents unconscious, she worried even more for the family she had left.

"That's what bothers me!" he grumbled. "Just leave me at the nearest human village, and I'll take care of myself. Anyhow, you've got to be tired of levitating your lanky uncle. It's not easy to navigate me through these oak trees, I'm sure."

"I don't mind!" she exclaimed, giving him a warm grin. He smiled back, wide and playful, unlike his usual serious self. She supposed it was freedom from the oppressive hidden surveillance back home that cheered him up. "Compared to lifting a rock fortress, you're a few grains of sand!"

"Hardly," he said and slowly lay his head back down.

"She wants to levitate your bed because she knows that once she stops, she's fair game for a lightning strike," Lahcen sneered as he surfed in between Khalid and her, splashing his sister's leg with water.

"You tickle me and I'll put you in a coma!" Qeriya swiped at the air behind him but failed to produce any coherent maneuver whatsoever. Instead, breathing into her cupped hand, she threw her breath like a ball at Lahcen's nose.

"That's disgusting! What'd you eat for breakfast, fish?" Lahcen shouted, choking on the flood of warm breath entering his lungs, coughing and sputtering as he spoke.

Qeriya picked up her pace uphill and then plunged down the other side. Doctor Michael clutched his blanket with white knuckles. They caught up to Khalid once more, his backpack snug against him as his strong arms fielded branches.

"Sorry about that crazy ride," Qeriya called to her passenger. "I had to get away from Lahcen before I did some real damage. She grinned. "Here, let me prop you up a bit so you can see everything." She thickened the air behind his back.

"Ah, that's better." He folded the blankets under his chin.

The cloud cover broke. Sunlight filtered through a colorful canopy, extending a few warm rays onto the chilly floor. Out of the corner of her eye, she saw someone moving in the woods. At least, there seemed to be a person in her peripheral vision, but when she looked, there was no sign of anyone. She stopped and listened, putting her hand up to signal the others to stop. They scanned the area, watching and waiting without a word.

"Perhaps it's a deer," Doctor Michael said at last.

"A deer?" Lahcen added.

"Deer meat's tasty, especially in a turnip stew, a specialty of the human village we're heading to next," Doctor Michael explained. "It's located past these hills, nestled in a meadow.

"Even though I've never tasted turnips, you make them sound so yummy I'm getting hungry," Qeriya said.

"We'll be there soon and you can get a nice meal. Certainly a nicer meal than anything you would get in the desert," Doctor Michael said.

"Nothing could possibly be better than home cooking! I miss the desert so much." A little pain flickered in her stomach as she spoke. "I especially miss maize tortillas smothered with beans and Khalid's salsa.

"You miss the desert, not just your parents, but the desert?" Doctor Michael asked, sitting up straight in surprise. "But it's such a hard life there."

"Hard? My life's been hard since I left. And I certainly don't miss my parents working in the salt flats, but I do miss home. Working hard for everything just made it taste better. There's no place more beautiful in the entire world, I just know it. Not even the rainforest."

"Sometimes I don't understand you." Doctor Michael sat up again, wearing a quizzical expression as he studied Qeriya. His short hair stood on end from a prolonged time lying down, while his brown eyes appeared empty as surprise and exhaustion canceled each other out. He resembled a boy forced to wake up in the morning for school.

"It's true," she said, drifting along at a steady clip. "I miss the desert. I just wish the Wadi wasn't drying up. I want to go back ..." she faltered.

Doctor Michael didn't answer, but bowed his head. She was glad he didn't say anything. Her grief was too raw. What she wouldn't give to curl up with her mom once again to a nice shoulder rub and a nighttime lullaby.

"Not an option to go back I'm afraid," Doctor Michael said at last.

Qeriya towed him ahead of the others and they led the procession for some time in silence. As they climbed hill after hill, the air thinned and lost humidity. More light trickled through the canopy. She saw movement. Branches snapped to her right. She scanned the direction of the disturbance and saw the familiar ten-foot frame of a giant soldier leap towards her. Spinning to her left, turning Doctor Michael with her, she darted out of the way.

"Soldiers!" she warned, but her brothers were already on guard.

Lahcen pounced upon the one who had attacked her. "How dare you hurt my sister!" His thick frame was slight compared to the giant. Still, Lahcen successfully pounded the attacker's face with his fists.

Khalid wrenched at another soldier's arm and flung him against a tree. The giant whammed into the trunk and wobbled back and forth before falling to his knees. Khalid drew a rock to his reach and smashed it onto the giant's head. Two more soldiers appeared from behind Khalid, grabbing his arms. He used their grasp to kick his legs high into the air, looping his knees over a low tree branch. Whipping them upside down, he slammed them to the ground. Summoning more rocks as a magnet would metal, he pummeled these onto the soldiers' heads.

Qeriya scanned for more lurking soldiers and found a few heads peering from behind trees. An unmanned hovercraft sat in their midst. She couldn't tell how many more were hidden. One sent a dart in her direction, but so sensitive was she to its flight through the air, she easily moved out of the way. It whizzed by her and stuck into a tree. She twirled air into mini cyclones that spun about the trees, uprooting the hidden figures from their hiding places. They whirled in circles until dizzy and she dropped them, disoriented, to the ground.

Three more soldiers pulled Lahcen from the one he was already wrestling. Before Qeriya could help, he drew water from the air to clap onto the soldiers' mouths and noses, suffocating them. They yanked fruitlessly on their death masks until they passed out and fell down. Their work done, the masks rolled off of their mouths and seeped into the ground.

The combatants Qeriya had disoriented were crawling onto their hands and knees, about to rise again. She and her brothers would have to run or else kill the lot of them. Before she could do anything, she heard Khalid call to her.

"Brace yourselves!" Branches slithered around her waist, and Doctor Michael's insulated container, gripping them tight. The branches then flung them forward, to be caught by more branches and flung again.

"Khalid, is that you?" she called as they were whisked from tree to tree, careening through the hilly forest. Rattled, she glanced back. Khalid raced towards her, but a soldier was close on his tail. How did the king find them? Where was Lahcen? She could no longer see him. As the sounds of conflict grew further away, the branches began to subside. They set her and Doctor Michael down by a meandering stream.

"The soldiers must've been camouflaged in the trees. Most of them were heading for you," Khalid told Qeriya, appearing suddenly beside her.

"It figures. I'm the weakest link since I have a passenger."

"You need to move upstream. Take Doctor Michael and hide. I have to help Lahcen."

Doctor Michael pulled himself back to a sitting position. "But—"

"No!" Qeriya hissed. "You need me, too! I can't stand by and watch you fight without helping!"

"Listen!" Doctor Michael tried again.

"You also shouldn't endanger Doctor Michael. Now get going!"

"Khalid!" Doctor Michael yelled. But Khalid had his hands full with the giant who had been in hot pursuit.

Qeriya forced a swallow. Khalid was right about Doctor Michael, but somehow that didn't make it easier. She flew, fast but careful, upstream with her passenger.

"I've been trying to tell you not to go this way!" Doctor Michael exclaimed, frustration plain in his voice. "They came from this direction! I don't think we should veer off course!"

"This is the way Khalid directed me," Qeriya replied doggedly. "Anyhow, if they came from this direction, they won't expect us to escape that way."

"Listen to me, you stubborn girl! I've been consistently ignored and now you need to listen!" the doctor ordered nearly in a fit of rage, in contrast to his usually controlled demeanor.

"Not now, later! We're going upstream! It's my decision! That's what Khalid told me to do and I'm not losing my brothers!" Qeriya snapped.

There was a pause that she chose not to fill with further argument. Doctor Michael had succeeded in calming his voice although his irritation was still obvious as he persisted in stating his case. Qeriya ignored him. All of her energy went to maneuvering far away from the attack. They flew up the creek for some time, along a valley carved into the hills.

Suddenly, she became aware of a strong presence behind her. Swinging Doctor Michael to the side, she flipped around to blast the enemy with hot air, almost colliding with ... "Lahcen!" Leaping off of his wave, he jumped over her head, leaving her snorting a nose full of icy water from his surf. Grimly, she maintained hold of her charge.

"What are you doing here?" Qeriya spluttered, coughing what felt like a quart of water from her lungs. "I thought you and Khalid were fighting?"

"We fought just enough until they backed off, then we escaped to come help you."

"Are you sure about that?" Qeriya asked, sinking to the ground, shivering with cold. "I'm not feeling all that helped right now." Glancing at Doctor Michael, she saw he was in no better state.

"I need to get you and Doctor Michael further away," Lahcen told her.

Qeriya pushed herself off a rug of brittle, brown leaves and stood up. Scanning the area, she could see no sign of anyone. Quickly breathing into her hands, she swirled warm air around Doctor Michael, wrapping him in a miniature tornado. Before long he was dry and she gently lay him down on the ground near the gushing creek, still wrapped in blankets, one tucked under his head, before drying herself off.

"Where is Khalid?" she asked turning to Lahcen, eclipsing Doctor Michael from both her sight and his for a moment.

"He's not far behind me."

"A moment later, she spotted Khalid leaping between branches to catch up, his worried face growing clear as he approached.

"Where's Doctor Michael?" he asked.

"He's right …" Qeriya began, but he wasn't where she'd laid him. She and Lahcen scoured the terrain, but there was no sign.

"He was just here!" Qeriya exclaimed.

"Let's fan out and circle around," Khalid whispered. "Whistle for help if you find him. They launched outward in three equidistant directions and circled around, leafing through the forest for some sign of their uncle.

Qeriya tried to suppress her growing panic as she completed her circle with no sign of him. Just as defeat settled over her, she heard Khalid's piercing whistle.

"There!" Khalid shouted, pointing as she and Lahcen hurried towards him. In the distance, two giants hoisted a now unconscious Doctor Michael into a camouflage hovercraft near a steep hill forming one side of the valley. One soldier climbed into the pilot's seat, while the other maneuvered the doctor.

Qeriya and her brothers lifted into the air, dive-bombing the craft just as it powered forward. Khalid landed on the front of the vehicle, blocking the pilot's view and forcing her to stop. Swiftly drawing rocks to rain down on the hovercraft hood, he leapt onto an overhanging branch to get out of the way.

Qeriya repressed a cheer as the small avalanche succeeded in puncturing a hole through the craft, but her relief was short lived. "No!" she screamed as a rock towards the outer edge of the cluster bounced off the hood, hitting the Doctor in the head.

Lahcen body slammed the distracted soldier holding onto Doctor Michael. The giant went down like a felled tree. Qeriya scooped up a limp Doctor Michael, and took to the air, putting as much distance between them and the scene as quickly as possible, her brothers following close behind as they sliced through the air in single file.

"Where are they?" Qeriya asked after a long and winding sprint.

"They're out of commission," Lahcen said. He moved up beside her. "There's no way they can catch us without their hovercraft. They're strong, but they don't move all that fast."

Khalid nodded in agreement. He gestured for them to depart from the stream and head for the hills.

"How is he?" Lahcen asked.

"He's breathing, but unconscious," Qeriya answered. She stopped on the gently sloping brae of the hill, lowered her uncle to the ground and cradled his head in her hands.

Khalid and Lahcen removed his outer robe, exposing his battered limbs. Scanning for injuries, they found nothing urgent.

"Here's where the rock hit his head," Qeriya said, gently probing the egg shaped swelling. "There's a big lump – but no blood."

"He's unconscious, but otherwise he seems all right," Khalid said, his eyes troubled. "Although ... look here, on his upper arm. I've never seen anything like it. It's a drawing!"

"Is that a lion head?" Qeriya asked.

"I think so," Khalid echoed.

"Maybe it's just temporary art," Lahcen said, squirting water onto it and trying to wipe it off, but the picture remained untouched.

"We'll have to ask him about it when he wakes up," Khalid decided.

"Who are you?"

Qeriya lifted her gaze to see two young men with pale hair standing above them. Bows and clusters of arrows were slung over their shoulders. It was the first time she'd seen hair as light as her mother's. The strangers wore soft, tan colored clothes, adorned with woven patterns of orange and red, matching the soft, autumn hues of the leaves falling around them.

"Who are you?" she asked.

"I believe we asked you that question first. You're humans in earth reaume territory after all," the taller of the two responded.

"You're earth reaume? Glad to hear it!" Qeriya breathed a sigh of relief, knowing that reaume were by nature peace loving.

"It seems I've answered you first. Now who are you? Are you lost?"

Qeriya shook her head. "We're travelers. We've just left the fire reaume. There was a battle between the king and the fire reaume at the volcano—"

"Yes, we know," the other reaume interrupted. "We were just on our way to see for ourselves how the fire reaume were doing."

"They're recuperating," Qeriya told him. "We fought alongside them. We won, but even so, just now we were ambushed by the king's soldiers."

"The king's here – in our territory?" The taller one asked, astonishment written across his round face.

"We left them a long way back," Khalid chipped in. "There were only a few soldiers. I don't think they mean to attack your reaume. It was only a skirmish. They almost got our uncle. We managed to get him back, but he's been injured." Khalid glanced down at the still figure, his eyes still troubled." Can you help us?" he asked. "He's alive, but he's unconscious."

"We have healers who may be able to help. Our village is a short ways from here, across the stream."

"Thank you," Khalid answered, relieved.

"So, what are your names?" Qeriya asked after first introducing her brothers and herself.

"I'm Karl, and this is my brother, Olaf," the taller of the two brothers said. His hair resembled strands of pale silk dusting strong shoulders and framing a cheerful face with a welcoming smile.

Olaf nodded, but stood apart from his brother, slender and quiet, hands dangerously close to his bow and arrows. Pale waves framed soft brown eyes that held a controlled strength. His movements were slow and calm, unlike the assertive hospitality of his brother and he appraised them carefully, not as eager to trust as Karl.

"And the man you're with?" Karl asked.

"His name's Doctor Michael. He's our uncle."

Karl moved closer. "Doctor Michael's your uncle you say?"

"Yes."

"I see he has a tattoo of a lion head on his upper arm," Karl noted, and Olaf gripped his bow. "Did you know that?"

"We just noticed it when we were inspecting him for injuries. He normally wears long robes that cover his arms, so it's not been visible before," Khalid said. "Why, is it important?"

Olaf slid an arrow out of his quiver and pointed it directly at the unconscious Doctor. The three siblings exchanged stunned looks, automatically bracing for an attack.

"Wait!" Qeriya said urgently. "What's wrong?"

Karl gestured toward the image. "That tattoo's reserved for people in the royal court."

"Would you ... would you like a coffee?" Einar stammered. His heart was in his throat. It surprised him that he'd got the words out at all. He'd figured he would just trip over his tongue and make a fool of himself, but it was better than stewing about her and never saying anything.

Alexis turned her lovely head of long, pale curls, caught by a bow clip at the nape of her neck, and smiled, displaying perfect, white teeth. "I'm afraid I don't drink coffee, but thanks." Alexis turned back to her lab write up.

Einar was trembling as it was, and now she'd said no. Her rejection zapped the strength out of his legs and he collapsed into a nearby chair, flushed and sweating. He had finally gone and asked her out. Hopefully this would put an end to his horrible panic attacks.

Chapter 2

Waterfall

"That's impossible! There's no way he works for the king! He's our uncle! He helped us escape from the royal family, and he's trying to help us save our parents! He gave us a book with maps to help us find them!" Qeriya begged as she faced them, her nostrils inflated, like a bull ready to charge.

Lahcen's feet brushed the ground, disturbing the leaves as he moved closer to the strangers. The gentle breeze grew stronger, swirling the rusted leaves about. Sweat dripped from Lahcen's brow as a gnarled twig snapped underfoot.

"Hold on, give me a second," Khalid announced, pulling the book from his pack. Qeriya couldn't see how that would help. If the two didn't trust Doctor Michael, then why would they trust his book? Khalid paged through the journal for Karl to see, as he and Olaf slowly lowered their weapons.. For the moment, the situation appeared to be diffused.

"Giving you this doesn't prove he's safe," Karl said, his eyebrows furrowed in suspicion. "Listen, I'd love to admit I'm wrong, but until we know for sure, we have to monitor him. He shot his brother a glance before turning back to them as Olaf nodded solemnly. "An ambassador from the king used to visit our village. He told everyone he was working on treatments for anomalies, and that turned out to be a lie. Your uncle may be a spy."

"A spy? Ridiculous," Qeriya mumbled.

"So, you have genetic disorders, like humans do?" Lahcen asked, in attempts to redirect the conversation.

"What?"

"The anomalies, they're a collection of disorders caused by years of genetic manipulation."

Karl frowned. "I still don't understand what you're saying."

"Oh, never mind. You call them anomalies, right?"

"Yes," Olaf said. "I'm concerned that our mom or dad may have ..." He paused abruptly, swiping his forearm across his eyes. Clearing his throat, he continued, "Anyhow, nothing ever came of the doctor's research. And any who go to the palace never return. Our mom was supposed to have a baby, but something went wrong. We're afraid they may've gone there out of desperation. Even after all that's happened, they can't accept that the king wants to harm them."

Qeriya softened her guard. "That's where our parents are too," she said with a mournful expression.

A wave of opal light overcame them as clouds closed ranks overhead. The colors glowed with concentrated abundance, rivaling those back home in the desert.

"There's still a ways to go before we get home, Olaf," said Karl, tugging gently on his brother's sleeve. "We need to start back." Addressing the others, he said, "We'll take you to our village, and you can stay the night with us. We'll have to watch Doctor Michael, but our healers can help him."

"Can you assure me they will help and not hurt him?" Qeriya interrogated Olaf.

"Of course! We'd never hurt him! We're only being cautious," Olaf asserted.

"Good!" Qeriya announced, standing stiff, her voice crisp.

"Well, definitely not human," Karl said to his brother.

They set off walking with their new acquaintances, Qeriya once more levitating Doctor Michael in midair for travel. Pretty soon, they found themselves passing from a forest of trees with leaves to one where bunches of sharp green sticks covered the branches. Lahcen felt the tip of one, flinching as it pricked his finger.

"You're not from here, are you?" Karl asked. The corner of his mouth rising in a half-smile as he glanced sideways at Lahcen.

"Why do you ask, don't I fit in?" he asked, throwing the green needle away with a certain amount of vehemence. He rubbed the slight sting from his finger.

Karl faced him squarely, the half-grin growing into a full sized smile. His eyes twinkled. "No, you don't fit in. No one here's afraid of pine needles. They're no different than leaves." Picking a needle, he demonstrated by poking it into the back of his hand until it snapped."

"Don't mind him." Olaf laughed. "My brother likes to mess with people."

"We'd heard there was an attack on the fire reaume when we were young," said Lahcen as they followed Olaf. "Do you know anything about that?"

Olaf nodded. "First to be attacked were the fire reaume, and then the rainforest humans. Many fire reaume were killed. They marched the humans into a desert prison. Grandmother can tell you more about what happened. She knows the history. We were only little when it happened," Olaf explained as they ascended a steep ridge.

"We grew up in that desert prison," Khalid informed them.

"Wow!" Karl added, admiringly. "You survived the wasteland?"

Qeriya's blood began to boil. She spun around to face the others, rolling her eyes and placing her hands on her hips. "It was not a wasteland! Why does everyone call it that? It may've been a prison, but it was home, and it was beautiful!"

"Don't mind her," Lahcen apologized, panting from the climb. He shot his sister a quelling look and grabbed a fast breath. "Qeriya, they don't mean to insult anyone. Let's not make things any worse!"

He smiled feebly at the reaume. "She misses home. But I'm just happy to visit places that have water!" He caught his breath and smelled the crisp air. It was cold and drier than the vast mist of the rainforest. He could smell clean water and heard it running in the distance, getting louder as they walked: far louder than the stream from which they had come. "What is that sound?" he asked, overcome with curiosity.

"That's a waterfall. We'll cross it shortly before reaching home," Karl answered.

"What's a waterfall?" Lahcen asked between gulps of air. His head grew hotter by the second, while his heart thumped all the way up into his brain from exertion. "It sounds fantastic, especially now. He sucked in another deep breath."

Karl's face swelled with pride. "It is! You'll see for yourself right after we climb over this hill. There's a gorge on the other side."

"I've got to see this!" Lahcen chuckled delightedly, rubbing his hands together in anticipation.

"If this Doctor Michael was in your desert prison, then perhaps he got in trouble with the king or else maybe he was sent there to spy on you all," Olaf reasoned.

"Neither," Qeriya said curtly. "He volunteered his time to serve there."

A short time later, they reached the top of the hill. Lahcen glanced down to find the source of white noise that had grown so loud he could no longer hear the others speak. Volumes of water tumbled down smooth boulders, turning from clear to plumes of white as it smashed against rocks in the pooling stream below. A large, wooden log was their path over this fast flowing wadi, a stream much larger than the one he had known growing up. But while the others walked across the log and Doctor Michael floated in the air, Lahcen elected to wade.

"No! Don't!" Karl yelled from atop the bridge. "It's cold, and the current's fierce!"

"He'll be fine," Khalid told him calmly. He laughed. "I certainly plan to take your advice, but Lahcen's precisely in his element."

Karl and Olaf panicked as Lahcen entered the frigid stream. Hurrying across the bridge they hopped down the steep bank to watch as Lahcen waded towards the middle.

"No! Don't do it! Don't go in!" they chorused.

Lahcen ignored their warning. As the water approached his waist, he giggled at the encroaching cold. The current took his feet from beneath him, carrying him swiftly downstream and he caught a glimpse of Olaf and Karl leaping like squirrels onto nearby pine branches.

"No! He's fine, really! Don't worry about him!" Khalid called, to no effect.

Lahcen stole brief glances behind him between close encounters with protruding rocks; Olaf and Karl were catching up. They resembled rainforest lemurs as tree branches propelled them downstream. But he was still too far along to tell the concerned brothers that he was all right.

Water had never tasted so fresh, and he savored every drop that splashed into his mouth. He felt the river surging down the steep grade. He sat upright and bent his legs to keep warm, using his hands to steer through rapids and avoid obstacles. Occasionally, the undertow flipped him and he righted himself. Forgetting everything else, he flew down the rapids, until he was plucked into the air by a pair of arms that grasped him around the chest and flung him onto the bank. Lahcen landed with a crunch on a pile of dried leaves. Above him, Olaf's legs were wrapped around a branch, his hands holding Karl's ankles. Olaf swung his brother to a nearby branch and both climbed down.

"Are you all right?" Karl asked, but Lahcen only laughed. "Quit laughing," Karl snapped. "It's not funny! You scared us!"

But Lahcen couldn't stop. The earth reaume brothers looked like a couple of spooked monkeys as they stared at him, pursing their lips in annoyance.

Khalid joined them just as Qeriya flew in.

"Am I all right?" Lahcen laughed delightedly. "That was great fun!" He scrutinized Khalid, Olaf and Karl as they stood towering over him.

Lahcen pushed to his feet and water rolled off of him and his clothes as if he were made of feathers. He stretched, noted Olaf's confoundment and simply patted his new friend's back. "It's complicated."

"I guess so," Olaf answered, leading them onward through the old forest. Suddenly he stopped, pointing to some bushes dotted with dark blue.

"You've brought us to a patch of wild blueberries! Let's get a snack and bring a bunch home for dinner while we're at it! We'll need to be quick, though, Grandmother will be worried if we don't hurry," he explained. "The clan didn't really want us to go and check on what was happening when we saw signs of battle at the volcano. They were even more dead set against us going when it erupted. It took ages for us to get permission to check it out. 'Course," he added, "We don't need to now we've met you."

"So how is it that the earth reaume didn't help?" Khalid asked, his eyes and hands drawn to the trees around him as if learning their names. "How come you were the only ones to come?"

"Earth reaume don't approve of the king's treatment of the fire reaume," Karl said, "but most don't want to get involved. We hate war, and while earth reaume are great fighters and weaponry craftsmen, we avoid conflict."

"Well, that reasoning sounds familiar," Lahcen said while Khalid and Qeriya nodded.

"Olaf and I believe that violence against the fire reaume is an attack on us," Karl added, thrusting his impassioned hands this way and that for emphasis, in contrast to his mild, soft-spoken brother. "We believe they attack all reaume when they hurt the fire reaume. The fire reaume have already had numerous confrontations with the king and so far we've been spared because we're cowards."

"No, not cowards," Olaf argued. "Pacifists. It takes courage to be a pacifist, Karl," he said, looking earnestly at his brother. He swung back to the three siblings. "Although, Karl and I believe that in this case pacifism is misguided. The king's out to destroy all reaume, and he's hurting our world. Most of the others don't seem to realize that that's a good reason to fight!"

Lahcen plucked a few plump berries and put them in his mouth, where they exploded into sweet, mildly tart juice. While the rest gathered berries, more ended up in Lahcen's stomach than in the expandable leather bags provided; he couldn't get enough. More bushes called to him, and he wandered away from the group like a child determined not to share his spoils.

Moments later, he bristled at a sudden noise among the bushes. "Don't you dare!" he warned, but there was no answer.

"Hey, I mean it!" Then he smiled. "Who's trying to scare me? Qeriya? Khalid?"

The only response was another rustling of branches. Swiftly surfing toward the sound, he saw an image disappear before his eyes. All he could make out was that it was either a person or a reaume, but that was the extent of his knowledge. Surfing back to the group, he found everyone still bunched together, chatting with one another.

"Okay, which one of you tried to scare me just now?" he asked. "I don't know how you did it, but it really freaked me out!" Blank stares greeted his words.

"Are you protecting the guilty party?" He grinned. "Wise move, because I'm gonna get them back."

Khalid shook his head. "We've all been here the whole time. In fact, we were just wondering where you'd wandered off to."

"You're messing with me?"

"No, honest!" Khalid looked to the others for support and they nodded in agreement, without even a glimmer of a smile.

"Maybe it was an animal, a small black bear perhaps? Bears love berries," Olaf ventured.

"It wasn't an animal!" Lahcen said exasperated. "Do you have ghosts in this forest?"

"No," Olaf said.

"Then it *had* to be one of you!"

"No, really, Lahcen, we've all been here the entire time. I'm perfectly serious. You're the only one who wandered off. Nobody tried to scare you!" Khalid insisted.

Lahcen was about to argue when Olaf interjected.

"I think we need to get back. It'll be dusk before we reach home at this rate," he said, setting off at a brisk pace. Left with no choice, the siblings hurried after him, mouths stained purple, clutching bags full of berries.

They forged ahead in silence for some time, Lahcen had refrained from asking how much further they had to go out of respect for his hosts. As he sensed the sun burrowing under the planet from behind the hills, he saw flickering firelight in the distance.

"Here we are," Karl announced proudly.

They entered an expansive clump of trees connected with woven vines and tree bridges. Shelters dotted the canopy, circling a clearing where a bonfire raged. Earth reaume conglomerated around tables and chairs placed around the fire, cooking their dinners on grates or in pots. They spoke quietly with one another, in contrast to the playful bustle of the fire reaume."

Approaching the fire, they found Olaf and Karl's grandmother stirring a large iron kettle. She wore a colorful shawl around her shoulders made from thick wool. Her hair was blonde and she looked youthful, more like their mother than grandmother. The earth reaume villagers were dressed in soft brown hide, male and female alike, but each carried different weapons or tools in packs similar to the one Khalid wore. The reaume studied them with intense interest, especially a gaggle of females who peered through infatuated eyes at Olaf and Karl. Camouflaged amid the greens and browns of the forest, hiding their faces and slipping behind obstacles to avoid a direct gaze, they sent penetrating glances at the visitors.

"The volcano's back to normal. The king gained control of

it, but the fire reaume fought back and won!" Karl announced proudly to everyone within earshot. His grandmother squeezed him and his brother in relief. The others slowly funneled into the open to lift their cups and smile at the newcomers.

"I've been so worried about you!" she exclaimed, giving them both a tight hug.

The pot held a fragrant smelling stew, simmering over a heap of hot coals, and Lahcen found his mouth gushing saliva as he savored the aroma.

"This is our grandma, Kari," Olaf introduced. "And Grandma, this is Lahcen, Khalid, and Qeriya." He paused. "They also rescued someone from the volcano prison. A man named Doctor Michael." There was a subdued gasp and some muttering from the gathering crowd as Qeriya floated Doctor Michael towards the evening fire.

"Doctor Michael?" Grandmother asked.

"He's our uncle."

Kari moved to Doctor Michael, eyeing and circling him for some time.

"The concern we have, Grandma, is that while he says he's their uncle and was captured by the king, he also bears the royal tattoo," Karl explained. He grasped Doctor Michael's forearm and positioned it for Kari to see clearly in the firelight.

Kari bent closer, carefully examining the tattoo.

Lahcen heard her gasp as the ladle dropped from her hand and she collapsed in a heap on the ground.

Oh no! Not again! It couldn't be happening again! Alexis had already rejected him once, what more did his subconscious mind have to be afraid of now? She was so beautiful, even walking down a dark, dank hallway. Leaning against the wall, he inched his way to the floor, his breathing constricted, his heart thumping, sweat pouring from him like tears; his body crying from humiliation.

She rushed over to him right away, squatting down, putting a hand on his shoulder, which made him feel even worse.

"Are you all right?"

He wanted to tell her that he'd be fine, but he could barely breathe. "Panic attack," he squeaked.

"I'll stay with you until you feel better."

He shook his head violently. "No! Please, no."

How could he possibly explain to her? He'd graduated top of his class, just like her. He was the essence of discipline and control. He'd withstood and excelled in numerous competitions over the years. He'd even been mugged while walking home from school without losing his head or suffering anything remotely approaching a panic attack. The first one came on when he heard her give a presentation in his nanotech grad class, and he hadn't even met her then!

He'd gone to counseling and the counselor advised him to try talking to her. "Just say, hi," he'd said.

Little did he know that his attempt at 'hi' would turn into: 'Do you want a coffee?' He'd jumped ahead of the program. In his defense, not much made sense when she was around.

"No, no, I can't leave you like this," she insisted.

He looked directly at her, with no other recourse. If he wanted to breathe again, he had to speak. "It's … you. You're the trigger. Go … and I'll … stop," he stammered, sweating profusely now.

"Oh!" Alexis blushed. Standing up, she walked out of his line of vision.

He doubled over and stared at the floor, humiliated.

Chapter 3

"Origins"

Grandma, you gave us quite a scare," Karl said, fussing around Kari. They were sitting on the ground, hoping the cool earth might help to revive her. "Do you feel ready to sit in the chair again?"

"Oh, yes, I'm feeling quite myself now. I must have got too hot by the fire." Kari tittered.

Lahcen thought she looked flustered and nervous as she began to rise. Karl and Olaf helped her into a chair. Lahcen, Khalid and Qeriya stood.

"I've never seen you faint before, Grandma," Olaf said.

"Yes, it's unusual, but there's a first time for everything," she said, chattering away as if nothing remarkable had happened.

"So, what do you think of this Doctor Michael? I thought he might be that ambassador sent by the king, you know, the one you told us about?" Karl asked.

Kari sat back in her chair, an incredulous expression washing over her face. "I know that to you, all old people are the same age, but this man's way too young to be the ambassador. He's your parents' age. Einar, the ambassador, was my age. I never met his wife, Alexis, but they were both scientists and medical doctors at the palace."

"Do you recognize that tattoo?" Khalid asked, once Kari was comfortably settled.

"Yes," she began and rubbed her eyes. "Yes, I'm familiar with it." She spoke with trepidation and offered no more thoughts.

"Do you know how our uncle ended up with this tattoo on his forearm?" Khalid asked.

Kari gave him a long look. "The only people who use this tattoo are royalty, and those in the royal circle. That's their trademark. It's the only way everyone knows they're part of the royal circle. That ambassador, Einar, had a tattoo much like the one on this man's arm. He showed me special markings on it that are particularly unique and can't be forged. This Doctor Michael appears to have them. Actually ..."

"Actually what?" Qeriya asked. She was met with silence as Kari moved to Doctor Michael and held his arm again.

Kari's gaze lingered on the tattoo for a long time. "It's just that this tattoo is a bit different ..."

"So maybe it's not royal at all?" Lahcen asked.

"It's just ... well, of course I'm not an expert on such matters, but Einar did go into some detail about the royal tattoos and ..."

"Grandma, please, just tell us what you're thinking?"

Kari seemed to come to a decision. "No, I won't speculate on things I know nothing about. I'll have to find more information."

"Einar shared quite a bit with me about the palace. He was a doctor in the royal circle, but he took time off to serve as an ambassador to the reaume," Kari explained to Qeriya, Lahcen and Khalid. She shook her head sadly. "We trusted him, but we were wrong to do so. He turned out to be an evil man."

"We need to get this man to our healers," she ordered with sudden conviction. Olaf, take them along, please.

Olaf led them to a wooden hut built on ground level, ducking inside, he held the long, beaded-string curtains aside as they entered. Two earth reaume, adorned with blue smocks, pulled plants and creams off of carts lining the far wall after a brief examination of the inert body. Their heads and faces were covered, leaving only eyes exposed. Candles flickered inside clouded crystals on shelves above where they worked, resembling bright stars illuminating the wooden shelter. The healers didn't acknowledge the visitors but went right to work on the doctor. They moved at lightning speed, lining his mouth with cream and putting patches on his head that gradually began to pulse in a distinct rhythm. Once the siblings were assured there was nothing to do but wait, they emerged from the tent with their new friends to return to the fire.

"He'll be all right," Kari assured them. "The healers can help, but it'll take some time to revive him. By the way, Qeriya, are you from the air reaume?" she inquired?

Qeriya glanced at her. "Air reaume, is that what I am?"

Kari furrowed her brows, as if puzzling how to answer. "You share their gifts. You hovered this Doctor Michael in the air. Can you fly, too?"

Qeriya nodded in response.

"Those are air reaume traits. I've only met one other from the air reaume, many years ago."

Qeriya was hungry for more answers, but Kari had picked up her pace.

"Well, let's eat. You all must be hungry!" She turned to her grandsons. "Some of your friends went hunting this morning and brought me a rabbit!"

"Rabbit! Not the cute, furry creature!" Qeriya wailed.

Lahcen squashed her foot but she shoved at him with surprising strength, forcing him to take a step to the side.

"Everyone's glad you're home safe," Kari said, wiping the wooden ladle she'd dropped before on a cloth and beginning to stir the pot of steamy stew. "I don't understand why you went. You could've been embroiled in a battle."

"We nearly were! But, Grandma, if we don't stick together with the other reaume, we'll all have to face the king in the end anyway, and he'll be stronger for having depleted the fire reaume. We have to make an alliance!" Olaf insisted.

"Alliances invite war. I hate talk of war!" Kari exclaimed. "It's just plain wrong, no matter how you slice it."

It was starting to get dark. The other earth reaume were enjoying their portions of after dinner herb tea and pretending not to listen to the ensuing argument.

"Everyone hates war. What's to like?" Olaf said. "But there's a difference between prolonging a war and fighting to end a war.

There're times when we need to look out for one another and protect what we've created! The king will milk the planet dry!"

Kari shook her head and raised her chin in defiance. "We care for the earth, for others, and for each other. We do not engage in fighting or any acts of violence."

"Pardon me, ma'am," Qeriya interrupted. "I'm afraid the fire reaume felt just as you do – until the palace captured all the adults and waged an attack on the children. We fought beside the children."

"Oh dear, children?" Kari winced.

"They didn't ask for it," Qeriya said, angry now. "They didn't want to fight. They had to, and the same will happen here!"

Again, Lahcen squashed her foot.

Kari's face paled as she ladled the savory soup into the carved, earthen bowls for each of them. The three cupped theirs gratefully, smelling the salty steam and sipping some broth before taking their first morsel. It was succulent and Lahcen greedily licked every drop of sauce from his lips.

"So, tell me about yourselves and your family," Kari said, changing the subject and smiling. "And don't worry, I always make a large pot just in case we have guests! You can have as much as you want."

"Thank you," Lahcen answered for all of them. He saw Qeriya eye her bowl, scowling at the pieces of rabbit meat. He elbowed her. "It really is delicious!"

"I'm not your punching bag, Lahcen!" she whispered with as much force as she could muster in hushed tones.

"Well, this might sound strange," Khalid commented, "but we seem to be learning more about our family from others than from our parents." While Khalid spoke, Lahcen studied the flickering patterns of light in the orange glow.

"Grandma, they're from the wasteland." Beholding Qeriya's cringe, Karl corrected himself. "I mean, the desert."

"The prison? You all are from the desert prison? But that

must mean you're human, and yet you have reaume traits?" She looked from one to the other, staring inquisitively, waiting for an explanation.

"We're human and reaume. It's a complicated story..." Khalid said.

"Kari's jaw fell a few inches. Really? Then it *is* a complicated story, and I imagine I know a great deal of it! Finding you three is why they imprisoned the humans in the first place. How did you escape the border?"

"Luck," Lahcen said. "We didn't exactly have much of a choice."

"I'm so glad you're all right," she said.

"For the time being," Qeriya added, sipping her stew. "You know who we are?"

"You're Aedan's children," Kari said, now ashen faced.

The siblings paused, staring at each other with disbelief. "How do you know that?" Lahcen persisted.

"I know your dad because I'm your grandmother's cousin, and she was my closest friend. Lourdes, your grandmother, was queen of the fire reaume."

"Lourdes, yes! We discovered that much when we were with the fire reaume," Khalid said. "She was our dad's mother."

"Lourdes and I grew up together." Kari's eyes were glassy and she gazed into the fire fixedly, as if it revealed pictures of the past. "You all and the boys are third cousins!"

"More cousins?" Lahcen asked, incredulous. "I can't begin to keep all of these cousins straight."

"Wait, she grew up here, with the earth reaume?" Qeriya asked, distracted enough to stop eating. Lahcen couldn't understand how she could forget to eat. No matter how interesting, nothing could distract him from Kari's rabbit stew. "Wasn't she a fire reaume?"

"She was also earth reaume. Our fathers were brothers," Kari explained. "I can't believe that I got to see Lourdes's grandchildren!"

"How did she die?" Qeriya asked, mesmerized, her half-eaten food balanced on her lap.

"She died in battle." Kari sighed deeply. "It wasn't until later that I discovered Aedan had married a human. Lourdes hadn't told anyone. She was strangely secretive about the marriage, so we weren't invited to the wedding. I don't know anything about the human he married. All I know is that after the battle, we figured Aedan must have been captured and forced into the desert with the rest of the human clan."

"Our father, Aedan, is now a prisoner at the palace, along with our mother," Qeriya added. She cupped her bowl and sat on the edge of a rustic wooden chair. "Not only are they prisoners, but they're both very sick with an illness that can only be treated with a flower called the paintbrush that grows in the mountains near the palace. That's where we're going now, to gather the flower and figure out a way to rescue our parents."

Kari's face fell. "Oh my! Poor Aedan and your mother. But rescue from the palace is impossible," she said, glancing from one to the other of them. "It's a fortress, like a planet within a planet. I've never seen it myself, but I heard about it from Einar. Its security is very tight."

"We don't have a choice," Qeriya said flatly.

Silence fell as they stared into the fire like a pack of cobras swaying along with the flickers. Lahcen suddenly came out of his reverie and peered towards the surrounding forest. He was certain that someone or something was lurking between the trees. But when he squinted, the image disappeared. Still, he'd stake his life on the fact that he'd seen movement. It had occurred just as a passing cloud released the moon from shadow.

"What is it, Lahcen?" Qeriya asked.

Lahcen raked his hand through his hair. "I don't know, but someone's out there. It's like before. I see someone in my peripheral vision, but when I look at the figure straight on, it vanishes."

"I'm sure there are lots of animals around. Perhaps searching for scraps of food?" Qeriya offered.

Lahcen glared at her. "I told you before, it looks human or reaume." He shook his head, curbing his irritation. "Then again, it's dark."

"Yes, it's getting late. I expect you need a place to sleep tonight," Kari said, rising from her seat.

"Oh, no, that's not necessary," Khalid said quickly. "I brought a tent in my backpack. We're planning to stay in it as we travel."

"A tent in your backpack? You really are earth reaume. I'm glad to know that Aedan prepared you so well. But you won't stay in your tent tonight. I'm sure you'll have lots of opportunity for that later. We have a guesthouse in our complex. Karl and Olaf will show you up there after dinner."

"Qeriya." Kari drew her aside by the arm as they were rising to leave. "I have something for you." She took a clear, small bottle out of her pocket and held it up to the firelight for Qeriya to see. It shimmered gold. "You're nearing the age for an air reaume to use this. I took it from the healing tent for you. I don't even know why we have it. Earth reaume certainly have no use for it."

"What is it?" Qeriya asked, lifting the bottle from Kari's hands, rocking it from side to side and watching the contents ooze around the container.

"Gold, gold cream."

"Gold? That has to be valuable, Kari! Why would you give it to me?"

"It is valuable, but not in the way you think. It's valuable to you. I don't know the proper way to apply it, but I know that all air reaume teens endure a rite of passage in which they apply the cream to their skin. Save it until you encounter them. They can show you how to use it correctly."

"What does it do?"

"I don't know. You'll have to ask them."

"I'll certainly keep it safe," Qeriya told her. "You've piqued my curiosity." She tucked it into a deep pocket of her scarf sling, a present from her fire reaume cousins, before following her brothers.

Catching up to the others, Qeriya walked towards one of the large trees circling the bonfire. Attached to and surrounding the tree was a wooden staircase that spiraled up the trunk into the lower branches of the canopy, where a platform awaited them. Extending from this platform was a web of rope bridges that linked a plethora of wooden tree houses nestled among the branches.

They traipsed across one rope bridge after another through what felt like an elevated maze cloaked in darkness, illuminated only by occasional solar lights along the bridges and on the numerous houses they passed. Each home had its own character, decorated in subtle but unique ways. Some were loaded with epiphyte gardens growing off the surrounding trunks and branches. Others had garden roofs full of flowers. There were large, spacious dwellings and small, cozy ones. Each one had a unique floor plan depending upon the nuance of the hosting tree trunk, and was carved with skillful designs.

"What are these guys doing?" Lahcen asked, having spotted a unique carving on a doorframe. He ran his fingers across the figures of Earth reaume curving downhill on tapering wooden planks. Thick clothing surrounded their bodies, heads and even their hands.

"Oh, I'm glad you noticed the artwork. My grandfather carved that scene. This structure is the bathroom. The figures you see are telemarking, a type of downhill skiing," Olaf said. "We ski in winter time, when snow covers the ground."

"I've heard of snow," Lahcen said.

Olaf beamed. "Before long the ground will be covered with a thick blanket of it. We also cross country ski with sleds, to harvest crops from our cold frames."

Khalid yawned and Lahcen followed suit. His stomach was starting to ache he was so tired. Thankfully, a short while later, Karl and Olaf gestured to a house.

"Here you are!" Karl said.

They entered through a doorway lovingly carved with flowers, opening out into a room with four small beds and cushions to use as back rests. There were crystal candleholders on the small tables between each bed, along with bowls and towels. Olaf immediately lit each candle, while Karl took water out of his pack and poured some into each bowl.

"Tomorrow you can sleep until breakfast's ready," Olaf said. "I'll wake you. We tend the harvest every morning," he added, "you're welcome to come."

"Yes, we'd like that," Khalid answered for all of them as the brothers left them to themselves.

Just as they snuggled down under wool blankets and lay their heads on the feather stuffed pillows, they heard a knock on the door. Lahcen stumbled out of bed. Opening the door, he discovered a glass globe, like a large bubble, glowing with light and harboring a letter inside. The globe levitated into the tiny house before Lahcen had a chance to register what was happening. Once inside, it went directly to Khalid and nestled into his arms as if it were an affectionate pet.

Khalid grasped the glass in his hands, looking as puzzled as Lahcen felt. He turned it around in circles and finally stroked it. Immediately, the top portion of the glass retracted and Khalid put his hand inside to retrieve the piece of paper. The message was short and to the point.

"It's Anna," Khalid said. "We're all safe," he read.

Lahcen sighed with relief.

"Be vigilant," Khalid continued. "We've been contacted through Orchid Pond. Friend or foe we are unsure. They send a message. The king has amassed an army at the ancient palace, an old human outpost strategically close to the Earth reaume. He's planning to attack. If you're with them now, watch your back."

Qeriya levered herself up into a sitting position and placed her head in her hands. "We should've listened to Doctor Michael when he said not to come here. Why do we not trust him when he's always right?"

"Einar, isn't it?" Alexis' voice sounded behind him. A familiar sensation began to creep under his skin, his throat clenched and he did not turn around to look at her or speak, but simply nodded.

"Were you by chance asking me to go out with you when you asked if I wanted coffee?"

He nodded, still looking the other way, frozen, the moment confining him to a state of irrational panic.

"I thought you were just asking in passing if I wanted some from the student lounge. You caught me off guard. I was in the middle of thinking through a problem. You asked me a question and I answered it without giving the situation much thought. Anyway, that's a long way of saying, yes, I'd like to go out with you to get a ... tea, preferably."

"He began to turn around, slowly, daring to peer at her face, her smile, and this time, he could breathe, though he still trembled.

"I'm so sorry that you suffer these ... panic attacks."

"Yes, well, thanks. I don't usually, only when ... when—" he began, twisting his hands together into a knot.

"When I'm around. Yeah, I gathered that when you were choking – that sounded way too casual, didn't it? I never knew. Just about everyone else did, though. They told me to avoid you, that's why I've tried not to talk to you. But I don't understand ... why me?"

"Because you're beautiful!" he blurted. Saying it was like opening a pressure valve in his chest. He felt better already. "You're the most wonderful woman I've ever seen in my life."

Chapter 4

Sacrifice

Khalid followed Olaf up a trail that wound through the leafy forest. The reaume had gathered this morning to partake in an offering up in the mountains. His siblings were a ways ahead with Karl, but he wanted to take it slow and admire the trees. He could sense that they were reserved, enduring, perhaps hibernating for the winter. They were so unlike the hospitable arboretum of the rainforest.

"The white bark trees are birch, those with large red leaves are maple. You'll see groups of both as we travel," Olaf explained as if reading his mind.

Khalid was excited to meet others like him. It almost distracted him from thinking about the news he'd received the previous night. They'd tried to warn everyone at breakfast, but like the fire reaume, the earth reaume had refused to leave. Nor would they do anything to prepare for battle.

Of course, the three of them could leave, but that assumed the king targeted only them. And what if they were wrong, maybe the earth reaume were his target after all? In that case they would need help.

"On the other side of our village are forests of elm, oak and ash. As we climb, we'll enter the evergreens," Olaf offered.

Khalid followed him to a birch tree, where he peeled a strip of bark. Scraping the inside of the bark until powder fell into his hands, he gave a pinch to Khalid.

"Taste it. That's birch bark flour. We use it to make bread. We use the outer bark to craft our containers," Olaf explained. "We collect this and other supplies on our way to the Hot Springs."

"So, what are hot springs? Did you say that they're natural pools of boiling water?"

"Yes, we're hiking up into the caldera of a volcano, only this one is many times the size of the one near the rainforest. It's an ancient temple. If it ever erupted, I doubt even the fire reaume would survive the— Hey, where are you going?"

"Stop!" Khalid called speeding off. There was someone there; he couldn't see who it was or make out any particular features, but there was definitely someone there. "Wait, where did you go?" he found himself addressing only snapping branches. "Did you see anyone, Olaf?"

"No. I didn't see anything," Olaf said, scouring the area with his eyes.

Khalid frowned. "I definitely saw someone. I can't describe anything about the figure, only that he or she was watching us, and when I looked over, there was nothing. It almost looked like—"

"What? Almost looked like what?"

Khalid struggled to find an answer. Grabbing the nearest branch, he swung through the forest scanning the area around where the figure had disappeared. Finding nothing, he retraced his path.

Shaking his head, he said, "I don't know, to be honest ... an apparition. Now it's gone."

"Gone as in ran away?"

"That's what's so strange. It's like he or she simply disappeared right in front of me first – and then ran away. It was similar to seeing something in the dark. You know how when you shift your line of sight to it, whatever you're looking at disappears? Only I saw the figure directly, not in my peripheral vision." He dry washed his face. "It's hard to explain."

"What do you want to do?"

"There's nothing to do. We'll keep going, and stay alert. I wonder if it's the same figure Lahcen saw?" Despite knowing he would find nothing, Khalid peered into the shadows among the trees. "I think we're being watched. Perhaps the king's sent soldiers to scout out your village and habits."

The sun moved in and out of the clouds, shifting between twilight and bright rays that sifted through the forest layers and danced along the ground. They walked, trading speed for attentiveness, harvesting wild mushrooms, acorns and apples.

"This is my new favorite fruit!" Lahcen's loud voice sliced through the quiet hum of conversation after biting into a crisp apple. He stuck out from the others like moss in a sand dune.

"We'll reach our garden plot soon," Olaf informed them, starting up a steep climb. "Hopefully the crops aren't missing this time."

"Did someone steal your harvest?"

He snorted. "Deer. We have trouble with deer and rabbit overrunning the crops. The predators are disappearing. The king's destroying them. He's unleashed a series of experimental animal hybrids on us. They prefer eating reaume and other predators to deer meat. Roast venison used to be a delicacy, but now we eat it all the time, as does our sister pack. Still, we'd gladly eat more rabbit stew and vegetables if it meant the noble predators could return."

"Did you say a sister pack? Is that what you call groups of reaume – packs?"

"No." Olaf smiled, climbing over a fallen tree. "We're it for the earth reaume. We're friends with a pack of wolves we call our sister pack. They guard our territory. In return, they get free hunting rights and we share food with them in winter."

"I've never heard of these hybrid creatures before," Khalid said.

"They've only been around for about five years or so. We were always able to kill them easily, but now they're growing more resistant to our powers. So far our sister pack has survived, but we're afraid for them."

As they crested a hill, Khalid beheld a meadow. Clusters of wild flowers dotted the ground in the sun soaked open space.

"The creatures are always bizarre," Olaf continued. "One was half-horse, half-venomous snake, if you can imagine that! Most of them must be purely experimental, because when we find their weak spot, they die quickly. Their lives are brittle to begin with, no stamina. None of us have died so far, but I'm afraid it's bound to happen soon."

"The king never seems to have enough power to suit him. Perhaps creating violent animals is his way of getting it," Khalid said.

They walked to a clump of trees on the other side of the meadow, most of which had buckets attached to their trunks. Olaf detached one of the buckets and emptied the liquid content, by way of a valve, into a skin that was in his pack. He then touched a swelling drip and gestured for Khalid to do the same. They both tasted the liquid and Khalid found that it tasted similar to water. He scanned further ahead, where Lahcen and Qeriya were taking a taste as well.

"We boil this for days to evaporate the water and it becomes a rich, sweet syrup."

"You eat tree blood?" Khalid clarified, contorting his face in horror.

"We make sure the trees are comfortable. We soften any discomfort they might feel during the procedure."

"How do you do that?"

"You don't know? You're so much like us. I figured you had that ability too. Perhaps you just need practice. It's a subtle influence, not a complete anesthetic. It happens when we feel compassion."

"Huh, I've experienced a bit of that type of power with the fire reaume. Their leader put me under a spell, and now I'm in love with her. I can't seem to move on no matter how hard I try." Khalid shrugged as he plunged into a deep well of longing. "And the truth is, I don't even want to. That's how much of a hold she has on me."

"But fire reaume can't determine your emotion, they only

influence what's already there. They tap into a person's drive. She may have influenced you all to remain with them, but she couldn't have made you love her. She can only magnify what you feel. Just like we can't take away pain, only soften it."

"Oh, no, she did more than magnify. She exerted a power on me, and it's unlike anything I ever felt!

"There's no way she could have you under any influence now. She's not even close! If you still feel that way, then you're genuinely in love with her." Olaf smiled widely as Khalid stood stock still, gaping, the idea obviously new to him.

They neared the top of a hill, skirting a sunken gorge formed by water erosion to his left. At the moment it was dry.

"This gorge floods every spring when the snow melts. The run off becomes a stream that feeds the waterfall we crossed before reaching our village. Other streams pour into it further down," Olaf said.

As Khalid climbed even higher, leaves were replaced with sharp, green needles, the evergreens. They must be close to the top.

"Olaf, the fire reaume said they were responsible for shaping and directing lava to form the planet. They received instructions from the sacred water they call Orchid Pond. Have you heard of it?"

Olaf dipped his chin in acknowledgement. "Yes, I've heard of it, we all have. The fire reaume claim it's sacred and we acknowledge it's an oracle, but we believe it's an extension of Hot Springs, sent to guide them. Hot Springs is home to the true Spirit, whose power bubbles from beneath the earth and floats into steam. It draws together lava, water, air and earth. It gives us instructions to plant life in every climate formed by the fire reaume. You'll see what I mean soon enough."

"W–well," Khalid stammered, "the thing is, we found out Orchid Pond wasn't sacred after all. It turned out to be a water computer. It was intercepted by humans, who recently used it against them."

Olaf shook his head. "I'm sorry to hear that. I've never heard of a water computer before."

"I'd never heard of such a thing either. Doctor Michael said that water computers are an old form of communication," Khalid said, surprised by Olaf's complacency. It was amazing how convinced Olaf was that his oracle was the "right" one. He appeared to have complete, unquestioned obedience to this Hot Spring. Why did reaume feel that the Spirit had to be contained at all? "Why would the Spirit give instructions to make the world like this? Why not leave it the way it was?"

"Mostly ocean? I think not. They tried to copy as much of Old Earth as possible, given its natural terrain, to assure that everyone could survive," Olaf answered.

"But aren't reaume native to this planet?"

"Oh, no, no. Reaume are from Old Earth, just like humans. We settled this planet together."

"Together, humans and reaume? Really!" Khalid halted, astounded. "The reaume were from Old Earth as well? Somehow it made more sense when I thought they were from this planet. So then how did the two species develop?"

Olaf frowned. "I don't know. All I know is the reaume migrated along with humans. We're natives of Old Earth. Once here, reaume used instructions from Hot Springs and the other pools to terraform this nearly lifeless ocean planet into another earth. The Spirit knew what we needed. We only had to obey and follow our instructions exactly as they were given. We've lived this way for many years. But now you've all come, everything will change."

"What do you mean by that? What kind of change?"

"I'm not sure. But you have a part to play in ushering in change." Olaf sought to move forward down the hill, but Khalid blocked his path.

"Part to play? What part?"

"There's an earth reaume prophecy. A prophecy that's so old, no one has any knowledge of its origin, but we remember it because it's our hope."

"A prophecy?" Khalid asked.

As Olaf spoke, the trees began to quiver as the slight breeze grew into a fierce wind.

"One will mend the worlds of reaume and human. One will overcome many, destroy destruction, heal New Earth. One will bring peace."

"What does that have to do with us?" Khalid asked, as the wind subsided.

"The prophecy speaks about one of *you*. It has to. You've already mended the rift between reaume and humans, just by nature of being born both. But I think it's clear that one of you will fulfill the rest of the prophecy."

"Our purpose right now is to rescue our parents. Anything else we accomplish is secondary," Khalid declared.

They soon reached the summit of a rim, the pinnacle of their climb, where the trees were small and gnarled. Khalid viewed the other side of the rim, looking down into the massive caldera. It was green with grasses, hills, trees, and decorated with winding streams. He didn't expect this volcano to be so unlike the other. Interspersed in this normalness lay steaming pools, some of which bubbled with boiling water.

"That's where we're headed." Olaf pointed to one particularly large hot spring. It appeared as a swirl of colors surrounded by white and yellow rock. The center of the pool faded to a mist of powder blue. It was beautiful. "Don't get too close unless you're prepared to sacrifice."

"Sacrifice?"

"Yeah, we bring the best of our harvest and offer it to the Spirit."

Khalid wondered what a pool of boiling water would do with maple syrup and apples but decided not to say anything offensive.

The crowd gathered around the edge of the steaming lake. The earth reaume began a deep bow in reverence, scattering their gifts of food across the white dirt and yellow rock along the shore. The steam smelled odd. "What is that odor?" he whispered to Olaf.

"That scent comes from a yellow rock called sulfur. It smells like eggs. You get used to it." Olaf inhaled to capacity.

Khalid searched for his brother and sister, and found them already standing alongside the edge of the bubbling pond with Karl.

The edges of the body of water were shallow on the outside, colored green and yellow. As his gaze moved towards the center the shades morphed to oranges, then reds, followed by the most brilliant azure he'd ever seen.

"This is Morning Glory Pool, the heart of Hot Springs, source of the great Spirit. Even its steam is healing. We take off our shoes on this holy ground and wade into the water, Olaf told him, doing just that." Khalid followed suit, along with his siblings, who straggled behind Karl some distance away, palpably unsure about the wisdom of wading into a pool of boiling water.

Khalid sighed deeply as he soothed his blistered feet in an inch of warm, yellow water, watching the earth reaume ford the length of the shallow area into deeper water to deposit a large harvest. Khalid retreated to where his siblings waded, but Olaf moved beyond Karl, sinking to above his knees in the near boiling, acidic water.

"Olaf, what are you doing?" Khalid shouted, no longer caring whom he might offend with his noise.

Olaf ignored him; trembling but calm, he took off his pack, released the drawstring and emptied it into the water. Out tumbled a mix of carrots, acorns, and more. The others did nothing but bow towards the center of the pool, even Karl. Qeriya was prepared to lift him out, but Lahcen put up a hand to stop her.

After depositing the produce, Olaf reversed and lifted his legs out of the water one at a time until he'd rejoined Khalid, who supported him out onto the chalky ground. Olaf collapsed, eyes tight shut, breathing fast. The skin on his legs and feet was already forming blisters and scattered with raw sores. Tears escaped from the outer corner of his eyelids and poured into his hair, but he didn't make a sound.

Lahcen and Qeriya crowded around Olaf and Karl. Khalid clamped Olaf's hand as his breathing slowed.

"You're easing his pain, Khalid," Karl said as he knelt beside them. "Only earth reaume can do that, but we usually don't after an encounter with Hot Springs. Pain's part of the process."

"But why?" Khalid asked in horror, his siblings' expressions equally aghast. "Why hurt himself like that? Why boil himself alive?"

"Sacrifice," Karl answered. "Sacrifice is the way we dare to approach the Spirit with a request. He made a petition for your safety."

"It's too fragile," Alexis said. "The protein folds won't allow for the insertion of even the tiniest nanoparticle." Having examined the data one last time, she spun her chair around to face Einar, who was pacing the floor.

"But that was our best strategy. If it won't work, that sets us back to stage one!" he exclaimed. It was enough to unsettle Alexis.

"Getting upset won't make it any more possible, it will only lead to you breaking something, probably a glass. Whenever you get upset, a glass breaks somehow."

"I need to play tennis, "Einar muttered savagely.

"Nothing's open. It's midnight. We just have to give up and start again tomorrow ... after you've played tennis."

"I'm too awake to sleep."

"Well, I can't very well help you with that. I'm frustrated, too, you know." She stood up from her chair and kicked off her high-heeled shoes with some vehemence. That was the extent of her rebellion. She gathered her papers and shoved everything into a large tote bag, ripping a page or two at the frayed edges.

"Of course, who wouldn't be? The king tasks the two of us with an assignment, unprecedented given our ages and inexperience. We finally have a chance to prove our worth, and we screw it up!"

"Speak for yourself. I didn't mess up. I'm just not done, that's all," Alexis said. "Perhaps we've been charged with an impossible assignment. Science, after all, has to be discovered before it can be manipulated. If the king wants alchemists, he shouldn't ask for scientists. That said, it's our job to explore the possibilities of science and see if such a charge is possible first. I suggest you set your ego aside and work the problem – tomorrow," she ordered, her voice full of irritation, and stormed out of the door, leaving her shoes behind.

Chapter 5

Abduction

Lahcen and Khalid joined a pack of earth reaume gathered by a pile of ashes, which had been a bonfire the night before. It was still dark, but the outline of trees against the sky was becoming more visible by the minute as light swelled into life.

"Olaf, you're here? How can you possibly walk after yesterday?" Lahcen asked as they approached the crowd of earth reaume who silently examined their equipment for the morning hunt: bows, arrows and knives.

"Of course I'm here. I hurt, but I'm not incapacitated. I can swing on branches just fine, and plan to keep my kill to squirrels or perhaps a rabbit."

It was a good thing Qeriya had decided against coming, Lahcen thought. She'd whine about killing rabbits and he'd end up arguing with her.

"Do we need equipment? We're just fine watching," Khalid said.

Olaf shook his head to Khalid's question. One of the earth reaume, with long, blond hair tied at the nape of his neck, stood apart from the others and raised his hand. He was apparently the leader as the others raised their hands in turn, one at a time, until all had sufficiently inspected their equipment and were ready to go. The leader made numerous gestures with his hands and arms that everyone but he and Khalid seemed to understand.

Olaf watched carefully. When everyone began to mobilize, he turned to Lahcen. "Sign language."

"So does that mean that someone is deaf?" Lahcen probed.

"No one here is deaf. We prefer sign language when hunting. We don't scare away the prey, and we hear our environment. "Listening profoundly connects us with the natural world."

Lahcen choked back a laugh. Noble as that might be, it would never work in his household.

Khalid joined the crew as he nimbly jumped to catch a nearby tree branch, flinging himself from one tree to another with incredible strength and precision. Lahcen trailed behind, embarrassed by his surf, which made more noise than the mass of the others combined. Olaf remained with him. The rest of them spreading out and sweeping through the forest, branch by branch. Some found squirrels or rabbits in a matter of minutes and then retreated back to the camp. Others closed the gap and forged ahead until they found whatever animal they were after.

They killed in whichever way they deemed most painless, most often shooting the animal through the head with an arrow. Their aim was impeccable. The rare times when they were not accurate, they whammed the animal on the head with a large stick.

"What do most of these hunters want to catch?" Lahcen asked.

"Some are out for deer, others are looking for elk. Still others might be lucky and find a moose. Finding a large animal is a much more time consuming process, but then you get a break from hunting come winter."

"I hope we spot large game!" Lahcen's eyes popped wide open with anticipation as he crested large waves, jumping over them and performing flips and spins before hitting the water again.

"All right, if you say so. We'll stick with it until we find big game. Although I might need help carrying the kill back to camp, given the state of my bottom half right now," Olaf said, eyeing his heavily bandaged legs and feet.

"Obviously," Lahcen said as he cruised beside Olaf. "I don't understand why you feel the need to hurt yourself when you pray. The world can be bad enough without you making it worse."

Because it's the all-powerful Spirit we're speaking to. There is no other acceptable way of approaching a Spirit that's so removed from our ability to comprehend.

"Why would a loving Spirit require such abuse, or do you not believe the Spirit is loving?"

"Oh yes, of course, but we don't want to take that love for granted. Our sacrifice forces us to confront the greatness of the Spirit and the seriousness of approaching the unapproachable."

Lahcen couldn't help but frown, and tried to keep his face hidden from his friend, not wanting to offend him in any way. This way of understanding the Spirit felt wrong, not just different, but truly wrong. Why? Why was he so convinced of this?

They moved along in silence for a long while before he could no longer hold his tongue. "We, too, have always worshiped the Spirit, but I believe the Spirit would rather us care for others than sacrifice ourselves for no reason. Sometimes caring requires sacrifice, but not always."

"Sacrifice is for our benefit, not the Spirit's."

"If that's the case, then make it count for something. There's enough need out there without creating new crises. My parents worked long hours in the salt flats all day, every day. Life was hard enough. Worship was joyful for us."

Olaf stopped to listen, but said nothing and made no gesture of any kind.

Lahcen's face filled with heat and he tried to hold back, but since he'd started talking the floodgates opened and everything in his head rushed out. "I mean, when we battled the king, earth reaume were nowhere to be seen. But now you give yourselves second degree burns to pray for our safety? If you care about the Spirit, then care about what the Spirit cares about! Help us, help the fire reaume!" Lahcen was breathing hard by this point, even though there were no hills to make him exert himself. He bit his tongue so that no more words came out.

Olaf stared at the ground for a long time. Light had blossomed into morning, though it was still early. Lahcen felt that maybe he should have stayed in bed. He could have avoided this confrontation. He might be right, after all, he usually was, but his anger was misplaced. Olaf's heart was genuine. He was just being obedient to his cultural practices. Why fault him for that, even if his cultural practices were ludicrous? It was too bad Khalid was so far ahead. He always had a better way of handling these situations.

Lahcen saw something out of the corner of his eye – movement. He turned to look. A woman became transparent before his eyes. She disappeared, leaving only translucent lines of her shape in her place. He surfed to where she had stood moments before, but there was no sign of anyone. He caught up with the others.

As he rushed ahead, Lahcen ran into Olaf's outstretched arm. His surf lapped an invisible wall of air. Searching the area in the direction of Olaf's gaze, he gasped. Down below was a majestic creature. Its enormous antlers were solid and somewhat flattened, extending out and upwards on either side of its head. It had large, droopy eyes that appeared almost sad. Its nose was long and rounded, almost like petroglyphs of horses he'd seen drawn in various caves around his desert home. Olaf eyeballed the animal as it looked in their direction, probably having heard him. It plodded with majestic strength on spindly legs and thick hooves.

"Moose," Olaf whispered.

Both Lahcen and Khalid held unnaturally still, copying Olaf's example. Lahcen grew stiff, and wondered when they were going to kill the animal. He glanced at Olaf and saw that the latter was moving, very slowly, to his quiver for an arrow, while at the same time lifting his bow into position. Olaf waited until the perfect moment.

Lahcen could hardly stand another minute of it. He wanted to jump out of his skin. The suspense of the hunt was bad enough, but the thought that there were invisible soldiers scouting them out for the king was even more insufferable. And what could he say? He didn't get a good look at the figure before she'd disappeared.

Finally, the moose turned its head to the side and immediately Lahcen heard the quiet thump of bowstring. The arrow lodged deep into the moose's head and the creature collapsed onto the ground, instantaneously dead. You could pierce the quiet with a knife it was so thick. Lahcen surveyed the other reaume. Their heads were bowed in reverent prayer for the life lost.

"So, uh, now what?" Lahcen uttered, breaking the heavy silence. Khalid crushed his foot and whispered, "You really know how to ruin a moment, don't you?"

"What? What did I do? I mean, the animal's dead, isn't it. Are we just going to stand here and gawk?"

"We always take a time of silence to pray, thanking the Spirit for giving us the animal," Olaf explained and Khalid rolled his eyes.

"Oh ... well ... I guess I could see how that might be a good idea. I mean, we take our eating seriously, too ... don't get me wrong," Lahcen stammered, flushing a deep shade of puce.

"I need to help," Olaf said and left the brothers to watch, both having forgotten their promise to help drag the animal back in the excitement of the kill.

The reaume had a tarp with handles they lay on the ground. A group of them grabbed hold of various body parts and lifted the moose onto the tarp. They used straps to secure the carcass, then got into formation around it, each taking a handle. Within minutes they were carrying the creature towards the village.

On a whim, Lahcen wheeled around to scope the forest behind them. There, accosting him, were a pair of familiar, steel-gray eyes. "There she is again!" Lahcen hollered as he surfed away, leaving his clueless brother in a spray of cold water.

Close as she was, within a few steps she had vanished. "Where did she go? She was right there only a minute ago! It wasn't as if she pulled her head behind a tree either. She just disappeared in a shimmer!"

"Who did you see?" Khalid asked as he ran towards him.

"We're being watched by the woman who tried to kill Qeriya. I swear it's her!"

"I thought I saw someone on the trip to Hot Springs, too. You got a good look at her?"

"Yes, but she disappeared."

"That's what I saw, too. You didn't see which way she went?" he asked.

"No, I mean she literally disappeared into thin air. I don't understand it. She just went poof!"

"I know, that happened to me, too. Could you tell at all if she 'poofed' to the right or left?"

Lahcen shook his head. "Poof has no direction! There's nothing we can do but watch our backs."

They made a beeline for the group and eventually reached the village. The crew let go of the tarp straps. Lahcen studied the once alert, now vacant eyes of the moose, and pondered for a moment the suddenness of death, how it crept up on this unknowing creature without warning, how suddenness meant less suffering, but it also meant not saying goodbye, not saying the things that should be said. What would saying goodbye be for a moose? Seeing this great animal fall made him think of Doctor Michael for some reason.

Hearing his name spoken, Lahcen peered around the village becoming aware of some sort of commotion. One of the medics who was speaking with an earth reaume spotted him and ran towards him. Pale strands worked their way out of her hair cover and sweat poured from her face.

"Come inside, quick, he's waking!" she called urgently. Lahcen and Khalid left the moose and stuck their heads through the entrance to see Doctor Michael restlessly twisting his head from side to side on his pillow. As they watched, he threw first one arm above his head, pulled it back down by his side and threw the other up. Qeriya was already there, sitting on the ground beside him.

"He's just started getting restless," the disheveled healer announced. Just then, Doctor Michael's eyes fluttered open, then closed for a moment; only to reopen to scan his surroundings.

"Lahcen?" His voice was a dusty croak. "I see Lahcen and Khalid, but where's—?"

"I'm right here beside you," Qeriya answered and he inclined his head towards her. "I've been here for some time. How are you feeling, Uncle?"

The Doctor grasped hold of Qeriya's hand, the act seemingly taking all of his strength because his lids slowly closed, his grip growing lax as he sank into deep slumber once again.

The healer started across the floor to check her patient but didn't even make it half way before a crack sounded above them. The structure splintered. Before he could blink, Lahcen was felled by heavy wooden shingles descending on him, pinning him to the floor. Struggling free, Lahcen crawled over to where the healer was fighting to escape from the rubble and began heaving aside the wooden slats.

"Thank you. I can manage now," she said a scarce few minutes later. "Help your sister!" She nodded to where Qeriya grappled with a pile of debris that trapped her legs. By now Khalid had freed himself and together they made short work of releasing Qeriya.

Turning to the bed, Lahcen froze as he realized there was no movement there. No sign at all of the Doctor trying to free himself. Beside him, Khalid muttered an oath as Qeriya pushed past them shouting, "Doctor Michael! Are you all right?" and began dragging aside pieces of wood. Lahcen and Khalid quickly joined her but as they dug through the mess it became increasingly obvious that the man they sought wasn't there. "Where did he go?" Qeriya asked, as they exchanged worried glances.

The other reaume had come running and suddenly, Olaf cried out, "Over there!" He pointed. "Doctor Michael's flying!"

"What a lovely place!" Einar said as he walked around her small but luxurious apartment. I see you have a flair for art." Set into the wall was a tapestry of woven colored light, appearing to slide into one another, parts of it converging to form white light, other parts exposing only dark. The collection involved complex patterns, both beautiful and stimulating.

"Yes, I collect light art. The light itself brightens my apartment. The colors are energizing and the patterns intriguing."

As she spoke, he admired her velvet curves, no longer hidden by the boxy lab coat, and his heart quickened. He reached out to stroke her hair. "You look lovely," he whispered. It was so hard to work with her day in and day out and not touch her.

She took a step towards him, gazing into his eyes, her own a radiant dark-blue in the shadow beyond the lab lights. He slipped an arm around her waist, a hand behind her head, and pulled her close: the closest he'd ever been to a woman. But it felt so natural. He'd dreamed of this moment for so long. Lifting her face, he kissed her on the lips, gently at first, then, an invisible force drawing her closer, deepening the kiss.

She squirmed in his arms and he held her steady for a moment before reluctantly letting go at last.

"Not now," she said. "While we're in the middle of this project it's not the time. You need to go."

He knew she was right but, somehow, he lacked the will. She extracted herself from his grip, pushed him into the hall and shut the door, leaving him hunched, his head against the wall, trying to collect himself. He was no longer a free man.

Chapter 6

The Palace

Rolph heaved his gear off of the hovercraft and watched as his soldiers hefted their packs also. He surveyed his towering, domed home with its endless height. While the others joked amongst themselves, he remained aloof. Isolation was the price of leadership. He lingered behind as the group scattered at a fast clip, excited to reunite with loved ones. They moved with anticipation, young and free, for a time, until the next call of duty. He remembered what it was like to feel like that.

The sun was settling, half into the mountains behind them, while the other half shone bright orange across the parched grassland and foothills. He wondered what his wife was feeling, having him home again. She used to meet him with hugs as soon as he entered the palace. She'd bring their son to see him. Some children hugged their parents, but Basra never did. He greeted his father with formality. As tempting as it was to grasp his son and hold him close, Rolph respected Basra's way of dealing with his father's absences and let him be. Their relationship became one of mutual respect, fellow soldiers as well as father and son.

When Basra died, Rolph's joy died with him. It should have been him. His wife never said it, but he strongly suspected that's what she thought too. He was a constant reminder to her of what she'd lost. She never said so, but he knew it was true. After all, that's how he felt when he saw her.

But is that what his son would want – his parents driven apart? The two of them were all that was left of Basra. Rolph wanted things to be different, but patterns were set in stone. The dread they felt seeing one another was instinctual. How could that ever change?

The approaching shuttle reached the entrance point. The station overlooked a wide and endless chasm, miles in breadth, surrounding the palace complex like a moat. The chasm was flush with the flat ground. If he wasn't careful he could easily step into it. There was no telling where the bottom might be. He'd die of thirst before hitting it. No, he wanted his death to be instantaneous. Before him stood the massive granite fortress he'd once thought of as the whole world. It was so large he couldn't see either end of it, and it extended back for countless miles.

The soldiers who had chatted on the hovercraft had quieted in his presence. They waited patiently for him to choose a seat then sat a few spaces away to give him room. His medals marked him as one who'd weathered a great many battles and who held a position of power in the military. Every now and then, over the years, he'd wanted to strip off his insignia and pretend to be one of them again. He'd wanted to tell jokes and complain about the commanding officer and share how he was going to make his mark on the world, but not today. Today he relished his space.

The speeding, snake-like craft zoomed along a rail on the edge of the narrow passageway, heading towards the front door of the dome. It was odd to feel rumbling underfoot, look out of the window and see nothing but black sucking up every bit of light. It felt as if the train would tip if he leaned against the side. That certainly didn't stop him from leaning.

Staring into the blackness below he thought about the king and this plan of his. It had obviously gone very wrong, and yet the king assured him he needn't worry, that there were layers to it, that despite everything they were on track. He couldn't see it. For the second time he began to doubt. The king had forgiven the evidence of his doubt before, and Rolph knew he must be cautious with his suspicions this time. Yet the king's plan had failed again. How many layers could it have?

Upon reaching the palace entrance a gigantic rock door opened and the transport docked directly inside. The boulder slid back into place as if sealing them in a tomb. It was a tomb in a sense. No one was allowed in or out without permission.

The granite structure was a massive, rectangular dome with windows forming the ceiling and upper sides. The entire middle was a large open space filled with markets, an amusement park, open-air offices and all manner of businesses, all containing a creative combination of spaces for giant and ordinary humans. Ponds stocked with fish were enclosed in clear barriers, along with small animals, plants, butterflies and other small life forms. The entire ark was a successful experiment in terrarium science, a perfectly balanced ecosystem; earth within earth.

He'd grown up living close to the entrance. His family one of many who's dwelling was tucked along the wall. Life was crowded and harried around the entrance. But as he moved up in rank and estimation, so did his paycheck. Eventually he could afford space and privacy in the exclusive community towards the back, behind the gardens, where the larger homes had more windows and quiet markets were nestled in residential areas. There were no lines and the produce was always fresh. That's where he'd met Kristen.

Everything appeared just how he had left it. Normal and giant sized humans lived in peaceful harmony, thanks to vast strides in perspective science and design. Large and small dwellings blended together seamlessly, embracing the once divided human spectrum. Children gathered in parks to play games. Vendors sold a variety of tapas in different sizes on every corner. He smelled fragrant curried lamb as he walked to the high-speed railway station but he didn't stop to buy. He didn't find pleasure in the foods he once loved anymore.

Besides, he never used to eat much coming home because his wife always made her incredible lasagna with bolognese sauce, his favorite. Nowadays she was more likely to dread him coming home, or worse, forget. Not that she had yet, but he was prepared for it to happen.

A wave of loneliness swept over him like noxious gas, a feeling he carried constantly these days. Kristen was all he had left in the world. The thought of her carrying on with life and forgetting all about him was insufferable. He continually put his life on the line to save her and everybody else here, and they didn't care. In fact, he was a burden, worth more dead than alive. He'd seen to that, having taken out a large life insurance policy for her. She at least deserved that. After all, he'd lost their son. It was under his command that his son had died.

He entered a courtyard where a silver train was waiting. Fortunately he could bypass the ticket line. Free rides when in uniform were one of the benefits of military service, as were tickets to events. At least the governing bodies appreciated his service on some level. He boarded, taking a seat next to the window.

These people, this place, everything was foreign, divorced from the reality that lay beyond these walls. He'd sacrificed his only son, risked his own life, and for what: to preserve a fantasyland? People lived in this biosphere, trapped inside a fortress, ignorant of the outside world. They weren't trapped by force but by fear, and they were right to be afraid. They were greedy, accustomed to excess and held the naïve expectation that the world owed them a long and happy life, with all the indulgences they could ever want. Gluttons, every one, and for a flicker of a moment he felt sorry for them.

The train sped up. To his left, he saw a carved stone structure with no roof, the stadium, and remembered his youth, before the service, when his dad would take him to watch the giants fight. His mother had believed the fights to be a bad influence and forbid him from seeing them, but his dad had snuck him out anyway. Rolph had taken Basra as well.

The contrast between the sheltered life he'd led under his mother's influence and the violence he'd witnessed since was stark.

Like his mother, his wife, Kristen, was also opposed to the fights and had even pioneered protests against the practice when she was in college, but the king insisted that the fights continue, and even encouraged attendance by lowering ticket prices and providing entertainment in between bouts. Rolph now realized that the fights served as a recruiting ground for military service.

His eyelids felt heavy, but he held them open, his gaze riveted to the sky. The carriage ceiling was a patchwork quilt of windows, bathing the interior in natural light as they passed fields of crops and orchards, all engineered to grow well in their particular environment, as well as the facilities where scientists made new discoveries at an alarming rate, the most formative of these being the successful genetic manipulation of DNA and nanorobotics.

Together, Einar and Alexis, outstanding scientists in that field of research, had discovered ways of weaving genes with artificial life through the use of viruses. It was a technology he had no means of understanding, but the king had ordered him to learn about it while on leave. Rolph wondered if it had something to do with the new weapon the monarch was designing. The man had already developed a series of living weapons, but his current project was much more comprehensive than any of the previous prototypes. Rolph let out a long, ragged breath. It didn't matter, none of it mattered anymore.

The train slowed to a stop and he emerged at a quaint station decorated with flowers. The exit was through a travel and gift store: one was never free of enticement to spend money in the ritzy part of town. Rolph made his way down the street, past the trolley car, electing to walk the rest of the way instead.

Stately homes and mansions for people of varying height lined the sidewalks. Everywhere he looked people were walking, running, pushing carriages, and frolicking about. The residents here were a mix of lucrative business owners and elite scientists and their families, with a mere handful of military elite. This was where the fear was strongest: fear not only of the reaume keeping the inhabitants prisoner but also the fear of losing one's wealth and being banished to live in crowded conditions among the commoners. It drove people to create legal loopholes to ensure that no matter how lazy their offspring became, no one could confiscate their property under any circumstance. Desperate to protect themselves, they had imposed such stringent security systems that they could hardly leave for fear they'd never get back in again. It always struck Rolph as ironic that in their quest to ensure their own safety, they'd imprisoned themselves. In their attempt to shelter their loved ones, they'd made them so dependent they would never survive outside of the neighborhood, much less the dome. Not that he had any reason to care.

At least he and Kristen had made a point of not sheltering their son. Basra had been comfortable in his skin wherever he went. While other parents spent their energy teaching their children impeccable social graces, he and Kristen had taken Basra on frequent field trips all over the dome. They'd procured a high level security pass so that he could visit the mountains, at first with them, and then, as a young adult, on his own. Basra had grown into an intelligent, capable young man who could survive anywhere and get along with anyone. Of course, in the end, Basra had died, while others Basra's age were taking their own children to school, worrying about stuffy noses and shots, preparing for their imprisonment in luxury. It was unfair, but then Basra had been a soldier like his dad. Despite the pain Rolph felt at losing his son, his pride in him had provided a small measure of comfort, at least until now. Now all he felt was regret.

Arriving at the small forest of evergreens that hid his home, he walked down the familiar pathway inhaling their fresh, pine scent. He'd always been awed by the quiet beauty before. This time it felt contrived.

Today it was impossible to escape the knot in his stomach, a knot he didn't even feel in battle anymore. There was a time he had been afraid. A time he was angry with himself for being afraid: angry that the king had let the reaume off so easily. They had robbed him of his son, his family, and his reason for living. But now all he could feel was this anxious pang on his insides.

The house was dark, no lights reached out to welcome him home from the opulent log cabin. His loneliness was so raw he felt completely numb. No matter, he was ready. His gun was loaded. His uniform was on. It would be quite straightforward. Perhaps he should write a note? No, he decided, there was no need. Who would care? He'd go and sit on the bed he had shared with Kristen.

The door was unlocked as always. Inside, he set his pack on the floor and walked into the big, open-plan space. It had been Kristen's design, encompassing a gourmet kitchen, dining table and living room, all done with sturdy appliances, rustic wood furniture and iron fixtures. Ancient farming equipment lined the walls, reflecting his interest in history, a hobby that now felt meaningless.

As Rolph pivoted towards the stairs, faint flickers of light on the table caught his eye. There were two small candles. The table was set. Serving dishes were placed on heated trivets that were built into the table. He moved closer and smelled his favorite dinner. Had she made lasagna? His gaze traveled upwards, his thoughts full of what he was planning to do, then back to the table. Deep inside, buried within the numbness of his heart, a flame sparked, a flicker of concern for his wife. Kristen had gone to the trouble of welcoming him. He'd eat with her first ... his last meal. Then he'd proceed as planned.

As if conjured up by his thoughts, she appeared at the top of the stairs and his throat constricted. Her hair was swept up into a bun revealing her elegant neck and the slope of her shoulders. She wore a black, sleeveless dress; jeweled in the front, and the red amber jewelry he'd given her for their twentieth wedding anniversary.

"You look—" he started, unable to finish as his voice choked up. Her dark eyes sparkled in the dim light and his knees shook.

Rolph allowed himself to drop onto the bench at the foot of the stairs. He didn't know what was happening to him. Where was his calm, his resolve?

"Welcome home," she murmured, settling herself beside him, wrapping her arm around his shoulders. His body suddenly felt weak.

"What's wrong, Rolph?" she asked, her forehead wrinkled with concern.

Rolph cleared his throat. "Did you make lasagna?" he asked, his gaze fixed on the red, patterned rug. It was a replica of the type of rugs common to the ancient Persian Empire back on Old Earth, though the modern version quietly siphoned any dirt off his shoes.

Kristen smiled. "Yes. That's still your favorite, isn't it? Or has living in a volcano for two years changed your tastes?"

"It's still my favorite," he said, his voice pinched.

"Rolph, what is it?" Kristen asked gently.

A tear escaped his eye, rolling down his cheek, his lower lip trembled. His heart was beginning to thaw, aching intensely as blood flooded emptiness, pain replaced numbness. Was he having a heart attack? He laid his head on his wife's shoulder in a rare moment of vulnerability and she stroked his hair like she used to do with Basra if he was hurt or upset.

"I thought you didn't care," he whispered.

"Of course I care," she said, and this time she was the one to tremble.

"Don't you blame me – for what happened to Basra?"

Her voice was no longer calm. It was strong and crisp, years of frustration behind every syllable. "No, I don't blame you. I gave you space because that's what *you* wanted, not me. You're all I have left. We're all that's left of our son. I'll always love you. And someday we'll all be together again."

Her words both stung and soothed like fire and water. His body clenched, choked, lurched. He was alive again.

"Trial after trial and nothing. No matter what protein we use, it will not fold around the nanobot!"

"Go play some tennis. Let off a little steam," Alexis said as she fiddled with the holographic images from the microscope, enhancing and turning, studying each rotation ad nauseam. "You're not a gladiator and this is not a fight. Getting upset will not clear your head so that you can think better. And right now, you need to clear your head before you drive me crazy."

"You're not crazy already?"

"No. My mind is clear. In fact," she lifted her head from the images to face him, "it's so clear, I have a thought."

"What?"

"Maybe we've been beating a dead horse."

"What do you mean? What are you saying?"

"Our assignment was to include a nanobot into the proteins, but we can't insert it and we can't fold it. Nothing we try works. It's just not possible, and I believe that we've adequately determined that."

"Yes, but that's our assignment! There have to be more possibilities!"

"Listen, just because it's our assignment doesn't mean it's possible. Let's think this through. Why did they give us this assignment? The king wants to infuse humans with reaume powers, but without the massive loss of life the reaume endured before their powers 'took'. My point is, if we can't accomplish the specific assignment, maybe we can find a different solution. Then at least we'd have something productive to offer."

"Not giving the king exactly what he wants is risky. We need to be more up front."

"I'm not so sure ... he'll probably just dismiss what we have to say. But if he sees us as helpful, we can influence what happens on a global scale. Our work will have meaning."

Einar paced, not convinced.

Alexis ignored him, lost in thought. "What if the solution was less complicated and risky than what we're trying to do now?" she continued. "Maybe we can find a way to infuse the nanobot into the fertilized ova? It would at least mean another option for the king to consider while pondering the bad news."

"It's a sound possibility, but the king wants it to pass down the genetic line."

"Well ..." she sauntered towards him, walking her fingers up his chest like a spider and whispered, "that may very well happen, but in the end, the king can't always get what the king wants."

Einar took hold of her hand and kissed it. She gave him a silky smile and his heart thumped.

"Alexis," he whispered.

"Yes?" she asked, looking up at him with doe eyes.

"Will you marry me?"

"Sure, why not."

His smile grew wider as she jumped to wrap her arms around his neck. He lifted her up and spun her around.

Chapter 7

The Chase

"She's getting away!" Lahcen pointed as a mass of earth reaume hammered in pursuit. Khalid joined them, leaping through clusters of ash, elm and oak. Lahcen and Qeriya passed the earth reaume, bolstered by a wind at their tail.

Doctor Michael hovered in the air, unconscious, astride a floating cloak.

"The person who has him flies like you!" Lahcen observed.

"Must be air reaume," Qeriya said curiously.

The figure looked astern to see them close behind. Under the setting sun, funneling through a clearing in the woods, Lahcen saw the outline of a familiar face.

"No!" Qeriya winced. "It's the woman who helped the prince try to capture me! She's a reaume?"

Lahcen was equally surprised in the recess of his brain not dominated by breathing and navigating branches. That didn't make any sense. How could she be a reaume and yet work for the king?

Lahcen grabbed a pool of water from midair and tried to throw it into the woman's face, but she ducked behind a tree and the water missed its target. She began evasive maneuvering, and was so skilled at it that Lahcen couldn't get a clear shot. If he could only get close enough to melt her … What did this woman want with Doctor Michael that she was willing to risk snatching him under the guard of an entire earth reaume village, including them?

Lahcen hoped that the woman would travel towards the stream so he could raise the water into a wall, but instead she journeyed the other way, deeper into the forest. The woman seemed familiar with the territory as she swerved without flinching. More likely she had some brilliant technology that allowed her to map a route through the brush. He and Qeriya struggled to maintain speed through the weave of trees and brush and could barely keep up, much less fight her. The chase dragged on and on, with little hope of letting up. Doctor Michael was chronically beyond reach. It was getting dark.

They heard a loud howl that nearly bowled them over in fright. Wolves dashed instantly across their vision, seeking to devour the black cloak in front of them, appearing as splashes of gray in the moonlight. The woman flew higher as if sensing danger, and the leader of the pack collected nothing but a torn piece of fabric from her robe. Lahcen saw Qeriya collide with fur in midair and was too close to stop. They hit the ground together in a tumbled blur. His head thwacked a tree. Arms and legs were flayed with branches. He was still for a moment, as if some chemical in his brain had paralyzed him, and afraid to move for fear he wouldn't be able to, but found that he could wiggle his arms and legs. Minus a few bruises and a wound on his shoulder, he was all right.

"Qeriya!" he called and heard a moan in response as she stirred a short space away. Once his senses functioned again, he remembered the wolves. The rest of the pack gathered around one who was not rising, the one they'd crashed into, who appeared unconscious. Lahcen's heart stung as he saw the pack's concern for their brother and knew how easily that could have been Qeriya. But he couldn't help the wolf by remaining. He called Qeriya out of her fog and they departed, dazed and behind.

Lahcen extended his water path into a thin knife before him. It reached forward like an appendage, catching up to Doctor Michael. Lahcen sliced the water in between them, trying to separate the bond she'd placed on the Doctor, but it was too strong. He then sought to smother the abductor, but she'd placed a protective barrier of air around herself and they flew over a few fallen tree clumps before Lahcen could form a coil of water to lasso them with. Lahcen quickly forced the flow down under foot, hoping to trip them and disrupt the bond, but the woman appeared to expect such a move. Keeping Doctor Michael secure in her grip, both with air and with her arm, she propelled them both into a midair somersault, effectively escaping his design.

Qeriya also fought to break the woman's hold, but it was no good. She quickly maneuvered the air around them into a tornado, but instead of being disrupted, the cloaked figure simply spun herself and the Doctor even faster, rising above the storm and moving ahead.

They were heading further into a forest neither Lahcen or Qeriya knew well, though the captor flew with precision and direction. They would need to surprise her. But how could they surprise a battle-primed soldier on foreign ground?

"Qeriya!" Lahcen called as he surfed over a fallen oak and moved closer to his sister. "Perhaps if you and I combined our strategy, we'd get further."

"Okay, shoot," Qeriya ground out.

He gathered water into a knife shape and moved to slice at the woman's arm. Qeriya lent force to the knife as it cut. Doctor Michael slipped out of the woman's grip and began a free fall to the ground but Qeriya was there instantaneously, buoying his fall and snatching him back. But as she pulled him closer, the woman swiped matter from the ground and whipped it at her face and Qeriya lost control of Doctor Michael as she clawed at her eyes, lacerated by a mass of dirt and dead leaves. The abductor quickly regained her grip of the Doctor and took off.

Qeriya nearly tumbled to the ground, but Lahcen cushioned her fall. He funneled water into streams and flooded her eyes, washing out any residual material despite her arms waving at him through the water.

"Go," she yelled. "I can't see anymore! Go get Doctor Michael!"

Lahcen apprehensively shifted between her and the fleeing

pair. He caught a glimpse of Khalid and the other earth reaume tailing behind and flagged them to attend to his sister before rushing ahead. The air reaume woman had gained ground. He zoomed ahead. Soon they reached a clearing where Lahcen had no trouble pinpointing the cloaked figure and her prisoner, even in the shadow of night. Tall grasses replaced thick tree cover to their left, marking the end of the forest. Now in the open, he lunged into the fastest surf he could conjure and was able to catch up again, but no sooner had he closed in, then in the blink of an eye, they disappeared. It was as if a mouth in the grass had swallowed them whole. One minute Doctor Michael was floating ahead of him, and the next he and the woman were gone. He halted and surveyed the area where they'd vanished.

"What happened?" Qeriya asked as she and Khalid joined him at the spot where the woman and Doctor Michael had disappeared.

"I don't know!" Lahcen exclaimed. "They vanished into the grass, but I can't tell where!"

They hunted back and forth for clues, aided in their search by the others as they arrived, but there was not much they could do in the dark. Lahcen fretfully paced the grassy meadow back and forth, as if walking would magically open a portal to the location where the woman with flint eyes held Doctor Michael.

"I know you want to pursue them," Olaf said, "but it seems that nothing more can be done tonight. It's dusk. Maybe in the morning we'll find something, a clue perhaps."

Lahcen sighed. "Yes, maybe. We'll need to camp here tonight."

"Sure," Olaf said, "we'll camp with you."

"Thanks," Khalid said, "but we don't have enough food for us all. I always carry a portion in my backpack, but it won't even be enough for the three of us."

"That's all right," Olaf assured him. "I could live for days on Grandma's rabbit stew."

"That's because you eat like a rabbit! Fortunately, I always carry a stash of jerky." Karl grinned. "We're staying."

"Thank you," Khalid said.

"Where did you get this tent?" Karl asked, as Khalid set it up.

"I don't know. Our parents brought it with them from the outside world. We've never seen this material elsewhere in the desert. It's patched in places and smells stuffy, but it's our home away from home," Khalid explained. Before long they'd finished setting up camp and were relaxing by a cozy fire.

"Hey, what's that coming towards us?" Olaf asked.

A bulb was slowly descending towards them. Qeriya tried to catch it but it eluded her, flying instead to Khalid, nestling in his arms like a pet in need of attention. Shooting the others a half-pleased, half-embarrassed glance, Khalid stroked it and it collapsed in his hand, releasing a piece of paper. He began to read.

"Anna," he said as he studied the letter.

"Well…?" Lahcen asked.

"She's wondering where we are, how Doctor Michael's doing. I don't know how to tell her what's happened," Khalid mumbled as he skimmed the first page. He tucked the letter under his arm and walked to a patch of bright moonlight in a nearby clearing, leaving the rest of them staring at the fire.

"Humph, must be love," Karl whispered, grinning at his brother, Olaf.

Lahcen could clearly hear them but chose not to take issue.

"Yeah, I suppose so," Olaf replied quietly as the others grinned.

"How did you guess?" Qeriya teased.

"I'm jealous," Karl said.

"I don't see why. Every girl in the village wants to date you," Olaf said.

"Who, me? You're joking. They never speak to me."

"Exactly," Olaf said.

"I'd say Olaf understands women pretty well," Lahcen added and Qeriya elbowed him.

"Seriously, what could you possibly know about women," Qeriya chided Lahcen.

"You'd have your pick of the litter, Karl, if you weren't so down on earth reaume women," Olaf continued.

"Well, maybe I'll have to re-evaluate." Karl stood, scratching his head, trying to make sense of this new revelation.

Lahcen gazed at the flames until his mind began to drift. He was fumbling with the zip on the tent, ready to retire when Qeriya tapped him on the shoulder. He looked up just in time to see Khalid lift the bulb containing his quickly scrawled reply into the air. It floated above the trees, shrinking as it moved away from them until it resembled a pale star creeping across the sky: a prayer for Doctor Michael floating across the heavens.

"I'm so sorry, Alexis. I'll be gone for six months on this assignment," Einar said, the strain heavy in his voice as he closed the door behind him.

"I know," she said from the couch where she sat. She put her book on the coffee table. "The others told me while you were in the meeting. It's going to be hard, but worth it."

"How fortunate I am that you understand." He sat down, looping his arm around her, clasping both hands around the front of her waist and pulling her close. "I'll miss you, but this is everything we hoped for – a chance to stop the suffering."

"Of course I understand. This is the culmination of our life's work." She stroked his forearm. "You're the king's ambassador, but you're also our ambassador. I want healing for them too. I'll do surgeries on any sick reaume you send here."

Alexis twisted her head around to meet his gaze. "Whether or not we're separated, we're together in Spirit because we share a common mission. When you leave, you take me with you."

"I love you as much now as when we first met," Einar murmured fervently, squeezing her tight and kissing her cheek.

"And without the panic attacks, thank heavens!" She chortled.

Chapter 8

Maze Rodent

Khalid tossed and turned in agitation. The ground had never felt so hard. Doctor Michael, the girl with the gleaming silver eyes and a host of other thoughts flooded his mind in a constant stream of questions.

If they'd been under surveillance in the desert, wouldn't their uncle also have been watched? Or had he somehow remained under the radar? Was he given a cloaking serum? Given the circumstances of her disappearance from the palace, it was likely their mother was given one. So, why not give Michael and their father the serum as well?

Whether their enemies knew who the Doctor was or not, he had suffered consequences when he gave his journal to them. He had risked his life to give them that information! He had also been insistent they avoid the reaume and press on and find the flower they needed. Had he known that they'd get sidetracked by the reaume? Khalid's brain fused images of wild flowers and paintbrush drawings from the journal into a myriad of combinations in his sleepy head until the red from the paintbrush flower glowed so brightly he aroused from that place of purgatory that was somewhere between slumber and vitality.

The red glow filled the tent with light as he rubbed sand grains from his eyes. He could already hear bustling outside and snatched a whiff of roasting meat as its fragrance wafted in through the mesh window of the tent. He'd slept in! They all had! How could they sleep in after what had happened to Doctor Michael last night? The earth reaume had already been hunting for breakfast.

"Lahcen! Qeriya!" He prodded his brother and sister. "Wake up!" They rolled onto their stomachs and prized themselves off the ground.

"We have to look for Doctor Michael!"

Khalid stumbled to the entrance and shoved his head outside to face a smoky fire and a mouthwatering smell.

"Don't worry, some of us were hunting and preparing the fire, but most were searching the area," Olaf explained. "So far, nothing."

"I can't believe we slept in!" Khalid exclaimed, harnessed with guilt, wishing it would inspire his adrenal glands so that he could move a little faster.

"Maybe you're getting used to chaos. You have to sleep some time. Anyway, you didn't sleep that long. Here, have some breakfast," Olaf urged. "It's squirrel."

"Yeah, chaos has become our new order," Khalid said as he, Lahcen and Qeriya each fished a portion of juicy meat off the skewer and drank some icy water. Even in their haste they ingested each bite with purpose, chewing slowly, offering silent prayers of thanksgiving.

After eating, they packed up their tent and joined the search party with Olaf. Karl ran to meet them, blond hair streaked with mud, clothes torn in places and dark circles painted under his eyes.

"Everyone's searched the area thoroughly but we've found nothing. I think we need to look ahead. It was difficult to see last night. They could've been further along than you thought," he explained and Lahcen nodded.

"We'll check in with you," Khalid said as the three readied themselves to set off. They hiked along the emerging hills on the right, the endless line of tall grass on their left, watching closely for clues. Their eyes adjusted to shifting waves of light and shade as clouds played peek-a-boo with the sun. Lahcen tapped his brother on the shoulder and pointed towards the sky. A bird with an enormous wingspan soared overhead.

"A golden eagle," Olaf said, not far behind them. "It nests near our village."

"It's beautiful," Qeriya said as she gazed at it. "I wish I could fly beside it."

"It would probably attack you. It sees this area as its private hunting grounds," Olaf explained. "I wouldn't suggest messing with a bird that could lift a small elk."

"An elk? What's an elk?" Qeriya asked.

"A big animal that tastes really good," Olaf answered.

"That works for me," Lahcen said, smiling.

The bird grew larger as it flew towards Qeriya and Khalid braced for an attack, but it didn't appear aggressive. Qeriya winced, but bravely extended her arm, strapping a cushion of air around her skin to protect it from sharp talons. The eagle was heavy and majestic. It nudged her hand gently until her fingers uncurled and then dropped a piece of raw meat into her palm, steaming and fresh from the kill.

"Thank you," she stammered as she stared at the dead creature in her hands. The raptor bowed his head and flew a short distance away. The others looked at the meat and laughed as bloody juice leached from it pooling into her hand.

"Enjoy your lunch, sis!" Lahcen teased, giving her a pat on the back.

"I can't believe this!" Olaf stammered. "Golden eagles are among the most solitary of creatures, none of the earth reaume have ever been able to approach one!"

Qeriya's eyes widened as they settled upon the beast, and the sizable offering it brought. "So, what do I do?" she said, voice quivering.

"This eagle has given to you part of her catch. It would be a sign of disrespect not to eat it," replied Olaf as the eagle's stare intensified upon Qeriya.

Her stomach contents began to churn like butter, but she willed herself to rip into the tender flesh with her teeth, blood streaming from the corners of her mouth.

The eagle bowed, appearing pleased with Qeriya's

demonstration. It turned away and soared up into the clouds, slowly circling the vast grassy opening in the dense forest.

"Hey! Look at this!" Karl exclaimed, gesturing to a clump of tall grass. Looking to where he had indicated, they discovered a narrow opening leading to a trampled path.

"Speaking of eagles, Karl. I think you have their eyes," Olaf said.

Khalid tailed him into the scrub. This was the most promising lead they'd found yet.

"Let's check it out. Now if only you had eagle eyes on a hunt," Olaf teased.

"I can shoot as well as anybody," Karl defended.

"I know." Olaf sighed. "It's spotting the prey that you could afford to work on."

"It gets boring lying in wait for hours at a time with nothing to do."

"I know. You want to kill the animal, which is itself unnatural for an earth reaume, but you lack the patience to wait for it."

"I'm not meant to sit around twiddling my thumbs in a deer stand," Karl said.

"If you're not meant to hunt, you're not meant to eat. You'd better marry a good hunter so you can be whatever it is you're meant to be," Olaf said.

"I'm meant to fight!" Karl answered, his eyes sparkling.

Olaf rolled his eyes. "Well let's just hope you're not meant to die."

"Not while I've got you watching out for me." Karl whacked his brother on the back and Olaf stumbled forward, coughed and then tried to swipe at his brother but Karl dodged.

"Hey, I thought reaume avoided fighting?" Khalid smirked.

"We do," Olaf explained. He cupped his hand around his mouth and pretended to whisper. "That's why he's weird!"

"Ouch!" Olaf yelled as Karl punched his shoulder. "I'm his body guard."

"My body guard? Fat chance!" Karl shouted.

"What kind of argument is this?" Lahcen asked.

"One we don't have time for!" Qeriya pronounced, her voice quivering with irritation. "Our uncle's missing! This is not the time to engage in useless banter!" The earth reaume brothers clamped their lips together and walked silently. Khalid clenched his jaw and saw Lahcen counting backwards, probably trying to refrain from sharing a few choice words with Qeriya. Nevertheless, he could understand her irritation. Doctor Michael was in trouble and the sound of bickering, even if it was silly and meant to pass the time, only served to distract from critical thinking.

They walked silently along a trail of freshly crushed grass in single file. The blades parted for Olaf and Karl just as they did for Khalid, while Lahcen and Qeriya swiped at grasses that tickled their faces like a cloud of gnats. Before long they all emerged, stumbling onto a wide, dirt path.

Qeriya flew upwards to survey the scene from above, but she bumped an invisible wall. "Ouch!" She rubbed her head. "I can't see much, but I can see enough to tell it's a maze, and it's huge! I can't make out where it ends."

Olaf and Karl eyeballed one another. "I bet it's the old palace maze!" Olaf announced knowingly. "We've never been able to find it. But now is not the time to be stuck in a maze. We should go around." They reversed towards the grassy passage from which they'd come, but an invisible force prevented them from penetrating the grass wall.

"We're sealed in here!" Karl exclaimed.

"What is this maze?" Qeriya asked.

"It was designed by an ancient king to test his enemies before putting them to death," Olaf said and shuddered. "That is, if the maze didn't kill them first."

"It better not have a minotaur," Lahcen said.

At that moment a loud squeal sounded from elsewhere in the

maze. The sound was so loud and harsh that it sent a shiver up his spine. He exchanged frightened glances with the others as everyone froze in place.

"I just had to say something," Lahcen moaned.

"One of the king's weird creatures appears to be out there," Karl said sarcastically. "What a demented hobby."

"Supposedly the old palace is abandoned. Although a sword forged by our ancestors is said to lie there," Karl explained.

"That's great if we get that far. Since we're prevented from leaving the maze, I'm thinking this might be a trap," Khalid explained.

"I don't see that we have a choice but to move forward," Qeriya said. "We're locked in, and it could be that Doctor Michael is in here as well."

"How would we get him out?" Khalid asked.

"We could try to pierce the wall somehow. Perhaps if we complete the maze then we can get out," Lahcen suggested.

"I'm so sorry that you all are stuck in here with us. This may be our path, but it's not yours," Khalid told Olaf and Karl.

"I think this is very much our path too," Karl declared.

"But earth reaume aren't warring people, and this will be dangerous!" Qeriya said, genuine concern in her weathered expression.

"No, we're not warring, but they are, and they'll hunt and enslave our reaume unless we stop them," Olaf answered. "This is as much our fight as it is yours."

"I told you," Karl added, "I'm ready to fight. I meant what I said."

"Thank you." Qeriya smiled, her eyes brimming with tears.

They heard a loud rustle in the reeds and another squeal, this time closer. Karl flinched, but pride enabled him to reclaim his brave face.

"What was that?" Lahcen asked.

"Danger," Olaf reasoned.

"We'd better hurry," Qeriya urged.

They cast votes on the direction and headed right. After traveling for some time, they heard another squeal further off. They'd escaped, for now.

"We should really find some way of marking where we've been in case we end up back here again," Lahcen suggested.

"Don't worry, we'll know," Khalid answered as he, Olaf and Karl caressed the tall grasses as they walked.

"So, do you guys talk to each blade?" Qeriya asked.

"Yeah, I ask each blade about new neighbors and if they have aphid problems," he teased.

"You know that's not what I mean."

"We don't talk. We just sense the plant's consciousness."

"Plants and grass are conscious?" Lahcen asked surprised.

"Yes," Olaf answered. "All life is conscious."

"What about the earth itself?" Qeriya asked Olaf and Karl.

"Plant and animal emotions are a bit like our own since we all have DNA, but earth and rock are governed by forces, and these are what we sense and manipulate."

"I can understand that." Qeriya considered. "I sense gasses in a way I can't quite explain. I never knew why others didn't. There are limitations though. I can't control the air in another person or animal unless I'm touching them."

They heard the familiar squeal again. This time it sounded closer.

"Why do I feel like I'm walking into that thing's nest?" Qeriya asked.

"We're already in it," Karl answered. "So we'd better gear up to fight!"

"I'll tell you what. You fight and I'll run," Qeriya suggested wearily and sped ahead with the others.

Around the bend they reached a wall of grass. They were at a dead end.

"Well," Khalid spoke for everyone, "this is a maze, after all."

They'd backtracked a few turns when Khalid glanced the way they'd come and caught sight of two blazing red eyes. Suddenly, the beast let out a demonic squeal and leapt from the shadows, revealing the twisted face of what appeared to be a wild boar.

"Run!" he screamed as the noise deafened their ears. Needing no urging to obey, they did just that, while Khalid brought up the rear. Lahcen surfed as fast as he could go, choosing a new path at the branch and succeeding forks. Qeriya blew their scent sporadically along various trails to confuse the creature. It worked. They ran until weariness overcame fright. When Khalid looked back, the brute was not behind them.

They kept going, now with the knowledge of what was hunting them. Nothing appeared but more grass lined turns and a dead end. Fear steadily wore at Khalid's patience as they turned yet another corner and were blown backwards by the sound of the fiend hunting them.

"Now I know what deer feel like," Olaf observed.

"That thing is awful!" Qeriya yelled.

"It's sickening," Lahcen echoed.

"I didn't see it. Lahcen rammed into me, but I did experience its breath. Pretty nasty," Khalid explained, trying to fight off the disgust in his gut.

"It's got a face to match," Qeriya said. "This is insane! Who knows where Doctor Michael is by this time. This maze goes on forever!" Qeriya exclaimed in frustration after unsuccessfully trying to puncture the ceiling with a hard kick.

"Maybe we should work on penetrating the wall another way," Khalid muttered. Lahcen looked at him in amazement. "You're kidding, right? That would be a complete waste of time. Not only will it not work, but whatever's after us will surely be able to spot our position."

"Not only that, but the creature would ruin the rest of the land. Nothing would be safe," Olaf argued.

"Even if we reach the end, it's probably a trap anyway. If we work on breaking out of here we can plan a better route, and deal with the creature then," Khalid said rubbing his swollen, itchy eyes – probably a result of an allergy to large rats.

"It's a waste of time, it won't work," Lahcen pressed.

"There's such a thing as barking up the wrong tree," Karl added, glancing at Khalid.

"Whatever that means," Qeriya commented.

"Hey, what's your problem?"

"Isn't it obvious? You want to fight. Your bravado talk makes me want to beat my head against this ceiling. Stop talking about how you love to fight when you've never really been in one. Fighting is not exciting! It's messy and painful and just plain evil. We do it because we have to and that's it," Qeriya snapped.

Olaf quieted his brother with a piercing glare.

"Where did that come from?" Karl retorted smugly.

"See, this is what happens when you shoot your mouth off. You make people irritated," Olaf said to Karl. "Just be quiet from now on."

"Stop! Everyone stop arguing!" Lahcen ordered. "We're losing our heads here, and we can't afford to do that. We know the woman took him through here, but we're stuck. Let's think of a solution instead of distracting ourselves with dribble."

Khalid sighed and thought for a moment. "If only we had a guide through this maze – wait, what am I thinking? Doctor Michael's journal!" He pulled it out of his rucksack.

"We may as well get a bite to eat while we have a moment of calm," Lahcen said and began handing out the remains of his food as the others hunted out any last morsels from their storage sacks.

"Maybe there's something in here about this place, or where we need to go," Khalid said and smoothed his hand over the soft cover.

"That's buffalo hide," Olaf commented as he looked at the journal. "That was made by air reaume." Olaf touched its patina and watched as Khalid carefully turned pages lined with gold ink. "That's a very fine gift."

Khalid studied the pages, Lahcen peering over his shoulder. Khalid traced their path through roughly sketched forest trees. He found the expansive grassland they were now in that bordered the forest and saw a vast body of water labeled, 'Ocean', beyond it.

"Dad spoke of the ocean in some of his stories," Lahcen said. "And we learned about it in school, of course, but it's hard to picture it."

Khalid surveyed the rest quickly. Direct light was in short supply, especially in a maze with towering grass walls. Flipping through the pages, he saw that each illustrated a portion of the map in close detail. Artistic doodles reflected samples of plants, animals and insects that Doctor Michael had seen in the respective regions during his travels. He recognized the acorn and maple leaf from the forest page and soon came to the grassland page. As he squinted, Khalid saw a faintly drawn maze sketched lightly over the grassland. It was drawn as an afterthought since it marred the pristine quality of the map, and it was so faint as to be barely visible, but it was definitely there.

He leapt off the ground, clutching the journal, a finger holding his place. "Hey! I know how to get out! Listen! If I can just figure out where we are on this map, I can get us out!" Everyone formed a knot around him.

"I can't fly up high enough to see much, but maybe if I look back I can recognize about where we are in here," Qeriya suggested. They nodded in silent approval. She pulled the air around her and shot up, careful to approach the top slowly with hands raised to avoid hitting her head. She squinted, her searching eyes soon opening wide. "Hurry! That thing's coming our way! I see where we are now!"

"Quick, before we go, Qeriya, where are we on this journal page?" Khalid pleaded.

Qeriya mastered her disgust long enough to peruse the map and point.

"What exactly did you see?" pressured Khalid.

"It! I saw it! Hurry! It's coming fast!" she urged, nudging them to action. "Move!"

They responded in a flurry. Khalid, desperate to work out their route, tried to keep up. He wondered what could possibly make his sister look like a skewered rabbit. The thought stirred his adrenaline and he ran faster, taking over the lead and guiding them confidently through each turn. Qeriya waved their scent along opposite branching paths to confuse the creature. It took her bait, but even so, the sounds grew louder; there were fewer branching paths the closer they got to the end.

Khalid lost speed as solid ground morphed into a quagmire beneath his feet.

"Karl, look! Sedges!" Olaf exclaimed. "And there's sphagnum moss! Phenomenal! Our ancestors set this in motion. I've always wanted to see it. It takes hundreds of years to create."

"We need to stop and fight before it reaches the bog!" Karl mused. "That thing will destroy it!"

"No! Keep going! Better it than us," Lahcen determined.

"But it took hundreds of years to form, and that thing will destroy it in seconds. No telling what kind of damage it'll do. We should stay on solid ground and fight!"

"You sound more concerned with the bog than our lives! If there's any chance of escape I think we should exhaust that option first!" Qeriya said.

"All right," Olaf said. "It's just that, what are we compared to this amazing work of art!"

Khalid's foot sank. He slumped to his waist in black muck. "Yeah, sure, a work of art; I'd rather not become a part of it," he squeaked. Qeriya grabbed his arms and wrenched him free, setting him gently on his feet.

Khalid, Olaf and Karl clung to the thick grass mounds,

thrusting forward to snag new clumps, keeping the tension tight to propel them along, trying to put as little weight as possible on the precious mud. Qeriya flew around, pulling them up when they got stuck.

Khalid dropped back with Lahcen, who brought up the rear, casually surfing, careful to milk water from a wide area of earth. Khalid noted frightened faces turning back much too often. "Stay focused on where you're going! Don't worry, Lahcen and I are behind you. It'll eat us first!"

The varmint soon caught up with them, brushing against the grasses flanking them in its pursuit, and, despite his warning to the others, Khalid glanced back in time to see it round a corner. It was so large the bog was nothing but a puddle to its strong legs. He'd never seen such a freak of nature. It resembled a cross between a disfigured rat and a wild boar, not unlike the one they'd feasted on in the rainforest, with large tusks astride its mouth. But it was fifty times the size. Its speckled black and brown fur was matted and clumped, spiking in every direction, as if it had been dipped in melted candle wax and scrubbed. Its dark eyes flanked a snout and it had pig ears. But its feet, tail and body were that of a giant rodent. He could hear the others squeal in disgust, but they could no longer outrun it; they had to fight.

"How did this *thing* happen? It can't be natural." Lahcen surfed above the strange animal and jumped onto its neck, trying to dig his hands into the fur and suck the water out of it, but nothing happened. "Whatever this coating is, I can't penetrate it!"

"The eyes or ears, Lahcen!" Khalid instructed his brother as the monstrosity thrashed to dislodge the parasite grasping at its slippery skin.

Lahcen maneuvered towards the ears. "It's coated with thick wax, even inside its ears! I can't get through it, and I can't reach its eyes from here," he exclaimed.

"I can distract it," Qeriya suggested, swallowing hard as the others looked on helplessly.

Lahcen leapt onto the swine's right tusk and poised to jump onto the left one. He planned to brush its eye with his hand on his leap across tusks. But before he could jump, the creature flung him off like a rock tossed overhead. Lahcen summoned water to cushion his fall into the murky depths, but only managed a splash. Half of him sank into the bog, which sucked at his limbs like a baby on its thumb.

"I'll distract it while you come up with a plan of attack!" Qeriya yelled to the others, emboldened by her brother's attempt. Plucking Lahcen from the muck, they flew in circles around the beast's head as it swiped its tusks at them. Slobber splattered in every direction from its flabby lips. Its teeth gnashed at them, narrowly missing her leg. Setting Lahcen down safely, Qeriya shot back to their assailant where she ducked, swerved and flew directly into a nostril.

"Qeriya!" Khalid screamed.

Embedded in the snotty cove, she sucked air out of the large nostril. It worked! The barbarian thrashed about as it choked. It walloped its snout against the maze wall and Qeriya was knocked from its nose onto the ground, covered in a membrane of mucous.

Khalid hustled to retrieve his sister from the ground before super-sized pig hooves crushed her.

"Are you okay?" he asked, stunned at her bold strategy.

"Yes, I think so," she answered, dazed, but unharmed.

Lahcen, capitalizing on the brute's fight to clear its airway jumped on its snout and tried to melt it, but nothing happened. Once more he found himself sailing through the air like a missile. "There's a barrier protecting this thing!" he warned as Olaf helped him up again.

"What are you doing now?" Khalid asked his sister as she flew from his protective arms. She spun about the behemoth like a mosquito hovering over its prey.

"Get us out of here!" Qeriya ordered Khalid, her voice spinning circles as she wound around the hellion.

They sprinted, using any means of locomotion possible. Khalid leading them along trails that wound through the darkening, misty bog. He flipped around to ensure that Qeriya had caught up with them and saw that Olaf and Karl were still trying to preserve the bog as they ran.

"Forget it!" Lahcen yelled. "That creature's making so much mess nothing you do will help."

"Why don't we keep fighting it then?" Karl shouted.

"Because we'd die."

"It's worth losing our lives if it means we can protect the bog!"

"*If* is the key to that phrase. Anyhow, speak for yourself. I'm not as convinced that this place is worth my life."

Try as Qeriya might to blow their scent away, the thing was close enough now to see them. It charged forward and caught Olaf by the britches with its tusk, tossing him high into the air. He hammered the ceiling and then pounded into the sludge.

Qeriya circled about until she could rescue him. The titan rushed on, heading for Karl next, tusks close to the ground, ready to charge. Karl swerved. Missing their target, the beast's tusks scored the ground instead, digging up a wad of acidic soil. Karl steered back toward the mammoth, grabbing a wad of grasses in the process. He ran a beeline between its legs and sliced its ankles, two at a time, having tightened the grasses into stiff blades. They cut through its flesh like knives; garnering paper cuts so deep they reached the bone – going by the measure of blood that poured from each leg. But the pain was not enough to stop the freak of nature. Fortunately for the thing, Karl had been unable to sever any key tendons or muscles and they could only watch helplessly as the monstrosity stampeded towards Khalid, screaming its rage.

"Watch out, Khalid!" Lahcen exclaimed as Khalid ran ahead. He leapt between grassy knolls as fast as he could possibly move; snaking along an alternate trail they had previously passed. No longer following the map, he tried desperately to lead the thing away from the others. He could feel the creature's heavy, hot breath on his back. Its putrid smell overtook him as the others raced to catch up.

"Khalid! Dead end!" Qeriya shouted.

With the beast on his tail, he ran at full speed for the wall then stopped dead, sidestepping out of the way as the mutant crashed into it headfirst. Despite the force with which it struck, it was merely dazed and pivoted to chase Khalid and the others again.

More by accident than design they reconnected with the trail they were on previously, following it even further into the bog, the deformed rat attacking them with unabated aggression. Abruptly, Khalid halted, swiveling around.

"What are you doing, Khalid!" Qeriya exclaimed in shock.

"Karl's right, it's time to face it head on!" Khalid's voice was determined.

"That's crazy!" she insisted.

"Perhaps, but at least we can focus on fighting instead of running and fighting. That thing's too fast. We can't outrun it!"

Before the creature had time to realize what was happening, he ran straight at it and jumped on one of its tusks. Despite his surprise maneuver, the thing shook its head like a wolf breaking a rabbit's neck and Khalid flew through the air. Qeriya cushioned his fall.

Olaf leapt onto an ear. Karl let the distracted animal pass and grabbed the tail. They clung fast, fingernails clawing the waxy fur, digging into skin. The miscreation squealed, slapping the ground with its tusks as it spun in circles trying to fling them off. But its efforts only served to tighten their grip and increase its pain.

Qeriya whipped around the animal like an electron cloud, pinching it here and there to distract it.

"I knew this would come in handy someday," Khalid said as he fished rope from his rucksack, tied a slipknot and formed a lasso. He twirled it overhead to build momentum and aimed for the head. "It's a good thing I got lots of practice."

"Yeah, it better be worth it after everything I suffered in the name of your lasso practice over the years," Lahcen said.

Khalid looped the rope around the thick neck and jerked. The hybrid spun and bucked against its new collar, Olaf and Karl holding on for all they were worth. "That should help," Khalid panted, transferring the rope to Olaf and then positioning himself to jump.

"Give me the rope once I'm up, Olaf. We're going to spin a web!" Khalid ordered, and leapt. Grabbing hold of a tusk, he held fast. The creature shook its snout violently, covering him in mucus. "Gross, there are boogers everywhere!" Khalid shouted. "How could you stand this, Qeriya! I'm gonna throw up!"

"Good idea, aim your vomit inside its nose!" Olaf yelled.

"That'll just make him madder. I might even get sucked into its sinus cavity!"

"That's not such a bad idea. You could do a lot of damage. Time to get a thicker skin, brother," Lahcen said.

"Yeah? You try it!" Khalid exclaimed.

The snout paused for a moment. In those few seconds, Olaf cinched the rope tight and tossed Khalid the slack. Khalid looped the rope around the abomination's mouth and nose a couple of times and held fast to the loose end.

"I can't access the nose!" Lahcen exclaimed.

"Karl!" Khalid called, ignoring his brother.

"I'm here!" Karl answered, still dangling from the mouse tail.

In spite of the situation, Khalid had to laugh at Karl's unfortunate placement.

Lahcen blasted the animal with random pinprick spouts of

ice-cold water. "You'd better not complain of boogers any more, Khalid. It could be much worse. Worse might yet happen to Karl, hanging on that mouse tail."

"I'd take booger slime any day to this end," Karl puffed.

"Pecking order," Khalid teased. He tossed Karl the rope.

Karl snatched the rope with one hand, clinging to the tail with the other. "We'll see about that!" The boar mouse lunged, sending claws, teeth and tusks in every direction. Red welts opened up on unprotected hands and arms, but they clung tight, using each pause to cinch the rope tighter.

The animal was beginning to weaken, finally it stopped its frantic dance and Karl spun a figure eight around the creature's legs, leaping precariously from one boney flank to another. Dropping swiftly to the ground, he pulled hard on the rope. The force cinched the rodent's legs together and the noose slid down over its knees, causing the beast to fall, thrashing, onto its side. Karl pulled on the rope and it slid down to the slashed ankles. The beast squealed in pain.

"I'm coming!" Lahcen surfed onto its neck. "Time to put you out of your misery!" He reached down to pry an eyelid open and touched the white of the creature's eye. The thing dehydrated instantaneously, leaving a chalk corpse that crumbled under Lahcen's weight, disintegrating into powder. Without the carcass beneath them, they found themselves in freefall. The chaff sifted away beneath them, while the water Lahcen commanded hovered in midair. Lahcen flung the water downwards, catching them in their decent and setting them gently on the muddy earth before dissipating back into the bog. Scattered ash, a pile of rope and stinging cuts made worse by the acidic soil were all that was left to remind them of the battle.

Olaf and Karl surveyed the wreck made of the bog and fell to their knees, paralyzed with loss. To them, the bog was a fellow soldier who lay injured from battle and they were powerless to help. Lahcen put kind hands on each of their shoulders. Khalid wanted to join him in consoling the brothers, but they weren't safe yet. He had to get them moving, fast.

"We should get out of here in case something else comes at us," he said and set off walking. Olaf and Karl grudgingly followed a ways behind.

"We're nearly there," Qeriya said after a while. She had floated up and was squinting around in the fast descending shadows of night. "I see the outline of the palace. Let's hope the maze lets us out of here."

A dozen or so paces later the bog ended and they climbed onto solid ground. "Nothing like an acid bath to give your skin that wholesome, healthy glow!" Lahcen announced to the others as they waited for Olaf and Karl to catch up.

Qeriya examined Lahcen and Khalid, frowning as she took stock of their appearance, knowing she looked far worse. Her hair hung in mud caked tails from under her disheveled scarf, and, like her brothers, her wounds were caked with acidic crud and her eyes felt gritty with exhaustion. Irritatingly, both brothers' hair was neat, their skin unblemished and the dirt barely registered on their clothes. "How can you guys come from that," she pointed to the mess behind them, "and look like this?"

"You just look like you fought harder, that's all," Khalid said.

"That's it, from now on I fight only clean animals," Qeriya announced.

It took them the same amount of time to finish the short distance left of the maze as it had to cover the entire distance they'd traversed with the hybrid at their backs.

"At least we can get out," Khalid said as they finally entered the palace grounds. They peered around cautiously but couldn't see much in the dark.

Lahcen cleaned and dressed their wounds as they sat in silence, exhausted. No one had the strength to set up camp and they simply collapsed in a huddle upon the grass near the exit. On the edge of sleep, Khalid felt a nudge on his shoulder and pried his eyes open to find a familiar fire bulb waiting for him.

"No way!" Lahcen exclaimed. "Now why couldn't that thing have brought us some serious firepower a lot earlier? Might as well be useful if it's going to find us holed up out here."

Khalid hurriedly skimmed the brief letter, reading aloud. "'We discovered the identity of the air reaume woman you wrote about. Her name is Mara. She is one of the king's generals. She'll probably try to lead you to the ancient palace. There's a massive soldier encampment there. It is also the site of an old reaume prison.

Don't follow her! It's a trap!'"

Einar walked slowly along the wooded trail. His earth reaume visit was drawing to a close. It would soon be time to send those with anomalies to the palace for Alexis to treat. Then he'd make his way to the rainforest. The water reaume were a scientific culture. He had only to explain the situation and the science behind their treatment in order for them to send their sick to the palace. They trusted him because he was a scientist. But the earth reaume were much harder to crack. He needed to earn their trust first, and he did, by befriending a woman with some sway in the community.

"Kari," Einar called as she walked along one of the nearby trails. "I was looking for you." She stopped to let him catch up. "Are you heading out for a walk?"

"Yes, I'm going to pick some huckleberries," she said and held up a large, birch basket.

"Can I join you for a bit?"

"Certainly, please do. So I hear that you're visiting the fire reaume next?" Kari asked.

"That's right."

"Please tell my cousin hello for me."

"Your cousin, in the fire reaume?" Einar froze in his tracks, utter perplexity painting his features.

"Yes." She paused. "She's the daughter of my father's brother, but her mother is queen of the fire reaume."

"But I thought that reaume couldn't—" He stopped, hunting for the proper way to express his assumption.

"Couldn't cross-breed?" she finished. "They normally can't, but the Spirit blows where it will. She's the first, or one of the first I should say. Her husband's the son of a water and an air reaume, but they're the only ones like this known in the reaume world."

"I didn't think that was possible."

"Nobody did. I mean, what are the chances they'd be able to conceive or even find one another?"

"Amazing! Anyhow, before I say goodbye, I wanted to tell you that it's been wonderful getting to know your reaume and spending time in

these beautiful woods."

"Thank you, Doctor Einar, for caring about our sick. I feel so hopeful putting my parents in such capable hands."

Chapter 9

Prophesy

Khalid awoke to frost in the early morning dew. He no longer fought to ignore his shivers, trying to stay asleep, but instead admired magnificent hues of pink and orange as the warm sun opened its sleepy eyes on the horizon. Allowing the meager rays to warm him, he turned over and studied the path they'd emerged from the previous night, carved clearly into the grass.

Angling his gaze left, he spotted a large building covered with broken stone reliefs of flying space ships, resembling humongous versions of the one that had brought contaminated tea to the desert games. As his trembling abated in the growing warmth, he climbed to his feet and surveyed the others. They were huddled together, still more exhausted than cold, and he left them to slumber in the blossoming sunrise.

There were no obvious soldiers, but he decided to scope the place carefully, just in case.

"Where are those spaceships going?" he muttered as he approached the palatial but dilapidated building. The surrounding stone paths and steps were disturbed by tall dandelions growing through the cracks, dislodging stones to form mini, jagged towers erupting from the ground.

He tugged at the handle of a large wooden door with metal moldings and it opened onto a vast space full of cobwebs. Paintings and fixtures were unrecognizable under the piles of dust. Khalid marveled at the black and white checkered flooring that appeared to spiral towards a magnificent staircase. It would have created an illusion of falling if not for the dust caked onto the floor, betraying scattered footprints, none of which looked any fresher than the others. People had been here, but he couldn't hear them if they were still present. Could this Mara be hiding here? Or were all of these prints old, with no breeze to sweep them away?

He sneaked inside. The doors to every room were ajar. Glancing inside a room off the rotund entryway, Khalid was stunned to see a portrait of a beautiful lady, dressed in animal skins, with long, dark hair blowing in a breeze and a chain of flowers on her head. She was walking up a mountainside, surrounded by wildflowers. A gloomy valley loomed below. The sky was gray, but clear. Khalid entered the room to take a closer look. Ornate furnishings speckled the rest of the space. No one was present.

"Khalid!" Qeriya screamed from behind him.

His heart jumped into his throat and, instinctively, he clutched at his ears. Turning, he saw his sister, Olaf and Karl trailed her into the room, closely followed by Lahcen.

"What happened to you?" Lahcen asked.

He shrugged. "I decided to explore the palace."

"We gathered that much, but what happened to sticking together?" Lahcen chided him, digging his index finger into Khalid's chest. "Next time you decide to go off on your own – don't. Wake us up. What if that woman had ambushed you? You could've been killed!"

"I suppose so," Khalid admitted. "I just wanted to let you all sleep. You guys looked so tired."

"You shouldn't be so nice," Qeriya added. "I was worried sick when I woke up and saw that you weren't with us!"

"Trust me! She was screeching like a banshee. It was not pleasant," Lahcen contributed as he stretched and yawned.

"We'd rather get Doctor Michael back than sleep a few extra winks, and our chances are better if we stick together," Qeriya explained, grasping Khalid's arms, standing squarely before him. It was as if he was three years old and she was Mom, giving him a lecture.

"We tried both stairways and the other rooms, but they're sealed. This is the only room we can enter," Lahcen told him.

"Then where can they be?" Khalid asked.

Qeriya scowled. "I don't know."

"Look at all of the footprints. More than two were here," Olaf surmised.

"Yes, and look at that portrait," Lahcen added. "Do you suppose there's a secret passageway behind it?"

"Don't be ridiculous, Lahcen!" Qeriya said irritably. "Khalid," Lahcen said, "why don't you study the journal and see what you can find out about this place."

Khalid's head snapped up. That's right, the journal, he kept forgetting about the journal. Props to his brother for remembering, although he wouldn't be nice and tell him so. Reaching for his backpack, he eased the journal out. Sitting down on a dusty couch, he coughed and began flicking through the pages.

"Hey, wait!" Qeriya walked over to the picture and pointed to the flower chain. "Khalid, Lahcen, look at the flowers on the woman's head. Don't they resemble paintbrushes? Are those the flowers we're looking for?"

"I was thinking the same thing," Khalid said, scanning pages and at last finding the flower sketch that Doctor Michael had made for them.

Behind him, Lahcen spoke into his ear. "Yeah, they do look a lot like the flower chain. There are others on the mountainside as well."

"That's the flower you're looking for?" Olaf asked redundantly. "That flower grows in the mountains on the other continent."

"We've heard that, but in what mountain range?" Lahcen asked. "There's more than one."

"The big ones. There are many ranges, but only a few of that caliber. I'll show you where they're located in your journal," Olaf suggested. Khalid removed a map that was neatly tucked into the journal and unfolded it on a short table for all to see. He pointed to where they were currently located.

Olaf traced his finger along the map from where they were to a large body of water beyond. "This is the ocean," he explained. Far out into the ocean lay a large island and beyond that rose another continent. His hand moved inland a ways and landed on a narrow mountain range spanning the length of the continent, north and south. He smoothed his finger across the range that lay along the side of the palace. "That's where they're most prevalent," he said, "in this patch of mountains. The elevation climbs above the tree line, but not so high that nothing grows. You'll also find the air reaume living near there. The flower looks like it does in the portrait. Each flower is a different shade of red or orange or a mixture of the two colors."

"We finally know where we're headed!" Lahcen exclaimed with satisfaction.

"That's a nice change from being chased by freakish animals everywhere we go," Qeriya commented.

"I don't know. I think that giant rat pig had a hankering for you, Qeriya," Lahcen teased.

"Yeah, he did, a hankering called hunger. Hadn't had a decent meal in a while by the looks of his scrawny body," she said.

"I never thought I'd hear two tons of rat pig flesh called scrawny. Anyhow, you wouldn't be much of a meal I shouldn't think. I, on the other hand, would've made a delectable feast with all of my strapping muscles," he said and flexed his arms.

Qeriya was about to jab him in the ribs when Khalid chimed in from behind her. "Yeah, muscle marbled with lots of fat's the tastiest kind of meat." He sniggered.

"Just you wait," Lahcen warned.

"Look here, on your map," Karl interrupted, "there's a gazebo with the sword and two sets of bows and arrows." He pointed to a structure in the journal that lay behind the ancient castle. In the margins were sketches detailing the weapons.

"Doctor Michael wrote something here about them. According

to him, 'This structure was created by the earth reaume for champions of the maze. It is said that no one who has survived the maze has yet been able to dislodge these weapons, but whoever does will hear the oracle speak.'

"Listen, I know it's a far-reaching hope, but well, why not? There are three of you. It sort of makes sense that you should at least try. Weapons could only help your chances of getting your uncle back."

They all shrugged. It wasn't part of their plan, but as long as they were here and had no leads whatsoever, how could it hurt?

"Where is it, again?" Lahcen asked.

"It's behind the palace. We saw images of it in Hot Springs," Karl said. "Occasionally we'd see images of strange places, like this palace and the sword here. We saw the weapon prophesy. It says that there has never been one to dislodge it, but when the time is ripe, one will come to extract the sword from its sheath, and two to dislodge the bows and arrows."

"Did you see anything else in there? Anything about us, maybe?" Lahcen asked.

"Why would we see anything about you?" Olaf asked bluntly.

"I only ask because the fire reaume we met grew up seeing images of our life in Orchid Pond. I just wasn't sure if your Hot Springs showed the same images."

"No." Olaf sneered playfully in return. "Nothing about you. You're not that important. But there was nothing about me in there either, so neither am I."

Lahcen knocked him on the head and the two began to wrestle.

"Hey, guys, there's no time for man hugs!" Qeriya quipped with a sparkle in her eyes. "I can understand the allure of weapons, but we should really try again to access this place."

But try as they might to penetrate the doors atop the main staircase, and the one tucked in a corner of the entryway, the thick passageways refused to budge. They were not only sealed shut, but reaume proof.

Finally, they gave up and wandered outside, behind the neglected palace. The stone gazebo that housed the weapons was detailed with many relief carvings. In one such carving, Khalid saw a human woman reclining on large cushions at a sandy beach while a group of reaume attended to her. A fire reaume kindled a fire beside her, while an air reaume woman flew above her, braiding her long hair. Meanwhile, an earth reaume brought her a meal, and humanoid creatures with fins flipped through the water as she watched as if putting on a show for her. Overall, it looked as though the reaume were servants to the humans inhabiting this palace. Unaware of this chapter in reaume history, Khalid turned toward Olaf and Karl to spy their reaction. However, they seemed to be focused only on the weapons, oblivious to the distasteful images. Concluding that what they didn't know couldn't hurt them, he returned to the group.

The sword was lodged in a large marble stand, fused to the stone floor, while two bow and arrow sets lay on shorter marble stands, flanking the sword. All were encased within a visible force field. They approached cautiously as if treading on sacred ground.

"It makes sense!" Olaf observed. "There are three of you and three sets of weapons!"

Columns edged the perimeter of the shelter. As they stepped between them onto the floor, embedded lights lit up from below, illuminating the space, and a deep female voice sounded.

"Welcome, you've survived the maze. Now you may test your worth. Grasp a weapon and pull."

"Wow, those bow and arrow sets look sturdy," Karl observed enviously.

Khalid, Lahcen and Qeriya approached the weapons, lining up youngest to eldest in front of the sword.

"I'll go first!" Qeriya yelled excitedly.

"All right, I'm second, then!" Lahcen chimed.

"Fine, I'll go last." Khalid sighed, resigned to the fate of the eldest and therefore most patient.

Qeriya gripped the sword and pulled, but it wouldn't budge. She attempted to pull it from side to side and even put her foot on the sheath for added momentum but it budged not a centimeter, it didn't even so much as rattle. Lahcen stepped up to take his turn and likewise, no matter what he did the sword would not move.

Finally Khalid placed his right hand around the hilt, added his left on top and took a deep breath. "Here goes!" he uttered and heaved as hard as he could. The sword slid free effortlessly, landing him on his butt, still grasping the weapon with both hands. The others flinched and scooted away from the paper-thin blade. The mass of marble soon ejected the sheath as well and Khalid rose to his feet to take it from its home.

"Congratulations!" The disembodied voice sounded again. "The rightful owner has at last claimed the Earthen Greatsword! Many have come before you and failed. But you who bring the worlds of earth reaume and human together forge a new future for all. Use the sword well, to defend justice, fight poverty, and usher in an age of peace."

Khalid was stunned. He didn't believe in oracles. To him it was obvious that the structure had been programmed to release the sword upon his mere touch. He didn't have to pull at all, but why release it to him? Was it because he was both earth reaume and human perhaps?

Lahcen and Qeriya approached the bows and arrows to free them, but they wouldn't budge. They switched places and tried again, but the weapons remained immobile.

"Hey! Why does Khalid get a weapon and we don't?" Lahcen complained. "We fought the mouse freak too! Why don't we get anything?" he grumbled, folding his arms like a sulky toddler.

Qeriya was not pleased, but managed to hang on to her

dignity. "Well, congrats on your prize, Khalid! The mound won't yield any prizes for us, but even so, yours was well deserved," she said meekly.

Olaf patted Lahcen's back consolingly as Karl studied one of the bow and arrow sets with awe. Khalid watched with interest as Karl gently stroked the fine, carved bow. It was sturdily built with a strong cord. He thrummed it, gently at first, and then with more force as he pulled the cable through the pulleys. When he let go it snapped into place without vibration: a powerful weapon. Adorning the ends of the arrows were sturdy feathers that didn't crush under the pressure of his hand. The tips were sharp. Karl circled a hand around the grip and lifted. To Khalid's surprise, it plucked free of its place without effort. He reached for the quiver of arrows and that also slipped willingly into his hand.

Olaf saw his brother holding the weapon and his eyes grew wide. He glanced at Lahcen, who motioned him forward. Olaf likewise grasped the other bow and quiver without difficulty.

The voice spoke once again, "Chosen earth reaume, defend and deliver your people! Once created by humans as slaves, you have grown into your freedom by the will of one more powerful, who would see all life free. Use your weapons to free your kind from the past and fully serve not your creators, but theirs, the author of all life."

Upon finishing these words the platform shut down, casting them into shadow. A cold breeze blew through the columns.

Einar opened the familiar fold of the letter, delicately scented with Alexis' perfume. Nestled on the bed in his tree house, his lamp glowing softly on a wooden table beside him, the faint rustle of liquid sunshine, as the fire reaume called it, slapping his thatched roof in the darkness, his heart pounded with longing. He missed her so much; he didn't know how he would bear this last trip to the air reaume.

'Come home! I can't explain in a letter,' she wrote. Einar sat up abruptly, hitting his head on a wooden beam. 'Drop everything and come home, it's urgent!' he read. Flipping the letter over, he searched the back and the envelope as if he'd got the wrong post by mistake. But it was from Alexis and it was for him. Something was very wrong.

Chapter 10

Attack

"Slaves?" Karl asked, his voice leaching disgust. "Created by humans? We're more powerful than any human!" There was no doubting the oracle's accuracy. The gift of the weapons was a sign of its truthfulness.

Lahcen's throat constricted, hurt at the favoritism bestowed on his brother. Karl and Olaf's prizes made sense, they were earth reaume, but why did his brother get the great sword? He might have earth reaume traits, but they all shared the same great-grandfather. He told himself it shouldn't bother him, but sibling rivalry flamed in his chest no less.

"What did the voice mean when it talked of reaume being slaves?" Qeriya whispered to Lahcen.

"I don't know." Lahcen shrugged. "The relief carvings seem to tell a story of such a history, but we don't have time to study them."

Khalid stroked his sword like he might a newborn child. He clasped the hilt as he wandered towards some nearby grasses to test its sharpness.

"Let me have the journal," Qeriya called after him. "I want to see if it says anything else about this gazebo."

Khalid dug it out of his rucksack with his free hand and threw it to her. Qeriya caught it and flipped to the map. She traced over the maze they'd just escaped and the palace.

"Look, Doctor Michael wrote a note about the weapons," Lahcen said and read aloud, "'I saw the encased weapons. None so fine were ever made. It's said only chosen warriors can extract them, but none have been chosen since their creation hundreds of years ago. Not likely to be anyone I know.'"

"If only he did know," Lahcen added, an edge to his voice.

"Lahcen," Khalid began, walking towards them. "I don't

know why it chose me to take it. It just did. And I'm not going to pretend not to care. But I have to know there are no bitter feelings." He waited until Lahcen stumbled towards him and offered a reserved handshake.

"Of course there's no bitterness. Did I say something wrong?"

"No, I just know how I'd feel if it was you that got it, that's all," Khalid said. "And I know Qeriya doesn't care for weapons, no matter how cool they are, but even she might feel a little resentful."

"Congratulations, Khalid," Lahcen said, his voice edged with a small note of sincerity. That was all he could muster. He couldn't help the way he felt.

"No, no. I'm just fine, Khalid," Qeriya said with an air of superiority. "I don't see that I need a sword. To be frank, it would get in the way. Now, let's get back to the task at hand. It appears from the map that beyond this small forested area lies an ocean." She gestured to the trees at the base of the steep, grassy hill.

"We've never seen the ocean," Khalid said.

"You've never seen the ocean?" Karl asked, thunderstruck.

Qeriya scowled, "Why would we? According to you, we grew up in a prison."

Karl shrugged in defense.

"Knock it off, Qeriya!" Lahcen ordered. "You're being rude. Karl's being nothing but friendly and your words are like salt in a wound."

"Sorry, Karl," Qeriya said. "These days I'm a little—"

"Tense? Yeah, I get it," Karl answered. "I'm not trying to offend you."

Qeriya's shoulders hunched forward. Ever since they'd left the rainforest, she'd had little patience for humor. The continuous fighting and running was wearing on her.

"The ocean's a large body of salt water that covers most of the world," Olaf continued.

"Most of the world?" Lahcen's eyes fluttered in disbelief as he searched the page. Growing up in a desert, it was difficult to imagine that large bodies of water even existed. "The ocean supposedly bordered our desert, but it was so far away that no one ever came close to it."

"You can't drink it," Karl said, seeing their amazement. "It's very salty. And it moves in rhythmic waves that crash on sandy or rocky shores. From what I've seen, Lahcen, it will be like paradise for you." Lahcen bent down on the pretense of brushing something off of his foot, embarrassed by his smile. Why, he didn't know. How could he not be excited? This hope was enough to lift the self-pity he'd come to resent in himself. He had always been discontent, frustrated at being chronically deprived of his element, like a fish living in a tiny bowl of water. He'd got a taste of freedom in the rainforest, but the ocean ... that sounded like a dream come true.

Just then he heard a slight whir and a snap overhead. An arrow clattered to the marble floor of the gazebo. It had hit the column where he'd stood just before bending down. His stomach lurched.

"Watch out!" he screamed at Khalid who was swiping grasses for practice. Lahcen scooted behind a stone gazebo support, quickly followed by Karl, Olaf and Qeriya. They craned their necks around, searching and waiting for any sign of movement, but all was quiet. The sun shone bold and bright while a slight breeze rippled around them. The perfect weather would be squandered if they were forced to do battle today, Lahcen thought, saddened. Odd how much his perspective had changed since he'd left home.

Qeriya pulled a mass of air forward and flattened the grass, revealing scores of soldiers. Caught off guard, some found themselves blown onto their hands and knees.

Olaf and Karl fired off a volley of arrows in quick succession before the soldiers could grab for their weapons.

"Guess we get to try out our prizes a little sooner than we'd bargained on," Karl said. "These arrows are really smooth and steady. They're slicing into the soldiers as if they were cutting through butter!"

"They certainly are powerful," Olaf added as he strung another shaft. "But that's a rather grotesque way of putting it."

Lahcen gathered water from the grass, collapsing the tall stalks. Qeriya blasted air. More soldiers stumbled. Lahcen plugged many of the platoon's mouths and noses with water and Olaf and Karl took out those left standing.

"Khalid's on the move," Qeriya said. Their brother zigzagged back out of the deep grass, taking out three rather rash soldiers who rushed him with his new sword. No trace of jealously remained. Lahcen was grateful Khalid had that sword now. Qeriya spun a barrier of air around them, watching as the other side's arrows and flamethrower blazes bounced harmlessly off her protective wall, some rebounding onto the shooters.

"Only one Khalid and who knows how many of them. That's not a fair fight! No more surprises. Time to see what we're up against!" Lahcen said. He drew more water from the grass where the soldiers hid, seeing the grasses wilt, steadily exposing soldier after soldier. Khalid pitted his sword against an army of giants, his super strength and speed lending him the advantage. Olaf and Karl fired arrow after arrow, their quivers seemingly holding an inexhaustible supply.

"Qeriya! There're more coming than we can fend off!" Lahcen called and lobbed water at the enemy's faces. "There's more air than water around here. Can you do something big … and fast?"

Qeriya blew out a plume of air, stirring it in a circle with her finger. As she stirred, faster and faster, the air obeyed this physical command on an exponential scale, gathering strength until the eddy pushed away, taking on a life of its own, culminating in a massive cyclone. She thrust the tempest toward the enemy, exhaling into it again and again, feeding the windstorm, infusing it with power as it sucked the giants into the air like a large, hungry mouth, only to spit them out again, letting them meet the ground with devastating consequences.

"Nice job, Qeriya!" Lahcen commented. "Khalid, come back!" he yelled. He put his fingers in his mouth and gave a loud whistle. Qeriya covered her ears.

"Where'd you learn to whistle like that?" Olaf asked.

"In our five-by-five foot house," Qeriya said. "It was his only non-water weapon. I now have permanent hearing loss."

Lahcen flung a disc of water at an approaching mob of soldiers with lightning speed, cutting into their stomachs.

"Where's the prince?" Qeriya asked. "He's mine if you see him. I've a debt to settle."

"Yes, Mam!" Olaf answered.

Olaf and Karl kept up a steady stream of arrows to cover Khalid as he sprinted towards them, a crowd of giants on his tail. As he ran, earth and rock lifted up behind him like a cloud, spraying dirt into the soldier's eyes. Qeriya raised her wrists towards the sky in an elegant motion. The air obeyed her thoughts, painting an invisible bulwark of whirling air behind Khalid. She brought the base of her palms down fast, her fingers trailing, shoving the air, earth and rock onto the soldiers still standing, knocking them down. But even as they fell, more of them poured across the flattened grass towards them.

"There are too many to block!" Khalid yelled. As they sprinted down the long and steep descent towards the forest.

Glancing back, Qeriya could see hundreds more closing in.

"Get to the ocean we saw on the map! I'll take care of the rest there!" Lahcen yelled.

"Sure, Lahcen, only five more miles to go with a hundred King Kongs on our tail!" Karl panted.

"Who's King Kong?" Qeriya asked almost instinctively.

Karl glanced up at her soaring effortlessly on the wind while he struggled down the grassy mound. "You mean to say you've never heard of King—"

"Never mind!" she snapped.

"Don't worry, Karl," Lahcen said. "It's not you. She's just a little bitter when it comes to men these days. The prince messed her up pretty bad."

"Do you want me to include *you* in the next tornado?" Qeriya threatened.

"It was a crush, that's all," Lahcen continued, ignoring her. "Then he went and poisoned everyone in our village. Later he tried to kidnap her, but she got away."

"Sorry to hear about your home," Karl said.

"Condolences later. No time now as you can see," Lahcen said.

"If we can reach the forest, we can use the trees to get to the ocean pretty fast," Olaf said.

"Or we could turn around and fight," Karl puffed.

"All of those soldiers?" Qeriya asked. "Are you crazy! Do you see how many there are? Anyhow, I'd rather escape than kill."

"We can't outrun them," Karl insisted. "It's not possible. They're too fast. We have to think fight, not flight. Our best chance of survival is to delay them so Lahcen can make a run for the ocean. We could take them!"

"You are not a normal earth reaume, Karl," Olaf panted. "But, you have a point. Lahcen would be much more powerful by the ocean. Why else did we get these weapons if not to kick some King Kong butt?"

"In that case..." Qeriya spun on her heel to create a huge, concave oval with her hands. The air obeyed her sign language and condensed on a large scale, encompassing a mass of soldiers coming at them from either side. She placed a hand on the newly formed barricade and pressed, sending a rampart rippling against the enemy, knocking them backwards, watching as many fell and didn't rise again. Others, though, hung on in close pursuit, gearing up to tackle Olaf and Karl, who brought up the rear.

"Watch your backs!" Qeriya yelled as the soldiers closed the gap on Olaf. The brothers notched arrows as, without breaking stride, they spun around, letting fly as giants leaped for them. Arrow after arrow hit their marks, soldiers behind tripping over their fallen comrades. Olaf and Karl resumed running.

"Nice job!" Lahcen yelled as he surfed. The water was no longer dissipating quickly, now it streamed forward, drawn towards the ocean.

"Keep moving!" Qeriya urged, her voice rising to a panic. "They're gaining. Lahcen, take Khalid!" she ordered as she swooped to snag the scruff of Olaf and Karl's collars, like a mother cat lifting her kittens. Lahcen likewise scooped up his brother onto his lap.

"Lahcen, let me tie myself to your back!" Khalid yelled, grabbing rope from his rucksack and looping himself onto Lahcen. He snaked around to Lahcen's back and cinched the rope. Now he could face the onslaught of attackers, while Lahcen got them to where they needed to be.

"I put up spinning air shields around each of us to protect us from their weapons, but I can't maintain them for long, Qeriya explained. "They'll be able to break through with enough persistence. We're going to end up having to fight at close range," she added anxiously. Then, to Olaf and Karl, "Watch yourselves. Their armor protects them from reaume power."

"Yes, even my water plugs dissolve after a time," Lahcen said, dragging a bit with Khalid on his back. An idea came to him and he bubbled water beneath Khalid to offset the extra weight.

"Not so much water, Lahcen! I don't have gills!" Khalid sputtered and Lahcen toned it down. "That's better! Hey, we're like a water hovercraft! Glad it's warm. Now, when I nudge your right side, turn right, when I nudge your left, go left, assuming you can, and my head back means lift quick. Lahcen slowed, listening and watching Qeriya as she turned to face the attack.

"We're a mobile battle station!" Karl yelled as the thick of the army descended on them.

"Yeah, I think I'll call us … the death comet!" Olaf announced, firing arrows in rapid succession.

"Don't make me laugh, I'm trying to concentrate," Lahcen half-chuckled.

"Lower him down, Lahcen!" Qeriya exclaimed. "He can't reach!"

Lahcen dropped, blind to the fighting behind him. He and Qeriya were the collective eyes towards the forest.

With Lahcen lifting him, Khalid found himself on par with the giants' height. Despite their size, as soon as he drew his blade strength flowed through his arms to exceed his enemies. His blade sliced one and then another, spearing them like the squirrels they'd eaten for breakfast the morning of their search.

Qeriya held her charges, not daring to try to make the two of them hover at the same time. Karl and Olaf shot a volley into the crowd chasing them, their actions almost a blur, turning what they did into almost a non-stop, circular motion, like wheels on a cart. Karl took aim, shot, hitting the shaft of an oncoming arrow, splitting it in two. Watching with satisfaction as it spiraled down to strike two giants running at full stride next to each other, catching one on his upturned face and another square in his Adam's apple.

"I got two with one arrow!" he yelled. "I've beat you!"

"This isn't some sort of sick competition, Karl. It's defense, that's all. Wipe that idiotic smile off of your face!" Olaf snarled.

"I know it's defense, but I'm going to make it interesting. These could be our last moments of life and I'm not going down without a roiling fight!" Karl's face reddened with resolve as he spoke. He plucked arrows like they were bones in a fish, shooting one after another with renewed vigor.

"Stop arguing!" Qeriya ordered. She was sinking. "You guys are too squirmy! And you're heavy! I'm picking up the pace and dropping you in the forest. Lahcen, I'm losing my grip on these two."

"Go ahead, we'll catch up," Lahcen said and saw Qeriya wince. It was obvious her hands were cramping.

"I have to get you to the forest before my arms fall off!" Qeriya said urgently.

The soldiers were barely managing to keep up with Lahcen's surf but Khalid was still locked in battle. Lahcen heard clanking and felt tugging. "What's happening?"

"Khalid just got three with one strike! He punctured the sword hand of one," Karl yelled as they steadily pulled ahead. "That was amazing!"

"That's my bro!" Lahcen said as he sped towards his sister. It was unnerving having to leave all the fighting to his brother, but Spirit willing, he would do his part soon. Luck was with them and they reached the forest without any casualties on their side. Qeriya descended fast. Breaking her force field, she dropped the brothers onto a towering deciduous tree. Karl and Olaf caught at the branches on the way down, then fired themselves, like living arrows, higher into the canopy. They settled into a fighting position and readied their weapons.

Lahcen heard Khalid sheath his sword and felt the rope loosen. Once they met the tree line, Khalid let go. Lahcen spun around to help but Khalid didn't need any. He gathered a mass of branches in each hand from two different trees to slow him down; the rope draped over one shoulder. Stopping, he bounced upward, then let go of one lot of branches to mount the other tree, tucking the rope into his belt, just beyond reach of the giants. As soldiers surrounded him, he hung from his knees and drew his sword once again, fighting upside down with as much ease as if he were standing.

Lahcen marveled at Khalid's dexterity. He pegged water at the oncoming foe, but the soldiers simply dissolved the water into mist.

Qeriya blew into her palm and began circling her hand, as if stirring an invisible cauldron. Immediately, air began to condense into a powerful tornado which she touched down near the hostile hordes, allowing it to grow as it careened up and down the enemy line, plowing the earth, sucking up soldiers and spitting them out only to be knocked unconscious or killed as they nailed the ground. Though Qeriya was doing a good job of eliminating the giants, many still managed to push forward towards them. Khalid rose into the canopy to avoid an onslaught. Olaf and Karl likewise climbed out of reach, all three lunging from tree to tree towards the ocean. Meanwhile, Lahcen garnered as much water as he was able.

"If I could get closer to the ocean I'd be much more use," he said, frustration coloring his voice. "My powers are useless without it!"

"Yes, you need to go!" Qeriya called to him. "We'll hold them!"

"I can't leave you guys on your own!" Lahcen argued. "Come with me!"

"We will, just a bit slower. We're in our elements here. You'll be more help if you hurry to the water. We can buy you time and I won't have to worry about protecting you," she argued. "Now go!"

Instead of leaving, Lahcen surfed close to the soldiers, drawing a mass of them away from the others in pursuit of him. They sprang for him, perhaps thinking he would be an easy target away from the others. Just as he veered away, a scream he easily recognized pierced his ears. causing him to back up. To his horror, he saw that some kind of dark blanket had swallowed Qeriya. Panic gripped him as he realized that his sister was captured. Abruptly, he saw the same type of blanket was about to close over him, too. He had no choice but to keep surfing. A terrible fear for his siblings wrapped its thick hands around his neck and squeezed as he fled, helpless.

"What is it Alexis? What's wrong?" Einar asked immediately, stepping across the threshold of their home. He'd been consumed by worry since receiving her letter.

His wife sat in their office nook, off the kitchen, interacting with the water segments in various colors and shapes that hovered in midair where she'd directed them. The scene resembled a shabby version of the abstract light sculptures she'd collected over the years.

"Einar!" She jumped to her feet and ran to embrace him, burying her forehead against his chest before staring up at him wordlessly. Tears smeared her cheeks. She held onto him tightly, shaking as if in a fever.

Einar slowly circled his arms around her as she struggled to speak. He was impatient to know what had upset her like this but he waited patiently for her to recover.

"It's the king, Einar! He's betrayed us," she sobbed.

"What are you talking about, Alexis?" He chuckled. This of course had to be a misunderstanding. They were the king's personal doctors now, and his best scientists. He'd made them permanent members of his royal court. He'd given them both lion head tattoos to signify their status as royal advisors. How could he possibly betray them?

"Einar," she whispered, collecting herself and pushing him away. "Let me explain."

"All right," he said, calmly sitting down.

"It's about the Nano-bot technology that we developed and adapted to heal anomalies."

"Yes," he encouraged. "The king wanted to use it on his offspring since it was less risky than old reaume forming technology, but the process didn't work. The ova proved too difficult to change.

"Right, but later we realized the uses it might have in healing anomalies."

Einar nodded. "We managed to eradicate anomalies within the palace walls."

"You've been visiting the reaume, establishing contact, sending the sick here for healing. And we did this because the king wanted to mend

relationships with the reaume," she said.

Einar nodded again. So far they were on the same page. "Yes, and although it didn't work with the air reaume, it worked with the other three groups, and the king granted me a paid sabbatical to act as ambassador, and extra resources to help."

Alexis nodded miserably. "He did, and he even let me meet the reaume here at the palace, to assure them that we could help them.

"So, then what are you so upset about?"

"Oh, Einar," Alexis' lips trembled, but she took a deep breath and steadied her voice. "He had them put into prisons. I didn't know, I didn't know anything until a few days ago!"

"Well ..." Einar was stunned, but his mind struggled to rationalize what he was hearing. "Maybe he's using the prison cells as holding cells. Where else would he put them otherwise? Or maybe the reaume weren't used to suppressing their powers and the King confined them to minimize the chaos."

Alexis didn't answer, only giving a hollow faced nod. "I wondered why my surgical team was in a state of constant flux. I felt so isolated. The patients came in and I never saw them again. I'd train in surgical staff and they'd be reassigned. I wanted to follow up, but I was told I needed to work nonstop, that there were so many suffering, so many lives at stake. I barely slept. Then one day I simply broke down and needed to know if I was doing any good.

"Recovery was in a building clear across the dome. I thought that it was odd to have it so far away, but there were so many reaume coming in, I figured there were few spaces available. I tried to enter the recovery station and found that it was locked and required special clearance. They wouldn't let me in, even though I was the chief surgeon! That's when I got suspicious and stole a nurse's uniform and badge from the locker room. I called in sick the next day, which I've never ever done before, even if I am sick, I never take a day off. I snuck into recovery with a group headed to work. The king was obviously trying to hide something from me, and I just had to know what was happening to my patients. It turned out to be a nightmare."

"Did ... you find them?"

"Yes, they were still unconscious, and they were not recovering at all!" Alexis covered her face with her hands, rocking in silent anguish. When she looked back up at Einar tears chased each other down her cheeks and her face was racked with pain. "They'd been dissected," she whispered. Einar, they were literally left wide open!" She moaned, her composure completely deserting her as she let out a terrible scream, banging her fists against the wall.

Einar gently pulled her close, waiting for the storm to break, but his own arms trembled and his gut roiled as he pictured the scene. The lovely reaume he'd come to know, whose trust he'd won, now worse than massacred, and all of it made possible by him.

Chapter 11

Cell 4C

Rolph stared at the painting hanging on the wall of the ancient castle. Next to him, King Sean seemed totally absorbed in it. What must he be thinking?

"Have you ever seen such a beautiful woman?" the king asked, but Rolph said nothing. He stood in the doorway of the room in full uniform, stiff and silent. That was not what he was expecting to hear. "I suppose that's not a fair question for you to answer, is it?" King Sean said.

"No, sir, that is not a fair question. I must maintain that my wife is the most beautiful woman in the world."

"For the sake of domestic harmony, of course. Yes, I understand." The king smiled faintly, his face growing serious as his gaze returned to the painting.

The full figured woman stood with knee length black hair blowing in the breeze. Her dark skin glowed in a haunt of gray clouds. Rolph could only guess how her image must disturb his monarch. How could she betray her own husband, he wondered? How could she betray their son? She was a reaume, who claim not to understand deception?

Rolph couldn't imagine how the king maintained his composure after finding out about his wife. The betrayal could mean his death, as well as the death of the prince. Everything Rolph had known of her had led him to believe that she was a loving wife and mother, a dear friend of his own wife. He couldn't have predicted what she would do.

And then there was Mara: transparent skin and eyes of pure metal such as he'd never in his life seen before. She had seemed so promising, reliable and incredibly capable for someone so young. He'd even vouched for her, praised her gifted leadership, her ability to get things done in a timely fashion and follow orders without question. How could his intuition have been so wrong? Even the King took note of her obedience, planning to attach her to his son in a marriage of convenience. Rolph would never have suspected her of being a spy.

"Where are they?" the King asked, still staring at the painting, his lips closing in a crooked line across his face.

"They're contained below. According to personnel, all of the cells required adapting for reaume prisoners."

"I'd feel better if you'd been in charge of the facilities, but that can't be helped. It was short notice for all of us. I'm glad you thought to come here when you did. Very sound anticipation. That's why you're my first officer." The king faced him, speaking as if stating a simple fact.

"Do you plan to see them?" Rolph asked, bowing his head in deference to the praise paid to him.

"Not yet. If I saw them now, I don't know what I'd do. No, someone more objective needs to deal with them, so that we can excise their usefulness. That means you, of course. You have license to make Mara uncomfortable should you need to, since she's a traitor," he sneered. "But not my wife. Never my wife."

"Now that we know Mara's a traitor, does that affect our plan?" Rolph asked.

The king's answer was prompt and full of conviction. "Knowing she's a spy doesn't affect the plan in any way whatsoever. As far as the siblings are concerned, whether Mara works for the prince or me won't matter. They don't trust either of us. We go ahead as planned."

"Sire, General Rolph!" A soldier had appeared at the doorway, his eyes wide.

"Yes," the King said, "what is it."

"We have a prisoner. It's the female hybrid. She's restrained, but we need to know where to take her."

Rolph was relieved that in the wake of disappointment, something had gone in their favor. But the king did not appear so affected.

"Which cell should we take her to?" Rolph asked. The guard shifted his attention to the King and awaited further instructions.

"Hmm, let's put her with Doctor Michael in 4C," the King said after a moment's thought. "It'll be interesting to see what happens. Install surveillance and communication lines if they're not already in place."

"Certainly, we'll have her down there shortly," the soldier answered, saluting smartly before hurrying away.

Rolph followed the soldier out the back door, to where the others stood. A quick glance over the battlements showed him that the battle still raged below. One of the soldiers carried a long black bag over his shoulder. The bag appeared surprisingly still considering what it contained. "Is she conscious?" he asked.

"Yes, sir." The soldier smiled thinly. "She's most definitely conscious. It took the lot of us to get her under control."

"Hmm." Rolph thought quickly. "Outside and around to the side entrance would be the easiest way, but since she's literally a flight risk, I say we bring her into the palace and navigate the stairs.

"I'll have the guards prepare for her arrival," he added. Heads nodded. He reached up to pull a holographic visor over his eyes. He could still see the others through a haze, as if they stood behind a veil. He was just getting used to the new contraption. Images overlaid his immediate surroundings, feeding him the information he required to enable him to make decisions quickly. The contraption attached to his uniform and was resistant to many reaume powers.

Rolph wound his way through a maze of locations and files using refined eye movements, until he found the old outpost prison and selected a cell number."

An image of a guard approached.

"Yes, General Rolph?" The guard asked.

"We have a prisoner ready for cell 4C, by order of the king," he told the figure. "We'll be down in fifteen minutes." The soldier nodded and Rolph notified the king before turning his attention to the soldiers.

"Follow me," he said, leading them inside and down a narrow, spiral staircase tucked alongside the wall. It was a tight fit, but they arrived into a confined, dimly lit hallway coated in stainless steel. They walked past a number of doors, each with a letter and a number, carrying the prisoner between them. Arriving at 4C, Rolph opened the door and stepped aside as the soldiers carrying the prisoner entered, reemerging again within seconds of dumping the bag onto the floor. Rolph shut the door promptly behind them.

Just as he was about to breathe deep with relief, another giant approached him, her hair pulled back taut behind her head. Instead of the traditional uniform, she wore a sleek, illuminated suit, one designed for soldiers who worked away from sunlight for long periods of time, as they did in the underground prison. Her head was bowed low and lifted just enough to talk to him without making eye contact.

"What is it?" he asked, alarmed by her demeanor.

"It's the other prisoners, the King's wife and Mara, sir ..."

"Yes, what about them?"

"Qu–queen Kanti and Mara ... They–they've escaped, sir! We can't find them anywhere. They've vanished," she stuttered.

Three hours had passed since she'd told him about the clandestine reaume experimentation, and they still sat on their couch, both sunk into their own thoughts. Einar was trying not to stonewall, but at the same time this new reality needed to sink into his psyche. It was so awful, so contradictory to what he'd thought he was doing. Everything in him wanted to believe she'd made a mistake, but then, Alexis would want to believe that as well. No, he had to face it, Alexis had seen this horror for herself and there was no better proof than that.

"What can we do?" Alexis whispered. "I don't know what to do."

"Most reaume with anomalies have already come. When no one returns, they won't send any more."

"They'll send a few back healed, I bet, just to give the illusion that healing is taking place. Reaume will continue to trickle in as new anomalies are diagnosed. We'll have to watch for them and try to warn them."

"If we can." Einar sighed. "We'll be watched closely now. I'm sure they won't let us leave the palace. I learned from the reaume how they communicate. They could reach us if they wished, and if they do, I'll warn them, but they won't trust me now. They won't know who to believe."

"They sent you away to gather reaume, but also to get you out of the way. They used me to teach students how to do the surgeries and use the technology, and flooded me with work to get me out of the way. I'm sure we've been watched all along. There's no escape for us, or for any future reaume who come here."

"No, there isn't, but we also don't have to work for the king anymore. The worst they can do is hurt us. If they threaten to harm us we won't bend. We'll have to be strong."

Alexis began crying again.

"Did I speak wrongly, Alexis?"

Alexis shook her head, "Not about us, no, but ... there's something else I haven't told you yet." She brushed the last vestiges of tears from her eyes and took a few deep breaths. Removing her bulky shawl, she flattened her shirt so that he could see a significant swell in her abdomen. She met his eyes, a bitter smile etched on her face. "I'm six months along now, Einar. You're going to be a father."

Chapter 12

Escape

Discomfort and exhaustion replaced the flood of adrenaline that had coursed through Qeriya's body. Her first priority was to get out of the sack they'd stuck her in. Tiredly, she began to pry at the bag.

"Let me help you with that," a familiar voice said.

Qeriya's heart skipped a beat. "Doctor Michael, it's you!" she exclaimed. She could feel the warmth of his hands as he started to work loose the knots in the ropes that clutched her inside the bag.

"I'm sorry I'm not here to rescue you as I'd planned. The others are outside fighting off soldiers. It's bad out there, Doctor Michael. We're overwhelmed."

The last of the knots was undone and the bag lifted over her head.

"Thanks," she said, rubbing at her gritty eyes with her knuckles. She surveyed the dingy, grey, prison cell. There was a veil of light emanating from the walls, but otherwise they were contained in solid metal.

Doctor Michael stared at her. "You came here to rescue me?" he asked. "Why would you do that? You have a mission to accomplish if you want to save your parents. Coming after me was far too risky."

"Doctor Michael, next to our parents, you're the only family we have. You're important to us."

"I'm not the only family you have. What about the fire reaume?"

"They are our family, yes, but we've only just met them. You're from home."

The Doctor sat down on the bed.

"You look sick. Your face is green," Qeriya observed.

"That's because I wish you hadn't come! Before I just had to worry about myself, but now that you're here, that complicates everything. We have to get out of here. Can you use your power?"

"No. I can't seem to move this air," she explained as she pushed and pulled at it, focusing on seams and crevices.

"I guess they thought of everything," he muttered. "There's no water anywhere, no access to outside air, no heat. This metal probably has a protective force field on it. My guess is that the cell is reaume proof."

Qeriya rubbed her sore arms and ankles where the ties had bound her. "We'll see about that."

"You have an idea?" Doctor Michael asked, getting to his feet and beginning to pace.

"I'm getting a few," she answered. "What happened after that woman took you? You were regaining consciousness when she captured you. Do you remember her flying you? It turns out that she's air reaume! We chased her to get you back and ended up doing battle here."

"Is that what happened? Well, you know more than I do then. One minute I was in the forest with you guys, and the next I woke up here. I may have become vaguely conscious some time in between, but I don't remember much, just a tent with people prodding me occasionally, and bright light."

"We ran into the earth reaume and stayed with them for a few days, waiting for you to regain consciousness. You stayed in their medical tent."

"Really? A lot happened while I was out. Where are we now?" he asked, looking around their cell as if to find clues.

"We're in an ancient royal outpost."

"Oh, yes, I know it well."

"You do? What do you know about it?"

"Way back, people didn't want reaume imprisoned in the palace, so they created this place. But it was easier to build high security prisons closer to home, so now there are prisons in the palace as well.

That woman must've taken you through the maze and put you in this prison cell. I wonder if she's still here? Why would a reaume work for the king?"

"It's difficult to say."

Qeriya focused her breathing and closed her eyes to concentrate, hoping she might have missed something that could help them break free. She moved her hands as if directing an orchestra. The air inside the metal cell listened to her, but it lacked strength. "I just can't manipulate the air in here for some reason," she said. There's nothing I can do to get us out. I'll have to wait until the door opens, if it opens, and they don't just leave us here to die."

"There's nothing you can do? Well, they captured you, and me for that matter, so they must want us alive."

"Somehow that's not comforting," Qeriya said.

"We do want you alive," a faceless male voice rumbled from no particular location. It was as if the walls were speaking.

Qeriya's heart raced once again.

"Who and where are you?" Doctor Michael asked as he and Qeriya hunted for the source of the sound.

"I'm General Rolph, second in command to the king," the voice answered, and where I am isn't important."

"What do you want with us?" the Doctor asked.

"I don't presume to know. The king has ordered that you both be held prisoner here, that is all."

"Is this the way he treats honored guests?" Doctor Michael answered sarcastically and Qeriya glared at him.

"Don't make him mad!" she ordered in a whisper. "Let's not make things worse than they already are."

"That's a wise idea. You should listen to the girl," General Rolph said. "This is a prison, you know. There are consequences for bad behavior."

"You didn't answer me. What does the king want with us?"

"He wants nothing with you. As far as we're concerned, you're expendable. We keep you alive only for the girl's sake. As for the girl, he wants her alive and cooperative."

"Why doesn't he just ask us to come to the palace?" Qeriya asked. "Why this war and killing and chasing?" As she spoke, Qeriya carefully surveyed the cell trying to identify any sign of imperfection in the metal, but the cell appeared to be seamless. "We'd never want to hurt anyone."

"No? You've already hurt quite a few."

"We were defending ourselves from *you*."

"Even if you don't want war now, you might later. Your children or your grandchildren may wish for control, and we wouldn't stand a chance against any such as you. The king can't risk such unchecked powers in his kingdom, not when the safety of the entire human race is at stake!"

"We are the human race! We are human! And why should it matter if we're human or not? All life feels pain and loss. No life should be so disrespected."

"You are more machine than life. You have a human mother, but you express machine traits. Any human blood you have is polluted."

"What are you talking about? Reaume aren't machines!"

"You're mistaken. Reaume have human tissue, but they're simply machines with genetic architecture, once created by humans to care for their children. Yes, that's the truth," the voice added as if it saw her surprise. "Reaume were created on Old Earth to care for human children. They were purchased by humans to be nannies."

"That's slavery!"

"It's slavery only if applied to a human, and reaume are not human. They were made by human hands in order to serve people, but are not and never were human. They were treated well, like a well-loved pet. For now, know that you're stuck here. This place has been fortified in order to contain you and will not budge. There's only so much air in there and I'd hate for you to suffocate before the king arrives. Of course, that's up to you."

The voice was silent. Qeriya and Doctor Michael listened for more but heard nothing.

"I think he's gone, or his voice has anyway," Doctor Michael said.

"What is he talking about? It's ridiculous!" Qeriya exclaimed. "Why would reaume need powers to care for children?"

Her uncle looked down at the floor and pinched his eyes shut, clearly not wanting to speak.

"Please say this is nonsense," Qeriya pleaded.

"Qeriya, he's right about the reaume history."

"What do you mean?"

"There's no time—"

"I'm afraid that's about all we have now."

Doctor Michael ran his hand through his thinning brown and gray hair. "Well in that case, I need to start by explaining why reaume were created. Back on Old Earth, as robot technology improved, people created robots capable of doing childcare tasks such as feeding, changing diapers and basic discipline. These artificial life forms were warm, looked and felt human ... but they weren't. Unlike humans, they didn't make mistakes."

"Lifelike robots cared for children?" Qeriya asked, sitting on the other bed, her legs folded together, head cocked in curiosity.

"Yes, but the robots turned out to be disastrous. Tech businesses willfully overlooked years of research on child development, thinking that infants should thrive with robots if they looked and felt human. It wasn't enough to fool infants, the bulk of whose young years are spent cultivating emotional development that only a true life form could provide. They would have fared better with animals. Research illustrated the need for infants to be consistently cared for by people who love them. They feed on love in much the same way their bodies feed on milk. Without the constant presence of a loving caregiver children suffered serious disorders of their psyche, and many didn't survive. Entire generations of children grew up with serious attachment disorders and antisocial behaviors."

Just as Doctor Michael finished his sentence, Qeriya heard hollering coming from somewhere within the palace walls.

"What was that?" she asked, sitting up straight.

"Someone's angry."

"Are there other prisoners here?"

"Probably, this is a palace prison after all. It was originally designed to hold reaume they found back when they used to hunt them down for extermination."

"It seems as if that practice never ended. Do you suppose that's another reaume?"

"I don't know," Doctor Michael answered.

Qeriya rose and paced the room, trying all of her ideas for escape again, but to no avail. Defeated, she sat back down on the bed. "So, what did they do about the robots?"

"They destroyed them. Scientists experimented with human DNA instead, crafting human-like figures, selecting for a high degree of empathy and docility." The Doctor sent her a tight smile. "Thus began the creation of the first reaume."

"That was allowed? It seems so wrong."

"There were plenty of protests, I'll grant you. Many people were also angry about the destruction of the robots. Some saved them from being destroyed and tried to give them decent lives. But they were ultimately sacrificed for the sake of progress."

"It amazes me how cruel and ignorant humans can be."

"Where there's demand and profit, ethics are often compromised. That's what happens when profit is your oracle and greed your guiding principle. Anyhow, genes related to the development of the frontal cortex were manipulated in these early reaume, minimizing intelligence and aggression of any kind, barely maintaining the instinct towards self-preservation. The DNA was human in origin, but the new creature was not.

Everything that makes humans what they are was missing."

"How cruel!"

"Yes, although most families adored their caregivers."

"And I'll bet most caregivers adored their families as well, but it doesn't change the fact that they were forced to be vulnerable, and that is the heart of slavery." Qeriya slumped onto the bed, pulled her knees to her chest and rested her chin on them, hugging her legs. It felt as if she'd received a slap alongside the face. It was outlandish to think that humans created reaume. "They were created to care for children? That doesn't make sense. Why would anyone caring for children need powers over water, air, earth and fire?"

"Those powers came hundreds of years later," Doctor Michael said. "Many years later earth had to be evacuated."

"Why?"

"That's a mystery we've yet to solve. There are only rumors I'm afraid."

They heard more yelling and grew silent for a moment. It was horrifying to wonder what was happening.

"So then what did they do?" Qeriya asked, desperate to escape her dark thoughts.

"They planned to terraform another planet. In order to do that, they needed creatures that could withstand the elements, but still think and communicate. They bred more of these early reaume for the purpose of experimentation, this time splicing their DNA with nanotech robotics, using virus technology, which gave them certain powers. In this way, reaume became part artificial and part cultivated life forms, capable of reproducing combined human and robotic traits. There were multitudes of trials before the procedures worked."

"So even more reaume died?"

Doctor Michael glanced away from her for a moment. "Yes, very many," he said finally.

Qeriya felt queasy just listening to this.

"During the years that New Earth was terraformed, the reaume grew in power, while humans remained in the safety of the ship. Many reaume died in the formation of New Earth. Only the strongest survived. Because of their heightened abilities, they were no longer trusted to care for children. Humans felt threatened by their powers. There was a mass effort to force extinction, but many reaume escaped and regrouped in the wilderness. They eventually split into their respective groups and went into hiding.

"Why didn't humans just leave them alone? Couldn't they see then that they weren't a threat? That they just wanted to live in freedom and quiet. They didn't take revenge or harm people in any way!"

Her uncle nodded. "Because of that people stopped killing reaume, but they were still afraid of them. They expanded the palace, which was in fact the ship in which they came to this planet. Some human villages sprang up outside of the dome, but they were a world apart from the dome dwellers. That's how reaume could remain hidden for so long.

"So how did they get re-discovered?"

During the many years of hiding, something happened that humans hadn't considered at any time during reaume creation or implementation. Reaume evolved, and did so at an alarming rate, far beyond the transformation that had occurred after terraforming.

"Occasional reaume became bolder and didn't stay hidden. While not mean, they pushed boundaries, a very human behavior, and were eventually discovered by humans. These particular reaume were captured and studied and it was found to be impossible to remove the robotic elements from their bodies. Because of this, and their vast capacity for power, there was a new push to exterminate the reaume.

"The last king decided to dissect and study reaume en masse. He tried to find a way of imbuing humans with reaume traits.

He would've wanted to study you and find out how you came to be, a human/reaume combination. His idea was that perhaps people could have reaume traits spliced into the bodies of their children.

"Does the current king want to do that, to experiment on me?" Qeriya asked, her face white with horror.

"The current king doesn't experiment in that grotesque way, no. He does see reaume as dangerous and believes it's necessary to kill them. He may have an interest in studying you and your brothers in some fashion, however, since a fusion between human and reaume has taken place naturally."

"In that case, I don't understand why the king didn't simply explain this and ask us to work with him."

Doctor Michael raked his fingers through his thinning hair. Getting to his feet, he started pacing again. "Given your power," he said finally, "I doubt the king ever considered you'd agree. His concern, I imagine, is that once you discovered the extent of your powers you would refuse to recognize the authority of the king. Even if you agreed at first, once you got a taste of power you might've changed your mind. The king, and humanity at large, would be vulnerable and unprepared."

"That is such a shame. Not everyone wants power, and certainly not us. Most people like us just want to make our way in the world, with basic comforts, family and friends. There's nothing wrong with power, somebody's got to have it, but the king's crazy obsession with it is making him out of tune with common decency."

"Well," Doctor Michael said, eyeing her with curiosity, "that very well may be. You've grown into quite an interesting young lady."

"Thanks." Qeriya half-smiled. "It's just … I miss Mom and Dad. I want to go back home to the desert with them and get back to normal life. But I suppose even if – when – we get them back, there'll be no going back, not really."

"You said before that you liked living in the desert?" Doctor Michael said. "I must confess, I find that difficult to believe. It was a hot, arid place with little food and very little water. Why would you want to go back?"

"Because it's my home. I'm finding out that life was hard there, but it was also simple. Nothing I've seen yet compares with the beauty of the giant arch gleaming at sunset, and nothing I've tasted rivals Khalid's salsa."

"I must say, I'd never have imagined you'd want to go back."

"I always thought that you enjoyed it," Qeriya said.

"I enjoyed it for a time, but I can't say I relished living there. Maybe I've grown stale in my old age." He guffawed.

Qeriya heard more yelling.

"That sounds like soldiers. It must be about one of the other prisoners," Doctor Michael speculated, his forehead knotted with worry.

"We've got to get out of here." Qeriya spoke softly, listening out for a clue that might help clarify if the screamer was someone she knew.

Within a matter of minutes, the door rumbled open. A soldier entered and immediately encased her in a force field, but not before she managed to subtly direct a thin layer of air around the edge of the door seal and lock with a simple twitch of her finger. The soldier was the one who'd accompanied the prince at the desert games. "What was his name?" she asked herself. Rolph, that was it! Rolph. The same Rolph whose disembodied voice she'd heard speaking a few minutes ago.

"You!" He gestured to Doctor Michael. "Come with me."

"Why do you need me?"

"You'll find out soon enough. Look around. Do you think you're in a position to ask questions?" Rolph's deep voice boomed and Doctor Michael cowered, slowly walking towards the door. Rolph escorted him into the hall. The door slammed behind them and the force field immediately disappeared from around her. Qeriya smiled slowly. She'd made the layer of air so thin that it was undetectable, but it was enough to allow a thin passage in which to pull more into the cell. Patiently, as if the cell were a choked lung, she sucked fresh air into it in a slow but inexorable trickle.

Worries and questions nudged at her brain, but she smothered them and focused on her growing strength. Once she was empowered again, she used her ability to slowly pull at the door. With a swell of fresh air inside the cell, she pushed it all along the door edges to force the lock and guide the door open, bracing for a fight with the guards. To her amazement there were no guards stationed, they were all milling about further down the corridor, arguing heatedly.

Silently, she slipped out, using air to buffer any sound as she shut the massive, heavy door behind her. As she crept down the corridor, Qeriya noticed that above the door to her cell was a light. There were other cells in the passageway, but none of their lights were on. The cells had a small window and Qeriya risked darting a quick look inside – empty.

In a turmoil, she stole silently along the corridor with no idea of what to do. She couldn't fight a mass of soldiers on her own in this confined space, nor could she abandon Doctor Michael. She had to think fast. The lack of lights probably meant that there were no other prisoners, so her uncle must be elsewhere. Maybe if she reached the stairs she could check on the other floors. She'd start in the basement. Decided, she moved along the shadowed edges of the wall to the spiral staircase and padded down a flight of stairs.

The stone hallway below was long, dark and winding, with no windows or hangings on the walls. She wondered if this underground passage led outside the old palace. Perhaps this was the best way to escape? Upstairs would be full of giants. It was risky, but this way held promise.

As she crept along the tunnel, she heard murmuring. There

were voices up ahead. Flying up to the ceiling, she allowed herself to float closer. The voices grew louder. She couldn't discern what they were saying, but she heard Doctor Michael's voice in the mix. Now was her chance. She had almost reached the corner, around which she'd no doubt find him, and a host of soldiers. She didn't have the strength they had, but she did have the element of surprise on her side, and she could fly like lightening.

Qeriya inhaled sharply and zoomed ahead like a rocket, moving so fast it was difficult to see her form as it streaked along the roof of the passage. She aimed directly for Doctor Michael and whisked him away mid-sentence. Completely unprepared, the soldiers stood dumbstruck, mouths gaping as she stole their prisoner from under their noses and took off like an arrow.

Fortunately she was right about the passage leading outside. They burst through a door hidden under a pile of dirt and leaves below an overhang of rock. Qeriya didn't slow as she carried Doctor Michael far away from the exit, into the forest below, where she set him on the ground. Throwing herself down beside him, she lay back, arms aching, and gathered her strength.

Doctor Michael was as white as the glare of sun on water. "Are you all right?" she asked as he sat, unmoving and silent.

"Yes," he answered, nodding, though she could see that he was trembling. "How did you escape?"

"When Rolph came in to get you, I formed tiny straws along the seal to suck air inside. Anyhow, I'm sorry I scared you like that, but it was the only way to rescue you." Qeriya bared her teeth in a triumphant grin. "We did it! We're free! Although, they'll be coming for us." She glanced around herself. "I have to find my brothers, but I need to do something with you first, to keep you safe."

"Oh, no, no. You should go and I'll take care of myself. I'll be fine now," he said. "I can walk to a nearby human settlement without a problem. There's one a few hills over."

"I can't leave you here!" Qeriya exclaimed and saw him give her a vacant smile, still in shock no doubt.

"The ocean's our best bet then," he suggested.

Qeriya nodded, her eyes on their surroundings. "It's surprisingly quiet, she observed. "The battle must be done. If they've escaped, the water's where I imagine they'll be. That's where we were to meet up."

"Makes sense," Doctor Michael acknowledged nervously.

Even though she was impatient to be in the air, Qeriya forced herself to rest until enough of her strength returned. Then, with Doctor Michael hanging like a limp mouse, and keeping under cover of the forest canopy, she flew, winding through trees, towards the ocean. But as they approached the sand, Qeriya slowed. There was no one on the shore, or anywhere remotely close for that matter. Her brothers were not here! She set Doctor Michael down with a heavy heart. Had they been captured too? She stared into the ocean, numb.

Part II

Ocean

"Clara, this is our new home," Alexis forced a smile, her hands on Clara's shoulders. They dragged their bags inside the already furnished living space.

"Not bad, for a prison," Einar commented. He ignored Alexis' sideways glance and characteristic pinched lips displaying her disapproval. But why was she annoyed? he wondered fruitlessly. Better to be above board with their eight-year-old daughter. She should know what was going on and learn to deal with it.

"It has a kitchen," Clara said, her sullen demeanor beginning to perk up. "And I have my own bedroom! I've never had my own bedroom!" As a little one she'd roomed with her parents, and as she got older had slept on the pull out couch in the living area. Living space near their workplace had been pricey, in employment with the king or otherwise.

"Why did they give us such a luxury space? I didn't know they had anything like this in prison?" Alexis asked.

"The king needs us, Alexis," Einar explained. "We're his doctors and pioneers of his most valuable technology. We've also cured anomalies in the dome, so we have supporters. He can't afford to alienate us. Even though he now knows that we know what he's doing, and how we feel about it."

"I suppose so, but it doesn't seem like prison."

"It's prison all right! We've strayed from our designated path – and they've discovered that I made contact with the fire reaume." He scrubbed at his chin, his voice heavy with sadness. "I had to explain ... I had to warn them and—" he broke off, looked around the room and shook his head quickly. Alexis seemed to understand and followed his lead, staying silent.

Clara came back to join them on the couch, standing in front of her mother, who slipped her arms around her daughter's shoulders and gave her a squeeze from behind. "Clara, you'll be escorted to and from school and whatever activities you choose to participate in. Your father and I will also be escorted to work. So essentially the routine part of our lives will stay the same, we'll just be watched."

"Well," Clara said, smiling, "at least we still have a kitchen, so you can still make cookies."

Chapter 13

Ocean Reaume

Qeriya shook herself awake on the ocean shore. She couldn't afford to waste time right now, but the rhythmic waves were mesmerizing. Much of the white sand was damp from a recent tidal wave that had swallowed the entire shore, reaching right up to the woods. Qeriya hoped that was Lahcen's doing, and that it had worked. It was bright and sunny, not a cloud in sight. She and Doctor Michael saw movement near the forest on the left side of the beach, but upon closer examination, it was only a large turtle flapping dirt into the air with its back feet, burying its eggs. The mother then waddled back to the water. There was still no sign of Lahcen, Khalid, Olaf or Karl, and hardly any evidence of a fight. No dropped objects, no weapons, no bodies or blood anywhere.

"Where did they go?" Qeriya exclaimed miserably.

"I don't know," Doctor Michael answered. They both scoured the beach with their eyes for the umpteenth time without luck.

Qeriya waited for clear-headed courage to override her despondency, but it didn't. "It's as if the ocean swallowed them all whole! What should we do?" She looked at her uncle, her unhappiness written on her face. "Should we go back and search the area around the castle? No, what am I saying," she corrected herself. "It's way too dangerous. I've got to get you out of here."

"Maybe we should check around the woods and see if we can find any clues as to what might have happened," Doctor Michael reasoned calmly.

Qeriya nodded as desperation clouded her mind. She fought against the tears swimming in her eyes, trudging wearily along after Doctor Michael toward the forest. They scouted the area for clues, their attention locked on where they searched.

Suddenly, Qeriya heard a rushing sound. Behind them a huge

wave, the size of a miniature tsunami, rushed toward them. Qeriya grasped frantically at Doctor Michael and flew into the forest. She was fast, but not fast enough, the wave swallowed both of them in mid-air, sucking them deep into the salt water, the force of the churning ocean pulling the Doctor from Qeriya's grip. Swiftly, she harnessed a bubble of air to surround them, cushioning them from the wave's crushing impact. They were engulfed by the water's twilight depths, and then spiraled upward, rising to the surface, immediately gripped by the current and carried deep into the ocean. Qeriya gritted her teeth and fought to lift them into the air, but the water held them like glue.

"I can't break this hold," she cried, unable to gain stability. The water rumbled as if hungry, and a stampede of breakers hit them at full speed, tumbling them around. Another giant wave crashed over them.

"Hold tight!" Qeriya screamed. The next instant their bubble ripped apart and Doctor Michael was torn from her grip. Qeriya choked and spat salt water, the blast disorienting her.

Striving to hold her breath, she somersaulted. Where was up? What was down? It was as if she were spinning in her own tornado. A mask came over her face and she pulled in the sweet air her lungs craved. Arms encircled her, pulled her deeper into the water. She was too weak to struggle. What was the point? She didn't know where Doctor Michael was anyway.

Limp and numb with cold, everything grew dark, her mind hazy. Had she been drugged? The unknown arms pushed her through a round metal drum and she was vaguely aware of an opening clanging closed behind her. A circular wall enclosed her. Freshwater sprayed the salt away. She shivered with cold, knuckling the remaining water from her eyes. As if reading her mind, a gale of a warm air enveloped her. She felt her hair; her head cover, a present from her fire reaume cousins, was gone. Relieved as she was to be alive, she couldn't fight back the tears, too tired to try to be brave anymore.

The circular wall opened into a comfortably furnished room, enclosed within the same thick, clear substance that had harbored the prince on the rock wall that terrible night of the competition. A faint glow of light penetrated the water from the surface. She could barely see through the ocean depths, just managing to make out a sandy bottom and creatures with claws crawling on the ground. Schools of fish brushed the underground tank. The submersed oceanic house teetered on the edge of a precipice. The floor extending out over a dark void.

Hearing a sound, she whirled around to see another door open. Doctor Michael appeared. "You're alive!" Qeriya cried and ran to hug him, relief flooding through her as he embraced her.

"What happened?" he asked, his puzzled expression mirroring her own.

Qeriya shook her head. "I don't know, I didn't see anything!"

"Look outside. It's amazing," he said.

Qeriya stared at the ocean floor mesmerized. Movement caught her eye and she discerned what looked like people darting past them. A few slowed to peer in at them. They had black, glazed eyes, and wore thick lenses that magnified them even more. Their skin was hued in various shades of brown to black, reminding her of chocolate they had in the rainforest. She had never seen anyone like them before. They didn't have dark chocolate people back in the desert. Lahcen was as dark as they came and he was what the fire reaume called milk chocolate. She imagined she must look something like toasted coconut to these creatures. Thinking about skin color in terms of food made her hungry. Why couldn't she think of anything but food? Of course, she realized, it had been two days since she'd eaten.

She scrutinized the beings more thoroughly. With hair shrouded around their heads like puddles of black ink, they were fierce and intimidating, with large, defined muscles, and digits that she could see had webbing ballooning like tiny sails in a wind. They were so fast and powerful in the water. Bright white teeth gleamed when they smiled, catching the glow of light from above.

"Could they be—" Qeriya began to ask when they heard one of the rotating tube doors open."

Lahcen, Khalid!" Qeriya exclaimed and ran into their arms. "You–you're okay!" she stammered, hugging each of them fiercely, trembling as tears of relief leaked from her eyes. "Where are we?"

"We're fine, we're safe," Lahcen hastily reassured her. "This is a water reaume base."

"We didn't know what to think when the soldiers captured you! But here you are, and with Doctor Michael, no less!" Khalid exclaimed.

"I escaped and managed to rescue Doctor Michael! We came to the ocean looking for you!"

"How? How could you escape with so many guards?"

"The guards were too confident in the abilities of their cell. They put me with Doctor Michael and then came to take him away. That's when I found a way to escape. We took a back door ... Anyhow, here we are and here you are, and nobody's injured. Are Olaf and Karl here?"

"No." Khalid frowned. "They stayed and fought so that I could get away to the water and join Lahcen," he explained.

"I hope they're all right," Qeriya said.

"They'll be fine," Lahcen said. "They were in the woods. That's their natural element. They're like monkeys in those trees. I doubt any soldier could keep up with them." He turned to the Doctor. "Hey, Doctor Michael, we have questions for you."

Doctor Michael lifted his eyebrows.

"When we brought you to the earth reaume, they noticed a tattoo. They said it meant you were in the royal circle."

"Well, I was, in part. My parents, your grandparents, are in the royal circle. While I'm a doctor by training as well, I'm not as brilliant as my parents. So the tattoo was accorded me primarily as an honor to them. It's slightly different from theirs.

"Well, it certainly caused a stir with the earth reaume, particularly Kari, Olaf and Karl's grandmother."

"Oh?"

"Yeah." Lahcen treated the Doctor to a measured look. "She fainted when she saw it."

"Interesting." Doctor Michael pondered.

"I suppose it makes sense considering the circumstances, that they'd be fearful of a human with a royal tattoo," replied Doctor Michael after a brief pause. Khalid and Lahcen nodded in agreement. "

Qeriya watched the figures outside swimming around the enclosure, staring at her, and felt very much on display.

Her gaze took in the vast, thick windows and low, comfortable looking couches facing out. She'd heard of fish tanks before, but it appeared that they were now the pets. "So how did you guys get here?"

When Lahcen drew the fighting towards the ocean, they surfaced and saw that he was up against a mass of the king's soldiers, and that he shared their powers. I'd reached the beach further up the shore and I ran down to join him. I was hoping that he could swim us away from the soldiers. We couldn't have lasted much longer. My idea was to hole up somewhere while we came up with a plan to rescue you. But before we could communicate, a killer wave hit us. Someone grabbed me and put a mask over my face so that I could breathe underwater, then they swam me here, the same as you."

"I led the king's men into the water to fight," Lahcen added, "and I was in the midst of battle when the giants shouted and just ran away. Within seconds I was blasted by a large wave from behind. The giants were instantly sucked out to sea and drowned while I was captured, or so I thought. One of the water reaume dragged me down into the sea and I was struggling to get free, but then loads of them swarmed around me and each grabbed a limb, pulling me down lower. As I went lower, I sprouted webbing, and the water pressure closing in on me triggered gills. They seemed to expect this, even though I'd no clue. They knew I was like them." Lahcen laughed. "Crowds of them came to gawk at me. When I entered the chamber my lungs kicked in again. Then I saw Khalid. They explained who they were and what had happened."

Qeriya nodded. "We saw the result. Another wave crashed way past the beach and into the forest to get us."

"We explained our mission to the water reaume," Khalid added. "Although our plan was to rescue you first. They offered to help and we were discussing a way forward when they spotted you two! Now that you're here and safe, I'm hoping they can help us prepare to cross the ocean. We need to get to the next continent according to the journal. And there couldn't be a better group to help us. It's all worked out well, now that you're both here."

"I suppose so," Qeriya said, seeing Lahcen staring out of the window. "What do you see?" she asked. "Are you looking for something?"

"Oh, nothing," Lahcen answered. "It just looks fun, that's all."

"Have you been swimming out there other than when they rescued you?"

"No, I haven't had a chance." He grinned. "I've had other things on my mind. You for instance."

"Well, go on then." Qeriya nudged him in the back. "I'm fine, Doctor Michael's fine. Go on and play."

Lahcen examined her face and she smiled to let him know that she was serious. "Well, all right, if you're sure. What a relief it is to have you back!" Smiling, he embraced her – to the point she could hardly breathe.

"Go away!" she squeaked, pushing him. "Go on you big

brute!" She whacked him on the back as he entered the dual shower/dryer they came through earlier.

On the other side of the window, beyond the circular room, a school of fish flashed by. Water reaume darted here and there as if playing a game she couldn't understand.

The Doctor smiled and pointed outside. "There he is."

Her brother, with his webbed feet and hands, was almost indistinguishable from the other reaume. His skin was a little lighter, but otherwise he blended in perfectly with his mer-family. Spotting them, Lahcen started to wave just as a female version of him pummeled him from the side, sending him into a spin.

"Why did she do that?" Qeriya said, alarmed. "She ran into him for no reason!"

"Don't worry, Qeriya." Khalid chuckled. "She was the one who rescued him in the first place, and I think he hit her plenty before the others came to help. She's just messing with him. They're cut from the same cloth, I'm afraid."

They watched the two figures chase and frolic in the water.

"Anyway, enough about him," Khalid said. "I'm sure you're both tired, hungry and have a lot of questions. The reaume here are very helpful. I will warn you, though, they have a lot of strange stuff that does things on its own. They're big into technology. Never seen anything like it."

"Yeah, I've got questions," Qeriya said. "How did Lahcen end up with a girlfriend so quickly? While we were in captivity, he was here romancing some girl?" she asked, her cheeks becoming flushed.

"It wasn't like that, Qeriya, and you know it," Khalid reprimanded.

"Humph." Qeriya's eyes narrowed and her arms crossed.

"We were both very worried," he assured her. "And Sophia was very supportive. But now that you're here, it seems her support has turned into flirtation, and he doesn't seem to mind any. I think Lahcen's found his siren after all. Listen, I'll go get you both some food. Also, the reaume mentioned that we should probably move tomorrow morning. There's an island not too far away from here. It's where they live most of the time. I need to go listen to the plan." Khalid paused. "I'm so glad you two are all right. We thought we'd lost you," he said. His lip quivered.

Qeriya threw her arms around him, hugging him. After a moment, she let him go.

"I, um, I'll go get that food," he said awkwardly, and hurried off.

Qeriya sat down on one of the couches and Doctor Michael ambled across to sit on another. The seating resembled those she had seen in the house on the western border of the desert. She gazed into the darkening ocean. The water reaume had left and everything appeared fairly still. Neither of them spoke. Glancing across, it seemed to Qeriya that the Doc was already half asleep. Maybe she was, too. Eating would have to wait. Placing a pillow onto one side of the couch, she stretched out her legs, tugging a large blanket that draped the couch over her for warmth. As soon as her head touched the pillow her mind began to drift.

Suddenly her body lurched awake as a question hit her. Why Doctor Michael? Why send your best general, who happens to be air reaume, to kidnap Doctor Michael under the noses of (supposedly) the three largest threats to humanity, and an entire earth reaume community? Were air reaume in solidarity with the king? It didn't make sense! Anyhow, it didn't seem like the king's sort of plan at all. Too reckless. Who was this Mara? Did she really work for the king or not? And what did she want with Doctor Michael?"

A small globe knocked on a weak spot of their prison wall, weakened using small tools Einar had managed to steal from the workplace, tools he'd also used to manipulate the surveillance in their bedroom. At least that one room was private now. Carefully, he pulled out a chunk of brickwork and reached through to grab the orb.

"Is she safe?" Alexis whispered, as he pulled his hand back inside. Einar tugged the parchment free, carrying it into their bedroom. There, he unrolled it and silently pointed to the words: Clara's safe, made it home! Both mother and father breathed a sigh of relief as they sat on their bed.

"We did the right thing. This is the only way to protect her and the reaume. The king has nothing to threaten us with anymore except each other, and we won't waver, not for each other," Alexis whispered.

"Although, even so, he still needs us. Our lives may not change that much. The fire reaume won't be sending anymore reaume, and I gather the earth reaume have figured things out as well, since they haven't been sending any more sick, either.

They sat on together as the darkness thickened. Alexis began to whimper, "My baby!" she murmured. "I miss her so much!"

Einar tried to place his arm around her to comfort her, but he had no strength, his arm was a weak and trembling thing as he, too, began to cry. He wanted to do something, to fix the problem, but he'd done all he could. He was indeed relieved to have his daughter out of the king's hands at last, but still, the solution was unbearable, unnatural. She was gone, and he had no idea if he'd ever see her again. They lay together in the dark and cried long into the night.

Chapter 14

The Island

"Hang on!" Lahcen said as he grabbed a brother and a sister in each arm. Squished into the same tube he'd once entered in fear, he now exited with excitement, launching into the submerged light of day. Khalid and Qeriya wore masks, goggles and thick suits. Attached to Khalid was a metal tank that fed his mask with air, while Qeriya could suck air into her mask from above. As they rose to the surface,

Lahcen wondered if Khalid and Qeriya should've gone in the boat the water reaume had provided for Doctor Michael. After all, this experience was brand new for him. Who knew what could go wrong. But his siblings had wanted to see the ocean and he could certainly understand that. If there was ever a moment of complete happiness for Lahcen, this was it. Swimming in this volume of water felt like rebirth. He stretched his arms and legs as if for the first time and marveled at how powerful and fast he was once his gills emerged. Although it was slow tugging his brother and sister along, he was glad to give his sister a taste of her own medicine.

Just as he thought he'd reached the pinnacle of happiness, he was approached by Sophia, her ink-black hair radiating around her face, her eyes large and round like obsidian glass.

"Can I help, Lahcen? I can take one for you," she offered.

"You again?" Lahcen teased. "But you kidnapped me. Why should I trust you?"

"Rescued you, don't you mean? I rescued you from a ridiculous number of soldiers. By the way, I offered to be your host and they've granted you to me, so stick close and you'll be fine."

"I didn't know I was anyone's to be granted," he said, playfully.

"Only to the highest bidder," she answered and her eyes twinkled.

Mesmerized, he stared at the sleek black beauty before him. "Well, here you are." He passed his sister to her as a peace offering. "Thank you for the offer!"

Qeriya struggled a bit, but soon reconciled herself to being shoved into foreign arms. The two mer-folk swam together, a helpless Qeriya and Khalid in tow.

"Where are we going?" Lahcen asked.

"We feast on an island up this way. We call it, Oneisia," she explained, as they swam a diagonal path towards the surface, ascending slowly despite their speed. "It's beautiful."

"I suppose anything that's beautiful is always a bit dangerous," he commented with a mischievous grin and she returned a sly smile.

"So, I hear you've never been in the ocean before? That you come from the desert? Is that true?" she asked.

"I've never even seen an ocean before," he corrected. "Our dad used to tell us tales of the ocean and creatures that swam in it, though, and we learned about it in school."

"Wow," she said and shook her head. "I can't imagine how this must feel for you. A water reaume growing up without water? Who ever heard of such a thing? We'll soon be at the reef that lines the island shore. You haven't truly seen the ocean until you've explored the reef. Come on, let's race!" she urged, swimming ahead with Qeriya, who glanced back nervously through a foggy mask at the brother who'd abandoned her. Lahcen's thighs burned as he kicked, but he learned fast. His webbed feet expanded into fins, propelling him further and faster each time. He moved alongside Sophia and she impetuously knocked him on the shoulder to unbalance him, causing him to let go of his brother, and rushed ahead. He soon recovered a discombobulated Khalid and bumped her back in return, his strong body sending her tumbling through the water, making

Qeriya into the helpless, roughed up bystander. Lahcen knew his sister would be upset, but it was worth it.

"Uh, oh," he gasped, bubbles escaping his mouth. He hadn't realized how hard he'd bumped her. His heart pounded as he swam over to help. Sophia wasn't moving, she was hunched over Qeriya as if doubled up in pain. Lahcen gently placed a hand on her elbow in concern and she straightened and burst forth, Qeriya in hand, then pummeled him in the arm, which made him let go of Khalid once more. Grasping his hand, she twirled him like a dancer, then flung him away laughing. Lahcen collected Khalid, reoriented and feigned sprinting after her, but he was laughing too hard to swim anywhere.

Regrouping, they advanced at a steady pace, eventually approaching a mountain, the tip of which rose above the water. Climbing a mountain had never been easier, as movement seemed almost effortless in the ocean. Sophia broke off from the group and plunged deep into a rocky maze of lava tubes cut into the underwater mountain. Lahcen followed and they wound their way in and out of the tunnels and into a dark crevasse. He was vaguely aware that his sister would later let him have it for handing her over to such high adventure, but he stuck close to Sophia as she wound her way through and around obstacles nevertheless. The world they travelled through was populated by strange creatures, one large, floppy animal with eight tentacles Lahcen remembered his dad telling him was an octopus, schools of fish passed them within touching distance and a brightly colored eel flashed by a fish with black and brown stripes on its tail. He danced through this playground with Sophia and then moved up to the surface to join the others.

Nearer the top and close to the surface was the most beautiful sight he'd ever seen. It was canvased with bright colors, light, clear water and abundant movement. Life was everywhere. Khalid and Qeriya wriggled like toddlers wrestling free of a parent's grip. Khalid stroked the plants and frolicked with a myriad of curious fish. He smiled at the coral and swam near a sea turtle devouring a jellyfish. Qeriya floated on her back for some time, enjoying the air and sunshine. Then she turned over to explore the reef and came face to face with a barracuda. She paddled feebly away and Lahcen couldn't help but laugh at his sister's expense. She was just fine after all. Seeing his siblings content allowed him to enjoy himself also as he raced with Sophia at high speed, winding through tunnels, flipping and spinning, playing chase and other wild games.

"Hey, let's watch this guy for a while," Sophia said and Lahcen stopped to look at a small fish meandering through the coral and patches of anemone. There was nothing remarkable about it as far as he could see but he was in a mood to indulge this ocean princess. Suddenly the sandy ocean floor opened its jaws and snapped the little fish up. Lahcen violently recoiled, caromed into Sophia and sent her hurtling in a fit of laughter.

"What was that!" he exclaimed.

"A fish," Sophia squeaked between howls of laughter.

Lahcen fumed like a bull ready to charge. Sophia backed up and squealed as he flew at her. She barreled about the reef, with Lahcen close behind, the chase faster and more intense now that they were free of passengers. They zoomed through the water like electricity. At one point, Lahcen cornered Sophia, but she skyrocketed through the water to an incredible height, dove behind him and spurted off in the other direction, winding through tight obstacles. In her haste, she brushed past Khalid and sent him into a pirouette. Qeriya saw them approaching in time to pull up into the air and hover until the threat was gone.

A horn penetrated the water and Sophia halted. Lahcen braked to a stop before toppling into her. "It's time to gather," she said breathlessly. "Oops," she tittered, seeing Khalid and Qeriya walking onto shore, "I guess we're the only ones left in the water." Both hurried inland. Lahcen emerged onto the island and found himself struggling to breathe. But within seconds his newly discovered gills had closed and sealed, invisible to the eye, as his lungs took over.

He regarded Sophia's transformation. Her large, webbed extremities shrank into long and slender digits and her hair quickly dripped dry. Water rolled off of her as if she were made of wax, just like it did him. As her long hair dried, it puffed into a soft halo around her head. Lahcen wanted to touch it, but thought better of it. This was not the time or place, and they had just met, even though it felt to him like they'd known one another for ages. Water evaporated completely from them both on their short walk to the fire. Some of the reaume had procured soft blankets for the new comers to use as towels, but these were rendered unnecessary as Qeriya blew a helical of toasty air around herself and Khalid. However, she did choose a small one to wrap around her head, clutching it under her chin.

"Poor girl," Lahcen said.

"What is it?" Sophia asked.

"Qeriya usually wears a head covering, all the women of the desert do, but it came off in the ocean. It's a tradition amongst us and it's also practical in the constant sun, but to Qeriya, it's more than that, it's a symbol of her commitment to Spirit. She's very devout and she sees it as a sign of her submission. I pray, but I'm nowhere near as dedicated as she is."

"Oh," Sophia said, her voice sympathetic. "I see. I could come up with a scarf for her to wear."

Lahcen smiled gratefully. "That would be nice," he said. "I'm sure she'd appreciate it. I know she seems a bit rude at the moment. She's mad at me. But once you get to know her she's nice."

"That's good to know," Sophia said. "She doesn't seem to like me very much for some reason. I'm sorry if I scared her on the journey here."

Lahcen pealed with laughter. "You gave her quite a ride."

"Oh, no! Was she frightened? I'm so sorry. I thought it would be thrilling."

"No, don't worry, she's fine. It's me she's upset with."

The fire was glowing nicely. Roasted fish smelled very different from boar, rabbit or venison.

"I guess I got out of work," Sophia said smiling.

Lahcen wondered at her voice. In the water it sounded like everyone else he knew, but now that she was on land, he could hear a thick, musical accent. "But I'm being a hostess. That's work, right?"

"Hostess? Yeah, sure. What kind of hostess puts her guests through what you just put us through?" Lahcen teased.

"I can't believe you've never been in the ocean! You certainly learn fast!"

"Thanks, I'm trying. You're a good teacher."

Sophia grinned widely. "That's right, it's all my doing isn't it?"

"Yeah, catching you is all the motivation I need." His eyes sparkled and Sophia impishly prodded his shoulder.

"You wish!"

"So, we're having fish for dinner?" Lahcen asked as he sniffed the fragrant smoke.

"Fish, and whatever shellfish, plants and roots we can find. Probably yucca, we usually have yucca or yams, figs and nuts. You should see the monkeys on this island. They've learned to take large rocks and knock the shells open to eat the nuts inside. I love watching them," Sophia told him. "Maybe we can check them out later!"

"Yeah, sure. We'd better eat first, and I need to talk to Doctor Michael," Lahcen said. As much as he was loving this interlude, there were a hundred or more questions that he needed answering. "You don't suppose we're related, do you?" Lahcen asked uncomfortably.

Sophia laughed. "No, we're not related. My grandparents knew your great-grandmother. She married an air reaume and left the water reaume. After that they didn't hear much from her. The air reaume are reclusive, more than the other reaume."

"I wonder why?" Lahcen asked.

Sophia shrugged and drew in the sand with her toes.

"Well, at least you know what an ocean is," Lahcen said.

"Didn't anyone teach you? Why didn't you ask more questions about it?"

Lahcen frowned. "They didn't teach us much, just a few basics. And we weren't allowed to ask questions about our history. It wasn't a rule necessarily. Taboo questions simply weren't answered. And we soon found out what we could and couldn't ask."

They sat down with the others gathered around the fire, smoke billowing like an offering to the cloudless sky, which was growing darker by the moment as the light glowed orange.

"We'll camp here," Sophia explained.

The island was sandy, with rock outcroppings dotting the shore. Palm trees formed a wall around the inlet and towering hills loomed behind.

Glancing at Qeriya, Lahcen saw that she hadn't yet forgiven them for her wild experience. Seeing Sophia, her face clouded over even more. "Thanks a lot, princess nightmare, for that exciting ride!" she quipped. "And thank you, brother, for passing me off to a complete stranger. It felt like we were plummeting down a waterfall that never ended."

"I was looking out for you," Sophia defended, sounding hurt.

"What part of me, exactly, did you look after? It certainly wasn't my body or my sanity. I felt as if I'd be ripped apart at any minute during your ocean escapade," she added. Turning to Lahcen, she snarled, "Pretty rotten thing to sacrifice your sister for a pretty face, Lahcen."

Lahcen stared at the sand while Sophia burned indigo. Around them, the others had grown silent, watching the exchange with guarded interest.

Qeriya took a deep breath. "Anyhow," she added in a calmer voice, just as Doctor Michael was about to speak.

The Doctor shook his head. "There's not much to tell, really. I woke up in a prison cell. And before long, Qeriya joined me there."

Lahcen watched as orange flames spit sparks, a blue glow emanating from the wood.

Doctor Michael sighed. "They were about to transfer me to the palace when Qeriya flew down the passageway like lightening, grabbed me, and flew us to the ocean.

"How strange," Khalid said. "Did you see Mom and Dad or hear anything about them?"

Qeriya shook her head. Doctor Michael stared at his hands. "No, nothing," he said finally.

"Do you remember anything before you were put in the prison cell?" Khalid asked.

Doctor Michael looked at Khalid. "I covered a lot of ground and I didn't even know it. Just as well I was unconscious or it would have been a nightmare." He paused, then said, "I'm sure they've taken your parents to the palace. But they still need medicine. The stasis won't last forever." He glanced around at the three of them. "Is the journal helping you? Are you following it?"

"Yes, very much," Khalid answered. "We should be able to find the flowers on the other continent. There's a range of mountains stretching from the northern part southward. That's also where the palace is located. Once we cross the ocean, we'll move way north of the palace and cross the grassland to the mountain range. That way we'll avoid detection. Then we'll climb into the mountains and work our way south. We'll harvest the flower and approach from there."

"Perfect plan!" Doctor Michael answered. "I couldn't have guided you better myself. But what else should I expect from my dear sister's children?" he said, beaming. "Now, I should go to my tent and get ready for the trip."

"Thanks for helping us," Qeriya said, tears forming and sliding down her cheeks. "You're a true friend, and I'm so proud you're our Uncle."

Doctor Michael patted her head with reserved affection, and Lahcen thought he saw him blink hard a few times. Lahcen wrapped a comforting arm around his sister and she laid her head against his chest.

"Of course," Doctor Michael said in a choked voice.

The Doctor had never struck Lahcen as a very expressive person, which is perhaps why he soon edged away from the fire.

"I'd better get back to my tent," he murmured. I'm very tired. I'll see you all in the morning."

"Doctor Michael," Khalid called as he began to leave. He spun part way around on his heel. "I'm thinking of asking some water reaume to join us on this quest. Maybe they could help find out more about this virus and develop the medicine for it."

"Not a good idea, Khalid," Doctor Michael answered. "Listen, yes they are excellent doctors, but if the king got wind of it, he'd certainly kill them. The king's after you and he'll kill anyone in his way. A crowd's easy to spot, while you three can hide easier and aren't a threat. You can't help your parents by fighting. The king's too powerful. You need to lay low and be inconspicuous. Find the flower and mount a low-key rescue effort. That plan has the most chance of success, with the fewest casualties. I'll be there to help you. And anyhow, I know how to make the medicine."

"If this virus is spreading, they would most likely want to know more about it. Also, I'm having doubts about undertaking this alone. No one else would need to go into the palace. I don't want to place anyone in danger. But I think it's wise to have a few others to help us reach the right place and brainstorm a plan. Could you at least talk with them about it?"

"Khalid, first of all, I'll be there to help you, and like I said,

I already know how to make the medicine." Doctor Michael put a hand on Khalid's shoulder, staring straight into his eyes. "Second, I know this is difficult, but you need to trust me. There's a lot you don't know about these reaume. It's too risky to invite them into your mission and your confidence, no matter how interested they are. Trust me! I'm the closest person you have to a parent right now, and I'm trying to help you save yours."

"The king wishes you to tutor his son," a giant explained from outside Einar and Alexis' door. According to the insignia he wore on his armor, he was from the Royal Guard, the king's right hands.

"Why us?" Einar asked as he and Alexis stepped out to join him.

"Sean, it seems, is academically gifted. The most advanced schools are still not challenging enough for him. He's causing trouble."

"But that doesn't explain why us," Alexis probed.

"Everyone knows you two are the most brilliant scientists of this century," the giant explained.

"We are?" Alexis asked.

"Yes, you're read by students everywhere in both science and history books. The king thinks you'd be good teachers too."

"Oh, well, guess we don't get out much …" Einar chuckled. "Well, maybe …" he observed Alexis, who nodded as well.

"Yes, we'll do it," Alexis said.

Chapter 15

Carnivore

For the first time in Lahcen's memory, sleep was a waste of time. Tomorrow couldn't come soon enough. The fifth time he awoke from a restless doze, it was to a gentle wind blowing the front flap. It felt odd to be awake before his siblings, usually he was the last to open his eyes. He left Khalid and Qeriya to snooze, and going outside found the water reaume stirring. He couldn't quite explain why his heart was beating so fast, until he found himself scanning face after face for Sophia, who, it seemed, was also looking for him.

"Lahcen," she called, skipping over to him, her smile revealing gleaming, opalescent, pearly teeth.

"Sophia!" he said, suddenly struck dumb by her beauty. An azure scarf was woven about the crown of her head, pushing her mass of hair back off her face and upward, into a large tuft that resembled wool. A sapphire dress highlighted her curves. Her skin was dark, like the chocolate he'd tasted in the rainforest, but no longer tinted blue. Her eyes were the same obsidian as they had been deep in the ocean. She was a daughter of the island, moving strong and graceful on land as in the water.

"Let's help gather food for breakfast. I know just where to look."

Her melodic voice turned his bones into sponge and he obeyed without argument, strolling beside her along the beach.

"Where are we going?" he asked.

"This way."

"Does 'this way' have a name?"

"You'll see."

The shore was decorated by pretty rocks and small plants as they ambled along. Bamboo stalks covered the thick forest and Lahcen caught occasional glimpses of creatures that vaguely resembled the monkeys he'd seen while hunting in the rainforest.

"We call those immortals," Sophia said, watching him stare with wonder.

"Immortals? Seriously?"

"Well, that's what we call them. They're a type of lemur that can eat new bamboo buds, which contain enough cyanide to kill any other life form."

"Wow!" He stopped and began to head in their direction, but Sophia took his hand and pulled him further along the shore.

"Let's keep going. I want to show you something. You have to see these plants," she said.

Plants were more Khalid's thing, but Lahcen wasn't about to suggest getting his brother to come along with them. He'd have to feign interest, which wouldn't be that hard to do as long as Sophia was showing them to him.

They came to a collection of beautiful flowers whose giant bud was a pouch, opened at the top to reveal a puddle of clear liquid with a few drowned flies inside. Sophia climbed a tree and perched on a branch above a collection of the plants. She beckoned Lahcen to join her and he followed.

"Are we collecting food?" he asked.

"Oh, we'll get to that later. Let's see how other creatures collect their food first."

"What creatures? You don't mean to say that these flowers gather food?"

"Shh," she said and pointed to the buds below them.

Lahcen did as told, but it was difficult to be patient and watch when he had no idea what he was supposed to be watching and for how long. So, instead, he debated in his mind whether or not to clasp her hand. This turned into vivid imagery in the deep recesses of his mind of what it might feel like to kiss her luscious lips.

"Did you see it?" Sophia whispered excitedly.

Lahcen ricocheted back to his senses. "Yeah, wow, incredible!"

he lied. She resumed her observation and he paid closer attention, hoping to see what he said he'd seen. Ants negotiated petals, seeking to caress the inside top of them without falling into the puddle. He saw one slip and land with a plop in the liquid below, joining a jumble of drowned flies.

"There goes another one for breakfast," Sophia said and Lahcen was relieved to discover that he had, in fact, seen what he was supposed to. "Isn't that amazing – a plant that hunts, eating insects for breakfast! They're called pitcher plants."

"Flesh eating plants?" She wasn't kidding. They were something to see. One insect after another crawled to a precipice, taking such a risk to taste the sweet nectar, naively creeping to their death. He marveled at how undisturbed he was by the destruction taking place for his entertainment. Although, to be fair, it wasn't the killing he enjoyed, it was the ingenuity of the plant, the way a stationary predator managed to survive. From a corner of his eye, he caught movement and saw familiar faces passing along the shore.

"Lahcen!" They called.

He pulled himself up to stand upon the branch and waved vigorously to them, not answering lest he disturb Sophia's reverie as she attended the morning massacre. Qeriya wore an azure headscarf like the one Sophia was wearing, but she wore it the same way she did in the desert. It adorned her head like a fabric jewel, wrapping her long dark hair. For an instant, he was awestruck, proud of how lovely his sister had become. She'd grown up so much since they'd left home.

Khalid and Qeriya saw him wave and veered to join him. Lahcen glanced back down in time to see a few tiny lizards perch close to the mouth of the plants and zap the oblivious insects.

"Oh, look!" he exclaimed in a loud whisper. "They're adorable!" As he knelt to sit down, he slipped and fell backwards off the branch. He braced himself to hit the hard ground, but instead splashed into a puddle. Hopping to his feet, he dared to open his eyes. He was enclosed in a bowl. There were no handholds with which he could climb out. The wall of the bowl resembled the inside of his tent, glowing orange in the morning light, but with no exit. The liquid felt itchy and acidic and he couldn't extract water from the walls. A wax coating made it impervious to dehydration both from within and without. He heard Sophia attempt to do the same on the outside.

"Can you find a long stick?" he called from the depths of what he determined must be a very large pitcher plant. "I think I'm this plant's breakfast."

"I'm looking!" she assured him.

Just then the petals snapped shut, as if the plant had heard their conversation and was determined to stop him escaping. The fumes were suffocating.

"Khalid! Qeriya! Help!"

He could hear panic in Sophia's voice. Then he heard Khalid unsheathe his sword.

"Don't puncture Lahcen!" Qeriya yelled.

Lahcen tensed, although at this point he might take a flesh wound if it meant getting out of the acid bath. From inside, Lahcen felt the plant lift itself and swing, knocking into someone while tumbling over.

"Ahh! My hand!" Khalid yelled.

Lahcen heard a distinct crack. The plant swung again but this time there was no impact. It was fortunate he hadn't eaten. Vomit would only have added to the acid. He heard another thump as two sticks punctured the petals near the top, prying them away. Choking fumes escaped. Lahcen urgently tried to reach the holes but they were too high. He could feel acid soak deeper into his legs and feet by the second, causing an intense itch, quickly escalating to a raw burn.

"Aim lower!" he shouted. He could hear scuffing outside and the plant swung repeatedly from side to side. He was beginning to suspect that none of it would matter for much longer. His legs were now agony.

"I'm coming, Lahcen!" Sophia yelled. Seconds later, the plant opened and plucked her off of its stem to join Lahcen.

"That wasn't very helpful."

"Well, obviously, it's not what I meant to happen!"

"Climb onto my shoulders," he ordered.

Gathering his waning strength, Lahcen lifted her onto his shoulders. Sophia tried to grab a puncture wound, where the wax had been penetrated, and dehydrate the creature. But before she could even lift her arms, Lahcen's strength gave out and she plummeted into the acid bath.

"Geez," he mumbled, "did you eat rocks for breakfast?"

"You're welcome for my trying to save your life!"

"I didn't ask you to save me," Lahcen spat. "You shouldn't have risked yourself. Now I have to worry about getting both of us out."

"While I just sit by and enjoy a session of digestion?"

"All right fine! Let's just try it again."

"Are you sure you're up to it, Pee Wee? I'm not looking for another tumble."

Lahcen ignored her and once more boosted her onto his back. This time his strength gave out even more quickly, dumping her into the liquid.

Just as Sophia fell, Khalid's blade cut into a petal, slicing upward to avoid hurting the two inside. The cut was lower this time. Grimly determined, Lahcen boosted Sophia a third time and she heaved onto his shoulders, stretching up as far as she could manage, catching at the new cut, clinging to it by her fingertips. Lahcen propped her up even higher and using every ounce of her considerable strength, she dug her fingernails into the petal, drawing water out of the injured, wax free surface. Under her onslaught, the petal and stem steadily disintegrated into powder, spilling them both, together with a stream of acid, onto the ground. Lahcen collapsed onto the wet earth, wincing in pain as he siphoned water from the surrounding plants to wash his skin. No matter how much he rinsed his legs and feet, the burning persisted.

"Lahcen your legs and feet! They look as if you've been in a fire!" Sophia gasped. "You need a healer!"

Qeriya hovered Lahcen in midair as they sped through the myriad of bamboo, palm trees and ferns.

"There, see the guy in white and blue? He's a healer!" Sophia exclaimed, pointing to an older gentleman. His hair was white and bushy and his eyes sagged wearily as he tended a fire surrounded by raised rock beds covered with large leaves and cushions. He looked frail, bordering on starvation, and was dressed in a white robe with a turquoise sash. Hurrying over to him, they unloaded Lahcen onto one of the raised beds.

"Burned by acid," Sophia told him.

The man's forehead pinched as he listened, as if he needed more information. "It was from an oversized pitcher plant," she added. "I've never seen one that big before!"

Lahcen's attention oscillated from one to the other, but the pain was intense and it was difficult to concentrate on what they were saying.

The healer didn't speak or bother to comment on Sophia's statement about the plant. He blew a whistle, and a flood of younger water reaume in sashes came surfing towards them from around the island to help. When the elder healer spoke, his voice though calm carried the weight of authority. "Flush his burn twice as long as standard protocol. Continue further acid treatment as normal."

Some of the other healers collected leaves to place beneath Lahcen, while others streamed water from the nearby vegetation to flush his burns as he'd done for himself earlier. One of the healers then poured the contents of a vial of fluid into the streams of water that poured mercilessly onto his tender skin. Lahcen bit his lip and stifled the urge to cry out.

Khalid moved closer and laid his undamaged hand on his brother's arm. Lahcen felt relief almost instantaneously.

"I know it hurts, but ironically that's a good sign," the elder healer said. "It means your nerves are still intact." He studied the injury, frowning. "But this acid might be a kind that doesn't simply wash off, so after irrigating we'll just have to watch," he said.

Lahcen grimaced. "It did hurt, but Khalid appears to have magical pain relief powers."

"It's an earth reaume thing," Khalid told him modestly.

"Why am I not surprised?" Lahcen exclaimed. "I want a cool gift, although I'd settle for a weapon. Do water reaume make cool weapons?"

The healer's eyes suddenly lit up like fireflies and he started to dig through a nearby wooden chest full of herbs and moss, creams and potions and other organic ingredients. "I've an idea for a cream that might repair the burn. I'll prepare it for you," he offered, collecting a few jars out of the chest, opening them and gathering ingredients from each into an empty jar before mixing them with a wooden stick. He threw the stick into the fire and re-joined them.

"So, how did this happen? What is this oversized pitcher plant Sophia is talking about?" he asked. "We've no record of such a plant in our catalogue of species."

"Hey, guys—" Qeriya began.

"It was just that, a giant pitcher plant, like I said!" Sophia interrupted. "He fell in backwards. I've never seen anything like it before!"

"Sorry to interrupt—" Qeriya said again.

"Sounds like one of the king's experiments." The healer sighed deeply. "I suppose we'll have to send a group to search it out, but from what you said, it sounds like we've been discovered."

"Um—" Qeriya persisted.

"That means – that means we'll have to relocate," Sophia

concluded as her brows furrowed.

The elder nodded. "If we have been marked, then I'm afraid so."

"Qeriya, do you have something to say?" he asked.

"We–well, yeah," Qeriya stammered. "My other brother, Khalid, crushed his hand fighting that monster plant," she said, thrusting Khalid forward.

Lahcen winced as he saw Khalid's mangled hand.

"Here you were helping my pain when you were dealing with this?" Lahcen squealed.

"Yikes, you're right when you say the hand was crushed," the healer said, taking out what looked like a thin metal stick from his red sash and examined the hand thoroughly. "It's broken in numerous places. But don't worry, this won't hurt much," he added, shooting something from the pen into the injured hand.

"I can't feel my hand," Khalid said as the healer put away the instrument.

The elder traced his right index finger along each of Khalid's metacarpals, then along different stretches of his hand.

"Wait!" Qeriya said. "What are you doing?"

"I'm healing the breaks." Noting her uncomprehending expression he opted to explain. "I'm drawing my fingers along various bones in his hand until I sense the breaks, then I heal them." It took some time before he looked up from his work. "There, that should do it. The numbing medicine will wear off in a moment. Be gentle with your hand, and when feeling returns, let me know if it still hurts anywhere. I may have missed a few breaks. Your hand was nearly shattered."

"But how? How did you do it?" Qeriya asked as Lahcen stared at the miracle before him.

"Time travel." The healer smiled.

"Time travel? That's seriously your answer?" Qeriya asked, cocking her head, hands on her hips, noticeably unconvinced.

"Yes, I'm not teasing you." He laughed, revealing straight,

white teeth. Each reaume has a unique trait. Fire reaume can tap into nonverbal communication to manipulate emotion, for one example. Earth reaume are able to ease pain. They can influence how the brain perceives painful stimuli. Water reaume have a capacity for creative problem solving. Our reaume are responsible for numerous discoveries connected to time. We create advanced technologies and manage information." He paused, shaking his head. "Air reaume gifting is a bit of a mystery to us – we've had such little contact with them. While they can't travel bodily in time, they can speed up development of a fire, for example. We've examined this process and can now mimic it for the express purpose of healing. When I traced my hand over your brother's injury, it illuminated the skeleton under his skin. I could see the bones and their breaks. I then pulsated particular micro-time waves to fast forward the natural healing process."

"That's unreal," Lahcen muttered, open mouthed, staring vaguely into the trees. "So that's how you heal?"

"That's one aspect of how we heal. Those of us who are healers study other aspects of medicine and surgery, using knowledge very different from time travel."

"How is that possible?" Qeriya asked again. "Lahcen's like you, and I've never seen him do any of this. I've certainly never seen evidence of a superior intellect," she commented as Lahcen glared at her.

"Perhaps that's because he hasn't been with us long enough to allow him to develop. He hasn't been allowed to practice his gifts. Can you manipulate time?" he asked Qeriya.

"No, not unless you include running really fast."

"I suppose that's possible."

Qeriya grimaced. "I'm just kidding. So the technology you're speaking of is in your hands? How can technology be in your hands? Are you saying that we have computers in our bodies?" she asked.

"Yes, years ago we learned to embed nanotechnology into

our very DNA. Human scientists long ago on Old Earth learned to splice artificial genetics into human DNA, but the practice ceased when anomalies became problematic.

Deep within the ocean we have an underground research facility. For years we've studied and recreated the science behind all of this in order to understand it, but now we're more interested in the future. When humans created us to serve them, they didn't consider us to be sentient life forms, they saw us rather as androids with human tissue. They also didn't conceive of the possibility that we'd evolve, and we are evolving – at an alarming rate. Our DNA is mutating and recombining in ways it never has in the past. Now there's no way to separate out the artificial components from our organic tissue."

"Doctor Michael mentioned something about reaume evolving when we were staying with the fire reaume. So reaume aren't the same beings as they were when created by humans?" Lahcen clarified.

"Certainly not. While we were created by humans, we managed to evolve in ways they could never have dreamed. We were a creation, but now we are a species!

"That's why we're being hunted. We represent a new hybrid, where the powers of the reaume and of human's have been combined into one," Khalid clarified. "Instead of seeing us as half-human, the king sees only a more powerful species of reaume that humans created, capable of taking them over."

"You mentioned a lab deep in the ocean. You said it was a research facility?" Lahcen asked. "What've you done there?"

"One project we finished a few years ago was to insert mainframe computers into our eyes. We researched the plan, developed it, a few of us tested the lenses and now we all wear them."

"What does that mean exactly?" Lahcen asked feeling his lips curl into a snarl. Being water reaume was sounding a lot less inviting if it meant he had to put something in his eyes."

"We've successfully installed computer technology into our corneal lenses. I was the test case, the first reaume to have them placed. The lenses we wear are individually tailored depending upon our occupation in the community. They help us store or access information and do calculations. We learn to operate them using specific eye movements, and we can even turn the computer on and off at will."

"I wish I could have that!" Qeriya exclaimed.

"That's disgusting!" Lahcen contradicted, a shiver running through him.

I'm not so sure about putting anything in my eyes," Khalid added.

"We don't feel any discomfort. In fact, they act as a protective layer for the eyes. Everyone looks forward to getting them."

"Yeah! I got mine a couple of years ago," Sophia shared, standing up a little straighter.

"What's your job?" Lahcen asked, staring into her eyes with a disgusted scowl to see if he could spot them.

"You look upset," Sophia surmised, obviously flustered.

"Why would I be upset? No, it's just that, well, your eyes are just a bit creepy," Lahcen explained, still searching for evidence of the lenses.

"That's what every girl wants to hear when a guy is staring deep into her eyes," Sophia commented, her voice flat and oozing with sarcasm. "Anyhow, I'm in training to be a librarian. My job is to catalog all of our information."

"We were taught that librarians were bookish sorts of people, although we never actually had a library of our own, so what would I know," Lahcen said.

"Not here! Being a librarian is one of the most active jobs." Sophia stood tall and proud, thoroughly animated. "My job is to identify and catalogue information. As I find different life forms, my computer pulls up any information we might have on them from our database. I organize what I see and resend the new or revised info back to it. Eventually I'd like to travel more on land to revise our old info."

"Hey, guys?" Lahcen groaned, with a renewed awareness of his discomfort. "Sorry to change the subject, but is this irrigation stuff done yet? I think the water's flushing away whatever skin I have left," he complained. The healer or doctor, or whatever he was, Lahcen didn't know or care at this point, came over to examine him again.

When he spoke, it was not only to Lahcen, but to the crowd of young healers in training. "It looks like we can stop for now and apply the cream. I'm going to try this combination of my own instead of the protocol remedy for this case." He took the top off the jar he had filled earlier.

"This is made from a variety of creams. One stimulates healing and prevents infection while the other is a basic agent to counteract irritants. The recipes for these ointments come from the fire reaume. They're known for their medicines."

Lahcen felt his throat tighten as he tried to restrain a litany of complaints. He felt as if he were sitting in on a lecture, that the whole procedure was designed just to teach these young healers in training, and he was about to say this out loud when the elder smoothed some of the cream onto his leg. His skin instantly cooled and the painful burning abated.

Any irritation he'd been feeling immediately turned to gratitude as the healer rubbed more cream onto his other leg. Breathing a deep sigh of contentment, he relaxed and soon found himself beginning to doze. After what felt like mere seconds he awoke with a start. They were flooded him with water again. Thankfully, this time it didn't hurt so much. He looked at his legs. "Wow!" he said, amazed. "You can't even tell how bad they were burned!"

"I know, isn't it incredible?" Qeriya agreed. "And Khalid's back to normal, too!"

"I'm so sorry, Lahcen," Sophia said, stricken. "I encouraged you to watch the pitcher plants with me. But I swear I'd no idea there was anything of that size and that dangerous out there!"

"Of course you didn't, Sophia," Lahcen reassured her, reaching up to stroke her hair. "I'm just glad you're not hurt."

Sophia gave a little sob and threw herself into his arms, crying on his shoulder.

Qeriya, Khalid and the crowd of healers quietly slipped away from the couple.

"I've had a wonderful time with you," Lahcen said, wiping the tears from her cheeks and pulling her into a firm embrace. "I've never been so happy as here with you, in this place. I have to help my parents, but then I'll be back to visit and you can show me more wonders."

"I'm afraid there won't be anything to come back to," Sophia said, pulling away from him. "The king knows where we are now since we took you back to our city. We'll have to make preparations to leave. I doubt we'll be able to get far without a fight." She halted, her face knotted with worry. "He has us just where he wants us."

"Sean, what a surprise! It's so nice of you to visit us!" Alexis exclaimed when she opened the door to their prison home.

"To what do we owe this pleasure?" Einar said, extending his arm to invite him inside.

"Any problems with the problems?"

Sean shook his head. "No, I just wanted to tell you all something in person before the news is announced."

Einar waved at the couch, "Sit, sit," he said, as he and Alexis settled into their own seats. "Okay – shoot."

Sean came straight to the point. "I'm getting married."

"Congratulations!" They exclaimed, surprised and delighted.

"My fiancé is named Kanti."

"Kanti? What a beautiful name!" Alexis said. "How did you meet her?"

"Well, that's hard to explain. You see, Kanti is air reaume."

Einar's jaw dropped a few inches as a jolt of what felt like electricity coursed through his body. "Air reaume! Well, Sean, you seem to have turned a corner from your father."

"Yes, his reign of torment is over." Einar detected a note of bitterness in Sean's tone, though he had never spoken of his father before, or even alluded to him. "I have a new solution to the reaume problem, thanks to you and your work."

"Oh? And that is?" Einar asked.

Sean studied them for a moment. "Reaume and humans have never been able to have children together," he said quietly, "but with your advances in nano-robotics and ova, I believe that you can change that. I've been studying the possibility for some time now. My father took advantage of your research to experiment with living weapons, but I'd like to use your research in a different way. I wish to use our reaume and human DNA to genetically engineer an heir."

Chapter 16

H2S

Lahcen popped his head outside the tent to find banana trees on one side and ocean waves licking the shore on the other. So it wasn't a dream after all. He surveyed the beach for the beauty who seasoned his dreams. While he couldn't afford to get involved with anyone until his parents had been rescued, if he was going to think about her all the time, he may as well enjoy being with her.

"Boo!" Sophia whispered, poking her head around the side of the tent and surprising him as the other two slept soundly. She stepped into view and Lahcen's heart pounded. Every time he looked at her, there was something to see that he hadn't noticed before. He stood rooted to the spot as if in a trance. She wasn't trying to be flirtatious, just her normal, playful self. But just being around her normal, playful self was about all he could handle.

"So what adventure do you have planned for me today?" he asked, trying to appear as normal as possible.

"Would you like to come with me while I work?" she asked. "The leaders are having a meeting to discuss what we're going to do, so there's not much going on around here."

"Of course I'll come."

"I have something to show you, follow me," she said, running into the ocean and leaping into the first substantial wave that hit the shore.

Lahcen followed; transforming within seconds and speeding into the deep after Sophia, whose fins he could barely see until she turned around to wait for him. Her face came back into view as she propelled herself forward to meet him.

"Don't worry, it's not far, but it is deep. I have a light." She turned away and Lahcen saw beams streaming from each of her eyes.

"How are you doing that?"

"You remember the corneal implants I have? They're mini computers and one of the tools I have now are lights.

"Come on." She yanked at his forearm. "You have to see this." Obediently, he followed close behind her. Light swelled as the sun rose, only to dim again as they swam deeper, but her eyes lit the way for them. "I can see in the dark with my lenses," she informed him. "I'm lighting the way for your benefit. Don't worry," she added, "you won't have any problems. The light waves are calibrated to travel through water."

Lahcen soon saw what he could only describe as an underwater wadi, surrounded by riverbanks, and a waterfall up ahead.

"How can there be a river underwater?"

She faced him, dimming the halo of light emitting from the whites of her eyes.

"There are so many parts to the ocean we haven't begun to understand yet. This is a current of water mixed with hydrogen sulfide. Don't touch it!"

It resembled a jungle waterfall in the murky twilight and he could hardly believe his eyes. "When did you discover this?"

"I found it a few weeks ago. I've been cataloguing what I see. The information goes into my computer and I release it to the water computer in our research facility."

"What is this water computer you speak of? Is it an oracle or a house of the Spirit?"

Sophia stared at him, her face unreadable, uncomprehending. "An oracle? What's that? And what do you mean a house of the Spirit?"

"You don't believe in the Spirit?"

"I've heard of the Spirit, but we don't believe in it, no. What is there to believe in? The other reaume worship this Spirit you speak of, but we don't believe in the supernatural. We're scientists."

"Oh, I thought all reaume – anyhow, the fire and earth reaume seem to believe in a supernatural Spirit that resides in their respective springs. But not everyone who worships believes that the Spirit is supernatural."

"What do you mean by that?"

"I worship the Spirit, but don't believe it's supernatural. The spirit is entirely natural. It created everything."

"What does that mean? It doesn't make any sense."

"My mom used to say that the Spirit is like a pregnant mother, and the universe is the womb ... or maybe it was a placental sac ... I don't quite remember," he muttered.

Various expression of surprise chased across Sophia's face, quickly turning to laughter. "So, to follow this analogy, humans are one twin and reaume are the other?"

"No, more like humans are one pinky fingernail of one twin and reaume are the other pinky – fingernail, that is."

"Guess I won't be clipping my nails from now on. Don't you think you're taking this analogy a little too far?" she pushed.

"Oh, no, nothing's more important to my mom than getting a spiritual metaphor correct," he said, chuckling.

"Strange. Why do people believe in a Spirit, anyway?"

"I don't see it as strange at all," Lahcen told her. "We're alive, and we birth life, or females do anyhow. Us men, we just sit around, eat macadamia nuts and watch it happen."

"But we couldn't have a child without you."

"Without me?" His eyes twinkled.

Sophia burned maroon with embarrassment. "You know what I mean!" She pushed Lahcen, who caught her in his muscular arms, laughing.

"I don't think it's so strange for scientists to believe in the Spirit," he said. "Life comes from life, so it's only natural to assume that we should originate from life. That life is the Spirit. But unlike the other reaume worshippers, we don't believe that the Spirit is bound by anything like a pond or a spring."

"It's something to think about," Sophia said, turning away to survey the river.

"So, how did you find this place?" Lahcen asked.

"It's my job. I found it on one of my sojourns. My lenses map the ocean floor for miles around. When I find something interesting, I dip down and explore it."

"You do this alone?"

"Sometimes, yes, sometimes, no. It depends on how far away I'm traveling. My readings automatically sync with the master computer."

"Everything you do is watched by a master computer? That's freaky, though no different than my life in the desert where they watched our every move." Her shoulder bumped his ribs and he rolled in the water. When he caught sight of her again, she'd darted away.

"Hey, no fair! You and your X-ray vision can see me anywhere I go, but I can't see you as well in what's left of the light down here!" he said, swimming cautiously, peering through cloudy water. He could hear distant, haunting sounds, and was beginning to feel his throat tighten with fear when she rammed into his side, having snuck up from behind him.

He grabbed her hips, pulling her close and wrapping his arms around the back of her solid frame. She pushed and flailed hard, but he wrestled her closer, burying his head in her neck. Sophia wriggled but he firmly held her still.

The more she fought, the more he was drawn to her, as if she were a magnet, locking them together. He could feel her heart thump, or was that his own, beating stronger, louder, pounding in his ears. He'd never been this close to a woman, nor had he intended to today.

Sophia was a wild, exotic species, a part of him he'd denied for so long. She tried to wrestle him, her laughter sounding like music to his ears, but she was growing weaker. No, not weaker, softer, more pliant. Her arms came around his shoulders and she stroked his hair, his back. Her mouth brushed his shoulder. Slowly, Lahcen lowered his head. Her lips were full and soft, they tasted slightly of salt. All thought and reason slipped away from his mind. She was his only reality.

But she wasn't his only reality. He had to maintain control. He relaxed his embrace and she relented, pulling gently away in turn. They stared into each other's eyes and in the subtle light, Lahcen saw that Sophia was equally surprised by what had happened.

"If only we had more time here—" he began to say, but she quieted him, pressing her fingers to his lips.

"I know," she said.

"We'll be more careful," he added and smiled. "I guess we know how we feel about each other."

She smiled in turn. "Yeah, no need to bother picking petals to find out if he loves me … or he loves me not."

"Such a waste of time if you ask me," he said, and placed her hand in his, holding it up on display. "Now we can spend more of our short time together doing this."

As he spoke, he saw something behind her, an unnatural rustling of water. He couldn't pinpoint what it was, just its movement.

"What do you suppose that is?" he asked, pointing.

Sophia pivoted in time to catch a glimmer of motion. Whatever had caused it was too far away to be visible. A shimmer of water, a craft that appeared invisible – now spewing bubbles as it sped away from them.

"Did you see that on your computer?"

"No," Sophia said softly, frozen. "It didn't appear to register at all."

Lahcen's stomach twisted. "A spy, it has to be a spy!"

"I do believe that we did it," Alexis told her husband, who was hovering over her shoulder as she made her final observations. "Now to place the embryo in utero."

Einar smiled, a wide, hopeful smile. "This could be it! This could bring our daughter back," he whispered.

"Perhaps, it's everything we hoped for and more," Alexis said. "This has the potential to bring about peace between humans and reaume," she added, taking off her glasses and giving him a hug, which he returned in full. "The ova is genetically both of theirs and yet fully air reaume."

"Although it's too soon to get our hopes up."

Alexis gave him a long look. "Maybe," she said, "but I'm going to get my hopes up no matter what, so we may as well celebrate." She offered him a mischievous smile.

"And how would we do that?" Einar asked.

Alexis pulled away from his grasp and circled around him. "Just for once, let's sneak out for a bit, just to walk around downtown. We told the guards we'd be in here the entire night. Who could predict it would be done so soon?" She lowered her voice to a whisper. "They know not to disturb us in this phase of the project. We could crawl through the air ducts."

Einar's eyebrows twitched upwards. "Why not!" he exclaimed in an excited whisper. "Let's do it!"

Chapter 17

Spy

Sophia surveyed around and behind her before slithering into the lukewarm water, careful to make as little noise as possible. She thought she saw ripples and heard a disturbance. Was it a watercraft? She combed the area as best she could, but saw nothing. She must have imagined it, she told herself. Nerves were no doubt clouding her judgment.

It was a normal night; pleasantly cool with a mild breeze and no clouds. Stars twinkled against black velvet, like tiny heart beats. Her lenses illuminated the path in front of her and she glided along the coast to a series of boulders rising above the sea, set apart from the shoreline. She stopped at one in particular, clapped her hands and feet to it like suction cups, and climbed out of the water. As she rose, her body morphed. Her suction pads turned to fingers grasping at crevices in the rock.

The top of a head with spikey black hair was revealed as she scaled the rock face. The woman nested in a depression at the center of the boulder, waiting, her pale face illuminated by the burgeoning moonlight, free of the awful makeup she sometimes wore.

"Mara, you came," Sophia whispered, a note of disappointment in her voice that she couldn't quite conceal. She extinguished her lenses.

Aside from having seconds thoughts about her task, it was difficult to talk with Mara these days. Mara was hiding something from her. She no longer offered any information about herself unless directly asked. It was incredibly frustrating. Their families had always been close, even though friendships between reaume groups were rare. Mara was like her big sister, a mentor. She'd hoped that Mara would trust her to keep any secrets. What she wouldn't give to have the old Mara back, or at least understand the new one.

"I'm sure you can guess why I called you," Sophia said. "We have visitors. They'd just arrived when I contacted you." She turned away as she spoke and pretended to busy herself finding the perfect spot in which to sit down. She was now keeping her own secrets and wanted to avoid Mara's piercing gaze. The rising moon was nearly full and cast a pale light across their faces.

"Yes, I know," Mara acknowledged, her expression concentrated. "All three of them?"

"All three. I've connected with one of them in particular. He seems really nice. They all do." Sophia attempted to speak with confidence but her voice cracked.

"Don't even think about it. Remember your mission," Mara said emphatically. Her eyes narrowed and her jaw squared into a menacing stare.

Sophia found her courage. "What do you mean? Were you the one spying on Lahcen and me in the ocean?"

"Not exactly …" she said.

"Then who was it … exactly?"

Mara watched her silently, her expression stiff with resolve.

"I know you got the intelligence from someone else, but you're not willing to tell me who," Sophia said.

"Pretty much, yes."

"Someone spying on your behalf?"

"Maybe …"

"Forget the secrets, why are you so concerned with them? The three of them are reaume, too, not just human. Why should they be a threat?" The muscles in Sophia's neck felt as if they were tied in knots. She had been excited about helping before, now she was scared and uncertain.

"You're too young to understand. I've become someone I hardly recognize. It's taken everything I have to work for the king, to follow horrendous orders from him. I've only been able to do it knowing my purpose. We can't afford to get distracted,

Sophia, or else all I've accomplished will be for nothing and I couldn't bear that." Mara wore a scowl so deep it was as if it were etched on her face.

Sophia knew Mara's anger was born out of hurt and sacrifice. She watched her dip her head to the ground, thinking, perhaps remembering. Sophia reflected on how much Mara had changed. Her eyes used to be bright and cheerful, but now they were always angry. Tonight, her transparent skin exuded a white glow under her straight hair, but it was often plastered with white and black makeup. Her tribe revered her as a daughter of the white bison. She had been chosen by the Spirit to lead her clan. And she'd lived up to that calling, at one time. She used to be full of fun and adventure as a young teen, younger than Sophia was now, and she was always determined to do what was right. That's what Sophia had looked up to when she was a child.

But now Mara's hair was dyed in ebony spikes and with gray lenses on her eyes and an armor of fangs overlaying her teeth, Mara had turned herself into a monster, and played the part of one. She'd convinced the king and his general of not only her allegiance, but also her capability. She'd accomplished so much for the cause, but now she was identified as a reaume spy after her capture at the Maze palace, and she couldn't return to the king's service. That role was over, and while she could now go back to who she was before, in all the ways that really mattered, she couldn't. Something in her had changed, a melancholy weighed on her mind. She kept the hair, even the eyes...

"Mara, what's happened to you? Did they hurt you?" Sophia dared to ask. It saddened her to see her friend trapped in this character she'd played for so long, and on top of that, there was her recent imprisonment. Sophia sat rigid against the rock wall, bracing for a brusque response, instead, tears dripped from Mara's bent head, falling onto her knees.

"It's hard to explain, Sophia," she husked. "My imprisonment at the ancient palace was short lived. Yes, they hurt me, but the pain wasn't any worse than when they loved me, and they did. They relied on me. The king wanted me to marry his son, even though I'm much older. He wished me to be the next queen! That's what made this so hard, for at the same time, they ordered me to hurt so many reaume, so many of my own. Hurting other humans would be bad enough, but orchestrating the destruction and pain of other reaume," Sophia drew in a long, trembling breath, "was beyond horrible." She raised her grief ravaged face. "Part of me is forever dead." As she spoke, her hands shook.

"Oh, Mara!" Sophia whispered, her own voice laced with tears. Scrambling across to her, Sophia pulled her into her arms, holding her tight, letting her cry it all out.

Finally, when the tears had stopped flowing and she was still, Mara pushed away from her. "You've no idea just how awful I am, the depths to which I've sunk, the betrayal of which I'm now capable. But I chose it. Now I see only one solution."

Sophia remained silent for a very long time, unsure what to say, figuring at last that maybe saying nothing was best. She'd been full of zeal for the cause before, but as she watched Mara suffer, her enthusiasm had dwindled. But she realized the importance of her commitment, and accepted there would be a price to pay. Fervor would have to be replaced with duty. Mara had sacrificed to protect the reaume. She was not going to disappoint her. "What's the plan, Mara?" she asked in the most determined voice she could muster.

Mara wiped her eyes and nose clean on her cloak, sniffing a few times and clearing her throat. She raised her steel eyes to Sophia and took a deep breath. "The king knows they're here. He has something planned. I want you to stay with the three of them, no matter where they go or what they do. That will be the most helpful."

"We know about the king. We found one of his weapons, an oversized carnivorous plant. We're leaving tomorrow."

"Good, just remember, our mission is to win the war, not the battle. You mustn't tell anyone about our meeting or speak about what you know. Stick to your plan! Don't get too attached or else everything will be ruined. Be vigilant. Go with the flow and learn as much as you can about Lahcen and their plans. Let me know what you find on the connection I spliced into your lenses, the one you call me with to meet here. I can't tell you what the resistance's plan is yet, but you'll know it when it happens, I can promise you that. Remember to stay with the three if they drift away. You have to remain close if we're to keep an eye on them," Mara said and a familiar smile emerged that Sophia was relieved to see.

The two sat quietly for some time, Sophia mulling over the possible cost of her silence on this matter. She had become attached to Lahcen. It was impossible not to, but she had a duty to do her part and that wasn't negotiable. She must follow through and suffer the consequences.

"If I have to keep this kind of secret, I should at least be allowed to know who was spying on me. Who was it, Mara?" she demanded.

"Fair enough, it was Kanti."

"The Queen ... you mean *that* Kanti?"

"The one and only."

"Why here? Isn't she loyal to the king?" Sophia asked, sitting as far on the edge of her seat as she could without slipping into the puddle below.

"No, she's a spy," Mara said. "Although her heart's too pure to be very useful. She's a classic reaume, pure and innocent. I'm not." Mara's lip curled into a scowl. Sophia cocked her head in curiosity, deeply disturbed by this confession from her mentor, but she didn't interrupt.

"Kanti and I managed to escape because a new prisoner distracted the soldiers. We didn't know it, but it was the girl, Qeriya, who'd been captured. They were rushing around getting things ready and wanted me in with Kanti. I slipped a layer of air into the doorframe to prevent it from sealing. Thank fortune we escaped when we did."

Sophia shuddered as she pictured the events in her head. She wanted to embrace Mara, like a mother might hug a child, and tell her that everything would be all right, but she knew better than to hug her again. Personal space was important to air reaume, a sign of respect. Instead she glanced earnestly into Mara's eyes, as a gesture of solidarity.

Sophia rested her elbows on her knees and set her chin in her hands, evaluating Mara as if the sallow air reaume were a specimen in a lab. Mara exhaled. Her eyes appeared hollow as the shadow of night engulfed them. Sophia imagined she must be exhausted, and she still had to travel quite a distance after their meeting.

"More reaume and human marriage might lead to more like those three," Mara said eventually. "That threatens the king and it's the reason he wants to wipe us out, or else enslave us."

"That's awful! I can't imagine what horrible things the king would put them through! He's evil to the core, this man who calls himself king!" Sophia's heart beat faster, thinking about what Lahcen might suffer, but then she yanked her mind back to the present.

"What can we do? What can I do?" she asked, fiddling with her knuckles to ease a pervading feeling of helplessness, knowing that there could be no happy ending to all of this.

Mara stared at Sophia thoughtfully. Placing her hand on Sophia's to halt her fidgeting. For a moment, it seemed as if she might cry again, but making a visible effort, she pulled herself together. "You're so brave, Sophia. I'd hoped I could spare you having to employ deception, but you're our only hope right now. Don't lose your heart or your will ... Lahcen's taken with you. We can use that to our advantage. We need them to fight with us, but there's no way they'll do that right now. The reaume can't win against the king without them. Lahcen needs to trust you," Mara said softly.

"All right." Sophia's voice was strained. .

"Travel with them. Don't let them go off on their own. I'll track you. Sophia, you must understand how important this is. We can't let them go. Just keep in mind what the king has planned for them. It may seem wrong, but we've no choice. They're much better off with us than with the king." Mara rose, stretching her legs. She rustled her cloak to shake the extra water off and flounced it to let air underneath.

"Are you leaving?" Sophia asked, suddenly feeling like a vulnerable child, subject to doubt, wanting a big sister to comfort her. After Mara had gone, she would be all alone, guilty of betrayal. Even if her betrayal was necessary for the greater good, it wasn't in her nature to act in such a way. And she really liked Lahcen.

As if knowing Sophia's thoughts and seeking to shake her from them, Mara adapted water reaume practice and pulled Sophia into a firm embrace. "You're a sister to me," she said. "I know you'll do what's right."

"Lourdes, I can't believe you're here. It's been years! Hurry! Come with us." They pulled her into their bedroom, away from any surveillance.

Alexis felt herself start to tremble. "Clara?"

"I don't have much time, but, yes, it's Clara I've come about. Don't worry, she's fine," Lourdes added hastily, seeing the fear on their faces. "I've come with exciting news. You are now grandparents! You have two healthy grandsons named Khalid and Lahcen, named in honor of the desert people who were separated from their rainforest family when they helped our reaume many years ago, cousins of Clara's foster family."

Einar and Alexis lowered themselves onto seats. Einar's heart raced inside his chest. His daughter was now a mother of two. Silent tears of joy and pain crept down his cheeks at her absence. Suddenly something occurred to him. "But wait, why did you come and tell us in person, why not put this in the message you sent?"

Lourdes smiled thinly. "There's more. I need to hide here while you find a way to procure a DNA cloaking serum. Can you do this?"

Einar and Alexis had only to glance at one another to know the other's thoughts.

"Yes, I believe so, but why?" Einar asked.

"Your grandchildren are natural born human and reaume."

"What!"

"Yes, Khalid and Lahcen are your grandchildren, but they're also mine."

"But, Lourdes, that's not possible!"

"You know my heritage, and that of my husband. Nobody thought that was possible. Your daughter married my son, Aedan. Their children are both human and reaume."

Einar sighed and leaned back. "Do the boys show reaume traits?"

"It's too early to tell."

"How did Clara meet your son? I thought she was with the human clan."

"She was. Clara and Aedan met by chance on the beach. When Clara's foster family took vacations to the ocean, my son was often

there. He expresses his water reaume heritage and frequently swam at their favorite holiday haunt on his own. He said nothing to me about Clara until they were already in love."

"Prince Sean is now king, and he's just married an air reaume. Sean wants to do things differently. He promises to help the reaume," Alexis shared.

"Alexis, that may be what he promises, but he hasn't set us free," Einar pointed out, tempering her enthusiasm. He's kinder, yes, but still judicious. We shouldn't entirely put our trust in him."

"But surely Sean— "

"Alexis," Lourdes interrupted, "Sean's father nearly wiped us out not that many years ago. I'm glad to hear your optimism, but just in case, I'd feel better knowing Khalid and Lahcen were free from DNA tracing technology. And I'd prefer to remain hidden until the serum is ready to take back."

Chapter 18

Journey

Packing for the trip across the ocean took an hour at most. Water reaume were fast and efficient once they decided to act. They were simple in possessions, vast in technology, knew how to organize quickly and turn the process into a game that made packing fun. Lahcen was proud to finally find his people, even if they weren't actually people.

The miracle cream the healer gave him had restored his skin and he was sleeping much better. Once Qeriya packed the tent and all were found to be well enough for travel, Khalid and Qeriya climbed upon a covered boat the reaume had instantaneously inflated from compressed material.

Lahcen relished the many colors of fish and anemone below as he trailed Sophia's winding path through the coral. Lava tubes wound in and out of the rock which made up the island mountain. Sophia's webbed extremities cut the water with enormous force and he improved, like a child learning to walk, as he absorbed her technique by the second, occasionally catching her ankle and sending her spiraling and doing tricks to get away, keeping him from getting too confident. He found that while his brother had super strength when they were on land, his was magnified in the ocean.

A powerful wake knocked him aside as something raced by at lightning speed. Lahcen was just in time to see something barge into their path from the side and whisk Sophia away. It happened so fast he couldn't tell what it was, but the creature was large and powerful. Lahcen set off in quick pursuit, following the disturbed water, but it soon became obvious he couldn't keep up. Panic gripped his chest like a blast of cold air. Moments later, the trail had disappeared.

He circled around and headed back toward the group for

help but as he accelerated through the water, another creature slid alongside and nudged him. When he swam, it swam with him, when he tried to slow down or turn, the animal mirrored his movements as if playing a game. There was no outrunning it. Lahcen wondered if this might be the same type of creature that had taken Sophia. Rather than trying to escape, he elected to stay with it, in hopes that it would take him to her. He pounced onto its sleek back, the skin surprisingly soft beneath his hands, and grasped tight. His arms stuck quite naturally to the animal's skin, and he whizzed through the water faster than he'd ever traveled. It would have been exhilarating in any other context. Right now though, he was consumed with worry for Sophia. Where was she? His mind started to paint pictures he really didn't want to dwell on but all he could do was hold on to whatever he was riding and hope. Within minutes the creature slowed. Lahcen scanned the area for any sign of Sophia and found numerous other creatures like his, each carrying one of the water reaume. Somehow, they appeared familiar, but he couldn't place why. As they slowed even further, he saw that each creature was rounded and adorned with fins, with heavy lidded eyes and a long nose.

"Sophia!" he called as she sailed by, clutching her own beast.

"Lahcen, there you are! This is my friend, Roger! He's a dolphin, in case you didn't know."

"Of course, I know all about dolphins," he fibbed. How could he have forgotten? He loved the old stories his dad used to tell about dolphins rescuing humans from shark encounters.

"Is that your boyfriend?" he teased.

"Yes, isn't he handsome?" She hugged Roger, patting his side affectionately.

"Very. Do I have a boyfriend too?"

"You have a girlfriend, silly, that's Sally! I wouldn't insult her, she doesn't take kindly to being called a boy." Sophia and Roger sped past Lahcen and Sally, bombarding the latter with their wake. Sally called to him in squeaks that he decided must be a command to hold tight because, not two seconds later, she bolted. He gripped her with his arms and legs tight against her skin and kept his head down as she sliced through the ocean. Water rushed against his ears as if he were running through a fierce wind. He held on for dear life as she wove through numerous dolphins, occasionally bursting through the surface to spout from an opening in her head and inhale fresh air before submerging. Lahcen and Sally eventually caught up with Roger and Sophia, now swimming with the others. The most Sally could do in such a crowd was to nose Roger on the backside.

"Are the others in there?" Lahcen asked when he saw a few harnessed dolphins pulling a large, floating platform through the water. He assumed the platform must be a boat, though all he could see from underwater was a flat bottom.

Sophia nodded. "All except Doctor Michael. Someone gave him a ride to the coast, near a human village."

"I see, did he say when he'd meet up with us again?" Lahcen asked, not quite understanding why the Doc. would be so eager to leave.

"No, not that I know of, anyway," answered Sophia. Days began to feel like hours as they swam across the ocean. They traveled fast and played games along the journey. Dolphins had a sense of humor to rival even his. Lahcen saw many creatures he'd learned about from his dad's stories. Once, he saw a blue whale in the distance as it lifted its massive jaws out of the water to inhale krill. A fleet of orcas sent the dolphins into a panic, and Lahcen wondered if dolphins might have fire reaume power after all as they rocketed through the water at super speed like gray blazes. The closer Lahcen hugged Sally, the easier it was to travel.

His dad used to talk about dolphins often, creatures who breathed air instead of water, who were adept at communication and rested half a brain at a time. If only he could sleep with half a brain, he thought idly. He felt Sally's warmth, and synced his breathing with hers, forgoing gills for lungs, and discovered he could hold his breath for a long time, though he wasn't sure if that was natural for him or as a result of a symbiotic bond they had formed somehow.

After a few interrupted nights sleeping in droves in the water and nibbling on raw fish and seaweed, they finally saw land. As much as he loved his new friend, he was relieved. He was tired of seafood. He wanted real meat.

"Time to tell Sally goodbye!" Sophia called to Lahcen and she descended into the water. Roger positioned himself upright, apparently knowing what was coming because when Sophia arose, she tossed a fish into the air. Roger leapt on cue to catch it. Lahcen likewise struggled to catch Sally a fish, but the slimy critters slithered through his hands one after another. Sally zapped one up for herself to save him the trouble. She nosed him a playful goodbye and joined her throng as they moved out to sea.

The water reaume entered a maze of intertwining paths that wound through barrier islands and grassy marshland. Shale covered some of the islands, like crunchy skeletons.

"It's nesting season. Look at the pelicans over there!" Sophia told him. "Keep your eyes open for more. Mmm," she said, eyeing the shore, "we'll have a feast tonight! Blue crab's my favorite, Lahcen! You'll love it!"

"Somehow blue and crab in the same sentence doesn't sound very appetizing." Lahcen curled his lip in disgust.

"Trust me, it's in your blood. You can't be water reaume and not love blue crab," she insisted.

Lahcen couldn't help smiling at her long eyelashes, fluttering at him. "All right, I guess I'll try anything once," he said sheepishly.

"Does that include biting ants?" Qeriya asked, peeking over the edge of the inflatable float. Her hair hung in stringy clumps, matted with salt and baked by sun.

Lahcen back paddled in alarm, as if not quite believing it was really his sister. Something about her resembled an angry squid. "Maybe for Sophia, but not for you," he told her, jesting.

"See, I told you, Khalid, Lahcen will do anything for a pretty face," Qeriya chided.

"What are you talking about?" Lahcen demanded, his defenses triggered.

"Oh, nothing," she answered. "It's just that you meet some ocean chick and now you've lost all your sense! We're your family, you know, and you abandon us like rotten tomatoes as soon as a cute girl comes along!"

He stared at her, affronted, but speechless. It didn't make sense. Why was she so critical of his new friendship? It was as if she was jealous ... his sister ... jealous? Well, why not? He always hung out with her, even if they fought a lot, and he was pretty distracted now.

"Where did Sophia go? She was just here!" He searched the water surface and found her harvesting a skein of seaweed nearby. She'd joined a group of other females as they moved onto land and collapsed on a rocky beach, pairing up to plait the weed into their black hair. "That's talent," Lahcen said to his siblings after hoisting himself onto the edge of the platform to join his brother and sister, who were now also watching the beauty shop.

"Reminds me of Raquel and Maria," Khalid reminisced, and the others nodded.

While the women fiddled with their hair, the men circumnavigated the barrier islands, scooping handfuls of blue crab and large cod into nets and complaining to one another how women never did any work and cared way too much about their hair.

"Reaume aren't so different from humans after all," Lahcen said to Khalid as they helped fish. Qeriya joined the women to supposedly learn how to braid, but Lahcen was convinced she was content just to get out of fishing.

The men finished gathering crab out of the murk and loaded the harvest onto a shale covered seashore. Some of them proceeded to set up camp along the beach. The women eventually joined in the festive preparations, collecting branches from dead shrubbery as well as dung, grasses and wood from further inland to start a fire. Others cleaned and processed the crab. Daylight waned. The siblings lingered on the shore, exhausted guests. A flock of white egrets appeared, luminous, on a grassy island across the water pathway.

Khalid, Lahcen and Qeriya corralled beside Sophia as she cooked crab and fish on a ring of cast iron placed over newborn flames. It was a thick ring, open in the middle so as not to smother the fire. As their dinner cooked, the fire huffed and puffed, growing bigger and hotter, spilling smoke into the cooling air. Lahcen thought he might choke from the fumes. Qeriya's expression mirrored his own. Within minutes, Sophia finished cooking and Lahcen scrambled to find something to hold his food, finally settling for his shirt. He pulled it away from his trunk in a makeshift basket to collect his dinner. He tasted his first fruits of the ocean harvest with anticipation and nearly threw up. Water reaume or not, the love of seafood was apparently not in his blood as Sophia claimed. He was sick of fish, especially raw, and this crab wasn't much better. But Sophia and the other reaume were weighing up his expression. He gulped and forced an appreciative smile, seeing Qeriya mimicking his response, while Khalid inhaled his food.

"Oh wow!" Khalid exclaimed as he teased apart and devoured blue crabmeat, crunching morsels of dried and salted seaweed in between. "This is delicious! I've never tasted anything so good!"

"Not again!" Lahcen whispered to Qeriya, his face turning green as more seafood was shoveled onto their shirts.

"Now where are your manners?" Qeriya quietly needled her brother, despite her own pea-green face. "This is amazing," she said. "I've never tasted anything quite like it!"

"Your astounding ability to lie is really disturbing," Lahcen whispered into her ear.

"It's called being polite," she muttered out of the side of her mouth. "Anyhow, I didn't lie. We've never had anything like it and it is *awfully* amazing."

Lahcen held back a sigh as everyone nodded with satisfaction and offered them even more. They managed to sneak the extra to Khalid when observing eyes were shifted to their own food or to one another in conversation. He ate enough for all three of them, murmuring praises late into the evening.

"I thought you were the water reaume, so why does Khalid like sea food so much better?" Qeriya whispered.

"I don't know," Lahcen answered. "All I know is, I can't stand the stuff!" Lahcen cringed. "What I wouldn't do for some more of that wild boar!"

"How unfortunate for you," Qeriya clucked, and their mutual distaste for ocean critters erased any lingering bitterness. "I don't like meat that much, and as much as I love coconut, I still prefer Khalid's dinners to any food I've tasted since."

"Hey, Qeriya, look!" Lahcen pointed to a figure standing in the distance. He reached over to tap his brother and Sophia on the arm. "Sophia, Khalid, do you guys see that?" A woman hovered above the water. Her long black hair draped over a blanket robe patterned in bright red, orange and black colors. The vibrant hues brightened in the light of dusk for a moment as the sun dropped an inch and the weight of shadow grew heavier than light.

Sophia squinted. "Where?"

Lahcen pushed to his feet and quietly walked towards the wood, motioning for them to follow, moving close enough not to lose sight of the stranger, but not so close as to alarm her. The woman's dark eyes pierced them with a purposeful stare. Unmoving, she let them absorb her features from a safe distance.

Then she ascended a little into the air, her blanket spreading into the massive wingspan of an eagle, and skimmed the shore.

"It can't be!" Lahcen exclaimed as the others gasped. "It's the woman from the painting."

"You've seen her in a painting?" Sophia asked. "That's Queen Kanti."

"She's leading us to the shoreline," Khalid observed and set off after her with the others close behind, hearing the crunch of seashells beneath their feet. As they reached the water, Lahcen gazed at the beauty of rolling waves on the horizon, smoky in the lingering light. Not even his overwhelming curiosity could compete with the intensity of feathered clouds over darkened water in crisp, pink sunlight. The shell lined beached popped with white and swirls of blue. The queen swooped along the water's edge and down the shore, and they stalked silently after her until she literally disappeared before their very eyes.

"Kanti," Alexis said, pulling her inside the house and directly into the bedroom, where Einar and Lourdes were waiting. "This is Lourdes, Queen of the fire reaume."

Kanti's face grew pale. "What are you doing here? You're in danger!"

"I know," Lourdes answered, "but it's urgent. I've come to get something— "

"That's why we asked you here, Kanti," Einar interrupted. "We need your help to make a DNA cloaking serum. We can make parts of it at work without suspicion, but we need you to finish the process and bring it here to us. It's for our grandchildren."

"We've discovered that they're part reaume!" Alexis added.

"Reaume? Really?" Kanti said, astonished.

"Yes, it's a long story – we can tell you it at a better time, but we need to get Lourdes out of here."

"Certainly, I can help."

"Thank you," Einar said.

"I just can't imagine that they'll need it, though," Alexis said. "After all, Kanti, you're carrying the king's child, a child we helped you conceive. Your child is the same as our grandchildren! We shouldn't need to keep this a secret from Sean."

"Now that he's King," Kanti explained, placing her hand on Alexis' hands, "Sean wants to do things differently, but— "

"He promises to help the reaume," Alexis persisted. "We don't need to worry anymore. He'll free us, and we'll be able to see Clara … won't we?"

Kanti held tight to Alexis' hands, which clung to her own in desperation. Alexis fought back tears, but some escaped down her cheek.

"Listen," Kanti said. "I love Sean, and believe that his heart is kinder than his father's, but he's human and he's King. His own father treated the reaume in horrific ways. Sean is different, he's not cruel, and yet he's afraid of the reaume and fear is dangerous. His loyalty is to his role as King over all people, and reaume remain a threat to humankind. He won't set you free because he's afraid. The people are

afraid. Most accept me, but they're afraid of those like me."

Alexis let her grip loosen.

"I didn't marry him with the kind of infatuation most young couples have for one another," she said slowly. "I love him knowing exactly what he's capable of doing. Because of that, I'll help, but we must keep this a secret."

Chapter 19

Trapped

Qeriya shuddered as a wet chill slithered over her mouth, wrists and ankles, binding them, dragging her from her dreams of sailing the skies into a real life nightmare. Her eyes opened to a shrouded figure pulling her out of the tent before she had a chance to do anything to resist. She tried to scream but no sound came out. She could still breathe, but she was completely unable to harness air, rendered powerless. The tall shadow dragged her onto a blanket, where she was wrapped tight and lifted onto the shadow's shoulder. She was unable to see anything, all she could feel was the rhythmic thump against what felt like a man's back as he strode along.

They walked for quite a distance before he stopped and pulled her off his back and she heard the sound of trickling water.

It was a brief matter of seconds before the wetness on her hands and mouth seeped into her pajamas. She was turned upright and away from the abductor's face and the blanket was stripped from her. Water eclipsed the sun's burgeoning rays as she sank below the surface. Strong arms encircled her waist and pushed her into the ocean's depths. Qeriya held her breath, not knowing if or when she'd get her next. There was no mask with which to siphon air from above, and the substance on her mouth prevented her from making any attempt to wield her power.

Along with her steady descent went any hope of survival. Her lungs were ready to burst and as her thoughts drifted to hysteria she felt bubbles gather around her mouth, streaming down from the surface, as if they knew she needed them. The tiny bubbles grouped around her and as they did so, their membranes fused, leaving a substitute mask around her face. Qeriya inhaled slowly, trying not to drown her lungs. The bubbles streamed faster, connecting to form a tube of air that fed her lips with life.

Her brain grew clear, her muscles strong, despite being bound. When she turned her head, the tube followed.

She twisted, trying to see her attacker, but all she saw was a person in black clothes. Objects resembling fish fins covered his feet, and a helmet covered his head. Eventually, her feet touched the ocean floor. The figure used one arm to open a nearby hard-sided vessel, cramming her inside first and then nudging in behind her. It was a small space. He closed the door and her air supply was at once cut off. Qeriya froze, but then she saw that the water was being pumped out. Her agitation turned to dread and she tried not to think about what might happen next. She needed to keep focused in order to find a way out. The man pulled off his outerwear, leaving a thin layer of black clothes underneath. As he lifted his helmet off of his head, a familiar shock of thick, black hair dropped down to curtain his shoulders, and the green eyes that had once made her heart quicken with interest now made it thump with fear. From the glimpse she'd got of the woman in the portrait, other than the green eyes, she could see a stark resemblance.

Neither she nor the prince spoke, managing only a few heavy breaths before they were showered with jets of freshwater and then buffeted with warm air, just as in the water reaume compound. Another door opened and the prince guided her inside, shutting the door behind him.

"You won't get away with this. When my brothers find out, they'll figure out where I am and you won't last two seconds in your flimsy house boat," she rambled.

The prince said nothing. He merely stretched and ran a brush through his hair. Turning to a set of compartments built into the walls of the snug vessel, he extracted something. Try as she might, Qeriya couldn't tell what it was and her stomach dropped, assuming it must be some type of torture instrument. Clenching her eyes shut, she fought a fresh wave of terror pooling in her chest. Instead, new, softer restraints replaced those that had clasped her during capture. He did the same to her ankles and set her onto a cushioned couch. She still couldn't move freely, but she was more comfortable, as comfortable as a prisoner in restraints could be in the hands of a murderer. Finally able to think, Qeriya swept her gaze over the tiny room, furnished only with the couch she sat upon, the likes of which she'd seen in the border house. Along with the couch she saw a control panel and a tiny bathroom, whose door flapped until the prince closed and latched it.

There didn't seem to be anyone else inside. He sat beside her on the couch. His arm encircled her neck, holding her head steady. Her heart pounded. What were his intentions? Pulling the goo off her mouth, he immediately slapped on another patch. This time the stuff molded to her skin, containing an opening so that she could move her mouth, and probably even make sounds, but she was still unable to manipulate air. What was the point of screaming, though? There was no one to hear.

His hand gently stroked her face. "So lovely … and so deadly. What a shame. These should hold you, though." The prince grimaced. "These restraints have unfortunately held others like you.

"Why hold me here? Why not kill me?" Qeriya mumbled around the mask. She could feel herself shaking and tried to hold herself still so that he wouldn't have the satisfaction of witnessing her terror.

"Kill you? I wouldn't dream of it. No, I want you very much alive. You have to understand … I don't know how to make you understand." He got to his feet and started to pace as he spoke, his fists clenched by his sides. Suddenly, he threw himself back down beside her.

"I could hurt you. I could do anything, and there'd be no one to rescue you. No one would know." He bore into her gaze with his own smoldering green eyes, sliding an arm around her, then, abruptly he removed his arm and moved a little away from her. "But I'm not like that." Once more he rose and started to pace again. "I can't stop thinking about you, ever since the race. You're so lovely … and as if that weren't enough … you're so much more. I can't bear for you to think of me the way you do."

"It's hard to believe what you say when I'm bound and my parents are prisoners in your house."

"Your parents? I thought they were—"

"Dead?" She finished for him, seeing him gawk. "You tell me, are they dead? Did you kill them?"

"No! No I've never even seen them, much less touched them!"

"Or had them harmed?"

"No, I swear, I did not. I don't know what you're talking about. Perhaps it's the king. Maybe he did something. I'm not my father, I'm different!"

"How? How are you different?"

"I don't want to torture, only capture or kill—"

"You mean, like right now?"

"This is different. I need you, and you won't listen."

"Need me to do what?"

"To help me defeat my father. He's dangerous. We have to work together for it to succeed."

"And you're not dangerous? Are you saying that what you're doing is justified? My brothers will be worried. If you need me then free my parents. Give me my parents back and I'll believe you."

"If that's true and the king has your parents, then I don't know where they are or how to get them."

"Come on! You're the king's son are you not? You're the prince. How is it you aren't able to use your influence, your wit, your charm, to get them out?"

"He doesn't trust me, ever since the volcano. Perhaps even before. He'd never tell me where they are, and I have no idea. But I do know one thing, if you think you know where they are, he probably arranged it that way. And wherever they are, he'll let you think they are where he wants you to go, whether they're there or not. Do you understand me? If he has them, then you won't really know where they are, because he lies."

"He hasn't told us anything."

"No? Then you're making an assumption that he's keeping them in the palace?"

"He does have them, we have a reliable source."

"Who, Doctor Michael? Is he your reliable source," he asked, scowling.

"Yes, Doctor Michael, our uncle. You should know that because you captured him, too."

"No, no," Prince Liam said. "*I* did not capture him. Let's get that straight."

"Excuse me, not you, but your girlfriend."

"She's not—" Liam sighed, glancing upward as if searching for divine inspiration.

"Okay, let's say you're telling me the truth and you are working to defeat your father," Qeriya said. "That doesn't mean you're on our side. It doesn't mean anything except that you wouldn't mind another weapon on your side of the equation. You could be as bad as he is, and disloyal to boot!"

He paused, hands resting on his hips. "So what if that were the case? So what if I wanted you to be a weapon on my side? If it meant that you could get your parents back alive, would it be worth it to you?" he asked, his green gaze scrutinizing her face.

Qeriya stared at him. He had her and he knew it. But how could she possibly trust him? How could she know if she'd really see her parents alive again? Whether she cut a deal or not, she might get a chance to escape along the way, and chances of a getaway were greater if she played along, at least for now. What other choice did she have? Despite what she'd said about her brothers finding her, no one would guess that she was down here, with the prince. Even when her brothers awoke, they'd probably conclude that she was exploring the area. Lahcen was too consumed with Sophia these days to care about her whereabouts, and Khalid was too interested in learning about the water reaume and gobbling seafood. Whatever the prince planned to do with her, wherever he planned to take her, they'd be long gone by the time anyone realized that something was wrong.

"Maybe you're right," Qeriya spoke slowly, trying to force a tone of resignation. There was no way she could outright lie and pretend that she was sold on the idea, but at least this opened the path to more discussion.

"That a girl," he said and sat beside her once again. "You've made the right choice. You won't regret it, I promise. Now, how about some breakfast? I can put some beans on a fried corn tortilla and top it with eggs and salsa."

"All right," Qeriya concurred.

"We'll start with scrambled," he said happily.

Qeriya watched him go into the kitchen and soon heard crackling. She tried to get to her feet to go and see what the source of the noise was but the restraints wouldn't let her move.

"Don't worry," he called, "just the heating element prepping your food. Did you learn about that in school too?"

"We learned about robots that cooked food," she said, noting that her speech was clearer, as if the patch had better adapted to her. If she craned her neck, she could see a large cooking surface with a vent above it that siphoned steam into the ceiling. The food spat and hissed.

"What kind of school did you go to anyway?"

"Most of our learning was science and math. We had great teachers, but our cultural learning was outdated. We learned about Old Earth and only some about this one."

"You had good teachers because when the old king, my grandfather, began his experiments on reaume, many of his top scientists refused to participate. They were sent to the desert community where they became teachers. That's when the prison was formed. Anyhow, I'm not so sure cultural learning at the palace is much better, aside from access to high-tech equipment and comfortable classrooms."

"You knew the desert was a prison?"

"Yes, but trust me, I didn't know to what extent. I knew there was some sort of surveillance because we could watch the games, but I didn't realize how invasive it was until after I left." He paused before adding, "I swear I didn't know what was going on with you or your parents. It wasn't until I returned to the palace and my mother told me the extent of what my father was doing that I came to the volcano."

"You almost kidnapped me there, with that woman – the woman who tried to kill me. Who is she anyway?"

"My fiancé," he answered, an edge to his voice.

"What do you mean your fiancé? I thought you were only sixteen years old?"

"I am, and she's in her upper twenties. My father married for love but he now believes that was the wrong decision for a king. He arranged a marriage of convenience for me. He planned for us to marry when I turned eighteen. Mara's a military genius. She was his best up and coming officer. I guess he didn't trust me to do the job."

"And she's horrific looking – those fangs!" Qeriya quivered at the memory.

"She's quite lovely in fact. Although the makeup does make her look scary, and the fangs are fakes," the Prince explained. However, a glimmer of doubt in his eyes betrayed his true opinions, Qeriya noted.

"So you see, I have my reasons for rebelling, and that's just one of them." He placed the food on a tray and poured water into two cups.

"I see your point," Qeriya said slowly. Somewhere in the transition from fear of dying to relief that she was being treated with kindness, her spirits had taken an upward turn and she found herself able to engage with him in a pleasant way. She decided to milk the situation. As long as they were getting along, he would ease up on his guard.

"Mara is not who she says she is," the Prince said.

"I know. I discovered that she's an air reaume when she captured Doctor Michael."

"True, but that's only half of it."

"She helped you capture me. Why her?"

"Good question. We shared the same interests." He picked up the tray, brought it to the couch and placed it on a low table in front of her. "And she didn't think much of the marriage idea either."

"She's helping you start a rebellion?" Qeriya asked, sitting up straighter to study the food. It smelled good and she found it difficult to be angry with such a delightful meal sitting in front of her.

"Start? Heck no! A rebellion's been brewing for many years. She's as interested in finishing it as I am. The king has too much power at his disposal, and I already got caught once trying to wrangle it from him. He doesn't trust me. He did trust her, but not anymore. Mara and I, however, no longer agree on how this rebellion should end." Liam surveyed her intently.

Qeriya bit her lip to keep it from trembling, she refused to show any measure of what she considered to be weakness.

"I know for a fact you're against him as well," Prince Liam added. "So see, we're all natural allies."

He sank down close beside her again, too close for her comfort, placing his arm along the back rim of the couch. "That might be the case," she answered, non-committal. "But why did Mara take Doctor Michael from us?"

The prince said nothing. He pinched his eyes shut and shook his head.

Not getting an answer, Qeriya continued, "Once you have the power, who's to say you won't feel as threatened by us as your father does?"

"You and your brothers are a threat, but not the reaume. My mother's an air reaume," he said. "You saw her flying yesterday. Remember?" His face hardened. "The king wants to decimate the reaume; meanwhile, his queen is an air reaume. Does that tell you something about him, about who he is? He's evil."

"I certainly can't argue with that," Qeriya told him. "But that doesn't mean that you're not. You're not hurting me because you need me, but if you didn't need me then who knows what you'd do. And who knows what you'd do once your father was defeated and there was only you."

"I don't want to hurt you," the Prince said quietly. "I'm like you. I have a human parent and a reaume parent. I want to protect you," he insisted, taking her hands and readjusting the restraints.

Her hands were now separate, but she still couldn't use her powers. Meeting his gaze, she said, "I want to believe you, but you have to understand why it's so hard for me to trust you. I'm in restraints. And just because your mother's an air reaume doesn't mean she's like me or the other reaume we've met. I've come to know the other reaume groups during our time with them and they're all quite different, but they've been in contact with one another. The air reaume, however, are more isolated. I don't know anything about them. The others are all wary of them." She reached for the food, slowly at first, tasting this and that morsel. It was delicious, the best food she'd tasted since home. Who'd have thought a prince could cook?

The Prince shrugged. "Air reaume aren't so different to the other groups. My mother married the king to make peace with humanity. My father wanted a child like you, but got me instead. He wanted a child with powers, but I don't have any powers. I'm just human. Research shows that every reaume and human attempt to mate has been unsuccessful, except for your parents and mine, and mine only with the help of modern science.

Though I believe my poor mother miscarried an awful lot before I was born, and after me, they weren't able to have another child." He shook his head. "I didn't really know any of this until I met you. Meeting you, and then losing you so suddenly made me ask a lot of questions."

"If that's the case," Qeriya said, her voice cold, "then why did you poison everyone at the race?"

"I didn't poison anyone! That wasn't me! I was as surprised as anyone when everyone collapsed, but they woke up again the next day! They're alive! When I left, they were fine, everyone was all right, I swear! We just couldn't find you or your brothers, or your parents, either. Whatever they put in the tea was as much of a surprise to me as it was to you. I discovered too late that the king was trying to flush you out. You said that your parents were sick?"

"Yes, sick and unconscious. Doctor Michael put them into stasis. And that's just as well. It means that the king can't hurt them. And that they aren't scared. We have time to do this right, or we did before you got me."

"Like I said, I'm all for rescuing your parents. I just know how powerful and clever my father is. We need to work together or else it'll be a bloodbath. I kidnapped you for your own protection."

"Okay, fine, you have me, so now what? Now what's your plan?"

"We'll join the others and they'll talk with you until you understand."

"That doesn't sound like a plan to me. That sounds more like brainwashing. But let's go, by all means."

Liam smiled. "We are going. The craft's driving itself."

Qeriya stared out of the windows into the black water seeing nothing, although, when she paid close attention she could hear a slight hum.

"The inner craft is a vessel within a vessel, insulated by

freshwater and carefully calibrated to balance the movement on the outside. It limits any tendency towards ocean sickness." He smiled again. "It'll take us a few days to get where we're going. I'm not risking exposure. We're traveling under any radar I can think of at the moment."

"At some point you're going to have to let me go if you want me to help you."

"Not really. You and your brothers are too much of a threat. Plus, I'm hanging onto you as a bargaining chip. Your brothers can be of help me. And we have the added advantage of knowing that you're safe from the king."

"My brothers need me," Qeriya protested. "They can't fight alone."

"Of course they can't," the Prince said, "and they won't. They'll have a host of others fighting with them, including me. That's more than you thought you had," he added, looking pleased with himself."

"We're only a threat if your intentions are to replace one dictator with another. Given that you seem to want to do just that, I suppose we are a threat. Still, I can't imagine how I can help you while I'm in restraints, other than as a bargaining chip."

"The help I need most from you is simply your company," he said quickly. Then his face darkened. "You have to realize, you're in serious danger from my father. Plus, as long as I have you, your brothers will listen to me. Believe me when I say that I don't want to restrain you, but you're dangerous and I can't risk you getting away. I know you don't trust me. There are things I know that you would never believe if I told you right now. Even if you were to escape the restraints, this pod is a reaume prison. There's no way you can get out of here without the code, which is in my head. So sit tight and enjoy the ride."

"What do you plan to do to us once we've helped you? Are you going to kill us?"

"Of course I'm not going to kill you."

"Then what are you going to do with me?"

"I'm going to marry you," he said. Taking her in his arms he drew her close.

Qeriya shivered as he pulled her near, gazing into her eyes. Unexpectedly, she felt a sharp prick in her arm ... and then nothing more.

"Liam!" Einar exclaimed upon opening the door. A young boy around seven years old ducked behind his mother's leg.

"Hi, Liam! We're so happy to see you!" Alexis knelt down to his level and smiled. Liam giggled from behind his mother.

"Kanti, are you all right?" Einar asked quietly as Alexis played peek-a-boo with Liam.

Kanti's eyes were bloodshot, her lashes glistening. "It's ... it's," her eyes wandered down to little Liam, still embroiled in his game with Alexis.

"What's wrong?" Einar mouthed.

Alexis kept her focus on Liam, but her gaze darted to Kanti every few seconds.

Kanti struggled to control her quivering lower lip. "No markers. He has no air reaume traits. They would show by now, so we tested for classic markers and there are none. None at all," she mumbled quietly.

"Markers and even traits aren't everything, they don't tell the whole story. This is an experiment. It could change when—" Einar tilted his head to indicate Liam "—gets older."

Kanti nodded her understanding. "I know, but it's not likely, and I just worry what my husband will do now."

"He's different from his father," Einar said.

"Yes, his heart's much better than his father's, but his sense of duty to his people is equal, if not even stronger. His father loved power too much, but Sean feels that he's the only one who can truly understand and protect his people. Who knows what he would do in the name of duty."

"Oh, Kanti!" Alexis finally stood and put her arm around her, guiding her to the couch. "Listen, we tutored him, and we made a connection with him. We've seen just how in love he looks whenever he sees you. He could never hurt you."

"Oh, no, Alexis, you're wrong. You don't know him as well as you think. He could and he would if he felt that his subjects were threatened."

Einar ducked into the kitchen to get a fresh baked cookie for Liam, who peered around secretively, appearing both elated and devious, as if he and Einar were getting away with reckless disobedience. Einar left him to nibble his cookie in the kitchen and came back out to the living room.

"I just can't see him doing anything to hurt you," Alexis said.

"Alexis, like I said before, I do believe he cares for me, but to Sean, duty trumps love, responsibility to his subjects comes before any personal love he might feel. Love has enabled him to think of a creative solution to what he sees as the reaume problem. He doesn't treat reaume as his father did, as unfeeling objects for experimentation, but ..."

"Oh, Kanti ..." Alexis cried.

"If his son isn't reaume, who knows what Sean will do? The truth is, I'm fairly certain that he's never going to give you your freedom."

Chapter 20

Kanti

"Where are we going?" Lahcen demanded the third day into the chase. They were following Kanti up a steep, wooded mountain, snaking a gorge, until trees exchanged their leaves for needles. Khalid swung down from the canopy and the brothers converged to walk for a while.

"Where is she taking us?" Lahcen persisted. "When we call for her to stop she keeps going, but when we give up she stops and waits! Why doesn't she just talk to us? Maybe it's a trap."

"I don't know, but I'm guessing it's got something to do with Qeriya. She obviously wants us to follow her," Khalid said, massaging his shoulder, sore after scaling endless branches." He frowned. "Doesn't it seem odd that a reaume hating king would have a reaume queen, especially after those relief carvings of reaume serving humans?" he asked.

Lahcen nodded. "Yes, it's odd, but nevertheless, where there's a queen there's bound to be a king. It's probably a trap," Lahcen repeated. "And how will we rescue Qeriya if we're captured?"

Khalid stared at Lahcen's feet, encased in streamlined puddles of water that insulated him from the ground. "What choice do we have?" he asked. "We have zero other leads. She's our best chance of finding Qeriya. It can't be coincidence that she showed up before Qeriya disappeared, and again now. We need to press on. We have to talk with her," Khalid argued.

"Maybe she'll kill us." Lahcen shrugged. "You don't suppose she's already—"

"We're not even going to consider it, Lahcen," Khalid added hurriedly before changing the subject. "Hey, what happened to your shoes?"

"You mean the leather ones from the earth reaume?"

"Yeah," Khalid said, pointing to Lahcen's water encased feet.

"They look like glass slippers."

"They're water reaume shoes. I learned about them from Sophia. They maintain a layer of water around the feet to act as shoes, and they can adjust the layer's thickness and temperature to suit the climate. Nice, eh?" He stuck out one foot at a time and tried to flutter his eyes, but his heart wasn't in it.

Khalid could relate. As if they hadn't lost enough already. Qeriya's disappearance felt like an amputation. "That's clever, but I'm partial to my moccasins," he said, eyeing his soft leather shoes, decorated with colorful beads. "I got these from the earth reaume. The beads came from the palace and are supposedly used to decorate air reaume clothing."

"Yeah, but these are better." Lahcen kicked a few pebbles at random. "See, it doesn't even hurt to kick rocks!" Lahcen's kicks grew slower and his shoulders slumped. He drew a long, heavy breath.

"We'll find Qeriya. We won't stop until we do. The air reaume may have taken her. After all, Kanti is air reaume. Also, I'm sure Sophia understands why we had to leave without saying goodbye." Khalid patted Lahcen sympathetically on the shoulder. "She knows Qeriya's missing."

Lahcen forced a grateful smile for his concern. "It might help if we could exchange globes every single day like you and Anna," he said out loud, looking enviously at Khalid, "but water and paper just don't mix."

"Neither does fire and paper," a musical voice said from behind them. "Maybe we should try it sometime."

"Sophia! What are you doing here?" Lahcen spun around, then stumbled sideways like a broken spring.

"What are you doing and why did you leave so suddenly without saying anything?" Sophia asked, her eyes full of hurt.

"Khalid's orders," Lahcen muttered in a disgruntled tone of voice. Khalid opened his mouth to argue and paused. He oscillated between the two for a second or so, and then closed his mouth again.

"A woman appeared and we followed her," Lahcen stuttered. "She's leading us somewhere. Her picture was in the ancient palace. We're hoping she'll lead us to Qeriya."

"You don't need to do this alone," Sophia assured him, placing a hand on his shoulder.

"It's too risky for you to be here. The king's after us, not you. They'll hurt you if you're with us. You need to go back to the others," Lahcen mumbled, his face warped by anguish.

Khalid could see his inner struggle and understood it all too well. Lahcen wanted to be with her, but couldn't bear to see her in danger.

"You could spend your time and energy making sure I go back, or you could focus on your mission. Plus, you'll lose whoever you're chasing if you focus on me."

"She's gone for now," Khalid said. "You can stay with us, but Lahcen's right, and you might be more of a liability than anything else if we have to worry about you getting hurt," he added, removing the journal from his pack to see if he could make sense of where they were located.

"Going without me is more of a liability for you," Sophia answered, meandering over to a patch of wildflowers.

Khalid propped himself against a lonely oak, set apart from the other trees as the forest thinned into a level stretch of meadow. It was here that they should turn west and begin another steep climb, according to the journal, but, of course, it depended on where the woman took them. "If the king has Qeriya, he's going to use her to lure us to him. In that case, she's almost certainly alive and most likely at the palace with Mom and Dad," Khalid went on. "We should stick with our plan to reach the mountains and then the palace. If the woman has a different location in mind, she'll lead us there. But I don't want to sit around and do nothing. That's insufferable," he told them.

"I agree," Lahcen said, downcast.

"If only Qeriya were here to see her brothers agree," Khalid said under his breath.

"Haven't we reached the mountains already?" Lahcen insisted as they huffed up another steep, forested hill.

"We are climbing some very old mountains, but these aren't the ones that have the paintbrush flower. Those mountains are much steeper and tower above the tree line," Khalid clarified.

Lahcen panted as they all chugged up the steep trail. "Well, old or not, they definitely count as mountains. They're sure steep enough."

"Oh, come on, buck up little brother."

"Buck up yourself, I'm going as fast as I can without surfing. Why are we walking anyway?"

"As we climb and become more exposed, I think we should walk," Khalid explained. "Moving slowly helps us to hide under the tree cover – in case the king's airships patrol the area. Kanti waits for us in any case."

Khalid sat on a rock to rest again, placing the journal on his lap and hunching over its pages, his index finger casting over a path. "Here, look at this. After the barrier islands come the thick, forested mountains. That's what we're in now. The ground flattens for a bit up here before climbing once again. Anyhow, after these large hills—"

"You mean mountains," Lahcen interrupted, while Sophia nodded vigorously.

"—We'll reach the grass planes," Khalid continued, ignoring the interruption. "The palace is located on the southern portion of the plane, surrounded by a canyon moat. We don't want to get too near the palace and risk discovery unless we absolutely have to."

"It's going to take us forever to reach the paintbrush flowers if we walk like this. We're wasting time," Lahcen said. "And after we get the flowers, we still have to get to the palace, and even then, we're not sure if Qeriya is there or not."

"Do you have a better plan?" Khalid asked.

Disgruntled, Lahcen wandered a few meters away, only half-listening while his brother spoke to Sophia.

"Listen, we don't want to scare her off." Khalid gestured to where they'd last seen Kanti. "Also, the king's looking for us. If he gets to us before we get Qeriya, then they'll have no reason to keep her. We just need to stay hidden as long as possible. We don't want to attract attention."

Sophia rambled towards some bushes that carried bright red berries. "Buffalo berries," she said, tossing a few into her mouth. They were in her mouth only long enough for her to swallow a bit of their juice, then she gagged and spit out every last piece of skin. The remaining juice ran down her mouth and onto her clothes.

"What did you eat, Sophia?" Lahcen asked.

"I found what I thought were buffalo berries, but they taste terrible," she commented.

Khalid surveyed the bushes. His cheeks went pale with horror. "That's because those berries you just ate are poisonous!"

Einar smiled. "You've come to ask us questions about your assignments, I presume?" he asked the long-haired teenage boy with green eyes.

"Do I ever? You know me better than that. I only come here for the prison food. You guys make it taste so good! Anyhow, I'm done with my homework," he said, kicking off his moccasins and walking inside. He touched a few buttons on the coffee table, then sat on the couch and propped his feet up. The music came on and a loud, raucous noise emitted from the speakers.

Einar and Alexis plugged their ears and Einar moved to turn down the volume on the coffee table controls.

"No, wait, you have to listen to Deathmarch loud, it's the only way to really enjoy it."

"Not in our house, you don't," Einar said, turning to Alexis. "I believe Liam's the son we never had, Alexis. Don't forget to turn the settings back to jazz when you're done."

"Sure, Pops, whatever you say. You got any of those yummy cookies, Lexi?"

"For you, Liam, always." Alexis said and hurried into the kitchen.

"Thanks, Lexi," he said, grinning.

"I think it's time we upped your homework if you have hours on end to listen to this."

"No, please! This is the only place I can go to relax, Pops! Every inch of my life is planned. You guys are the best part of my day."

"Now how can you not appreciate that … Pops?" Alexis chuckled, emerging from the kitchen with a tray of cookies and milk.

"Ah, thanks!" Liam said, pulling her down beside him on the couch, tilting his head onto her shoulder.

Alexis leaned her head against his and patted his knee.

"That calls for a Liam sandwich," Einar said and squished himself on the other side of Liam. Liam just chuckled and they soon scooted over to give him space.

"You know, I never knew my dad's parents, the king and queen.

They died before Mom and Dad were even married. And from what I've heard, I'm glad I never knew them. So, I guess what I'm saying is, I feel like you're my grandparents. I just wanted you to know that."

Chapter 21

Scorpadillo

"Poisonous?" Sophia said, blanching. She pulled her ears forward to make sure she'd heard correctly, resembling a cute, baby jerboa. She'd hoped it was a joke, but Lahcen and Khalid's faces only mirrored the shock she was starting to feel. What could she do? She examined her body, while Khalid and Lahcen waited for her to vomit, stop breathing or double over in pain.

"Oh no, I feel itching! Something's happening!"

"What?" Lahcen demanded anxiously.

"Never mind, they're just mosquito bites."

"Wait, I think I'm going to be sick!"

"You want to throw up?" Khalid asked

"No, now that I think about it, I'm just hungry."

They waited in silence for some time, but eventually Khalid's alarm gave way to hunger, sleepiness, and the more practical aspects of life.

"Well, I realize this could be my end," Sophia said, "but it's getting kind of late. It'll be dark before too long. Let's just set up camp. I think we're worn out."

Khalid thought he saw a flash of the queen's robe swing into sight from behind another tree a ways off. He hurried off to check but found nothing. Had he really seen something or were his eyes playing tricks on him? Perhaps he was just overly tired? He was starting to think that Kanti was playing some sort of game with them and wouldn't really lead them to Qeriya, or anywhere for that matter. But he couldn't afford to think that way. Nothing good came of despair. Surely, she wouldn't just waste her time like this? She had to be leading them somewhere important. But did he feel safe sleeping when she was around? When he was tired enough, he thought, it wouldn't matter anymore, and he was starting to reach that point.

Lahcen and Sophia found a comfy spot under a tree and sat down together to talk.

"I'll get firewood while you guys set up camp," he said, loping off to scour the woods for fallen logs and kindling.

He had only been hunting for a short while, when a grey bird with no distinct markings appeared from the undergrowth and began to hop alongside him. Everywhere he went, the bird followed. Carrying an armful of wood, Khalid headed in the direction of the camp and was amazed to see that the bird still trailed him. Suddenly he heard a shrill, piercing whistle and the bird rose into the air.

Khalid's eyes narrowed as he scouted the area looking for whatever had frightened the bird. Staring at him from only feet away was a massive arthropod, armored shell resembling thick metal. Nodules covered its large, rounded body and many segmented legs. Without warning, it struck at him with its two pincers. Khalid darted out of the way, quickly tracing the creature's body to its thick tail he saw that, sure enough, it had a stinger on the end.

This had to be revenge for all the scorpions he'd eaten over the years, Khalid thought, surveying his options. Grabbing the branch of a nearby tree, he charged into the monster.

A pincer swiped the branch, slicing it from the trunk, allowing it to fall, pinning Khalid to the ground.

"Help!" he yelled frantically as the pincers dove for him again. Hurriedly scooting out from under the branch, he crawled away, twisting and turning in every direction as the pincers repeatedly snapped at him. Two points of agony developed on his torso as pincer teeth dug into his abdomen and squeezed. Khalid gasped, fangs and a slimy tongue dripping with saliva grew inexorably closer by the second. Every muscle in his body squirmed, but he was powerless to escape. In a kind of dumb acceptance, he closed his eyes and screamed as the creature speared him, lifting him into the air. The next instant, he dropped to the ground, free from the pincers and the threat of slimy teeth. He heard a strange noise and the creature recoiled. Khalid rolled out of reach.

"What is that?" Lahcen asked arriving on the scene.

Sophia wasted no words, instead picking up a sizeable branch and hitting the thing with it. The creature's legs waved angrily but it held its ground. As they stared at it, the beast convulsed and began thrashing around. Clasped to the creature's tail were the jaws of a fifty-foot alligator covered with scaly green skin. Its many teeth were embedded into the lower body of the predator. The lizard was equal in size to the monster it fought. It dragged on the brute, rolling on the ground, twisting and turning the creature like a crustacean windmill. But while the attacker's scaly skin looked like armor, it was leeching a great deal of blue blood. The scorpion's pincers had found their target. They sank deep into the alligator's neck, forcing the fearsome jaws to let go.

"What is what? Which one do you mean? The green scaly thing that looks like an alligator? Or do you mean the big scorpion-like thing that almost killed me," Khalid choked.

"It looks like a cross between a scorpion and an armadillo, don't you think?" Sophia asked.

"A Scorpadillo?" Lahcen answered. "I can't begin to imagine how those two got together!"

Sophia surfed over and did her utmost to capture the poisonous stinger. Khalid drew his sword and waged an attack on one of the pincers to distract it from her. Lahcen flooded the brute with water, but the armor was too stiff for it to penetrate. The creature was astoundingly fast and avoided all his attempts to suffocate it.

"This thing's quite the multi-tasker," Lahcen growled.

Khalid fought both pincers at once. Sophia wrestled with the large stinger. Lahcen scanned the area for ideas to help him fight the monstrosity. Catching sight of a particularly thick bush with sharp briars covering most of the tangled branches, he poked a stick at a few of the creature's many legs to get its attention, and then ran towards the patch.

"Thanks a lot brother!" Khalid called, seeing Lahcen turn tail while buckets of sweat poured out of him as he fought to subdue the brute.

"Trust me!" Lahcen yelled. He buffered himself with a slick layer of thick water and crawled into the thorny brush.

The creature thrust its stinger this way and that, trying to dispatch Lahcen but Sophia thrust it away. When Lahcen was fully entrenched, Sophia let up on her efforts. The stinger took Lahcen's bait, plunging into the sharp briar patch to spear him. Lahcen desperately burrowed even further into the briar just as the stinger lunged. It missed Lahcen but it was caught, unable to withdraw itself from the prickly snare.

Khalid fought both pincers with every ounce of his energy until someone stepped up to engage the other pincer.

"Lahcen, is that you?" he shouted, unwilling to take his concentration away from what he was doing for even a split second.

"It's me!" Sophia yelled. No sooner had she identified herself than she shrieked.

"What?" Khalid turned his head to see that the other pincer had clasped onto Sophia. The thing's mouth bared teeth, dripping copious amounts of saliva as it brought her to its jaws. Khalid redoubled his efforts, slashing furiously at the other pincer.

Lahcen struggled frantically to disentangle himself, trying to avoid the imprisoned stinger.

The distracted creature let down its guard for a moment to attend to Sophia and Khalid swung his sword putting everything he had into the blow, slashing at the thick pincer he was fighting, managing to sever the tip, watching with some satisfaction as it thumped to the ground. The monster squealed in pain, squeezing Sophia all the harder with the other pincer. Khalid saw her face whiten.

Sophia curled water into the claw and tried to burst it open but without effect.

Khalid raced to her side and hacked at the other pincer. Terror lent him strength and the sword bit deep, releasing Sophia. She thumped to the ground as the pincer clattered elsewhere, lying limp and still. But even as he reached for her, what was left of the beast scooped her into its mouth.

"No!" Khalid screamed He dropped his sword and wrestled to open the huge jaws.

"What's happening?" Lahcen yelled, still extricating himself from the briar patch.

"It's swallowed Sophia!" Khalid yelled, panic permeating his voice. "I can't ... get its jaws open!"

Lahcen tore free from the patch of thorns, lacerating his skin in his haste. Rushing over, he began to help Khalid pry open the creature's jaws but they refused to budge. Whatever they tried just reverberated throughout the armor and did nothing to encourage it to open up.

With each passing second, Lahcen's hopes spiraled into a chasm of despair. Then, without any warning, the creature abruptly collapsed to the ground, where it kicked once and then grew still. Lahcen again pried at the now limp but extremely heavy mouth. "Khalid, help!" he yelled. Together, they eased the jaws apart, using all their strength to keep them open.

Peering into the thing's gullet, they could see a lump. The lump stirred, a low moan escaping it.

"She's moving!" Khalid muttered through clenched teeth as he maintained pressure on the bottom jaw. Lahcen only grunted, his eyes fixed to Sophia as he held onto the creature's gaping mouth. Sophia slid upwards, a slimy hand emerged, then another as she clawed herself out, covered with a wet mucous membrane, like a newborn.

She spilled out onto the ground and, birthed from her slimy dungeon, she sucked in a deep breath, and a few moments later rose to her knees before summoning water to wash away the thick layer of muck covering her body. Relieved of their exertions, the other two collapsed beside her, panting, while Khalid clutched his bruised ribs.

"How did you kill it?" Lahcen asked bewildered.

"She's poisonous." Khalid sputtered, jokingly.

"Yeah, it does seem that way," Sophia echoed. "Are you sure it was me that killed the scorpadillo?"

Khalid shook his head, and slowly struggled to stand. "I'm not entirely sure, but it collapsed shortly after it swallowed you whole, didn't it? Do you want me to find another dangerous creature to swallow you to test the theory?"

"I don't think that'll be necessary!" Lahcen shuddered. He glanced at Sophia. "You ate those poisonous berries, and you never did get sick, much less die. You must be excreting the poison."

"You're just like a rainforest tree frog," Khalid said. "The poison's leaching through your skin."

Sophia stared at the hulk. "Well," she said. "I'm glad the poison didn't do that to me! Guess I'll be taking a bunch of those berries with us for the next disgusting experiment we need to battle." She scoured the bushes and, finding what she was searching for, picked a handful to wrap in a scarf and tucked them into a pocket of her indigo tunic.

"How's that alligator that saved you, Khalid?" Sophia asked.

Khalid and Lahcen found the alligator standing a short ways away, still bleeding. "I guess he did save me, didn't he? I wonder why?"

They approached cautiously, and Khalid observed the wound. "Lahcen, can you clean it with water? I have a few drops of medicine from our time on the island. I'll put a few drops into your irrigation."

"O–kay," Lahcen nervously answered.

"What's wrong?" Khalid asked, noticing his brother's hesitation.

"It's just that I remember irrigation and I'm not so sure it'll feel any more pleasant to a fifty foot alligator. And I don't particularly want to make him mad."

"It needs help," Khalid insisted, "and it did save my life. I can't just leave it like this." A sudden thought came to him. "Tell you what, I'll stand beside you and if it gets mad, I'll jump in the middle."

"So it can take us both out?" Lahcen clarified.

Khalid smirked. "Captain always goes down with the ship."

"Who made you captain?"

"You follow me ... so that makes me the captain."

"What is it with guys and pecking order?" Sophia asked.

"Well, it's only natural to follow the lead of the eldest—" Khalid began.

"And therefore smartest?" Lahcen stated cynically. Sophia remained quiet, staring from one to the other.

Khalid thought carefully about his answer. "If you insist. Now come on, Lahcen, he's losing blood."

"All right," Lahcen grumbled. He aimed a stream into the wound while Khalid added cleansing drops. Despite his concern, the creature didn't even flinch.

"How do you know it's a boy?" Sophia asked. "Or do you just assume something that looks that scary could only be a boy?"

"Not scary, fierce. Yeah, an animal that fierce has to be a boy." Khalid ribbed her. "Scary? Then it'd have to be a girl."

"Humph," Sophia said. "It's probably a love struck female."

"Yeah." Lahcen smirked. "And as for scary, well I'd have to agree with Khalid."

"I bet you don't make a habit of agreeing with Khalid. Why start now?"

"You did just poison a two ton monster. When you think about it, it's the pretty creatures like you that are most scary, because it's easy to underestimate their wrath until you've suffered it."

"Never thought I'd want to be scary, but sounds as if there are advantages," Sophia said.

Lahcen went to give her a hug, but then halted and stepped back. Just the sight of her made his stomach turn. "You're awfully slimy still. Maybe you should take another bath."

Sophia ran at him with open arms and he laughed for the first time in the three days Qeriya had been missing, but it was short lived.

"Let's hurry and make camp. It's getting darker by the minute," Khalid said. "Sophia, you're exempt. You can wash off like Lahcen suggested. Sorry to say it, but that Scorpadillo saliva smells putrid."

Khalid and Lahcen set too. Khalid erected the tent while Lahcen collected a bundle of fallen logs and kindling and cleared a spot sparse of growth to build a fire. The infant flame engulfed a tiny bit of fuel and Lahcen fed it more until it slowly sank its blue claws deep into the bark of the large logs and flourished into a steady blaze.

Khalid watched the mesmerizing glow, refreshed by its warmth in the nighttime breeze. As he sat quietly with the others, tiny claws dug firmly into his shoulder. He flinched.

"No, Khalid, stop! It's just a small bird, don't hurt it!" Sophia exclaimed.

Khalid sat quite still as she lifted the bird off of his shoulder and cradled it in her lap. "It seems to want your attention."

"That's the same gray bird I saw before the scorpadillo came!" he exclaimed.

"Look, there, on its leg!" Lahcen pointed. "There's something attached to its leg!"

Removing the message, he skimmed through it. "It's from Karl!"

"What does it say?" Sophia peered over at him.

"Everyone's fine. It seems that they've met up with the fire reaume and some members of the ocean reaume. They're all starting to talk with one another."

Lahcen grunted. "Finally, it's about time they cooperate," he said. "And they've learned a lot by exchanging information with one another," he relayed. "Still no air reaume present," he continued. "And that got them talking … huh?"

"What do you mean by huh?" Sophia asked, gently releasing the bird onto the ground.

"Well, this is certainly strange. Remember the general that worked with the prince, General Rolph? He's the king's right-hand man. Anyhow, he had a son named Basra who was killed a couple of years ago by the fire reaume during a skirmish. That's why General Rolph is so poisoned against the reaume."

"Basra? Interesting name," Khalid commented.

"It turns out that Basra was secretly married to someone in the air reaume," Lahcen explained.

Sophia's jaw dropped. She clenched her abdomen as if she'd been hit in the stomach. "General Rolph's son? The military general's son was married to an air reaume? Who was it?" Sophia looked as if she might choke, a distinct look of betrayal on her face.

"General Rolph's son was married to the woman who took Doctor Michael from the earth reaume village. Her name's Mara, the woman with the steel gray eyes. Isn't that the woman who tried to kill Qeriya?"

"No! That's impossible!" Sophia cried. "That can't possibly be true!"

"There's more," Lahcen said. "Not only did they marry, but they had a natural born daughter."

"I want to go on a trip by myself." Liam explained to Einar and Alexis as he leaned against the breakfast bar of their kitchen.

"Would your father let you go on your own?" Alexis asked, sliding fresh scrambled eggs onto a plate in front of him.

"I think he would."

"It's a little risky, don't you think?" Alexis asked while retrieving her homemade salsa from the refrigerator.

"I'm taking soldiers. General Rolph's going with me," he explained, now pacing along the length of the bar.

"Where do you want to go?" Einar asked, pouring milk into a glass and casually setting a stool down next to Liam.

"The desert," Liam said, biting into his steaming breakfast. His mouth flew wide open at the heat and he panted a few times before swallowing.

"The desert prison, why there?"

"I'm going to see the desert games in person. I watch them every year anyway. The people there are so different, so hearty. I'm curious, I guess."

"You're curious, and young, and naive," Alexis finished. "It's not going to be a fun trip, you realize. You're planning to visit a prison. It's not a spectacle. Why not travel somewhere else?"

"Well..." he said, then nibbled at his eggs. "I've been eavesdropping on my father."

"Why? Surely you could just ask him what you want to know."

Liam stared at them for a long moment. Then, not meeting their eyes, he said, "I don't trust him. I don't trust what he'll tell me. I know he's waging war on the reaume and I hate it. If I said anything, he'd only try to justify his actions and then he'd want to train me to follow him. My dad keeps a lot of secrets, too many in my book, given that I'm his heir to the throne. That's why I'm spying."

"And what have you discovered?"

"I found out that there are three others like me, teens around my age, half-human half-reaume. He believes they're in the desert prison. I think that he might be searching for them. I want to go and see for

myself if I can find them. I figure with their powers, the games might be the way to start my own search. They might want prize money in such a place. Also, it offers me an excuse to visit without arousing the suspicion of my father."

Chapter 22

Air Reaume

"We should travel quickly today, before we meet up with any more animal experiments. If that thing yesterday was one of the king's inventions, then there could be others," Khalid announced the next morning as they packed up their camp.

Clouds in the sky parted and the sun's light broke free from its prison. Before setting off, Lahcen irrigated the alligator's injury again and formed a thick pocket of saline to put pressure on its wound, amazed both by its docility and by the fact it had stayed with them throughout the night.

They progressed silently, except for the muffled sound of an occasional stick snapping beneath their feet as they climbed up the steep, forested mountainside. They tried not to use much of their power. Khalid decided to bring up the rear, just in case Lahcen got lazy and tried to surf. After they had been climbing for a while, he turned back to see how far they'd risen, and almost leapt into the air. The alligator was creeping determinedly up the mountain behind him.

"What are you doing?" he asked. The greenish mass stood stock-still. Khalid gingerly extended his hand to touch its scaly back and it didn't so much as twitch. "Why are you following us? Why did you save me?" The alligator simply stared back at him, uncommunicative.

"Go home, boy," Khalid said and gently pushed the animal, but without response. "It's not safe for you to come with us. You need to go home."

"I don't know how safe it is back there, especially if scorpadillo happens to have a family," Lahcen commented. "Maybe it figures it's safer with you."

"But it'll freeze where we're going."

"Well, then, get rid of it," Lahcen answered, waving the back of his hand at the rock-like statue behind Khalid. Khalid glanced at Sophia for advice.

"Don't look at me," she said, grinning.

Out of options, Khalid reluctantly continued, occasionally looking back to engage in a one-sided argument with the creature about why it should return home. It passively accepted the lecture like a large pet and followed him anyway.

A flash of robe came into view. The queen was back! She led them over endless hills until the trees grew sparse. Aside from a few rest breaks on large rocks, they persevered. The forest thinned and they at last reached a line of trees buttressing a vast grassy plane, uninterrupted for miles.

"According to the journal, the palace inhabits grassland near the foothills of the mountain range," Khalid said. "We'll head for the mountains, and eventually follow the ridges down to the palace. There's no sense in walking now. We're all exposed out here anyway," he added. The three sped ahead, surfing and leaping along the tall grasses. Khalid glanced back, certain they would have left the alligator behind by now, but incredibly, somehow it had kept up. The sun shone bright overhead and the plane fluttered gold beneath them with increasingly longer stretches of short, brown grass dotted with sagebrush. The wind increased, growing to a point Khalid hadn't experienced since the desert windstorms. Fortunately, they were without the sand that scoured them back home.

Khalid caught up to Lahcen, who was alone for a rare moment. There was something that had been bothering him since the previous evening. "Lahcen, how do you suppose Sophia knows Mara?" he asked. "She didn't give us any explanation but it was obvious from her reaction that she was stunned. You have to know someone for news to hit you like that." He looked at Lahcen frowning. "And Mara captured Doctor Michael..." he trailed off. "I'm just not sure what to think."

"I don't think it matters," Lahcen said. "She was just reacting to the whole situation, that's all. I mean, Mara's an air reaume and Basra was the general's son. It's shocking to even consider such a match."

"Yeah, but, Lahcen, we have to be careful. Sophia seemed particularly affected by the revelation, as if she'd known this Mara well. I think maybe you should try to see what she knows."

"It's fine, Khalid!" Lahcen said curtly. "I know you're worried about Qeriya and so am I, but so is she! You can't blame her for what's happened to our sister and start reading into things that mean nothing! She's shaken up just like the rest of us!" Lahcen kept his voice low so that Sophia wouldn't hear. Khalid noted the dark circles weighing under his brother's eyes and could relate to the worry he was feeling. He himself had been unwilling to consider Anna as suspect back in the rainforest, so he couldn't blame Lahcen for overlooking Sophia's suspicious reaction.

They rested once they reached the border between the grassland and the planes. The alligator keeping close to Khalid, while Kanti maintained a distance, although they could see her quite clearly without tree cover. "She's keeping to the route we planned to take anyway," Khalid said.

"Well, Khalid," Lahcen said, eyeing the pet monster with a grin stretching the width of his face, "you always did want a lizard. Now you've got one you can't get rid of."

"Yeah, I guess I did want a lizard, didn't I? But this one got into some fertilizer. There's no way I could keep it fed!"

The journey across the planes was long, with little to eat and even less to see, except for a lone bird circling the air further ahead. Khalid started to tell Lahcen and Sophia about it, but they were engrossed in conversation.

Sophia picked a sage leaf and tasted it, only to spit it out in disgust. "I thought these were edible?" she said, her expression twisting into knots.

"They're usually used as an herb to flavor food. Of course, I like them plain." Khalid reached down and picked some leaves to chew, patting his stomach and smiling at Sophia, who grimaced.

"Hey," Khalid uttered, pointing, "what's that?" The horizon was distorted by gray smoke rising to join the white clouds in the sky. Surrounding the scene were numerous flying creatures, circling the air like vultures over a kill.

"Do you suppose that's—" Khalid began.

"Air reaume," Sophia finished. From out of the smoke rose what looked vaguely like a bird. It flew across the vast, uninterrupted distance and as it grew closer and larger, they expected that the form would reveal a face from the clan, but instead they saw the distinct shape of a bird, like the one that had approached Qeriya before their journey into the maze. It flew towards Sophia and she extended her arm as a perch. The bird tenderly bowed its head and nudged her free hand open to deposit a large slab of meat.

"The golden eagle," Lahcen said.

"Thank you." Sophia smiled. "We're very hungry. Is this a gift from them?" she asked, nodding at the miniatures in the distance. The bird gave her a blank, uncomprehending stare. Instead of flying away, it flew to the alligator and perched on its scaly green back. The calm and steady alligator snapped at it, exposing treacherous teeth, but the bird sat unperturbed. The alligator twirled in a circle, nipping repeatedly at the bird, like a dog on a quest to catch its tail, but the bird was too fast and hastened into the sky, circling above.

"Did it bring elk this time?" Lahcen asked.

Khalid inspected the strange gift. "No, this meat looks different. I've never seen it before, but then again, there's a lot we've never seen before."

Maybe we should build a fire and cook it while it's still fresh," Lahcen suggested.

The eagle hovered until the alligator resumed its statuesque stillness, then it eased once again onto the alligator's back, this time behind the thick neck. The alligator snapped again at the large bird, but it dug its talons deep and held on as if taming a wild horse. No matter what the huge creature tried, the bird clung fast until the gator finally relented, consenting to give the bird a ride.

"Sophia, would you guys help me get that bird off of Al?" Khalid asked. "He's being annoying."

"That bird just brought you and Al dinner. I should think you'd be more appreciative," Lahcen argued.

"We could have got our own dinner," Khalid said.

Lahcen pointedly looked around. "Where? All you'd find is field mice and snakes, and frankly, I'd rather eat real meat. If you're going to complain, Khalid, then go find your own dinner and leave us the fresh meat!"

Khalid salivated as he ogled the large portion. He carried on grumbling quietly for a while, but decided to leave the bird alone for the moment.

"I wish we had our fire reaume cousins here to cook it for us."

"We could boil it," Sophia suggested.

Lahcen chuckled, "Yeah, we could, as in able, but no. Boiling would ruin it!"

"Works for seafood," Sophia said.

"We are not boiling this juicy piece of prime steak. Let's stop here for lunch, but no fire. We'll eat it raw. We don't have time to spare," Khalid said and the others shrugged, disappointed, but concurring.

They filled up on raw meat, the brothers trying to guess what animal it came off from their dad's stash of stories.

"Bison. We're in the planes after all, it's got to be bison," Sophia said definitively and the others nodded in agreement. After all, there was no sense in arguing with a librarian when it came to accurate information.

Rested, they resumed what was beginning to seem like an endless journey, almost like chasing mirages in the desert. The more distance they covered, the further away the pack ahead of them drew. After hours of traveling, the sun grew large on the horizon and in the burgeoning shadows they beheld pointed structures sprouting up amid the rolling plane. A fire ignited in the midst of the dwellings.

"Those are teepees," Sophia declared excitedly. They have to be air reaume! A nomadic tribe who communicate with eagles, eat bison and live in teepees must be air reaume," she decided. "Assuming they sent the meat."

"I'm guessing the queen must be from their group as well," Khalid said. "I don't see her anymore, so I guess she's joined them." He frowned, shooting a quick glance in Sophia's direction. "I hope we can get some answers and some information."

"I wish we had an idea how much longer it'll take to reach their camp," Lahcen wondered, squinting into the distance. His mouth curled to form a scowl. The dwellings seemed ever further away.

"Now that we're closer and can see more clearly, our guess on distance should be more accurate," Sophia encouraged.

"Still, I think we'll need to stop and make camp before it gets dark," Khalid said.

"Yeah, I suppose," Lahcen agreed. They set up their mildly mildewed tent while the eagle clipped at Al's nose.

"Do you suppose they're playing?" Sophia asked, nodding towards the animals.

"The eagle is," Lahcen commented.

"Yeah, and it's a risky game to play with an alligator," Khalid said.

It wasn't long before the three nodded off. Khalid drifted back to the ocean in his dream, swimming among the coral. His brother and Sophia frolicked nearby. His sister sunned herself on the water's surface and he weaved in and out of vibrant colored clumps of anemones and shoals of marine life. As he sculled through the water, he noticed a glint on a rocky island nearby. He paddled towards it, but, even though he increased his speed, he couldn't get there, as if twenty feet were really twenty miles in disguise. He didn't know why he needed to get there, but somehow, he knew it was important that he did. What he most needed was in plain sight, it was within his grasp but somehow he couldn't reach it.

He awoke to movement outside. Remembering his promise to always wake his brother, he did so, putting fingers on his mouth to quiet him. Lahcen, in turn, woke Sophia. Khalid motioned for them to listen. They could hear shuffling steps and carefully lifting the edge of the flap, Khalid glimpsed the woman with the colorful patterned cloak, the woman who Khalid recognized from the painting. She stood a few feet away holding a lit candle.

The three of them edged out of the tent but before he could speak, Khalid heard a murmur. It was only the slightest whisper, but something wasn't right. Keeping his eyes fixed on the queen, he shifted his attention beside and behind him. Before Kanti could say a word, Khalid reeled in a half-circle and knocked someone to the ground. Out of a corner of his eye, he could see Lahcen and Sophia engaged in battle with more invisible attackers, who were quickly felled to the ground where they lay unmoving. When they turned back again, Kanti was gone. They put their backs together and braced for more attacks, listening acutely for any odd noises.

"What was that about?" Lahcen muttered. "Either it's beyond dark out here or else whatever we hit was invisible, because I hit at black air and down came an air reaume." He shook himself. "Creepy!" He stared out into the night. "Well I'm certainly not going back to sleep any time soon," he said. "It's a miracle you woke up when you did, Khalid."

"I suppose I heard a noise," Khalid said somewhat bemused himself.

"We need to move fast, before they reconvene," Lahcen said. "Why do they want to attack us?" he added, puzzled. "It doesn't make sense! Why not just talk to us like normal human beings?

Well ... scratch that last part."

Fortunately it was nearly dawn and a modicum of light served to help them navigate packing.

"We'll head back to the forest where we can hide easier and find another route," Khalid said, slamming his supplies into his bag, severely disgruntled at the turn of events. Without another word, he bounded away like a cheetah, clearing long stretches of land with each stride. Lahcen and Sophia surfed after him. Nearing the forest, Sophia flagged Lahcen to set down.

"Sorry, out of breath," she panted as they all stopped to rest. I haven't surfed in a while, since we live in the ocean and all of my assignments have been there."

"They must have decided not to risk a fight to capture us," Lahcen said.

"I guess we know who probably has Qeriya," Khalid said. "I almost wish they'd succeeded in catching us. At least we might be with her now."

"Maybe or maybe we'd all be trapped without a means of escape," Lahcen reasoned.

Through the blossoming light, an invisible pair of hands grabbed hold of Khalid and hoisted him into the air as he made out the shimmering form of the woman they had been tailing, Queen Kanti. It happened so fast that Lahcen and Sophia hesitated, their brains running to catch up with their eyes. They hurled water in Kanti's direction, but Kanti held fast. Khalid drew his legs up, arched his back, kicked and swung into a backward somersault. His foot struck Kanti alongside the shoulder and he felt himself falling.

"Lahcen!" he called, plunging toward the ground.

Lahcen rebuffed another glimmering form with narrow picks of ice which sliced into the aggressor's face, escaping long enough to surf over, catch Khalid and plant him on the ground.

"We need to get back to the ocean," Khalid ordered. "The other water reaume are there. And you and Sophia will have an advantage."

"You don't have to tell me twice," Lahcen said, relaying the order to Sophia.

Khalid bolted for tree cover like a panther, but fast though he was, it wasn't fast enough. Nameless, invisible arms caught him off guard and lifted him off the ground."

"Don't even think about it, ghost-man!" Lahcen snarled from behind as a wide body of water cut through the air between the apparition and Khalid. The strategy had failed to work on Mara, but this time it severed the hold the air extended over Khalid. Lahcen flung Khalid ahead, into tree cover, where he caught at the branches and swung towards the ocean, followed by Lahcen and Sophia riding their waves.

Khalid propelled himself rapidly from tree to tree. Glancing back, he spotted distortions in the forest. More air reaume! Plunging into the trees had scattered most of them, but clearly some were persisting. There was surely no way they could determine which direction he, Lahcen and Sophia might travel.

It didn't take long to descend to the ocean. During the short journey the sun had fully claimed the sky and the hazy distortions they assumed were air reaume fell away.

"Did we lose them?" Sophia asked.

"It couldn't be that easy," Lahcen answered. "What else is going on, I wonder?"

Sophia surfed high above the trees to scan the area, pivoting around until confronted with a view of the ocean. She screamed, her face morphing into a mask of utter horror. "No!" she cried, anguished. "We're under attack!"

"Liam, it's early, what's wrong?" Einar asked, ushering the trembling teenage boy inside the door.

"He needs to be stopped!" Liam yelled. The veins on his temples swelled. Einar put his index finger to his lips, motioning him to be quiet, and pulled him into their bedroom, where Alexis awoke with a start and bolted upright in bed at the sight of Liam.

"Now, son, speak quietly, we're being monitored out there," Einar whispered.

"Monitored? Has that always been the case?" Liam mouthed in return, grasping the door handle, his rage momentarily replaced with surprise.

"Yes, but it doesn't work in here."

"He'll stoop to any depths to get want he wants."

"What does he want? What's got you so rattled?"

"He captured all of the fire reaume adults. It was on their sojourn to the volcano. Then he waged war on the children. He's slaughtering children! It's evil!"

Einar and Alexis both gasped.

"He's a monster! He tells me I don't understand what I'm up against, but I do, and it's him! It's time for a new King!" Liam struggled for control, saying a little less heatedly, "Also, I've found the three he's looking for. I knew as soon as I saw Qeriya run. She was so fast. Unlike me, they all have reaume powers. They're running from my father and are now fighting him alongside the fire reaume children. I think that it's time I paid my mom's family a visit ..."

Chapter 23

Rolph's Weapon

"Pardon me sire," General Rolph addressed his king as they floated in the sky towards the ocean.

"Yes, Rolph, what is it?" They were encased in what appeared to the king like an oversized hamster ball, the kind his son had owned at some point in his youth.

"I'm clear on our objective to defeat the water reaume, but why now?"

King Sean attempted to stretch his long legs, one at a time, in the close quarters. The seat was clearly designed for average sized humans, but small as he might be against Rolph, Sean was tall enough to find the seat uncomfortable. Nevertheless, cramped as he felt, he didn't want to show a hint of dismay or anything that might resemble disappointment in his loyal general.

"For different reasons. The water reaume are weak from their long journey. They're also vulnerable so far from home, and, while they have the three with them now, I have reason to believe the resistance is involved and will try to capture them. The battle will draw the resistance back into the fight and they'll relax their guard over the three. It'll also prevent the reaume from guiding them further since they'll be distracted with battle."

"I see." Rolf dipped his head deferentially. "Well, the design of this ship seemed the most useful for fighting water reaume. But I'm sorry that your seat is so cramped. I realize now that I should've done more to ensure your majesty's comfort. Please don't assume that my mistake extends to the function of the ship as a weapon."

"Certainly not, Rolph," the king said crisply. "The designs you adapt are always flawless. I was hoping you wouldn't notice my mild discomfort."

"Of course I notice, but not because you make it obvious,

only because I'm a giant living among small humans. I'm often aware of cramped quarters. But I believe that your confidence in me will be well placed. This ship may be cramped for you, but the craft are comfortable for the soldiers flying them. They're designed to move between water and land, while having an accessible weapon."

Rolph had become the closest thing to a best friend Sean had since Kanti's betrayal. In Sean's estimation, he was the perfect blend of intelligence, strength, wisdom and integrity.

"Yes, you think of everything, and that's why you're my top general. But how do the ships work? How do they move between high in the air to deep underwater?"

"The design teams employ Bernoulli jets on the craft," Rolph explained. "The container we sit inside is formed of a composite material designed to encase a layer of fluid around its surface, 'fluid' meaning the medium that matches the surroundings, air if in air, water if in water. The engines move the fluid at the necessary speeds to pressurize the craft for its environment. There are additional engines all around the craft to direct and propel it."

"And it's transparent?" The king could see other shimmering spheres like the one they were riding in, outside the expansive window, which were barely visible.

"The designers studied air reaume transparency technology and its application. It involves bending light in such a way that an object appears to be invisible when looking straight at it. The effect mutes the image, giving an appearance of shimmer, like a bubble, transparent but distorted, with visible edges."

"And what about its weapon system? How does that work?"

Rolph touched a scope about the same size as the king, sitting in between them. "This is the laser gun. In the other craft it's fully rotational. The soldiers are harnessed in and can spin in any direction to shoot. The composite material and fluids allow lasers to pass through unaltered. Soldiers can shoot through most of the craft's surface. That's why we only have one soldier in each craft, except for this one. We're equipped with a weapon in here, but this is primarily a transport craft."

"They'll be effective I'm sure."

"Oh yes, quite water reaume resistant."

He was right to have favored Rolph with his position. Rolph knew how to get things done and he was trustworthy. Still, despite their camaraderie, Sean kept their relationship formal.

Kanti was the only one to see the real him. And while she'd betrayed the king, she had never betrayed her husband. She was an enemy of the king, but she was still his wife. He pictured her now as he cradled one of the pottery mugs she'd made for him, etched with a geometric design and painted in vibrant colors of summer. She'd taken to pottery like a horse to oats. Her designs were so intricate, streamlined, clean, a perfect marriage of form with function. He missed her in his life, loved her despite everything. She was still the most beautiful woman he'd ever seen. He was sorry he'd put her in such an impossible position. Nevertheless, he must do whatever he had to in order to protect his people, and particularly their son.

"Pardon, sire," a light flashed at the dashboard of his seat as a voice spoke. King Sean secured his treasured cup and pushed a nearby button. A miniature hologram flashed within the small space in front of him. A tiny soldier stood at attention in the three-dimensional image of a room, all other features and chatter blocked out. The soldier was quiet, waiting for his prompt.

"What is it?"

"Our scans of the water reaume have not located the three you wanted, sir," the hazy figure explained. "Records indicate the arthropod weapon was triggered by three figures, but the girl was not Qeriya. Instead, the two males are traveling with a water reaume female."

"Curious," the king answered, and paused before adding, "Did the weapon record anything new?"

"Yes, between the pitcher plant, the maze rat and the armored scorpion, we have amassed a great deal of data on the hybrids."

"Excellent." Sean again shifted ever so slightly in his seat.

"Are you working on another weapon?" Rolph asked.

"Yes, it's nearing completion. I imbued it with artificial intelligence, so the more data I feed it about specific reaume fighting capabilities, the better able it is to calibrate its own fighting style."

"I can't imagine how you created such a weapon," Sean mused. "But it'll take such capability to be rid of the hybrid threat. Any other activity detected?"

"Only subtle movement in the ocean, not far from the water reaume camp," the soldier answered.

"Do you know what might be responsible for the movement?" the king asked, his brows furrowed in concentration.

"It's difficult to say because normally our equipment overlooks anything natural to the ocean. But in this case, the movement registers as that of a humpback whale."

"In these waters, at this time? That's unlikely. No, that 'whale' you've located is my son," King Sean said, concluding with a deep and frustrated sigh.

"Your son registers as a humpback whale?" the soldier stammered in surprise.

"I'm familiar with the 'whale' you picked up on the scan because I commissioned it," the king explained. "I helped design the vessel in my youth, in order to avoid detection on some of my outings away from the palace. I imagine he's got Qeriya. Send someone to follow him and see where he's taking her. That is all."

"Yes, sir." The soldier saluted smartly and the hologram disappeared at once.

"Reckless boy," the king muttered, shaking his head. "My son insists upon endangering his future."

"Why did he take Qeriya?" General Rolph inquired. "I realize he's enamored with her but why capture her? I assume she wouldn't go with him on her own."

The king shot him a tight smile. "Yes, he certainly was enamored. He showed his hand at the volcano trying to rescue her. And yet … perhaps this move he's made is purposeful. You're right – she would certainly not go with him willingly. She believes that he poisoned her village. He would have to capture her. But the only reason he would frighten her like that is if he had to, most likely for a strategic purpose. He just might be growing up after all, thinking ahead. He may have the wrong motives, but at least he's showing himself to be less impetuous and more capable of planning than he has before. It's likely that he's joined the resistance, along with his mother. Killing Qeriya would only incur the wrath of her brothers against the resistance, and the resistance needs them in order to win. She may yet provide him with a bargaining chip in dealing with her siblings, in forcing them to fight with the resistance."

Rolph reflected on the volcano battle and the toll it took on his soldiers. Such a battle offered proof of the danger the three were to the human race, and even to the reaume. If they acquired real power then there would be no possibility of stopping them.

"You think Liam may have joined the resistance? Do you think his mother recruited him? Why would she do that to her own son when it's decidedly not in his best interest?"

"Bitter though I might feel about her treatment of our son, she places him in second priority to the life of the reaume because that's what reaume do. They sacrifice one for the whole. She can't help it. It's simply her biology. And she's not much different from myself. I'd protect my people at any cost. But aside from being my son, he's to take over my role as a protector of the people. He must come to understand his duty, that despite his reaume heritage, of which he shares little, he's to become the next human king."

For a moment his gaze was snared by the hazy horizon,

signaling the promise of an ocean. They were getting close now.

"Why would the resistance seek to manipulate the three half-breeds? Why not just recruit them? Don't they share the same ends?" Rolph asked.

"They don't share the same ends," he said. Their ends and our ends are more similar. We're both afraid of unlimited power and the damage it can accomplish. They, like us, realize that the three are a threat because they have much more power than humans do. The resistance recognizes them as dangerous, and they are wise to do so. No matter how my son might feel about Qeriya, it seems that he, likewise, does not underestimate the damage she can do. The resistance might need them to fight us, but they certainly can't trust them to enter the inner circle. The fact that my son knows this, in an odd way, is progress. He's perhaps not so immature as I once thought. Nevertheless, he is acting as a reaume king and not a human king. He must be made to see the error in his judgment."

"How do you propose to change his mind, to make him see your point of view?"

"I've run out of ideas, Rolph." The king sighed, rubbing his eyes. "I'm afraid it's time for more drastic measures, and they involve you. But that discussion is for another time. It appears we're nearing attack position," the king noted.

"Yes, that we are." Rolph adjusted his mouthpiece to speak to the soldiers at large. "We're nearly in position," he said. "When I give you the signal, you may proceed as planned. Fire at will. Kill every last one of them."

"I've been in contact with the air reaume, and we have a plan," Liam explained to Einar and Alexis in their bedroom. "But I need to make a strong statement to the world, to solidify my message that from this time forth, human and reaume will be under one umbrella. Reaume are vulnerable. Humans need to confront their barbaric fears of both reaume and the outside world. We need to live as one. I must overthrow the king."

Einar rubbed his thumb along his chin. "That sounds like a grand vision you have, but how do you propose to do it?"

"I'll begin by recruiting more people into the resistance, here in the palace, and I have a pretty good idea where to start looking. We need a large enough group to challenge the king. The air reaume have more experience with humans, so they'll be capable of fighting, but the other reaume are more of a liability. They'd get themselves killed or get the air reaume killed protecting them."

"What about Khalid, Lahcen and Qeriya? They might be able to help," Alexis said.

"The fear between reaume and humans is so volatile, it's difficult enough for them to accept one another as it is. These three have traits of both."

"But that should help, shouldn't it? The fact that they are both reaume and human should endear them to both!" Alexis pressed.

Liam gave Einar a pleading look.

"It should, but it won't," Einar interjected, finishing Liam's thought for him.

Liam's face reddened and he studiously avoided Alexis' gaze.

Chapter 24

War

"What attack?" Lahcen called up to her.

"They didn't communicate with me. They didn't want me to come back and help." Sophia's voice choked and she surfed at full speed into the sky.

"Look!" Lahcen pointed. "Let's get to that high bit up there. We'll be able to get a better idea of what's going on." From their vantage point, they could see water reaume pouring into the ocean in droves, driven by barely visible spheres. They dove into the swell of oncoming waves and melded with the water. A few minutes later, Sophia returned to them, her face a mask of grief and anger.

"The scorpadillo was probably a ploy to distract us from this!" Lahcen said. "They were planning to attack all along. The queen lured us away so that the king could attack!"

"It does appear that way," Khalid agreed.

"Queen Kanti would never do that!" Sophia exclaimed. "She's estranged from the king. She would never do such a thing!"

"How could you possibly know that?" Khalid asked.

"I just do!" she hissed, jaw clenched, flames in her eyes.

"That's not an answer," Khalid said and gave a significant nod to his brother, who turned away.

Soldiers gushed forth in their supersized bubbles, while foot soldiers invaded from the shore. Lahcen blinked to break his shocked trance. Khalid threw his arms forward, willing beach sand to arrange into a flat plane of grains, dividing the bulk of foot soldiers from the reaume still on land. The grains organized into tiny frontline soldiers, rapidly climbing on one another's shoulders until they towered above the top of the giants' heads. Khalid smashed the entire wall of sand, sending it spilling over the king's soldiers, hitting them with such force sand penetrated their protective gear, irritating the skin and eyes of those who failed to lower their heads in time. Khalid grunted with satisfaction but he knew he'd had surprise on his side this time, now they'd be prepared for him.

"Move up shore away from the fighting, Khalid," Lahcen called. "This battle will be in the ocean and you won't be able to help for now. I'll come get you when we need you."

Khalid sighed and shrugged, resigned to his fate.

A tsunami arose in the water as more reaume teemed into the ocean. Sophia and Lahcen charged into battle as Khalid retreated. The wave broke, scooping soldiers into the deep as many more bubbles burrowed underwater. The spheres vaguely reminded Lahcen of the glass globes the fire reaume had used to escape the poisonous volcano after it erupted. Only these, he suspected, weren't made of glass. How, he wondered, were the soldiers able to fight from inside them?

At that moment, a bright stream of color emitted from one, aimed directly at a water reaume, shooting into the ocean without any damage to the bubble. Another of the vehicles forced the now stunned water reaume to the surface. Getting a closer look, Lahcen saw that it was the same elderly healer who'd treated his acid burns from the plant. He skimmed across the surface to go to his aid. Fire slapped his thigh and he somersaulted, singed and discombobulated, into the ocean. He resurfaced to find the healer struggling to roll off the clear sphere and back into the ocean, but his body was too frail.

"NO!" Khalid screamed from where he stood. He summonsed a rock from the forest and swung it hard and fast at the clear surface of the bubble, but the wall merely absorbed the impact and the boulder fell into the ocean. Lahcen could do nothing but watch as the vulnerable reaume caught another neon light through his chest. The soldier then tilted his craft to dump the still form back into the water.

Lahcen dove for the healer and dragged his body to shore,

placing him in Khalid's care. "Help him, Khalid, he's still alive!"

Khalid carefully carried the elder further up the beach as Lahcen, exhausted, followed, pulling in ragged gulps of air.

"Stay with me," Khalid told the frail old man, grabbing his hand to ease his pain. The healer's expression visibly relaxed. Opening his eyes, he looked at Khalid and managed a smile. Angry tears streamed down their cheeks as they tended to him. After a while, he spoke. "You are the future, the way things should be. I am hopeful." He closed his eyes again. Khalid shook his head, the old man's breathing was shallow and rapid and it was only a matter of time. All they could do was ease his pain and help him to die peacefully. A short while later, the elder took his last, rattling breath.

Lahcen stormed to his feet. "How could you possibly justify killing such a gentle man!" he yelled to the deaf objects of destruction now littering the water. Khalid released the healer's hand and slowly stood. He lifted more sand to throw at the soldiers.

Lahcen waded into the water and ducked below to find Sophia. His search took longer than he would have hoped but he was fortunate to find her at all, immersed as she was in the thick of battle. He paused, taking stock of the scene. An endless number of bubbles containing soldiers shot beams of death in all directions. The shooting was random and continuous and the noise was deafening.

The reaume tried to scatter as at the same time hordes of soldiers poured in from the ocean side as well as the shore, having been dropped from aircraft. What the enemy lacked in accuracy, they made up for with sheer numbers.

"What can we do?" Sophia cried. Her voice rang high and shrill, like a knife cutting into Lahcen's eardrums. He wanted to help, but there was hardly time to think and he hadn't been an ocean dweller for long enough to have developed any real strategy.

"I don't know," he whispered helplessly.

"Wait, I'm getting instructions! Come on!" she yelled, grabbing his hand and pulling him with her. They sliced through the water to join a host of other reaume huddled together like a school of fish and began circling the perimeter of the battle, fast and entirely in sync. They spiraled around and around, creating an eddy. Sophia and Lahcen linked arms to keep together. As they sped up, the eddy grew into a massive funnel of water that sucked the manned bubbles into the center and forced them onto the ocean floor. The inner ring of water surrounding them coalesced. Lahcen made his way towards the center in order to see better, dragging Sophia with him.

The whirlpool guzzled the spheres, sucking them from the surrounding area. They hit the bottom of the ocean with incredible force, dropping into a vortex which compressed all matter unto it, those at the bottom cracking like eggshells. When enough vessels had been crushed, the reaume changed their strategy, bolting upward while pulling the massive water tote full of invaders to the surface. Harnessing the force of the water, they pitched the load into the air then watched as the bubbles flew upwards before crashing back down into the ocean. A few of the craft escaped from the cluster unscathed and resumed their shooting rampage. Others aimlessly bobbed on top of the water, their pilots having been knocked unconscious.

"Nice work," Lahcen muttered. They had not only eluded the trap, they had also succeeded in thinning out the enemy. For the moment, they could regroup, recover and make some plans. Because as sure as fish had fins, this wouldn't be the end. The king would hunt them down and destroy them, one by one if need be.

"Khalid!" Lahcen recollected. Slicing swiftly through the water, he hurried towards the shore, holding his breath in anticipation, praying that his brother was okay. Lifting his head free of the waves, he searched up and down the beach, seeing nothing at first. Then he spotted him, hidden in a cluster of trees down shore, and he quickly headed in that direction.

"Khalid," he whispered, "how's everything going?"

"Other than a whirlpool and an explosion of bubbles across the ocean, I can't make any sense of what's happening," Khalid said, tension and worry etched into every line of his face.

"Good, then I don't have to worry about you doing anything stupid," Lahcen said shortly. "Just hang out here, don't go anywhere and I'll know where to find you if we come up with a plan. Capiche?"

Khalid scowled. "Do I have a choice?"

"Not if you want to be helpful, you don't. And we may need you soon. I won't forget you, I promise," Lahcen said. He ducked underwater and swam back to the place he'd last seen Sophia.

"Lahcen, where did you go? That's the second time you've disappeared on me!" she said exasperated.

"I just went to check on my brother," he apologized.

"Well, tell me next time, why don't you!"

"All right, fine, I'm just not used to—"

"Being accountable? Well that's obvious!" she flared, streaking away, leaving him to trail behind her.

A glint in the water caught his eye. "Sophia!" he shouted, throwing himself at her. He shoved her out of the way, both of them tumbling head over heels as a ray of light exploded where an instant ago Sophia had been swimming. "Go!" he yelled as, capturing the craft's attention, he spurted away.

Sophia jockeyed around to the back of the sphere, kicking and beating at it with her fists repeatedly with no result, except to once more make a target of herself. Lahcen battered it from his side, drawing the soldier's attention back to himself.

Sophia darted to a nearby ledge of rocks. Hefting a few jagged edged ones, she threw them to Lahcen who propelled each rock into the clear outer skin at high speed, only to watch as they bounced harmlessly off, while the barrier barely sustained a scratch. Their best hope, he decided abruptly, was to pound the ship and try to knock the pilot out.

"This isn't working! Sophia, help me contain this thing!" Lahcen yelled. Once more the water coalesced at their bidding. With a joint wave of their hands, they dragged the craft towards the rock ledge, dodging it's laser rays, and whammed it numerous times against the rocky cliff. While it did nothing to dent the shield, the pilot eventually bumped his head, and they saw him slump unconscious in his chair. Lifting the globe with a net of water, they flung it high into the air. The ship sailed over the shoreline and landed somewhere inland.

Sophia and Lahcen stared at each other, breathing hard. "One down, a few hundred more to go," Lahcen commented.

"At least the reaume are able to scatter now. I hope they'll find places to hide." Sophia leaned against a rock to catch her breath.

"Can we call them back if we figure something out?" Lahcen asked.

"Figure something out? What do you mean?"

"We have to fight back, but we need a strategy first," he said, repetitively swimming in circles.

"A strategy? You think we should attack?" Sophia asked, incredulous.

Lahcen shook his head. "It's a little too late for that. They've already done the honors. No," he said, "I think that a defensive battle is a losing battle. We need to surprise them with an offensive plan. Let's get behind cover," he added, pointing toward a clump of seaweed.

"Cigarette snails," Sophia said. Lahcen paused in his swimming.

"What did you say?"

"Cigarette snails. They're poisonous and live fairly near where we are now."

"What is a cigarette snail, and why are you talking about library science at a time like this?"

"I'm *using* my library science. There's a difference. You said that we need a plan of attack, a way to surprise them. The snails might just work. These soldiers are going to be ready for any water force we throw at them, right? So we need something unexpected."

"Yes, precisely. But ... snails? Can poisonous snails breach the impenetrable containers that hold these soldiers?"

"I thought I'd let you figure out that part. The snails would be a great way to incapacitate, but not kill the soldiers after the containers are broken." Sophia nodded to Lahcen, indicating the presence of another bubble. Quickly they hid themselves behind skeins of seaweed and the globe sped past.

"We certainly need to think outside the box, but that's outside the entire arena, Sophia," Lahcen told her. "We can take the soldiers down. It's those containers that are the problem." He frowned. "I don't know, Sophia, I'm worried about the water reaume managing to survive this attack. And you're more intent on figuring out how *not* to hurt the soldiers than on staying alive."

"The cigarette snails are our best chance at a humane attack," Sophia said, yanking him out of the way of a stray light beam.

"Yeah, snails sound real menacing," Lahcen chided.

"Are you being sarcastic?" Sophia said, irritated by the fact that he was dismissing her idea out of hand. "Maybe I should sting you with one and then see if you laugh."

"Listen, Sophia, we need to think more than one step ahead," Lahcen insisted. We have to come up with a more comprehensive plan."

"What do you mean?"

"We have to penetrate the barrier on those craft. We don't know what sort of material these bubbles are made from but whatever it is, it's strong."

"Maybe we could get them to eject," Sophia suggested.

"How do you propose we get them to throw away their only

protection from us?"

"I don't know."

"Heat!" Lahcen said, an idea dawning on him.

"No, it's too dangerous. We could harm everything in the vicinity if we heat the water."

"Not if we use precision. We'd need to get the water reaume to make another funnel, only this time we'd heat up the water around the craft."

"But that would boil them alive!" Sophia stared at him wide-eyed, horror covering her expression.

It made Lahcen feel like a monster to see her reaction. Suddenly a whirring sound alerted them to the battle going on around them. They rushed around the clump of seaweed they'd taken cover behind, and found themselves bushwhacked by a mass of light beams. Grabbing her arm, Lahcen pushed her back behind the seaweed. The rays sliced down, exploding all around them and Lahcen couldn't hold back a cry as one found its mark on his forearm. Sophia retaliated with another waterspout, whisking the bubble down to the ocean floor. Quickly, she rushed over to Lahcen.

"You're hurt!" she screamed. She held his bloodied arm carefully, tugging him further into the forest of weeds.

"See," he argued, "we only have so many options here. We can't concern ourselves with what constitutes an acceptable death."

"I'm so sorry you're hurt," she said, ripping a skein of seaweed to knot around his forearm. "I know they don't care if we suffer, but boiling them to death is too horrible!" Sophia's mouth trembled, her skin developing an unhealthy, gray tinge.

"Come on, think, we need more options. If only we could get something to deflect those blasts, like a mirror. That might reflect the blast back onto the ship and disable it. Then we wouldn't be killing at all. Less suffering," she mumbled, her voice shaky.

"Well, it's better than snails," Lahcen admitted. "But where on earth would we find enough mirrors for the entire water reaume clan in the next twenty minutes?"

"We'll just have to capture a vessel," she explained. "We could analyze it and find its vulnerabilities."

They crept cautiously from behind the seaweed.

"Now how on this earth are we supposed to do that?" Lahcen asked.

Within seconds of coming into the open, Lahcen spotted another craft. The things were everywhere! He wrenched Sophia back behind the seaweed again. Spotting a small cave, partially hidden from view, they crouched inside.

"I might have an idea," Sophia whispered. "You remember the lava tubes that we swam through on the island?"

"Yes, but they're too far away to be of any help to us."

"Those are, but there are underwater caves under nearby islands that could be just as good." She chewed at her lip. "We need to get a bubble to chase us."

"I–m not liking the sound of that," Lahcen said. "Very dangerous."

"Dangerous it may be," Sophia agreed, "but it would be worth it if we could isolate one of those things long enough to find out what powers it. I know it'll be hard to crack. We saw how difficult it was to fracture the others, and there's just two of us."

Lahcen scratched his cheek. "So we need to trap it. Do you have some way of getting the information we need?"

Sophia nodded. "My lenses can take readings if we can keep it still for a while first and..."

"And what?"

"...Keep it firing."

"That settles it. I'll be the bait while you wait to ambush it when it gets stuck."

"I couldn't let you do that." Sophia's face was set, stubborn. "It's my idea. I'll be the bait."

"No. You're too valuable," Lahcen said. "I don't have a computer built into my head like you do. The plan only works if you're able to get the readings."

"I'm a faster swimmer."

"I've learned quickly. I'm almost up to your speed. Plus, I don't want to outrun it, just keep ahead. I'm bait after all." Lahcen smiled crookedly. "Don't worry, I'll keep my distance. Now show me which tunnel will work best."

Sophia reluctantly nodded.

This time when they peered out, they saw that the bubble which had been pursuing them had given up its chase. Keeping to the shadows and darting behind cover at every opportunity, they raced through the minefield of enemy craft to a network of tubes similar to the ones Lahcen remembered. This time he saw them with new eyes: strategic, calculating. They would need to find the right size tubes to have any chance of success.

"What do you see?" he asked Sophia. "Can you estimate what will fit where?"

"I can do better than that." She grinned up at him. "I can pull up my memory of one of the globes now and calculate its dimensions. Her memory materialized as tiny flecks of light pouring from her eyes and molding into the familiar form of an enemy craft. "Unfortunately, my memory is missing key details," she said. "I didn't manage to see what powers it." The flecks of light swirled out of the shape they were holding, reforming into lines that streamed back into her eyes."

She remained still, floating in the water, her soft hair a black halo around her head. Then all at once she scooted off, snaking back and forth through the tubes without speaking as Lahcen schlepped along without question, letting her think and calculate in peace. Finally she came to a halt by the entrance to a passage.

"I've established a map of this spot," she said, so I can lead the craft here. Since I have the map literally in my eyes, I really need to be the one to lead the bubble. However, if you want to tease it after it gets stuck, then I can take measurements."

Lahcen couldn't argue. She was right. He wouldn't know where he was going. But that didn't mean he had to like it. "Please ... be careful," he begged.

Sophia smiled. "Don't worry about that. I like my life."

Lahcen nodded, trying for a smile that didn't quite make it. His gut twisted as he watched her depart and positioned himself to take over.

It was a very long fifteen minutes before she dashed into the tunnel just ahead of one of the spheres. Lahcen had to give it to her, she'd selected the perfect trap. The tube at first appeared navigable, but had a slight surprise angle with a rocky protrusion. Sure enough, as Sophia swam through the outcrop caught the craft without a hitch as Sophia disappeared into the murk. Now it was his turn.

He had positioned himself to look as if he was stuck a short way in front of the tank. Making sure he had the pilot's attention, he dipped into a volcanic depression as the light beam flashed overhead. When it ceased, he sprang up from hiding to stimulate more firing, only to feel his heart leap into his throat as the rock holding the craft prisoner ruptured and it charged towards him.

"Lahcen, watch out!" Sophia screamed as he ducked and dived this way and that to avoid a battery of blasts. He changed directions, briskly shifted speed, shot upwards, then dived down again, anything he could think of to get out of its line of fire, but no matter what he did, the thing stuck on his tail, the blasts missing him by a fraction. Sophia had reappeared and did her best to run interference but the pilot ignored her, concentrating solely on Lahcen as he entered the lava tunnels again, hoping not to fetch up at a dead end. The tunnels took him into a maze below the island and spit him back into the ocean. But the craft stayed on his tail. He dipped into another tube and tried to be unpredictable, but his muscles were beginning to cramp and he was unable to swim any faster. He knew the weapon was waiting for him to get sloppy, and, alarmingly, he was starting to get sloppy. The exhaustion of relentless pursuit with no plan, no end in sight, was taking its toll. Lahcen stopped thinking beyond the next bend, knowing there was little hope of relief. His pace slackened as he reached the end of the maze. He flashed out of the exit and spotted Sophia there, waiting. She forced a boulder into the tunnel just as the craft prepared to exit, firing in his direction. It worked! The enemy plowed into the small boulder, skewing sideway and wedged against the spherical wall. To Lahcen's relief, the capsule was firmly stuck again!

Muscles aching, he nevertheless rushed to catch Sophia who had been thrown back by the sudden impact.

"You all right?"

"Yeah! This is our chance!" she yelled. "You distract it!"

Lahcen groaned but obediently flitted around the craft, dangerously provoking the pilot to fire on him, and fire he did, mercilessly.

"I've got it!" Sophia called.

"Thank the Spirit," Lahcen panted, beating a hasty retreat.

They both reentered the lava tube from the back to get a closer look at the enemy from the rear. The soldier, thoroughly engaged with the problem of how to remove the boulder, didn't register their presence at all. Meanwhile, Sophia's lenses released their tiny lights. Baby fireflies made a beeline for the craft and burrowed, unobserved, into every surface, the nanobots nimbly darting out of the way of the soldier's gaze. Sophia pulled Lahcen out of sight as the pilot turned towards them, and they waited impatiently for the bots to finish. Soon, Lahcen saw them trickle back to their hiding place and rearrange to form a blueprint of the craft in the tunnel. Beside him, Sophia was silent as she analyzed the information.

"Bernoulli engines," Sophia identified. "That's what they are, and that's how the craft can go from high in the air to deep underwater without cracking. I've heard of them in theory, but

I've never seen them." They left the craft to an unknown fate and headed out into the ocean.

"What does that mean in non-scientist speak?" Lahcen asked.

"Bernoulli engines circulate fluids at varying speeds around the craft to maintain a constant pressure. If we can knock out the engines, the bubble will crack from the water pressure. We need to short them out."

"So they're electric?" Lahcen swam alongside her at a leisurely pace while they regained their strength from the chase. No one was in sight, though they each kept a sharp look out.

"Yes, they're electric."

Lahcen shook his head. "Anything I know about electricity is entirely theoretical. And I saw an electric light once. That's my exposure in a nutshell."

"We need to overload the circuitry," Sophia explained.

"Overload, you mean add more electricity?"

"Yes, but the real question is, how?"

"How? Well, where do you get electricity around here?"

"Where, yeah, that's the right question. Not how, but where … Thanks, Lahcen, I think I've got an idea!"

"Already?"

For answer, Sophia quickened her pace, enough that Lahcen had to push hard to keep up with her.

"It just so happens – remember that river I took you to visit?"

"The hydrogen sulfide river?"

"Yes, that one. Well, there's another. It isn't far from the eel spawning grounds. It's nesting season …" she began, then trailed into silent thought.

"I can't begin to make sense of what you're saying," Lahcen said, swimming along with her. "Can you try explaining?"

"I could if I knew—" She stopped suddenly and shot up to the surface. "Isn't this where you left Khalid? Hey, Khalid? Do you hear me, Khalid?"

"Sophia?" Khalid answered. "Did you call me?"

"Yes. I need you to help me research something. There are electric eels nearby, and I need something that can magnify the electric shock they can give so we can short circuit Bernoulli jets. There are lava tube tunnels and a hydrogen sulfide river nearby. I can't think of anything else at the moment, but if you look at the map of the area, you might see more.

"Sure, I'm on it."

"Sounds good, and, take this." Sophia passed him a mouthpiece. "Use this to communicate with us!"

"Sophia, look out!" Lahcen yelled, jerking her back into the water as another sphere started firing.

"Thank the stars that thing has horrid aim!" Sophia said. She quickly mobilized a nearby boulder, crashing it into the bubble as they launched themselves up onto the beach again. Making a dash for it, they ran along the beach and crouched behind a conveniently placed cluster of rocks.

"Sophia? Lahcen?" Khalid's voice sounded in their ears.

"Yes, we're here," Sophia whispered, handing Lahcen an earpiece.

"I'm not sure if you can use this, but I found out that hydrogen sulfide is a superconductor when it's cooled dramatically. I know that Lahcen can adjust temperature, but I doubt he can change it that much."

"A bunch of us could lower it that much," Sophia replied thoughtfully.

"Fantastic," Khalid answered. "If you can capture the electric eels, then the combination just might work."

"Thanks, Khalid. I'll be in touch." She considered a minute while Lahcen watched her in anticipation, not wanting to disturb her thoughts.

"I think I've got a plan!" she finally exclaimed, louder than she'd intended. "Do you think it's safe to go now?" she asked, bouncing up and down.

"Safe? No, but it might be worth taking a peek," Lahcen said and slowly peered around the rock cluster.

"The plan will take two of us and we'll need to find the electric eels. They come down river to spawn in the nearby estuary."

"But what about the battle? I feel as if we're ditching everyone," Lahcen exclaimed.

"I know, me, too, but like you said, this battle is a lost cause if we don't think outside the box."

"Sphere in this case," Lahcen clarified.

"We can't win by force. We have to outsmart them," Sophia echoed his thoughts.

"Right! So, remind me again why the river's useful? What does it have to do with the eels?"

"If you remember, the river's primarily made of hydrogen sulfide."

"I hope offering sacrifices to the river isn't your plan," Lahcen muttered.

"What are you talking about, Lahcen? That's just ludicrous," Sophia said, impelling him onward.

"You've no idea how good it is to hear you say that!" Lahcen told her, relieved she didn't share the rigid beliefs of the earth reaume.

"Here," Sophia said, "let me explain. Electricity and hydrogen sulfide alone won't do much to hurt those spheres. However, in extreme cold, hydrogen sulfide becomes a super conductor. In that case, the two together could do some serious damage."

"That makes sense, go on – no – never mind, come on!" Lahcen called as another globe drifted into sight. Fortunately, he'd seen it first and they had time to run.

Sophia yelled over the water rushing by them, "The enemy craft depends upon electricity to power the Bernoulli engines. And they're vulnerable to overload. We need to short-out the lot of them."

"So, we gather the water reaume and lead all the soldiers to the river, then what?" Lahcen asked.

"Then we focus our energy on cooling the river. Most of us together should be able to get the temperature down pretty low," Sophia said, picking up her pace as another enemy craft appeared. Lahcen quickly whisked up the sediment from the ocean floor, clouding the bubble's vision. Sophia pressed a button on a console attached to her wrist. A high-pitched whistle rang throughout the ocean. The next second, a group of swordfish appeared at their side, lunging at the bubble with brute force until the hull was pierced, flooding the inside with water.

"Nice one," Lahcen commented, only for Sophia to grab his hand and keep swimming towards the river. After putting some distance between them and the bubble, Lahcen resumed their conversation, "So, you said the low temperature makes the river a superconductor? But then what are the eels for?"

"If the eels mix with the river water, the shock will be massively magnified. It'll cause an electrical shortage to the jets with minimal damage to the soldiers inside."

"Seems like it could work," Lahcen said, panting as they zoomed away from the war zone.

"I can communicate with the other water reaume," Sophia elaborated, "but not well enough to give them instructions. They'll need a visual plan. We'll need Khalid to be our command central and feed the plans to everyone so that we're coordinated. We can communicate with one another through our lenses, but something this exact needs the motherboard. First, swim with me to the lab. You'll need to know where to bring your brother, and be careful!"

"You mean we haven't had to be careful already?" Lahcen teased.

"There'll be more of the enemy hot on our tails. Khalid should be fine once we get him in the lab, though. The water reaume will make sure they're not followed when they go there."

Sophia slithered like a shapely fish in front of him, descending into the deep waters until the light was nearly gone. Lahcen memorized the features of the underwater mountain they traced so that he'd remember where to take Khalid once he found him.

He hoped Khalid was safe. They'd left him on shore all alone because the fight was in the ocean, but what if the soldiers found him? This thought drove him on despite his growing exhaustion. He had to hurry.

Sophia signaled him in the gloomy dimness before disappearing under a knoll in the rock face. He followed suit and saw a hidden entrance beneath. Entering, he found the familiar freshwater cleanse and air-dry system he'd experienced at the first water reaume base.

The room was big, full of lab tables and chairs. Clear walls lined the perimeter. Inside the walls were creatures living in large, holographic habitats, each environment tailored to its species. Sophia went straight to the most central table and Lahcen saw that water lined the top of it. Sophia stirred it with her hand and it appeared to recognize her. Images materialized in the space before them, along with a catalogue of her old searches. Sophia brought up the hydrogen sulfide river.

Lahcen stood tormented, his heart pounding. He had to go find Khalid, but the thought of leaving Sophia alone in the midst of battle, even for a moment, terrified him. He gathered her up in his arms, disrupting her computer search, and folded her close, boring into her eyes with his own. His strong arms cinched around her waist and held her steady. Her stiffness eased and she softened into putty for him to mold at will. Wrapping her arms around his broad shoulders, she stroked his hair. Lahcen kissed her full lips, her cheeks, burying his head against her neck. Then, as quickly as he'd grabbed her, he let go, bowing his head and edging out of the door, forcing himself not to look at her lest his resolve weaken.

"I'll be back soon with Khalid," he husked. "You get everything ready." Turning, he forced himself to leave.

"You have to understand that the three pose a threat not only to the king and his subjects, but also to the reaume! Listen, I'm already part of the resistance, and I'm telling you they're wary of them. Qeriya, Lahcen and Khalid are a threat. They're also in danger on so many fronts. They've too much unchecked power, and at this point they see my mother and me as enemies. I need them to fight with and not against us or else to not fight at all. They'll be safer if they don't fight at all."

"Safe from whom?" Alexis snapped. She shook her head and sat rubbing her hands together as if peeling off glue.

Einar paced the floor, running his fingers through tufts of grey hair. "We've come to care for you, Liam. You're like our own grandchild, and that despite the betrayal of your father, and your grandfather. Don't destroy our trust in you."

Liam stared at them. "I don't understand. You might disagree with me, even greatly so, but how would this destroy your trust?"

"Because they're our grandchildren, Liam!" Alexis cried.

Einar's face flashed alarm while Liam's whitewashed.

"Your grandchildren! But how?"

Alexis glanced from one to the other. She'd done it now, that was supposed to stay a secret. "Our estranged daughter, Clara, she's their mother."

Liam wiped his hand across his mouth. "This is a shock. I hardly know what to say. I'm so sorry..."

Chapter 25

Electric Eels

"What on earth?" Lahcen asked as he stumbled into Khalid's hiding place amid a grove of trees on the shoreline. The damp sand was carved and molded into complex spires and tunnels.

Khalid breathed a sigh of relief at the sight of his brother, his thick muscles glistening like polished cacao, his hair dripping liquid crystals in the sunlight.

"This is what happens when you have time on your hands and no Anna to distract you," Lahcen teased.

"I was waiting, like you told me to, obeying my little brother's instructions. You don't know how hard that is."

"Sure I do. I have a little—" He couldn't finish, his sister's absence quelling any attempt at playfulness. Please let her still be alive, he prayed silently. Considering the abductor risked removing her rather than killing her, or them, it was likely she was unharmed. He comforted himself with the thought. But how were they treating her? Was she scared and alone somewhere? He couldn't think about that. There was nothing he could do at this moment, and he had to stay focused on the battle.

"There are no more soldiers approaching by land. They're all dropping from the sky." Khalid gestured to large vessels similar to the ones they'd seen in the desert, but these were high in the sky, unreachable, releasing the last of the bubbles into the air.

"I need you to come with me," Lahcen said. "We have a job for you. It's deep underwater. Fortunately it's in a lab on the ocean floor that's filled with air. You'll be glad to know you can breathe while you work."

"That's convenient." Khalid smirked, stretching out cramped muscles.

"Even though it's away from the battle, I need to beeline through the water to get there. No lingering on the surface until we reach it. Someone may be watching. I don't want to take any chances. Catch a big breath and leave the bag here."

"I can do better than that, and I never leave my bag anywhere," Khalid said, riffling through his pack. "You should know that by now."

"The journal will ruin in the water, and Qeriya isn't here to protect it," Lahcen said.

Khalid's shoulders slumped momentarily. "Can't you put a layer of water around it and pressurize the air inside to make a bubble? Then the water could act as a container."

"You're too smart for your own good, Khalid. Yes, I can do that, but—"

"Do it then."

"It's extra weight. It'll slow us down. You won't last," Lahcen said anxiously.

"I'll last," Khalid said, removing something that resembled a jellyfish from his pack. Placing his scattered belongings back in his pack, he hung it from his shoulders.

"What is that?" Lahcen asked, his face contorting with disgust as Khalid slipped the translucent, wobbly mass into his mouth. Reluctantly, he encased the pack in water, buffered it with air, and sandwiched it against Khalid's back.

"One of the reaume gave this to me before the ocean journey, just in case we went underwater," Khalid explained out of the side of his mouth. It lets me breathe by drawing air from above. Let's go!" he said wading into the water. Tiny air bubbles rose from the substance on his mouth as he descended.

"Hold on," Lahcen said, clasping Khalid's forearms criss-cross about his chest to get a secure grip. Lahcen cruised as if he'd always had fins and they descended unhindered to the knoll where the entrance was hidden.

Lahcen searched the area to make certain that no one was following them. When he was sure they were alone, he slipped into the cave entrance and opened up a well camouflaged door.

Once inside, they went through the familiar rinse and dry cycle.

"Khalid! Good, you're here. The system's ready and the plans are drawn," Sophia told him."

"What plans?" he asked, looking around the brightly lit room.

"We're planning a counter attack – and you're going to lead it."

"But I just got here," Khalid exclaimed. "I've no idea what's going on. Why me? I'm not water reaume." He noticed Lahcen staring and his eyes fastened on the water computer and the holographic images formed by nanobots of various shades of light.

"That's precisely why you'll be leading. You can't fight with us. The ocean isn't a friend to you," Sophia explained. "But we need a command center, so you're it. Just listen and I'll show you what to do," she added.

"The water reaume will be able to hear you and can access the plans with their lenses. This is where we are now," she told him, pinpointing their location on the lit up map and then tracing her finger to another location further down shore and deeper into the ocean. "We need to get the reaume to lead their pursuers here, near the river," she said, describing the formations and strategy to him and demonstrating how the technology worked.

Khalid repeated the information back to her to make sure he understood.

Satisfied, Sophia shifted her attention. "Here, on the shelf, I have some drops that'll form temporary lenses for you, Lahcen. We use them if we need replacements or repairs. They'll work for now."

"No way am I putting anything in my eyes!" Lahcen exclaimed in horror.

"Lahcen, get a grip!" Khalid hollered in his face.

Lahcen was feeling a lecture coming on and was about to argue when Sophia put her hands on her hips and spoke first, her tone confident and genial.

"Well of course you are, Lahcen. There's no other way." She spoke as if he'd said nothing contrary whatsoever, and to his own surprise, he shut his mouth and listened. After all, they couldn't afford to argue while her family was being hurt.

She rummaged in a bin of supplies hanging on the wall and removed plain eye drops, dropping some into her own eyes to demonstrate.

Lahcen swallowed his squeamishness and attempted the practice drops. They weren't bad at all, he decided, and, after a few attempts, they even felt quite pleasant. Once he had it mastered, he dropped the liquid lenses into his eyes.

"Can you hear me?" Khalid asked, testing the communication system. A flood of reaume answered. "Good," he said, turning to the two of them. "I can do this." He turned back to the map. "Hold on everyone, we have a plan." Khalid heard murmurs, too many to pinpoint what they said. As they spoke, lights appeared on the nanobot hologram, representing each of the reaume in the ocean. "I imagine they must be both curious and relieved to have some leadership," he said a little pompously. Sophia and Lahcen waved to signal that they heard him.

"How can they hear me?" Khalid asked.

"The lenses broadcast sound vibrations that are heard via bone conduction," Sophia explained.

"Why did I bother asking?" he asked Lahcen.

His brother shrugged and mumbled, "No idea."

Khalid shook his head and returned his attention to the task at hand. Now was the time to address everyone at large. "Listen," he began. "I know that most of you are hiding. There are too many of these things to fight and they're most likely immune to most water reaume powers. But we need you to be brave. There's an underwater hydrogen sulfide river not too far away from the estuary near where we were camped. I'm providing a map to illustrate where it is for any who don't know. Children, hide or stay hidden. The rest of you, hide for now and wait for my signal, then lead the soldiers to the river. Once you've got them there, Sophia and Lahcen have a plan to disable their weapons and communications.

Lahcen readied himself with a degree of apprehension. He didn't like leaving his brother alone in the middle of the ocean, with bubbles raining death on the loose. Thankfully, the lenses weren't so bad. He was already getting used to them. They somehow accessed his brain, either that or they picked up on even the most subtle eye movements. When he wanted to talk to Sophia from a distance, he only had to think of her, speak, and she alone could hear him. They had only just left the base when he noticed a creature gliding past and vaguely wondered what it might be, when, in response, the phrase, 'Tiger Shark', popped into his peripheral vision.

"We're heading around the estuary," Sophia explained as they swam, "to the electric eel spawning ground. We'll need to capture a whole bunch of them," she added. "They're actually a freshwater species, but they come to the river to give birth in brackish water."

As they approached the river, they spied a craft chasing down an elderly water reaume woman. She was no longer fast, but maneuvered with skill through the water. The sphere shot at random, coming unnervingly close to hitting her numerous times. Sophia broke away, skirting by the vessel closer than the fleeing woman, interrupting the fatal dance and causing the soldier to go after her instead. Light beams nipping at her heels like a puppy.

"Sophia!" Lahcen called, helpless. He had to think fast. Fortunately she was good at evasive maneuvering, since there was no way to outrun it.

Lahcen spared no time in catching up to Sophia. Approaching from behind, he coalesced the water around the globe and dragged it towards himself. When the craft reached him, he squeezed hard, putting pressure on the bubble from all different sides except in the direction of the hydrogen sulfide river. The dome shot forwards like a projectile, soaring through the water before melting into putty in the acidic stream. He waved to the woman as she hunched in the water, pulling in ragged, labored breaths and she managed a weak wave of thanks in return.

"We'll meet you at the hydrogen sulfide river!" Sophia told her before they resumed their mission.

They'd only gone a short distance when Sophia cried out and flinched, grasping at her leg. More light beams chased across the open space towards them. Lahcen pulled her from the line of fire and dived deep, half-carrying Sophia until they had put a good distance between themselves and the fire. When they judged it safe, they surfaced and Lahcen carried Sophia from the water over to some rocks on the nearby beach. He hurried to sooth the wound by leaching filtered saline and attaching it like a bandage to halt the bleeding.

"Are you all right?" he asked anxiously.

Sophia nodded, tight lipped and gray but composed. "I'm fine."

Lahcen peered out from cover, relieved that there was nothing in sight. Behind him, he heard Sophia scream.

"Lahcen, help!"

Suddenly aware of something above him, he glanced up to see one of the ominous spheres descending on them. Instinctively, they scattered but Sophia wasn't fast enough and Lahcen watched, horrified, as the capsule crushed her against the rock.

Lahcen drove a fierce force of water at one side of craft, not only rotating the globe but Sophia as well, flinging her into the depths. After spinning the vessel until the pilot was dizzy, Lahcen paused to coalesce the water around it and catapulted it towards the river, just like he'd done to the one chasing the elderly reaume.

He rushed to Sophia. "Not again! They keep hurting you! There's no way you're all right this time!"

"Of course I am," she said, her skin gray.

She was clearly shaken, despite her insistence she was okay, but what could he do? There was no other option but to keep going. Lahcen made an about face and clasped her arms around his neck. She was a great deal lighter than his brother and he navigated the shifting currents with ease, following the map provided by his lenses.

"These lenses feel as if they're plugging directly into my brain."

"They are in a sense," Sophia agreed. "They're made up of tiny nanobots, which are a type of artificial intelligence," she explained while clinging to his back. Her voice was weak. "They learn to read your most subtle nonverbal cues and act as an extension of your mind."

"Do you ever worry that they'll take control?"

"No, should I?" She chuckled.

"Yes, you should. What if they develop consciousness?"

"Sorry if I offend you, but it's so like a human to think that the hierarchical step after intelligence is consciousness. Consciousness has nothing to do with intelligence. In fact, intelligence can get in the way of consciousness, and in humans often does."

"Wow, you really have a bone to pick with humans, don't you?"

"Are they not trying to blast us into kingdom come?"

"Point taken. Although, they would have to want control in order to take it. Do artificial life forms want control?"

"Perhaps not, but the humans that program them do. Who knows what remnants of humanity bots might reflect."

"Yeah, I suppose."

They swam carefully, plucking unsuspecting spheres from the ocean and propelling them towards the river along the way, as if harvesting peppers from a garden and tossing them into a basket. Suddenly Sophia's grip on him slackened.

"What are you doing?" he exclaimed, feeling her arms slip off him and a wave of water cross his back as he was in the midst of blasting another sphere out of the water.

"There's one behind you!" Sophia yelled.

Lahcen couldn't see, but trusted she was attending to it and focused on getting the job done with the one he had in his sights, rocketing it through the water to join the others in the river.

Spinning around, he was not prepared for a second bubble to attack, both nearly cornering Sophia. She headed straight towards them in an attempt to protect him from being seen, then veered away and drew their firepower. Now there were two of them after her. Lahcen fought to catch up as the two spheres repeatedly targeted Sophia. Each beam erupted in a sonic boom at the end of its path, narrowly missing her every time.

"Ouch!" Lahcen's calf burned as he inadvertently scraped a rock. Wincing with pain, he glanced down to assess the damage. His calf was gouged open. He slapped on some pressurized water to act as a bandage and frantically searched for Sophia. Where did she go?

There she was, hastening this way and that amid rocky protrusions. As many and as frequent the blitz of laser fire, she was faster. Lahcen couldn't help marveling at her dexterity in the water, while simultaneously feeling a heart attack coming on at the danger she'd put herself in. Finally, he was in position to clutch one of the things and fling it at one of the nearby rocks. The craft smashed to pieces against the jagged coral, while a little stream of red oozed from the cockpit. Meanwhile, Sophia whammed against the remaining craft in time to send its beam, presumably meant for him, into the abyss. Before the globe could regroup, Sophia sucked the capsule down towards her and sent the vessel careening in that direction.

"How are you holding up?" he asked, worried. "Can you swim?"

"I'm fine," she rasped. "Just a bit weak."

"It's the loss of blood," Lahcen told her. "Thankfully, you haven't lost too much, but losing any is a big deal when you're being pursued by two globes," he said, picking up speed as he carried her along.

"You're fast," Sophia said. We're nearly there. We'll see it in just a moment."

Sure enough, within minutes he saw a pile of sediment that was the river delta.

"Look out for spawning eels. They're the big ones," Sophia ordered. "When you see one, enclose it in freshwater, and leave a funnel open to the surface so that they can breathe."

"They breathe air?"

"Yes, they breathe air. They have gills, but the gills don't work very well. Most of their oxygen comes from air."

"How much odd information do you keep in that beautiful, big head of yours, madam librarian?" Lahcen smiled.

"Big head? Is that supposed to be a compliment?"

"It is when the head is as beautiful as yours."

"Hmm!" Sophia grunted, clearly unconvinced. "I'll transport the eels deeper into the ocean while you watch out for an attack," she said. "For now, let's find them. They look like long and thick catfish."

"Catfish?" Lahcen exclaimed. "That sounds like something the king cooked up in his lab. There's no way I'd have thought to put those two together. Don't cats eat fish?"

"Ah, yes, I suppose they do," Sophia said, laughing. "You've never seen a catfish I take it."

"We may have eaten one once, but it was cooked and decapitated, not exactly the same as seeing it wiggle."

They searched for some time until Lahcen saw a creature matching the description Sophia had given him.

"Is that one?"

"Yes, you found one!" Sophia whispered and scurried towards it. She extended her hand and willed freshwater to seep out of the ocean and materialize around the eel within the seawater. She then placed a ring of water around the babies for protection.

"Eels don't pack a great deal of charge, but we're only hoping to short their systems. We shouldn't need too much. Still, we're going to need a bunch more if we want to inject a large enough electric shock to turn off their pressure stabilizers."

Lahcen thought about the implications their plan had for the soldiers but decided to keep that to himself for fear Sophia would abandon the plan. Maybe she was in denial, which wouldn't hurt in this case. Nevertheless, being crushed to death seemed no better to him than being boiled.

After finding a few more eels and encasing each in its own freshwater container, they wound through the ocean, tanks in tow, towards the underwater river.

Sophia had chosen a much longer path that skirted most of the battle. The journey was steady, but not as slow as Lahcen had imagined it would be. They arrived at the river to find a swell of globes fighting the water reaume. Taking cover, they watched the scene from behind a clump of anemones.

"We need to move fast. The reaume are fatigued," Sophia said.

"You ready?" Lahcen asked her.

She nodded. "Yeah. Khalid, do you hear me, Khalid?"

"Yes, I hear you, "Khalid answered.

"We're in position. Go ahead and give the order."

"Okay." The order, it turned out, was visual. Khalid illuminated a simple diagram. "I don't understand how this funnel strategy works," he said.

"It's all right, you'll find out," Lahcen told him. "The important thing is that the reaume know. Didn't know you could draw," he added, clearly pleased.

"It's Sophia's artwork."

"Oh, that explains it."

"So, we essentially do what we did before?" Lahcen double

checked with Sophia.

"The toilet bowl," Sophia said.

"What's that?" Khalid asked.

"It mimics the basin of water used to dispose of personal waste products," Sophia described.

Khalid groaned. "Oh gross, don't remind me. We almost drank from one of those! They didn't cover that sort of cultural learning in school. We didn't know what they were until our stay with you."

"Anyhow, it's what we did at the beginning of the battle," Sophia said.

"We make a whirlpool again?" Lahcen asked.

"Yes, only not as much of one, we only want to force the bubbles into the hydrogen sulfide river below, not to the ocean floor."

"Looks as if half the water reaume are to dam the river and work together to cool it down, is that right?" Lahcen asked.

"Yes, and then come the electric eels," she explained. "We'll expose them to the river very fast. The sudden burst of cold will scare them into giving off an electric shock."

"The electricity will then short out the jets," Lahcen confirmed.

"You got it! Without the jets, the containers can't take the deep ocean pressure."

Lahcen rubbed his hands together. "Okay! Let's go pop some bubbles!"

Sophia circumnavigated the fighting to join a good many other reaume as they dammed the river, containing it in a water barrier and collectively focusing on cooling the hydrogen sulfide. The other reaume circled as they'd done before, creating a massive whirlpool around the dam that sucked in the orbs, one by one, as they whirled out of control. A fast spinning barrier of water bounced the light beams off and back onto the crowd of spheres, which readily sank into the hydrogen sulfide.

"Lahcen, the eels!" Sophia called.

"Lahcen tossed an eel into the icy dam, frightening the creature and eliciting a charge. He withdrew it again fast, once discharged, it had no further use and he lifted it out before it was exposed to its own shock The superconductor sent electricity careening through the entire conglomerate of vessels in their icy bath. They lit up like a network of fireflies under water. Tiny jets exploded in rapid sequence, rendering the spheres vulnerable to the vast pressure of the ocean floor. One by one the bubbles popped, extinguishing into darkness.

"Yeah!" Lahcen cheered. "It's just like fireworks!"

They circled again, weaving a water barrier around the defunct weapons, then lifted and catapulted the lot of them into the air and clear across the ocean. As more spheres closed in, they repeated the process, funneling more of the vessels into the vortex, throwing in a different eel each time. As more of the enemy hurried to destroy them, they continued the procedure until only a pile of broken, blood-stained shells remained, those few still intact beating a hasty retreat.

Soon, there was nothing left but a few tired reaume migrating home in a murky ocean.

"At last," Sophia said and unleashed the dam, letting the hydrogen sulfide river flow once again.

It was a short trip back to deliver the eels home, though matching each with the right set of babies took a bit of time, but Sophia managed it. They made their way back to Khalid in silence. All along their journey were remnants of the destruction that had taken place. Fortunately, the losses were not huge, but casualties weren't simply numbers, but faces, Sophia's friends and loved ones, and those who'd rescued and nurtured Lahcen's own family. It brought back the memory of his sister. He was glad she had been spared the fighting, but how was she feeling, alone, out there somewhere.

Abruptly, his attention snapped back to the present as he realized that he was experiencing a strong drag, the scenery increasingly moving at a slower and slower pace. He found himself expending a great deal of energy to swim in one place.

"Are we being carried by a current?" he asked, now noting rocks drifting in the wrong direction. "We're going backwards!"

Sophia shifted restlessly. "I can't break free!"

"We're trapped!" Lahcen said, thrashing in every direction, only to encounter a strong, invisible barrier of air, surrounded by a layer of water. But nothing he did worked, he simply couldn't penetrate it. Sophia wrung her hands, clearly afraid.

"Khalid!" Lahcen yelled, but his ability to communicate had gone.

"What is this?" he snarled. "I don't see anything?"

Sophia frowned. "Me either. Feel along the walls and see if we can spot a weakness."

Moments later, Lahcen felt a sharp prick on the back of his arm, and before he had a chance to warn Sophia, all conscious thought floated away.

"Alexis, you haven't touched your dinner again, that's the forth night in a row. And I know for a fact that it's not my cooking."

Alexis dropped the empty fork from her hand and it clattered onto her plate. "Oh I know. It's just that ... oh, Einar, I don't know what to think. First Sean and now Liam, it seems that each generation is just as deluded as the next, and we get our hopes up every time." Alexis sank her head into her hands at the table.

Einar sighed, putting down his own fork. "Yes. It's so hard to know that Clara and her family are in danger, and yet be so helpless. Now Liam..."

"Hope is not lost." Alexis straightened. There is someone who shares our interest, someone who's decided to contact me at great personal risk," she whispered, shooting a frightened glance at the surveillance camera.

Einar's eyes widened. "Who?" he mouthed.

Alexis shook her head. "I don't dare name them. You'll find out soon enough. This person is in a position to help."

Chapter 26

Khalid vs. Rolph

"Who's there?" Khalid asked as he slid underneath the marble table, one of many in the lab that was attached to the floor. He wouldn't have noticed anything if it weren't for a moving reflection on the metal jars lining the shelves.

"Khalid," said a deep, rumbling voice, so deep it didn't appear human at all. The giant was attempting to sneak up behind him.

"Who are you? How did you get in here?" Khalid demanded, controlling any hint of fear or surprise in his voice. Snatching a metal container from the shelf he let fly at the giant's head, but the figure swiped at the air with a gloved hand and it smashed against the shelf and dropped to the floor.

The giant bared his teeth in what passed for a smile. "General Rolph, at your service," he sneered. "I've come to arrest you, and you'll see how I came in when I take you back out with me."

"Is that what you call yourself, a general?" Khalid taunted, slipping off his pack and tucking it in a corner. "A general of genocide perhaps. How did you find me?"

"It wasn't that hard."

"Then how?" Khalid asked. He crawled behind stools, staying under tables, moving to put distance between himself and his assailant.

"Does it matter?" the general asked, following Khalid's voice.

Khalid surveyed the metallic counters and grabbed the first item he saw, a jar labeled sodium nitrate. Hoping it wasn't explosive, he stood up and threw it with all of his strength, but the general simply swiped the object away, as if with his mind. The jar hit the wall and crashed to the floor, spilling its contents.

"What is this strange power you have? Are you a reaume too?" Khalid asked, as he skirted the perimeter of the room. He landed close to a water faucet behind a large kiln in the middle of the floor.

"Of course not!"

Hidden by the kiln, Khalid stretched up to get a cup from one of the cabinets, leaving the door open a crack to avoid any noise, and lowered himself back down. He was a few feet from the faucet, but the giant had spun around and was now approaching. Khalid scooted under a table.

"Then what power is this you possess? You must be air reaume. A reaume attacking the others? Perhaps so that you'll have all the power for yourself?"

"It's reaume that want power, and you are the more dangerous for not realizing that," the general uttered in that crackly, deep voice that sounded so unnatural. Rolph curled rope into his hand as he rounded a corner to confront Khalid. Within seconds he had it looped around Khalid, squeezing him so tight he could hardly breathe.

Khalid dropped the cup to the floor, where it rolled around. Casting his strong arms outward, he managed to slacken the rope off momentarily but Rolph immediately tightened it again, entangling Khalid's arms and knocking him to the floor before securing the scraggly ends.

"That should do it," he said.

"You'd like to think I'm helpless," Khalid said leaping onto his feet, then high into the air, aiming himself at the general as he landed, both booted feet trampling Rolph to the floor. The general went down heavily, the reprieve giving Khalid the space he needed to wrestle free of the rope.

Khalid snatched the cup off the floor and threw it at Rolph. It hit the giant square in the gut, knocking the wind out of him. Khalid sprinted to the shelves and shook them with all his strength. Lab equipment slammed onto the fallen general. Khalid hoped for one piece to be heavy enough to penetrate the general's helmet and knock him unconscious, but he was not so fortunate.

"Not so fast," said Rolph, lifting the debris into midair with his metallic, glove-covered arm, sending it flying back towards Khalid.

Khalid dipped under a table and hurried back towards the faucet, grabbing another cup from the open cabinet.

"If you destroy this lab, we both die," Khalid said and placed the cup in the sink.

"Is that a promise?" the general asked. He was on his feet again and rushed in Khalid's direction. "Because I'll gladly die if it means taking you down with me."

"You're bluffing," Khalid said, trying to calm the panic in his heart while scurrying a few tables away.

"Am I? You don't know anything about me. How can you predict an enemy you don't understand? Meanwhile, I get you, Khalid. I get where you're coming from. I know how much you want to save your brother and sister; that you're searching for your parents. I know that we have them."

"Where are they?" Khalid asked, momentarily distracted from his fear.

"Well, I'm about to take you to them right now. That's what you want, isn't it? I'm just giving you what you want."

"Okay, I'll take it!" Khalid ran directly at the general, jumped and flattened him using his super strength. The general struggled, trying to wrap his arms around Khalid, but Khalid pummeled Rolph's face and arms until the latter could barely breathe.

"Didn't expect me to attack with my bare hands, did you? Not used to getting a beating from someone a lot smaller than you, I imagine." Khalid's voice was thick with menace, his face etched with hatred. He punched General Rolph in the stomach, once, twice, ducking out of the way each time the general tried to grab him. Wham! Khalid blinked as he found himself smacked alongside his head. A monstrous, metallic arm reached for him, but making a supreme effort, he rolled free.

"And that is where you underestimate me," the general said, his voice calm but determined. "I spend my life rooting out threats to humanity, especially ones like yourself."

"Humanity, with the power to manipulate objects through the air? You've got to be reaume, or hasn't that occurred to you yet?"

"What I have is technology, designed to fight you. All of those creatures you've defeated have not been conquests. In fact, they've given us the means of developing the technology you see me using to fight you."

Khalid edged toward the sink, now on the other side of Rolph's view. He filled the cup with water and as Rolph came closer, he bolted towards the spilled sodium nitrate and waited, hoping his attacker was too blinded by rage to register his objective.

"Haven't you wondered about those creatures you've been fighting? They were research. You're a lab rat. Collecting detailed information on your powers enabled us to emulate some of them. But enough of this mindless chatter," the general sneered, lunging for his prey.

Khalid dropped to the floor, scooping up a handful of sodium nitrate. He shoved the substance under the general's helmet, and immediately threw the water at him before dashing to the other side of the room and burying his face in his arm. He heard a rumbling scream as the general's neck and chin blistered. Rolph ran to the sink frantically splashing water onto himself.

Khalid searched the room for some way of ridding himself of the giant. He willed the shelves to empty, pummeling the giant with metal containers as he rinsed his skin, but despite his pain, the general reacted by deflecting the missiles. Using his gloved hand, the general ripped the metal scaffolding of the underwater chamber down on top of Khalid.

"You sure you're willing to die? If this building goes, so do we," Khalid warned.

"Maybe, maybe not." The giant turned away from the sink.

"I have friends in high places, you know," he said coldly. From somewhere, a large metal coil appeared in his hand and he sprinted for Khalid with the intention of twisting it around him.

Khalid's mind churned desperately. A metal container lay within reach of his fingers so he grabbed and threw it. The canister smashed into Rolf's sternum and clattered to the floor. Stunned, momentarily unable to breathe, Rolph ground to a halt.

Khalid seized the rope the general had used on him earlier from the floor. Hastily removing the metal glove, he trussed the general up tightly, carefully securing each limb away from his body. He stared at the giant lying on the floor unable to move. Then he went to the corner and retrieved his pack, shrugging it onto his back.

"You think you can escape," Rolf grated. "But there is no escape from the king. No matter what happens to me, he knows where you are and he knows I would willingly die here."

"Why," Khalid said flatly. "Because you blame the reaume for killing Basra, and you want to bring me down in retaliation? I didn't grow up as a reaume! What kind of justice is that?"

The general's face grew pale. "You do not have the right to speak my son's name."

"Don't I, even after you tried to hurt and kill me, unprovoked? You blame the reaume for killing your son, but aside from being shortsighted about the reaume, you're just plain wrong about me. If I have to suffer for being reaume, then how come I wasn't able to enjoy any of it, and how come all the people I love are human?"

"You're a threat," the general spat.

"Either you're as evil as the king, or else you've been deceived by him." Khalid spoke quietly. "You're so sure you know me when you don't even know your own son."

"I said, don't speak his name!" Rolph yelled.

"Or maybe you do!" Khalid said as a light flashed in a dark corner of his mind. "Maybe you do know your son!" His mind was searching for something ... Anna had sent him a message a few days ago. She'd written about Rolph. What had she said again? It was something about Rolph's son. Basra married an air reaume named Mara, the same girl who tried to kill Qeriya and capture Doctor Michael, the girl with the silver eyes. He'd always thought she worked for the king, but what if that was just a cover? Scales were falling from his eyes.

"You play your part well, Rolph!" Khalid smiled thinly. "You're not working for the king at all! You're in league with Mara, aren't you!" He circled Rolph, who had grown suddenly still.

Things were starting to make more sense. Didn't Anna write that Basra and Mara had a child together? They had a daughter, half-human half-reaume. Did she have powers? The letter didn't say, but he was guessing probably so. What would the king think of his best general with a granddaughter more powerful than his son? He wouldn't like it at all, especially since Liam didn't have any reaume powers.

"Mara was a high ranking soldier wasn't she?" Khalid sought out what little of the general's squint he could find. "And now it turns out she was married to your son? I'd assumed you didn't know when I first found out, but you did know, didn't you?" he said, connecting the clues he'd accumulated. "You and the air reaume have an alliance against the king!" Khalid snapped the final piece of the puzzle into place while Rolph lay bound. "It's you who are leading the resistance!"

"You're speaking nonsense! You can't goad me!" Rolph shouted.

"Perhaps you're not so much anti reaume as against me. Lahcen, Qeriya and I are a major threat if you have designs on the throne for yourself, and eventually for your granddaughter."

"Granddaughter? You're full of lies!"

"Where does Prince Liam fit into this scheme?" Khalid asked, ignoring the giant's outburst. "Will Liam and Mara's daughter be king and queen eventually, or will you try and supplant Prince Liam? What about Queen Kanti? Are they willing to stand down for you?"

"The king will rend you limb from limb, if I don't get to you first!" Rolph hissed, wrestling with his bonds.

"Mara and the prince attempted to capture Qeriya together, but she was a spy and he was ... well, young and naive. Perhaps Liam and Kanti believe the resistance fights for them, but you have plans to betray them, don't you?"

"They are the betrayers!"

"Do you want to take power all for yourself?" Khalid goaded. "How far does the deception go? I never would've considered the possibility of reaume fighting for power before, knowing what I do about their peaceful nature, but then again, Doctor Michael did say the reaume had evolved. Perhaps the air reaume are ahead of the others in their evolution. Perhaps they see you as their best chance for survival."

A vague noise sounded in the ceiling. Rolph stopped struggling. Khalid broke off his questioning to look, but he could see nothing unusual.

"When did you first find out about Basra and Mara, or did you always know? They were poised for leadership, a human married to a reaume, just like the king and queen. But they had a natural daughter, conceived without science, like us. It makes sense why you hate my family now. It's not because we're a threat to humanity. We're a threat to your grandchild! You mean her to claim the throne! You're not here for the king, you're here for yourself. You're the traitor!"

Rolph stared at him speechless. He appeared as breathless as Khalid felt, his face red with rage, his eyes darting about, searching for any possible escape.

"That's why the air reaume won't work with the other reaume groups. They're working to destroy the king and perhaps they know that the others would be a liability. Why did Mara take

Doctor Michael from under our noses? To bargain with us so we would help you fight? Then you'd kill us? You have Qeriya! But your resistance would be no better, just another evil power to replace the evil king."

Khalid heard another noise. It sounded like something had hit the outside of the lab but he couldn't pinpoint the exact location. More of the enemy, he thought, as if the general wasn't bad enough ...

"Is that the king or the resistance?" he sneered, but the general declined to respond. The sound came again. This time whatever was making the noise punctured the lab in one corner.

"You're right," he said, looking at Rolph, "the king is willing to sacrifice you, because once that blows we're both dead."

In an instant, the general disintegrated into tiny shreds of light. The pieces sifted out of the ruptured corner and he was gone. Khalid froze, unsure of what he just witnessed. Frantic, he checked around the table, but there was no sign of him. Another bang pounded the outside hull, denting and stretching the metal. Khalid knew it couldn't hold much longer. With an iron will, he turned his mind away from the chaos around him and lifted his face to the ceiling.

It was too late to escape and a search for the gel mask turned up nothing. It must have been lost in the skirmish. Once again the banging was repeated, like a massive heartbeat, stretching the lab wall to breaking point. Khalid pulled metal from anything he could in the room, forming a seamless barrier around the holographic animal landscapes.

That done, he closed his eyes and tried to imagine the vast, blue sky back home, resigned to his inevitable end. He gave a fleeting thought to his brother, sister, parents and to Anna, lifting them up to that blue sky in his mind, an offering of love and affection, a wordless cry to the Spirit to care for them, imagining a gentle breeze carrying them higher and further away, and this perfect love he felt cast out all fear from his heart.

The next thump ripped the metal container apart as if it were mere fabric. A flood of black water gushed in. There was no time to think as the water swiftly rose, the relentless pressure smashing him against the wall. Instinctively, he tried to reach for something, anything, a way out, a way to the top, but as he thought through every scenario the certainty of his situation crept over his heart and his lungs like a cold bath, trapping him, pinning him to the wall, covering his face.

Darkness filled him and he slipped deeper into its hold. Strangely, it didn't feel how he'd imagined drowning to be. Was he dying? What was happening?

"Einar," Alexis called to her husband, "come quick."

Einar walked to the window, holding his early morning mug of coffee. Outside, the sunrise was bright pink, glinting off a multitude of large ships, their gray, metal shells appearing black in the colorful sky.

"They're heading for battle. So many of them ..." Einar whispered.

"Yes." Alexis clutched at his arm. "We'll need to be strong."

Chapter 27

Kari

The flames leapt high in their fiery dance as Doctor Michael sat beside Kari for after dinner tea. Around them, earth reaume milled about cleaning up from the meal, drinking tea and working on crafts as the light dwindled to dusk. Some weaved birch bark baskets while others carved utensils or knitted clothing from woolen yarn.

"I taste huckleberry," he said, sipping out of a wooden, carved mug.

"You taste right, huckleberry tea with maple syrup is one of my favorites." Kari drizzled maple syrup into her drink, stirring it with a wooden spoon.

Doctor Michael saw that her hand trembled ever so slightly. Was she perhaps shaky from age?

"I'll forgo the syrup. The pure huckleberry flavor's enough," he said and smiled.

"To each his own." Kari nodded amicably. "It's so good to hear about everything that happened after you were taken. I've been so worried. And now my grandsons are home, though it sounds as if I've every reason to worry about that. They had quite an adventure chasing after you!" She gave a high-pitched laugh and eased herself into her chair.

Doctor Michael came to his feet. It was time to address why he'd come. She'd seen the brand on his arm, but how much did she know? She certainly appeared not to know anything, but was she pretending?

"The truth is," he said, "I came to talk with you. It's urgent and private. Can we take a walk?"

"Oh, c–certainly," she stammered.

"Do you have something to do first?" he asked, calm, patient, trying to put her at ease.

Her cheeks dragged into jowls as she stared, alarm, or was it fear in her eyes? "Ah, no, no, it's fine," she decided.

He smiled, reaching for his mug, carrying it with him. "I'm glad the water reaume were able to vouch for me," he said. "You know now that I'm trying to help Khalid, Lahcen and Qeriya, but you only know half yet of who they are," he explained as they left the warmth of the fire behind. Kari led him towards a trail as dusk grew into night and a full moon rose overhead.

"I know that they're Lourdes' grandchildren. Is that what you wanted to tell me?" Kari asked, parting some branches and holding them out of the way for him. Her voice sounded hopeful. They joined a trail lined with layers of pine needles. He could see the uncertainty in her shadowed eyes as she glanced at him.

"Yes, you're correct, but there's more. They are also Einar and Alexis' grandchildren. That's what I wanted to clarify."

"But ... that's impossible! How could they be Einar's descendants? I mean, Einar was a – he was an agent of the king, an enemy of the reaume—" She stopped in her tracks and he followed suit, interrupting.

"He's not a traitor to the reaume. He was genuinely trying to help them, but he was manipulated by the king at that time." He paused to let this information sink into her brain. He could no longer see her expression clearly, but he heard her small gasp and saw her clutch her chest, standing quietly, considering this possibility. He began walking again, encouraging her to move along, hoping to find a clearing, some moonlight to illuminate her face. He needed to read her, to know what she was thinking, how she was responding to him.

"It's true," he said quietly. "He and Alexis have been on house arrest ever since Einar returned home from here."

"I figured that they were Lourdes' grandchildren. And I knew they were part human, but they're Einar's grandchildren as well? How could this be?" Kari asked. "How could they have possibly connected?"

"Lourdes didn't doubt Einar as you did. She maintained a relationship with him. They sent their daughter, Clara, to live among the rainforest people to keep her safe. That's where she grew up, and eventually met Aedan."

"Then why didn't she tell me, argue his innocence?"

"Probably to protect everyone. It was safer for Clara if everyone believed that all reaume distrusted Einar and Alexis. Sometimes it's better not to share what you know. Protection was more important than absolution."

"I can't believe this!"She stumbled over her words, twisting her hands in knots as she spoke. "I can't believe that they're Einar's grandchildren. It's ... earthshattering," she mumbled.

"Is that all that's earthshattering?" he fished.

"No, that's not all!" She edged further along the path. "That means you must have been in the royal court. Your tattoo – that's how you knew about Einar."

"Yes. I lived in the palace before my time in the desert." He paused again. "I was in the royal court. My marking might be a little different ..." he said as he pulled up his sleeve, displaying the tattoo in a patch of moonlight. "You see," he held his arm up, letting her see it clearly. She drifted closer, her eyes fixed on the mark, flinching at the lion's mouth that appeared to roar.

"It's true," she uttered to herself in a mere whisper.

"You see, it's essentially the same as Einar's," Doctor Michael said.

She took a few rapid steps backward and tripped over a mass of dried brush. Doctor Michael extended a hand to help her up, but she ignored it, and rose instead on her own. She stared with unmistakable surprise at the lion head. It morphed as his arm muscle flexed, appearing almost alive in the moonlight. It was not the same as Einar's.

"The truth is, Kari, I can't tell you how I know Einar and Alexis, but I do. Suffice it to say I'm in a position to know," he said as he pulled his sleeve down again. "I can't tell you how

I know the children or why I regard them, but I do. There are others who are concerned with the three siblings, others I can't tell you about. Just know there are those who take a special interest in the children you're trying to protect."

"Interest? What kind of interest?"

"I'm not at liberty to say," he answered.

Kari edged away from him as she spoke. "Oh, how Einar has suffered." She put her face in her hands and swung her head from side to side. When she spoke her voice shook. "To think that I've thought ill of him all this time, when he and his wife sacrificed their livelihood and even their daughter for us. It's insufferable. I didn't realize that humans could be so selfless."

After a moment, she started walking again, Doctor Michael following close behind. They reached a fork in the trail and Kari steered to the right. They entered a clearing where moonlight illuminated her face. Doctor Michael could at last see her haunted eyes. Her face was pale.

"You know I'm not their uncle, don't you?" he asked slowly, studying her expression. She nodded, her lips pursed, disapproving. "But you never mentioned it to anyone?"

"No, I wanted to be certain. Why do you pretend to be their uncle?"

"An uncle is someone they can trust without a complicated explanation, and trust me they do, implicitly. You have to understand, for everyone's sake, they can't know the truth!"

A breeze blew through the needles of the lodgepole pines. It sounded akin to a soft waterfall. Kari shivered.

"You cannot repeat anything you know to anyone, including reaching out to Einar. You'll put everyone at risk if you do."

Kari paused, frozen in space and time, unreadable. "I see now that I've been a fool. I see that in my desire to avoid war, I've nurtured a path to it. There's no hope for escape. Poor Einar! If you're indeed telling the truth, and I do believe that you are, he's been alone!"

The Doctor stared at her for a long time. Finally he said, "Now, will you promise to remain quiet?"

Moonlight shone through a clearing in the trees, momentarily illuminating Kari's stone cold expression.

"I will do what I need to do. How are the children?"

"I don't know."

"If anything were to happen to them, the reaume would find the courage to fight, and that would not bode well for humanity," she declared, a boldness to her voice very uncharacteristic for her.

"It will come to that in time, regardless of whether the reaume find the courage."

The breeze blew as if whispering wisdom into the space between them. They stood, staring at the other, not bothering to move. What more could be said? What more could be done? The children were key to everything. War was coming to the reaume. He would return home and prepare.

Recent bestsellers from Lodestone Books are:

AlphaNumeric

Nicolas Forzy

When dyslexic teenager Stu accidentally transports himself into a world populated by living numbers and letters, his arrival triggers a prophecy that pulls two rival communities into war.

Paperback: 978-1-78279-506-3 ebook: 978-1-78279-505-6

Shanti and the Magic Mandala

F.T. Camargo

In this award-winning YA novel, six teenagers from around the world gather for a frantic chase across Peru, in search of a sacred object that can stop The Black Magicians' final plan.

Paperback: 978-1-78279-500-1 ebook: 978-1-78279-499-8

Time Sphere

A timepathway book

M.C. Morison

When a teenage priestess in Ancient Egypt connects with a schoolboy on a visit to the British Museum, they each come under threat as they search for Time's Key.

Paperback: 978-1-78279-330-4 ebook: 978-1-78279-329-8

Bird Without Wings

FAEBLES

Cally Pepper

Sixteen year old Scarlett has had more than her fair share of problems, but nothing prepares her for the day she discovers she's growing wings...

Paperback: 978-1-78099-902-9 ebook: 978-1-78099-901-2

Briar Blackwood's Grimmest of Fairytales

Timothy Roderick

After discovering she is the fabled Sleeping Beauty, a brooding goth-girl races against time to undo her deadly fate.

Paperback: 978-1-78279-922-1 ebook: 978-1-78279-923-8

Escape from the Past

The Duke's Wrath

Annette Oppenlander

Trying out an experimental computer game, a fifteen-year-old boy unwittingly time-travels to medieval Germany where he must not only survive but figure out a way home.

Paperback: 978-1-84694-973-9 ebook: 978-1-78535-002-3

Holding On and Letting Go

K.A. Coleman

When her little brother died, Emerson's life came crashing down around her. Now she's back home and her friends want to help, but can Emerson fight to re-enter the world she abandoned?

Paperback: 978-1-78279-577-3 ebook: 978-1-78279-576-6

Midnight Meanders

Annika Jensen

As William journeys through his own mind, revelations are made, relationships are broken and restored, and a faith that once seemed extinct is renewed.

Paperback: 978-1-78279-412-7 ebook: 978-1-78279-411-0

Reggie & Me

The First Book in the Dani Moore Trilogy

Marie Yates

The first book in the Dani Moore Trilogy, *Reggie & Me* explores a teenager's search for normalcy in the aftermath of rape.

Paperback: 978-1-78279-723-4 ebook: 978-1-78279-722-7

Unconditional

Kelly Lawrence

She's in love with a boy from the wrong side of town...

Paperback: 978-1-78279-394-6 ebook: 978-1-78279-393-9

Readers of ebooks can buy or view any of these bestsellers by clicking on the live link in the title. Most titles are published in paperback and as an ebook. Paperbacks are available in traditional bookshops. Both print and ebook formats are available online.

Find more titles and sign up to our readers' newsletter at www.johnhuntpublishing.com/children-and-young-adult
Follow us on Facebook at https://www.facebook.com/JHPChildren and Twitter at https://twitter.com/JHPChildren